"I can tak

Noah touched Wendy's ... know you don't *need* anyo... *want* anyone?"

She shivered, and he rubbed his hand up and down on her arm, like he was trying to warm her up. He didn't know that she wasn't cold. That she was, in fact, on fire. If she was shaking, it was rage. Or that stupid ever-present lust. Or some goddamned combination of the two.

The hand that had been rubbing vigorously up and down her arm slowed. Came to a full stop on her shoulder. Then slowly, slowly, it started to make its way up along the side of her neck until it came to rest on her cheek. She wanted to look away, but she wouldn't allow herself.

His eyes burned, but it didn't seem like there was any anger remaining behind the heat she saw in them. And his hand, in contrast to all their fighting words, was so gentle on her cheek.

So she leaned into his touch. Just a little.

But it was enough to shift everything.

PRAISE FOR THE BRIDESMAIDS BEHAVING BADLY SERIES

ONE AND ONLY

"The book's addictive combination of memorable characters, polished writing seasoned with deliciously acerbic wit, and some off-the-charts hot love scenes aptly demonstrates that when it comes to creating unputdownable contemporary romances, Holiday is in it to win it."

—*Booklist* (starred review)

"Get ready to laugh, swoon and fall in love.... A sweet and spicy read that kicks off a new series in style!"

—*RT Book Reviews*

"Delightfully sexy and sweet, Holiday knows how to deliver the perfect combination of sexual tension and happily-ever-after."

—Lauren Layne, *New York Times* bestselling author

"*One and Only* is fantastic! A great start to a new series. Compelling characters, tons of heat, loads of heart. I highly recommend!"

—M. O'Keefe, *USA Today* bestselling author

ALSO BY JENNY HOLIDAY

The Bridesmaids Behaving Badly series

One and Only

IT takes two

BRIDESMAIDS BEHAVING BADLY

JENNY HOLIDAY

FOREVER
New York Boston

Copyright © 2018 by Jenny Holiday
Preview of *Three Little Words* copyright © 2018 by Jenny Holiday

Cover design by Elizabeth Turner Stokes
Cover photography by Claudio Marinesco
Cover copyright © 2018 by Hachette Book Group, Inc.

Forever
Hachette Book Group
1290 Avenue of the Americas, New York, NY 10104
forever-romance.com
twitter.com/foreverromance

First Edition: June 2018

Forever is an imprint of Grand Central Publishing. The Forever name and logo are trademarks of Hachette Book Group, Inc.

The publisher is not responsible for websites (or their content) that are not owned by the publisher.

The Hachette Speakers Bureau provides a wide range of authors for speaking events. To find out more, go to www.hachettespeakersbureau.com or call (866) 376-6591.

ISBN: 978-1-4555-4242-0 (mass market), 978-1-4555-4241-3 (ebook)

Printed in the United States of America

OPM

10 9 8 7 6 5 4 3 2 1

For Sandra Owens, my fellow soldier.
There's no one I'd rather be doing this
with than you.

Acknowledgments

Thanks to Andie J. Christopher for making sure Wendy and Noah weren't violating attorney-client privilege when they did their legal bantering and to Alyson Geary for helping me figure out what their half marathon times should be.

Sandra Owens and Emma Barry read a very early draft of this book and helped enormously in the project of making it into something better.

But the queen of that process was Lexi Smail. I always appreciate a good, hard edit, but boy did this book need one. (They don't all come out perfectly sparkly on the first try, but let's just say this one needed some major glitter cannon action.)

Thanks also to everyone at Forever Romance for making this book, from the story inside to its exquisite cover, shine.

And finally to my agent and friend, Courtney Miller-Callihan, who makes everything happen.

IT takes two

Chapter One

*T*he phone rang.

Wendy jumped, cursing herself for forgetting to turn it off before her meeting. Her client, Mr. Frederick Brecht, jumped, too, his solemn tale of woe interrupted by the highly unprofessional "Who Let the Dogs Out" ringtone Wendy's best friend Jane had set for herself on Wendy's phone.

"My apologies." Wendy fumbled to silence the phone and sneaked a glance at the time. It was late Friday afternoon, and Mr. Brecht was...thorough.

She eyed the now silent but still ringing phone. Historically, her heart had always done a happy little bleat when she saw the name *Jane Denning* on her call display. Wendy and Jane had been friends since the first day of fifth grade. Wendy still thanked her lucky stars that Jane had marched up to her in the cafeteria that first day and said, "Sit with me." Jane had made Wendy's first day at a new school better. Just like she'd made every day since better. Because Jane was all the things a best friend should be: a good listener, a straight talker, and a hell of a lot of fun. That phrase, "like a sister"? It wasn't enough to describe how close they were.

Lately, though, her best friend was *also* one other thing: a bride-to-be. To be fair—and fairness was Wendy's stock in trade—Wendy couldn't accuse Jane of being a bridezilla. She wasn't making her bridesmaids do any bullshit crafts or anything. They all, Jane included, still had bridesmaid PTSD from their friend Elise's wedding last summer. As a result, all Jane had instructed was that they wear the black dress of their choice to her wedding. So in a letter-of-the-law sense, a person couldn't accuse Jane of being a bridezilla.

But...spirit of the law. Even though Jane wasn't obsessed with the perfect wedding, she was sort of fixated, paradoxically, on the idea that she *wasn't* obsessed. She was constantly talking about how her wedding, which would be held at an amusement park she and her fiancé loved, was going to be "low-key."

It turned out that being "low-key" actually required a shit-ton of mental energy.

The phone's display continued to show Jane calling. Mr. Brecht pulled out a diagram of his apartment on which he'd marked—and annotated—every instance of rodent infestation that had occurred over his five-year battle with his landlord.

Wendy looked at the clock again.

She weighed her options, then mouthed a prayer of forgiveness. Because right up there with fairness, Wendy valued honesty.

"Excuse me for a moment, Mr. Brecht; I have to take this."

She braced herself and answered the call.

"Wendy! I thought you were never going to pick up!"

"Good afternoon, Ms. Denning," Wendy said in her best professional voice. "Could you hold for a moment, please?"

Jane giggled. "Of course, counselor."

"I'm so sorry, Mr. Brecht. Something has come up with another client." Wendy made a show of looking at her watch, though she already knew it was 4:58 p.m. "And given that the day is almost over, might I suggest that we pick this up next week?" She stood, ushering him out as she spoke. "We're all ready to go for your appearance before the board."

Wendy felt guilty about shuffling Mr. Brecht off—what he needed more than a lawyer was someone to listen to him—but not guilty enough to endure another hour of rats when it was 4:58 p.m. on a Friday and her best friend was on the phone. She was going to get Mr. Brecht's eviction overturned. She was good at her job—no, she was *great* at her job—and the fact that a rat had appeared under his sink at precisely 7:43 a.m. last Tuesday would have no bearing on the outcome of his hearing.

Once he was gone, she slammed her door behind her and sank into her office sofa, letting that lovely Friday feeling overtake her. "Hi!" she said, hoping that she was going to get Friend Jane and not Bride Jane.

"I need you to send me your bio."

Damn.

"My bio?" Wendy tried to ask the question in a way that masked her real question, which was: *What the hell are you talking about?*

"For the website?"

Wendy did a lot of pro bono defense work—witness Mr. Brecht and his rats—but she was also an associate at one of Toronto's most prestigious criminal law firms. In that capacity, she had a bio on the firm's website—an impressive bio if she did say so herself. But she was pretty sure Jane didn't care that Wendy was a top-notch criminal litigator with special expertise in the Extradition Act.

"Your bio for the *wedding* website?" Jane asked.

What Wendy said in response was, "Riiiight." What she meant was, *damn it all to hell*. The wedding website was part of Jane's "everything about this wedding is super fun and low-key" philosophy. She thought if she had a website with all the pertinent details, it would ease logistical challenges for the guests. Not sure about parking? Check the website! Want to see some funny pictures of the bridal couple that demonstrate how fun and low-key they are in a way that looks effortless and un-curated but is actually the result of several hours with a professional photographer? Check the website!

Wendy hadn't realized, apparently, that the wedding website was also supposed to include bios of the wedding party.

"And you're coming to the website photo shoot tomorrow morning, right? That's why I'm nagging you about the bio. I want to give the bios to the photographer in advance so she can get to know the members of the wedding party a little before she shoots you."

Whoa. Bios and, apparently, *portraits*.

Wendy wanted to ask if there was any way the photographer could *actually* shoot her. Because at this point, a quick and painless death would probably be less excruciating than what Jane was suggesting. Wendy could not imagine anything worse than spending a beautiful spring morning sitting for wedding portraits.

"I was going to get some bagels and cream cheese for

people to snack on while they wait their turn with the photographer," Jane went on, "but do you think I should have something more solidly brunchy catered in? I'm not good at this stuff like Elise was. Will people expect, like, eggy things?"

Stifling a sigh, Wendy hoisted herself off the sofa and went to her computer to check her calendar for anything that looked remotely like "photo shoot/brunch/eggy things" listed for tomorrow. She was guilty of maybe not totally paying one hundred percent attention to everything wedding related. But in her defense (pun intended), she was pretty sure she had taken note of all the major events that required her presence, if only because she was determined not to *appear* to be the disgruntled bridesmaid she actually *was*.

She found an entry that said "Ten a.m.—Jane's." Vague enough that it could have meant anything, including, she supposed, "photo shoot/brunch/eggy things."

Wendy wanted to ask if she could skip it—she was training for a half marathon and had been planning a long run tomorrow. Could she send a selfie or her law firm portrait and be done with it?

But no. Of course not. She needed to up her game here. Yes, she wasn't into all this wedding bullshit. But the bigger issue was that in her heart of hearts, she wasn't into the wedding itself. She was, selfishly, sad that Jane was getting married. She had nothing against Cameron, Jane's fiancé. Well, nothing that would stand up in court. He had started out as kind of a jerk, and what Jane saw in him remained a mystery to Wendy, but anyone with a brain could see how happy he'd made Jane.

It was just that it had always been Wendy and Jane against the world. The Lost Girls, they used to call themselves. The Dead Dads Club. They were a duo.

And now they were going to be...not that.

But that train had left the station, so Wendy put on her court face, even though Jane couldn't see her. Wendy's court face was like a poker face, but a lot more badass. "Sorry the bio is late. I'll send it within the hour. And, no, I don't think people will expect eggy things. Why don't I bring the bagels?"

"You don't need to bring anything except the questionnaire."

"The questionnaire is different from the bio?"

Her question was met with silence. There were messages encoded in that silence, though. Messages that only two-plus decades of best-friendship could interpret. Wendy had failed Jane. She wasn't quite sure how, yet, but the disappointment in Jane's silence was unmistakable.

"Right, yes, the questionnaire," she lied, typing "questionnaire + Jane" into the search field in her email and coming up with a message from two weeks ago about how each member of the wedding party was supposed to answer a few "fun, low-key" questions. The answers would be posted next to their bios on the wedding website. The bio that Wendy had forgotten all about.

Wendy sharpened her court face. "Of course the questionnaire and bio are totally different things. I'm sorry; I just got confused for a moment. It's been a really long week."

Mollified, Jane made a sympathetic clucking noise. "When is your next trip?"

Wendy sighed. She could feel herself getting itchy. "Nothing until the big one."

"Wow," Jane said. "That's like four months away. Have you ever stayed put for that long?"

It was a fair question. The wanderlust was strong in Wendy, and it hadn't been indulged for a long time. But in the fall, she was taking a six-month sabbatical and traveling around the world.

She. Could. Not. Wait.

But it also meant that she had a shit-ton of work to get done before she hit the road. "I have to be in court starting next week, and I think it will be a long trial. Plus I have this side thing I'm doing that's going before the Landlord and Tenant Board on Wednesday, so I'm already going to have to clone myself somehow. So, alas, no trips for me until the big one."

"Landlord and Tenant Board?" Jane echoed in a skeptical tone—the Landlord and Tenant Board was not Wendy's usual scene, and Jane knew it. Wendy was a high-powered defense lawyer, but she frequently volunteered her services in other, less glamorous contexts. "Who's your latest downtrodden?"

"My hairdresser's uncle. His apartment is infested with rats."

Jane cracked up. "You're a superhero, you know? Getting white-collar criminals off by day, de-ratting the city by night."

Wendy's friends found her pro bono work amusingly incongruous. Elise had even suggested she did it to balance out the karmic scales. But that wasn't it at all. Wendy believed that everyone—*everyone*—had the right to a rigorous defense. And, sure, she did her pro bono work because it wasn't fair that rich people could afford better defense than poor people. But the essential act of advocating for someone—defending them—was the same no matter the circumstances. Still, she'd long since stopped trying to make her friends see that logic when they launched into their speeches about how "cute" it was that she made two hundred grand a year and still signed up for volunteer shifts at Legal Aid clinics.

"Dang, I love you." Jane's voice had gone all moony, almost like she was talking about her fiancé rather than Wendy.

"I love you, too." It was the truth. It was why she was so torn up about this wedding. Inexplicably, her eyes filled with tears.

Which was mortifying. Wendy was not a crier.

"You know who else I love?" Jane sniffed. The impulse to cry must have been contagious.

"Who?"

"My brother."

You and me both.

Okay, that wasn't true. Not anymore, anyway. Not since she was fifteen. And that hadn't been anything more than a girlish crush. Still, adrenaline surged through Wendy as it did every time Noah Denning's name was mentioned.

"I wish he could come to the photo shoot," Jane said.

Right, so Wendy had to correct a previous thought. It turned out she *could* imagine something worse than spending a beautiful spring morning sitting for wedding portraits: spending a beautiful spring morning sitting for wedding portraits with *Jane's brother*.

"But of course he's coming to the wedding itself, and that's what matters," Jane said, sniffles transformed into glee.

Noah Denning: one more huge-ass reason Wendy was not looking forward to Jane's wedding.

Usually, when Jane's brother came to visit, Wendy managed to be off on one of her trips. When she couldn't avoid seeing him—he was her best friend's brother after all, and she had practically lived at the Dennings' house when she was a kid—she had to armor herself so extensively that it was exhausting. And that was just for short encounters—a dinner, a brunch, church with Wendy's aunt Mary.

A week, though?

How was she going to survive?

"I'll let you get back to your rats, Wendy Defendy," Jane said, using the nickname she thought was so hilarious.

Wendy Defendy had to take a couple deep breaths to get her shit together.

"Okay," she said once she had succeeded. "I should get a bit more done before I knock off for the night."

Wendy defended people. It was just what she did.

Too bad she didn't know how to defend her heart.

Chapter Two

"Oh my God, you totally saved the day," Jane whisper-yelled when Wendy arrived for the photo shoot the next morning bearing not just bagels but several bottles of prosecco and a gallon of fresh-squeezed orange juice. "Everyone is standing around waiting for the photographer to finish setting up her equipment, and I *knew* I should have done more with catering."

"Nah." Wendy flashed Jane a smile. "We'll just get 'em drunk. Much more efficient."

Elise approached and gave Wendy a quick hug before relieving her of her bags.

"Is Gia in town?" Wendy looked around for the fourth member of their close-knit group.

"She's at a Givenchy shoot in Rio," Elise said.

"But she sent a picture!" Jane pulled out her phone. "She asked me for specs on how these shots were going to be done, and she had *Steven Meisel* shoot one of her in the same vein. Like, in an off moment during the shoot. Can you imagine?"

"I really can't." Wendy took the phone to better see the photo and refrained from asking the obvious question: *Who is Steven Meisel?* And also from wondering why she hadn't thought to fake an international high-fashion photo shoot this morning. That was probably the only thing that would have gotten her off the hook today.

"Hi, Wendy." Jane's fiancé Cameron approached.

Wendy tried not to stiffen as he leaned down to peck her cheek. Cameron was such a *guy*. He was a former soldier with all the tattoos and muscles that stereotypically went with the gig. Now he was working construction. He was also in university part-time, though, which Wendy had to respect.

Wendy sighed as Cameron placed his hand on Jane's butt and Jane shot him a big, besotted smile.

Wendy needed to try to muster some genuine enthusiasm for this wedding. She couldn't keep half-assing everything and forgetting shit or she was going to hurt her best friend. And Wendy could not afford to lose Jane. Since her mom had died a couple years ago, Wendy was an honest-to-God orphan. She could star in her own Charles Dickens novel.

So, even if everything was going to be different—and by "different," Wendy meant "worse"—when Jane got married, Wendy *needed* Jane.

"Wendy, why don't you go first with the photographer, being the maid of honor and all?" Jane's gaze traveled up and down Wendy's body. Wendy tried not to squirm—she'd done as instructed and shown up in jeans and a white top, but the bride's silent appraisal made her feel like she'd made a mistake.

"What?" Wendy looked down at her white silk blouse. "Too dressy?" She probably should have just gone with a straight-up T-shirt. But the only actual T-shirts she owned were from the races she'd run, so she'd resorted to the only white top in her wardrobe, which was something she wore under her work suits.

"It's fine." Jane's tone suggested that it was not, in fact, fine.

"If you have a spare shirt, I can change." Jane would pretend not to be too invested in the photo shoot, but Wendy suspected her friend had a backup shirt or two stashed somewhere in the house.

"Well, I do have a couple."

Bingo.

"Which I just got in case anyone spills orange juice or something on their shirt."

Wendy refrained from pointing out that since she had surprised Jane with the orange juice, her logic was flawed. "Give me one. It'll look better—more in tune with everyone else."

Jane tilted her head. "You sure?" But she was already pulling a shirt out of an Old Navy bag sitting on the kitchen counter. "Elise is in the bathroom, I think. You can go change in my bedroom."

Wendy glanced around. Everyone else had gone outside—Jane's house was tiny, and it looked like the actual picture taking was happening in the backyard. "Nah, I'll just quickly change here. Shield me." She whipped off her offending garment and reached for the new shirt. "What size is this?" she asked as Jane turned around and put her arms out in an "airplane" stance in an attempt to provide privacy to Wendy's presto-chango.

"Small. But if it's too big we can pin— Oh my *Gaaaawd*!"

Not only did Jane's airplane arms crash, she ran away, leaving Wendy exposed as she struggled to turn the new shirt right-side out. Once she succeeded, she jammed her arms into the sleeves and lifted the shirt over her head, but the fabric was still twisted so she got stuck.

"Noah!" Jane shrieked. "I can't believe you came!"

Danger! Danger! Wendy's body screamed, reacting in such a clichéd way, she might as well have been a cartoon. She could feel her jaw drop, her eyes widen. All she needed was for her cartoon-heart to literally hammer its way out of her chest. And perhaps an anvil to fall on her head and put her out of her misery.

He wasn't supposed to be here. Not yet. He wasn't coming until the day before the wedding.

She peeked over the edge of the shirt. There he was, tall and handsome and freaking *perfect*, framed in the doorway of Jane's kitchen like it was no big deal.

She was not prepared for this. She wasn't wearing her armor. Hell, she didn't even have a goddamned shirt on.

"Janie." Noah's voice was the same warm baritone it had always been. He had teased Wendy with that voice. Cheered her on at her softball games. Yelled, "Race you!" when they used to go running together. Wendy's attempts to avoid Noah as much as possible in the seventeen years since he had left Toronto for New York had been largely successful. She'd only spent a handful of hours in his presence in all those years. But that voice was as familiar as ever. It made her feel, unnervingly, like no time had passed. Like she was still the nerdy, shy loser standing alone under a disco ball in the high school gym.

Wendy considered whether she could somehow run away. Her arms were caught in the T-shirt high above her head, so maybe he wouldn't recognize her.

But no. She *wasn't* that nerdy, shy girl anymore. She'd killed that girl off.

"Hey, Wendy." His voice slid under her skin and diffused through her body like a drug.

Wendy had no protection against Noah Denning. She might as well have just handed him her renegade heart and said, *Here's my heart. Break it. Again.*

∼⌒∽

The first thing Noah saw when he sneaked into his sister's house to surprise her was Wendy Liu taking off her shirt.

He sucked in a breath. It had been a long time since he'd moved away. You would think that all those years would have been enough to kill his infatuation with Wendy Liu's breasts.

And more to the point, he was an adult now. He had gone to college and law school, built a career, bought an apartment, had relationships come and go. He had lived an entire life in those years.

To be fair, it wasn't like he was *trying* to ogle her. Clad in an off-white satin bra, she writhed as she struggled with turning a new shirt right-side-out. It wasn't cooperating with her, and she was making such a fuss, you couldn't *not* look.

At least this time, he could look his fill without feeling like a pedophile perving on his little sister's best friend.

Well, technically, she was still his little sister's best friend, but these days, she was of legal ogling age. And nothing was ever going to come of it. It was a long-ago childhood crush. Not even a crush. Just a weird...fondness. Or protectiveness. Or something. None of them had had an easy childhood, and Wendy was like a fellow soldier.

So it wasn't even ogling. It was more like...objective

aesthetic appreciation. He was a grown-up. He could admire a beautiful woman without it having to *mean* anything.

Just for a minute—what could it hurt? So he let himself lean to the side, the better to see around the barrier his sister was trying to create around Wendy as she changed.

God, she was lovely. Whereas time had etched lines around his eyes and slowed his metabolism so that he had to run like a fiend to make sure he kept fitting into his slim-cut courtroom suits, Wendy appeared immune to the ravages of time and gravity. That pale, smooth forehead was unlined. Her pretty brown eyes as she rolled them at something Jane was saying were as bright as ever.

And her breasts. Oh, those breasts.

Okay, it wasn't objective aesthetic appreciation. It was ogling.

Noah and Wendy were both runners. They used to go running together back in the day. So Noah had seen Wendy in lots of tight tank top–type things. They had given only a tantalizing hint of what lay beneath. But this bra...well, this bra confirmed that his teenage imagination had been spot-on. Because Wendy's breasts looked exactly as he had pictured them back when he was a raging sack of hormones: small, perky, and gorgeously shaped. The perfect handful. A man could reach out and just cover them with his hands, and none would go to waste. They were—

"Oh my God! Noah! I can't believe you came!"

His sister launched herself at him, throwing herself into his arms, which was, on the one hand, exactly what he'd meant to have happen by surprising her. But on the other, it caused her to abandon Wendy, who froze partway through putting on the new shirt.

"Janie." Noah's arms did what they were supposed to do, which was hug his shrieking sister, but his gaze remained pinned to Wendy. Normally, coming home and seeing Jane was like taking a deep breath. She calmed him, grounded him, reminded him what was important and why he worked so hard.

But this particular dose of his sister was apparently not enough to counter the power of Wendy Liu's breasts. Because he was...not calm as Wendy, still stuck in the shirt with her arms over her head, peeked through its neck hole, her eyes twin missiles locking on to his gaze.

He cleared his throat preemptively so his voice would sound casual. "Hey, Wendy." When she didn't answer, he asked, "What's your half marathon time these days?" but immediately wanted to kick himself. *What's your half marathon time these days?* What was *the matter* with him?

The question seemed to unfreeze Wendy, though. She struggled the rest of the way through putting her shirt on before answering, "An hour and forty-nine." Her eyes narrowed and then traveled quickly up and down the length of his body. He would have liked to flatter himself that she was checking him out as he had been her, but he knew she was merely assessing his current fitness level. He waited for her to ask what his time was, because that's what he and Wendy did: compete with each other.

"Oh my God, Wendy! I'm sorry!" Jane jogged back over to the kitchen. "I left you totally exposed there. I was just so surprised."

"No worries. It's only Noah."

"It's only Wendy Lou Who," he said, deploying his old nickname for her. The endearment had been a play on how her name—Wendy Liu—sounded like "Cindy Lou Who," the little girl from *How the Grinch Stole Christmas*. Wendy hadn't shared any physical characteristics with her cartoon alter-ego, except one—she'd been adorable.

He wouldn't necessarily call her adorable anymore. No, that word was too anemic. Her teenage ponytail had been replaced by a straight curtain of dark hair so shiny she could have starred in a shampoo commercial, and her snug curves were perfectly showcased by a pair of skinny jeans and that white T-shirt he'd watched her do battle with.

Once Jane was assured that Wendy was properly covered, she came back over and hugged him again. "I'm so glad you came."

God, he loved his sister. He was so glad she was getting married to someone as reliable—and, he hated to say it— badass as Cameron. Every time he thought about the fact that his soon-to-be-brother-in-law was former military, his insides unknotted a little more.

"What are you doing here, Noah?" Jane gave him an extra-hard squeeze before letting him go. "I thought you couldn't get away. Aren't you in the middle of a trial?"

"The defense's key witness has shingles, so we adjourned for a week." Which was probably not true, and normally Noah would have insisted on proof, but given how hyper Jane was over this stupid wedding website photography session, he'd decided to swoop in and surprise her.

"And you fell for that?" Wendy, now (alas) fully clothed, asked. She sniffed. "Losing your edge, counselor?"

Noah was ramping himself up to spar with Wendy— there was something deliciously familiar about it—but Jane's glee derailed him. She clapped her hands like a kid on Christmas morning. "Well, real or fake shingles, I'm so happy you're here! And look at you, doing something so impulsive!"

"I can be impulsive," he protested.

His sister rolled her eyes affectionately at him.

Okay, maybe he wasn't the most spontaneous person in

the world, but what was wrong with that? He had responsibilities in New York. Not everybody could—or wanted to— go flitting off at a moment's notice.

"Did Clarissa come with you?" Jane asked.

"No. We, ah, broke up."

"What?" Jane hit his shoulder. "Why? I *liked* her!"

Noah shrugged. "Why does anyone break up?" Was it too much to hope that his sister would be distracted enough by the day's events that she wouldn't force a big conversation about the demise of his relationship with Clarissa?

"Well, I don't know about 'anyone,' but *you* sure do it a lot."

Yep. Too much to hope. And she wasn't wrong. Noah was a serial monogamist. And the answer to Jane's question was that things had progressed enough with Clarissa that Clarissa had started, reasonably, pushing for more—she'd wanted to move in together. And Noah, ultimately, had been unable to pull the trigger. Which pretty much described the demise of all his relationships, really. He should probably feel bad about it—and he did. But he'd be lying to himself if he didn't admit to some relief. Noah spent his life worrying about people: his clients, his sister. With Clarissa gone, there was one fewer person on that list. Which made him sound like a dick, but it was what it was.

"Can we not talk about this now?"

"Fine. But only because I have to go tell the photographer to expect one more!" Jane narrowed her eyes at him. "Those jeans are okay, but you're going to have to put on a white T-shirt. There are some extras in that bag on the counter."

Once he was left alone with Wendy, a touch of awkwardness descended. Which was strange. It was just Wendy, after all. It was probably because he'd seen her shirtless. Should he apologize? He wasn't sorry it had happened, but should he fake apologize? He opened his mouth to say something, but his mind went blank. Which was also strange. Unprecedented, really. He couldn't remember one single time in his life he'd been struck dumb in Wendy's presence. Usually it was the opposite—usually she brought out his most combative self. Made his arguments sharper and his thinking clearer.

Wendy slid an Old Navy bag across the counter to him. "Welcome to the doghouse."

"Well, I wasn't planning on coming, so I guess I missed the white shirt memo." He pulled a men's cotton shirt out of the bag. "What's your excuse, counselor?" There—he was fine now. Back on familiar footing. It was funny that he'd become a prosecutor and Wendy a defender. It was like they were made to argue with each other.

"Oh, I arrived in a white shirt. It just wasn't the right *kind* of white shirt." She flicked her gaze down herself, which caused his to follow, once again getting snagged on her chest. Her shirt was a plain, crew-necked model, so it wasn't even like there was any cleavage on display. There was no reason to go all slack-jawed. "Apparently."

That *apparently* caused him to jerk his eyes back to her face. She raised her eyebrows—she had busted him checking her out. Well, fine. Noah was no slouch either, if he did say so himself, even if his half marathon time had slipped a little compared to hers. So he grabbed the back of his T-shirt, preparing to pull the offending not-white garment off. He and Wendy had always had an almost-confrontational "what's good for the goose is good for the gander" thing going. Which right now he was interpreting to mean that if she could tell he'd been ogling her, he was going to *make* her ogle him.

"Hey, Elise is out of the bathroom." Wendy pointed over his shoulder. "You can change there."

"Nah. I'm fine here." He grinned and whipped his shirt over his head, the cool morning breeze coming in from Jane's open kitchen window causing his skin to pebble. "Try to control yourself, though, when you see my naked chest." Now that they'd broken through that brief initial awkward patch, teasing her came as naturally as it had when they were teenagers. Sparring with Wendy Lou Who was one of life's simplest, purest pleasures.

Except she didn't clap back at him the way he'd expected. She just rolled her eyes and walked away.

—◦⌒

Holy God. Not only did Wendy not have any armor against Noah's unexpected arrival, every weapon she had in her arsenal just up and vanished once he took off his shirt.

She tried to think when she'd last seen Noah shirtless. Probably not since they used to run together back when they were kids. He had been on the cross-country team before his dad's death forced him to drop all his extracurriculars, but he would occasionally strap on his running shoes between school and work shifts and head out with her. And as a boy, Noah had been cute in that wiry way that runners often are.

But this was Noah the *man*. Those sculpted shoulders. That sculpted *everything*. Unlike most of the male lawyers Wendy worked with, Noah was clearly hitting the gym at night instead of the bar.

Well. It didn't bear thinking about. Because she had done a hell of a lot of growing up since the night he broke her heart. So she wasn't allowing herself to be flustered by him. No, the way she related to Noah Denning now, on the odd occasion she couldn't find an excuse not to be around him, was the same way she always had: by harassing him. It was a familiar groove.

Except today that groove was lined with more irritation than usual. She hated the way he expected to waltz in here like the big savior. They were all supposed to fall all over themselves squealing with joy—return of the prodigal son or some crap.

Of course, he *was* the family's rock, given the way he'd stepped up and supported his mom and sister after his father died. He'd worked nights and weekends—a *lot* of hours—at a grocery store. He often worked the eleven to seven night shift and then went from the store directly to school.

So, he was a good guy.

Kind of.

Selectively.

When he wasn't standing up nerdy, besotted, vulnerable younger girls at the prom.

The tips of her ears burned. The humiliation was still there, even all these years later. His job back then had been important, but she had never imagined that he would choose it over her. But it had been a good, if harsh, reminder of where she'd stood with him. It had been too easy back then, given how much time she spent at the Dennings' house, to assume that she had a claim of sorts to him. Like he was her honorary big brother.

Or something.

"Wendy!"

She jumped as Jane's voice pierced her little stroll down bad-memory lane. "I'm sorry, what?" Oh, shit. Everyone was looking at her.

"I was just explaining," the photographer said, "that I

don't want to force anyone into anything they're not comfortable with—some people's natural faces are quite
somber—but is there any way you could try to look
less…pained?"

Wendy winced. "Of course! I'm sorry." As Jane had di-
rected, Wendy had gone first with the photographer, and
she'd been in the middle of posing—while the rest of the
wedding party looked on—when she'd fallen down the rab-
bit hole marked *Noah Denning*.

"Usually, Wendy has the opposite of resting bitch face,"
Elise said. "She's usually smiling."

Was that true? She was going to have to work on that. In
court, anyway.

"Unless she's mad at you." Jane joined the assessment.
"Then watch out. But that's not resting bitch face; that's
more like *active* bitch face."

"*Terrifying* bitch face!" Elise laughed as she nodded in
agreement.

"The point is," Jane said to the photographer, "Wendy
isn't a shrinking violet, so just tell her what you want her to
do."

Embarrassed not only because everyone's attention was
on her, but because her friends were discussing her like they
were at parent-teacher night—though probably the word
"bitch" didn't come up so often in parent-teacher night—she
tried to look away, up, over their heads.

But of course her gaze snagged on Noah's. He was at the
back of the crowd, lounging casually against a tree in his
jeans and his pristine white T-shirt like he was the star of a
Lands' End advertising campaign.

"You never told me what your half marathon time was,"
she called.

"Have you made partner at your firm yet?" he parried, his

greeny-brown eyes twinkling the same way they had when he used to tease her.

"What do you mean *yet*?" Annoyance flared in her chest. She was only thirty-two—no one made partner that young. But then she was annoyed at *herself*, because clearly he was trying to redirect her—and he'd succeeded. He hadn't answered her question about his time, and he'd gotten a rise out of her.

He shrugged, perfectly, irritatingly nonchalant. "How many weekly billable hours are you doing these days?"

"Seventy, roughly." She'd like to see him top that. He was a public prosecutor and so he wasn't under the pressure lawyers at private firms were to bill a million hours a week. "You?"

He raised his eyebrows. "I get my work done in sixty."

Wendy rolled her eyes.

"What?" He pushed himself off the tree and stood up straight. He had dropped the nonchalance. Good. She'd gotten to him. "I live for my job." Wendy was startled by the vehemence that had crept into his speech. "It's the most important thing in my life." His eyes darted around until they rested on Jane. "Present company excluded."

She wasn't surprised, if his devotion to his stupid grocery store job back in the day was anything to judge by. "Yeah, well, all I'm saying is that seventy is nothing. That's lawyering lite."

"Remember when you used to be shy?" Noah asked, the question a curveball that gave Wendy pause. She did remember. Jane had, just now, told the photographer that Wendy wasn't a shrinking violet, but that had not always been the case. When Wendy and Jane first became friends, Wendy had pretty much been the definition of a wallflower. Her dad had just died, she and her mom had moved, and she was at a new school—her whole world had been turned up-side down.

She also remembered the day she decided to *stop* being a wallflower. It had been that day on the dance floor. The day she decided to harden herself. The day she'd become un-hurtable.

It had been his doing. But Noah didn't know that. So why was he asking this? What possible relevance could it have?

Except, maybe, to make her feel self-conscious, and though she and Noah had spent years sparring, their banter didn't usually have a genuinely mean edge to it. Or at least the banter that came from his side of the court didn't.

"Shy?" Cameron saved her from having to answer. "I've only gotten to know Wendy in the last year or so, but she seems far from shy to me. Curses like a sailor, this one."

That's right. Thank you, Cameron.

Noah, who had been looking at her really intensely, like he was trying to solve a riddle written on her face, shook his head as if he'd been woken from a dream. His adversarial grin returned. "Is that so?"

It wasn't like she went around looking for opportunities to swear, but yes, it was sort of an occupational hazard. In fact, Jane had gone through several phases of trying to curb Wendy of the habit with various swear jar scenarios. If Noah hadn't known she cursed often, it was because she went out of her way to avoid him now that she was an adult. The first few times Jane had announced Noah was coming home from college to visit, Wendy had conveniently man-aged to be out of town. Then she'd just kept it up. The travel itself had become a genuine passion, though, as she'd be-come more adventurous, more confident. As she'd grown up and seen more of the world, she'd continued the dewallflowering project that she'd begun the night Noah stood her up.

"You turned into a bit of a potty mouth, did you, counselor?" Noah asked.

She raised her eyebrows to match his. "I sure as shit did." Then she put her hands on her hips. "Counselor."

"Okay, great job!" The photographer interrupted their little stand-off. "Who's next?"

Wait. What? Wendy looked around, confused. She hadn't even realized the photographer had started shooting again, and now Jane was shoving Elise toward the makeshift outdoor studio. "That's it?"

"Yeah, there was some great energy flowing there, and I got some nice shots of you." The photographer was talking to Wendy but already working on arranging Elise.

"So you can put away your claws, both of you." Jane shook her head and looked between them, her smile fond despite her admonishment. "Honestly, I forget how exhausting you two can be sometimes." She made a shooing motion at Wendy and began fussing over Elise.

Fine.

Wendy would put away her claws—for now. Because, honestly, she was exhausted, too.

Chapter Three

"Noah, can I have a word after you get your drink?"

Noah turned from the bar at Finnegan's Wake when Cameron asked his question. "Sure." After he collected his Guinness, he hoisted it in a toasting gesture and said, "Lead the way." The pub was full of little alcoves, and he followed Cameron to one around the corner from Jane and her girlfriends.

"I spoke to your mother before I asked Jane to marry me." Cameron fiddled with a cardboard coaster on the table. "But now I'm thinking I probably should have asked for your blessing, too. I know Jane asked you to be in the wedding party, but I should have spoken to you myself."

That hadn't even occurred to Noah. He would freely admit that he was a little . . . intense when it came to his sister's well-being. It was just that taking care of her had become a habit. So when Jane had called ten months ago, all hemming and hawing and embarrassed, and told him that she had a boyfriend, *and* that he was a big beefy former-military dude, Noah had practically done a dance of joy in his Manhattan living room. Jane had only ever had one boyfriend—a loser she met in college who, like a persistent infection, stuck around for a while after graduation.

After that, she'd been single for years. So when she'd brought Cameron along on a visit to New York a few months later and the guy had lived up to—no, *surpassed* expectations—on the whole "capable of taking care of Jane" front, Noah had practically gone out and bought a ring himself, in order to speed things along.

"No worries, man. You have my blessing."

"I'm not going to be working construction forever." Cameron picked up the pace on his coaster-fiddling. He was clearly uncomfortable having this conversation with his future brother-in-law. "You know I'm working on an engineering degree." Noah nodded. That Cameron had gone back to school later in life was admirable, but it didn't elementally change Noah's stance on the guy. "Jane is always on me to quit my job and go full-time, because at the rate I'm going, it's going to take me a while to get through, but I don't feel comfortable taking her money."

That was a great sentence. Noah *loved* that sentence. Jane was always assuring Noah that she had plenty of money. She'd even taken to mailing him copies of her royalty statements to prove it, which she attached to the uncashed checks he persisted in sending her. He understood with his mind that his sister was more than capable of taking care of herself. But sending money to her and to their mom was a habit so ingrained in him that he couldn't stop.

It had started with him sending money home when he'd left Toronto for college in New York. It was the only way he felt comfortable taking the full ride that NYU had offered him. He'd been determined to keep sending them as much as he'd made working at the grocery store in Toronto, so his absence wouldn't be a burden. Then when Jane had gone to university, he'd tried to help with her tuition as much as possible, and he just...hadn't stopped.

Because he couldn't.

The fact that her novels had been successful didn't reassure him the way, say, her taking up a stable corporate job with benefits would have.

And, really, why shouldn't he want a secure, comfortable life for his family? They certainly hadn't had that in the old days. He had that now—a predictable life he was in control of. It had been hard won. Was it so wrong to want the same for Jane?

"I'll be the first to admit that I haven't always been an angel," Cameron said, drawing Noah back to the present. "Especially as a kid. But one thing I've always done is worked hard and pulled my own weight."

Damn, this guy was too good to be true. Grinning, Noah clapped his sister's fiancé on the back before he could do something stupid like engulf him in a bear hug. "You're a stand-up guy, Cameron. I'm glad Jane has you." He lifted his beer.

Cameron heaved a big sigh, like he'd been in confession and received absolution, and reached for his own drink to clink against Noah's. "Thanks, man. But I don't want you getting a false impression of me. Jane has her shit way more together than I do. If anyone is getting the long end of the straw in this relationship, it's me."

"Let me ask you a question. Is my sister going to go hungry while she's with you?"

Cameron's eyes widened in surprise, and Noah held up his hand to forestall what he assumed was going to be the same argument Jane always made, that Jane made plenty of money. Yeah, yeah, he'd read the royalty statements, so he understood that, or at least the rational part of his brain did. The part that had brought home old veggies from the grocery store that had been destined for the dumpster before stir frying the hell out of them in order to put dinner on the table? That part did not. Neither did the part that went through undergrad on scholarship *and* took out loans *and* worked full time in order to keep the money flowing homeward.

"Hypothetically," Noah added, "say my sister's publisher goes out of business. She can't sell a new book. Is she going to go hungry on your watch?"

"Are you kidding me? Hell, no."

Ding, ding, ding. "And what will you do if someone hurts her?"

Cameron didn't hesitate. "I will find that person, and I will end them."

Noah chuckled in satisfaction. This guy was batting a thousand. "Then I think we're done here." He started to push back his chair, thinking they would go back and join the others.

"Not quite." Cameron leaned in closer. "I also read all your sister's books and tell her how amazing they are— because they *are*. And when she's stiff from sitting in front of the computer all day, I rub her shoulders. And when she's on a book tour, I move mountains to arrange my schedule so we can Skype every night."

"That's, ah, great," Noah said, because it was what he was supposed to say. It wasn't that he didn't care about that emotional shit. He wasn't a caveman—he wanted his sister to be happy. But he'd spent more than half his life worrying about her physical well-being, about whether she was going to bed hungry and if she had enough money for the clothes she wanted to buy so she wouldn't be embarrassed at school. You couldn't just turn that off like a water faucet. Worrying about Jane wasn't a burden he could simply set aside. But, hey, he'd gladly share some of it with Cameron.

He did the back-clapping thing again, not, this time, because he was afraid he'd spontaneously hug Cameron, but because Noah was done with this little moment of bro-sharing. Cameron had passed with flying colors.

—⟋⟍

Wendy saw her opening and seized it. As unobtrusively as possible after she'd slipped the server her credit card, she started gathering her stuff. Jane had insisted that the wedding party go out for drinks that evening, and there had been no way to get out of it. But Jane had just left to go to the bathroom, and Noah had also disappeared somewhere.

Noah's presence had been making her jumpy all evening. She'd purposely sat far from him. Tried not to look at him, even, but it turned out that actively *not* looking at someone was more work than you might think. The night was winding down and now that both siblings were gone, this was the perfect opportunity for a stealth getaway.

"Oof."

If by "stealth," she meant crashing into the very man she'd been trying to escape, causing him to spill his beer all over her white-but-not-the-right-kind-of-white shirt.

"Oh, shit, Wendy! I'm sorry." His hands shot out to steady her. He probably thought she was stumbling, when in fact she was quite consciously stepping away from him. The collision had taken place in a small hallway that would take her to the pub's main room and exit. She had been so close to freedom!

"It's okay." She tried to use the force of her mind to get him to take his hand off her forearm.

His large, warm hand, which was now doing some kind of rubbing thing on her arm that felt way too good.

"I was just on my way out anyway, so it's not a big deal," she said.

"*What?*" It was Jane, who had sneaked up on them while Wendy's attention was on her little arm massage. Wendy quickly snatched her arm from Noah.

"You can't leave!" Jane whined. "It's not even ten!"

"And you can't leave until you let me pay you back for this evening." Noah dug into his back pocket and produced his wallet. He turned to Jane. "I tried to give the server my card, and she told me a Ms. Liu had already left her card info to pay for the entire tab when we close out."

Jane, who rarely drank, had had two glasses of wine. She turned to Wendy, her eyes all moony. "Aww. That was so *nice*."

"Nice, but not happening." Noah tried to hand Wendy a wad of cash, but Wendy held up her hands. It was a reverse robbery, the suspect trying to give her money instead of take it.

"I'm the maid of honor," she said.

"And I'm the brother."

"She's my best friend."

"She's my sister."

"You guys, *stop*." Jane showed each of them a palm. "Were you always this bad? I can't remember."

"I just want you to have the best wedding—and wedding-related events—possible. I'm just trying to do my job." Wendy was lying through her teeth. There was no rule about

maids of honor paying for random wedding party drinks
three months before the wedding. Maids of honor were supposed to, like, go dress shopping and plan showers. Neither
of which she had done. She should probably get on that.

"All right. Listen." Jane turned to her brother. "What's
the tab at now?"

"Roughly two hundred."

"Okay, it'll probably get to three hundred before everyone leaves. So you guys split it." She pointed at Noah. "Give
her a hundred and fifty bucks."

Wendy and Noah both started protesting, but Jane held
up a single finger and said, "Do what I say, or I'm paying
for the whole thing."

"But I'm leaving, and what if the tab gets up past three
hundred?" Wendy said. If they were splitting the bill, they
were *splitting the bill*.

"Oh my *God*, you guys." Jane sounded annoyed, her
happy buzziness from before no longer in evidence. "I
promise that at the end of the night, I'll make sure you
each pay half. Down to the penny if you want, you freaks."
She turned to Noah. "Give her a hundred and fifty dollars."

He grumbled, but he did it. Wendy made sure their fingers didn't touch as they made the transfer.

"Thank you." Jane put her hands on her hips and
swiveled to face Wendy. "More importantly, you are not
leaving yet."

"I have a trial starting next week. I have to go home and
work."

"You are *not* leaving."

Wendy moved on to plan B. "I mean, I *wish* I could stay,
but..." She gestured to herself. Most of what had been a
full pint of very dark beer she suspected was Guinness—her

favorite, ironically—had spilled on her. She had surpassed damp. She was full-on wet.

In a white, paper-thin silk shirt. *Oh, shit.* She crossed her arms over her nipples, which were standing at attention, almost like they knew Noah was in the vicinity.

He cleared his throat. "Don't leave because I'm a klutz. Tell you what. I have a T-shirt on under this hoodie." He unzipped said hoodie. "I'll give it to you and put the hoodie back on, and we'll be good."

We will not be "good"! Wendy wanted to protest. But she was struck dumb by the sight of Noah taking off his shirt for the second time today. He went fast this time, though, and the moment she'd adjusted to the eyeful of—she hated to say it—hunky manflesh, he was slipping his arms back into the hoodie.

Damn. Wendy realized with a start that it had been *months* since she'd gotten laid. Her most recent friend-with-benefits had broken things off six months ago, when he'd met another woman he was serious about.

"Noah!" Jane laughingly scolded. "Did it not occur to you to go to the bathroom to change?"

"Nah. We're in this back hallway. No one saw—it's just you and Wendy Lou Who."

Wendy Lou Who. Jane called Wendy "Wendy Defendy," but that was a nickname that had taken root in adulthood, after Wendy had graduated from law school. Noah's nickname for her was much older. It had flattered her back in the day. Now it just annoyed her. She wasn't that girl anymore.

He held out a heather-gray T-shirt. "Your turn."

Was she mistaken, or did something flare in his eyes when he said that?

"Public nudity aside"—Jane punched Noah's upper

arm—"this is the perfect solution." She beamed as Noah pulled her into a side hug.

When Noah transformed the half hug into a full-on one, lifting his sister off her feet and banding his arms tightly around her, Wendy's heart did a funny little flop. Jane and Wendy had bonded, as kids, over the fact that they both had dead dads. They were the founding—and only—members of the Dead Dads Club.

They called themselves the Lost Girls, a là Peter Pan. Wendy was, of course, the name of one of the protagonists of the books, but the girls had discovered that in the Disney movie universe, Wendy had gone on to have a daughter called Jane, who spent time with Peter in Neverland, too.

But the difference between the two Lost Girls, was, ultimately, that Jane wasn't really lost. She'd always had Noah—steadfast, strong Noah. And sure, Noah had played surrogate big brother to Wendy back in the day, alongside all the bickering. He would drive her along with Jane to the mall. He made sure no one—except him—picked on her when she was a freshman, that sort of thing. Hell, he'd even attended Wendy's softball games sometimes, despite the fact that Jane was not on the team, simply because, she suspected from the vantage point of adulthood, he'd known that if he didn't, no one else would. Wendy's mom had been too busy working, and her aunt, though she often came over in the evenings, rarely attended games because they conflicted with choir practice at the church that was the center of her life. And that had been it for Wendy in those years: one over-worked mom and one over-Jesused aunt. So Noah had taken up the slack.

Until that horrible night he broke her heart, leaving her standing on the sidelines at the prom in that awful silver dress watching everyone else dance to goddamn Matchbox Twenty and trying to look like she didn't care that she was alone.

The memory was a good reminder that ultimately, neither Jane nor Noah had ever belonged to Wendy the way they did to each other.

And now Cameron had been thrown into the mix.

Wendy was the last Lost Girl left standing.

"Hello? Earth to Wendy?" Jane waved her hand in front of Wendy's eyes.

Wendy looked up to find the sibling hug that had triggered her little existential crisis had ended. Noah was still holding his T-shirt.

"Take this, and then give me your shirt," Noah said. "I'll have it cleaned."

"You don't have to do that. I really should just go, because—"

"Take it." Noah's voice was softer than she'd heard it all day. "Stay."

She took the shirt.

Then she went into the bathroom and put it on. He'd always smelled like a Christmas tree back in the day. What were the chances he still wore the same cologne he had as a teenager? She sniffed the shirt.

Dammit.

⎯⎯☙

Well. If seeing Wendy in a beer-drenched shirt had gotten Noah riled up, he'd had no idea what he was in for. Because when she strolled out of the bathroom wearing his shirt, his dick took note. Which was ridiculous because the shirt was too big for her. The size differential between them meant that the "short" sleeves came almost to her elbows and the hemline halfway to her knees.

He got up from where he was sitting at the end of the big semicircular booth they were all crammed into and motioned for her to slide in. She paused, uncertain, with the wet shirt in one hand. He grabbed the other end of the shirt and pulled, intending only to dislodge it from her grasp so he could take it home with him and get it dry cleaned. But since she didn't let go, the result was a tug of war. It went on until Jane cleared her throat and glared at them like a put-upon mother. Wendy stopped pulling, but she didn't let go, so he ended up tugging her closer to him. Close enough, in fact, that his T-shirt she was wearing brushed his chest. Damn. He'd had a girlfriend once who liked to sleep in his shirts. She'd seemed to kind of get off on it. He'd never really seen what the big deal was, but suddenly, he got it. If he squinted his eyes and blocked out their surroundings, he could almost imagine Wendy was wearing his shirt because she had just woken up.

Stop it. This was *Wendy*, for fuck's sake. She'd always been cute, and yes, he had kind of perved over her running attire back in the day, but he had always kept her firmly in the "honorary little sister" category.

Which was why the next thing he said made no sense at all: "You should come to New York with Jane next time she visits."

What the hell was *up* with him?

"You're a big traveler, right? That's what Jane says. I'm surprised you've never come with her before."

Eff *off*—he needed to shut the hell up.

"I need to go..."

She was about to agree. Wow, that had been easy. For some reason, he'd expected her to put up a fuss, since putting up a fuss was Wendy's default mode when it came to him. It took him a moment to adjust to the fact that she was actually agreeing with him. "Great. I can show you some off-the-beaten-track stuff in the city."

She made an inarticulate *hrmph*ing noise. "I meant *home*. I need to go home."

When she finally let go of the wet shirt and hoisted her bag on her shoulder, Jane protested loudly from across the booth.

"I have to. This trial isn't going to prepare itself." Wendy wrinkled her nose at Noah. "I'll even let him pay more than half if it gets me out of here."

"You have your witnesses all prepped, don't you?" Jane asked. "You said as much the other day."

Noah could feel the tension rolling off Wendy. She really wanted out.

"I do, but I need to work on my opening. It's a tricky case." She turned to him. "Vehicular manslaughter. No DUI; tox screens all negative; plaintiff is abject with remorse, but he took out a teenager."

"Texting?"

"Surprisingly, no. Just an old-school moment of inattention."

He whistled. "Yeah, that is going to be a tough one. What's the guy's story? What does he do?"

"Stockbroker."

Not a profession that garnered a lot of respect in the post–Wall Street bailout era. "He have a family?"

"Nope. Single."

"Nieces or nephews? Involvement with charity? Anything you can use to humanize him?"

"Nope, nope, and nope. He pretty much just makes money all day and spends it all night."

Noah wasn't really sure why he cared. If he practiced law in this jurisdiction, it would be his job to put this guy away. Hell, if he practiced here, he and Wendy would very likely have ended up on opposite sides of the courtroom from each other every now and then—arguing professionally, not just personally. The thought was...disquieting. But also strangely stimulating. He cleared his throat and turned to the table. "Sorry guys, Wendy has to go get ready for court." It was the truth. Not that he doubted her abilities, but she had an uphill battle with her case. Anyway, the case aside, she clearly didn't want to be at the bar anymore, so, as her honorary big brother, he felt duty-bound to help her make an exit.

"I really should call my aunt, too," Wendy said.

"Okay, fine," Jane moped. "I can't argue with that one. Aunt Mary needs to be called."

Noah turned to Jane. "Church with Mary tomorrow before I fly out?" Wendy's family and his, both having lost their fathers, had become close when the girls were kids. Almost like in-laws. So Noah always tried to pay Mary a visit when he was in town. Went to church with her if his visit spanned a Sunday.

"Yes!" said Jane, even as Wendy said, "No!"

Jane ignored her friend's protest. "Okay, Wendy, you're excused for now. We'll pick you up at eight thirty tomorrow."

She blew Wendy a kiss, and Wendy mimed catching it and pressing it against her heart. The sight was a jolt. They used to do that all the time when they were kids, but he'd forgotten. Seeing the adult versions of those girls performing the same ritual of devotion did something to him.

He cleared his throat. "I'll walk you to your car."

She made a dismissive gesture. "I'm taking the subway."

"Then I'll walk you to the station."

"Noah, I'm *fine*."

There was an odd edge to her tone. Like she was genuinely pissed at him. Too bad. He didn't wait for further protest, just took her arm and started for the door. Toronto was a remarkably safe city for its size, but seeing Wendy and Jane doing their kiss-catching gesture had made something turn over in his chest. Both girls had been so vulnerable back then, losing their fathers within a couple years of each other, and at such impressionable ages. He was glad they'd had each other. They'd even created the Dead Dads Club if he remembered correctly.

He hoped what little he had tried to do to help them, to smooth the way when they started high school, to make sure they had a sort of parental attention—or at least the best approximation of it he could muster—had made a bit of a difference. His mother had been too distraught over his dad's death in a car accident—and by the fact that it had been caused by his drunk driving—to pay much attention. And Wendy's had been too busy working.

"There's a subway entrance like a block from here." As they descended the steps of the pub, Wendy pointed at what was indeed a lit-up sign indicating the subway. "You don't need to walk me." Her tone was clipped. She was still mad.

"It's nice to get some fresh air," he said by way of deflection. It was funny how reflexively he slipped back into the caretaker mode when he was back in town. After his dad died, his mom fell into a spiral of grief, and his sister went totally silent, he'd had no choice but to grow up—utterly and immediately. To bow to the yoke of responsibility as he became everyone's caretaker. Worked forty hours a week while keeping up his grades for the scholarship he knew he'd need. Not that he regretted any of it. He'd done what he had to do. And, really, even though he'd regarded it as a duty, keeping Wendy company had never been a difficult one. It still wasn't.

"Well," she said when they'd reached the station entrance, "I hope you enjoyed your thirty seconds of fresh air. Bye, Noah!"

The level of enthusiasm in her good-bye, especially when she'd seemed out-of-proportion pissed at him just moments ago, put him on alert. Wendy didn't do chipper. She leaned in for a hug. That also wasn't normal. She was definitely up to something.

Before he could figure out what it was, she was skipping down the steps to the subway.

It was only hours later that he realized she had, in a kind of reverse pickpocket move, given him his hundred and fifty bucks back.

Dammit. Point to Wendy Lou Who.

Chapter Four

The next morning, when Jane texted Wendy that she and Noah were waiting for her outside her building, Wendy had her armor on.

Noah, in the passenger seat, got out and started to move into the back of Jane's tiny hatchback.

"No, no," Wendy said. "You'll never fit back there."

He waved away her protest. "I'll be fine."

"Noah, your sister drives a tiny toy car, and you're six-three."

"Are you two fighting about who *doesn't* get shotgun?" Jane shook her head. "Honestly. We're going to church. Try to control yourselves."

By the time Jane was done scolding them, Noah had gotten into the back seat. He did not, in fact, fit, but he arranged himself so his back was to the door and extended his legs along the back seat. He smirked at Wendy as she climbed into the front.

"I haven't seen Mary since Easter dinner at her place," Jane said as she pulled away from the curb.

Neither had Wendy, and that had been more than a month ago.

Shit. She was a terrible niece. She had no excuse other than that life just got busy. Wendy was devoted to her job, and Mary was devoted to the church she attended as a congregant and worked at as an administrator—and somehow the weeks slipped by. But Mary was Wendy's sole remaining family connection, and Wendy loved her fiercely.

After Wendy's dad died, her mom had taken on his shifts at the convenience store they owned, which had meant she was *always* working. They'd moved so they could be closer to the store—it was at her new school that Wendy had met Jane, which Wendy counted as an extremely lucky break. Wendy had basically been raised by the Denning siblings with a big assist from Aunt Mary. She'd go to the Dennings' after school. Then she'd go home, where Mary would meet her, give her dinner, and oversee bedtime. Even when Wendy had gotten older and had protested that she didn't need supervision anymore, Mary still came more evenings than not.

At church, they approached Mary, who was working as a greeter that morning, and she lit up brighter than a dozen communion candles. "Wendy! Sweetie!" And when she realized Jane and Noah were here? Make that a hundred communion candles.

Something squeezed in Wendy's chest, and she vowed to do better by her aunt.

"Oh my goodness!" Mary tugged Noah down and kissed him on the cheek. "What are you all doing here? You're going to give an old lady a heart attack from excitement."

Noah picked the petite woman up off her feet as he

hugged her. "I'm visiting Jane for the weekend, so we thought we'd surprise you."

"Well, you did!"

The pressure in Wendy's chest intensified. Noah could be so charming when he wanted to be. But that wasn't really the right word. *Charming* implied a note of falsity, of manipulation. There was none of that. His interactions with Aunt Mary always seemed one hundred percent genuine. Unlike Wendy, he had an easy way with people. In high school, he'd been the rare person who could move between social groups and be welcomed in each of them. He'd been as at home with the jocks and popular kids as with the chess club—or with the nerdy friend of his little sister. For as much as he'd sparred with her, he'd taken care of her—*and* her little family, such as it was.

Her moment of wistfulness was cured, though, when the collection plate came past them. Wendy usually dropped ten bucks in, and so did the Dennings when they came. This time, though, Noah dropped a huge wad of cash in the plate and shot her a smug look.

He was putting in the money she'd given back to him last night. And there wasn't a thing she could do about it. She tried to lean over Mary to protest, but Mary elbowed her in the ribs and said, along with the congregation, "Accept this joyful offering as a token of our abiding love."

Goddammit.

Point to Noah Denning.

—☙

"You guys want to come to my place for brunch?" Jane asked as she pulled away from the church. "Cameron's cooking."

"Nope. I want to go running before my flight." Noah twisted around to face Wendy in the back seat—she had won the "reverse shotgun" battle for the return trip. "I was hoping to convince you to come with me. I brought my running stuff." He pointed at a gym bag he'd stashed in the back seat. "You in?" He didn't really know why he wanted her to come. She was going to wipe the floor with him.

Well, he did know: bastard that he was, he wanted to see grown-up Wendy in running clothes.

"I'm training for a half. So I'm doing eleven miles today." She raised her eyebrows like she doubted he could keep up.

She was not incorrect in her assessment. But no way in hell he was going to back down from an implied challenge like that. "That's cool," he lied.

"I'll need to get my stuff, so why don't we both change at my place?"

"How come you're not inviting me to go running with you?" Jane tried to pout as she altered her route to head downtown toward Wendy's, but she couldn't even get the sentence fully out before she cracked up. Everyone knew that Jane was allergic to exercise.

When she pulled up in front of Wendy's building, Jane physically pushed Noah out of the car even as she stuck her tongue out at Wendy in the rearview mirror. "You two freaks do realize that most people go for carby brunches after church, right? Cameron is making eggs Benedict for us *right now*. Last chance."

Wendy hovered with one foot on the pavement and one foot still in the car, as if she were tempted by the idea of brunch.

"Come on," Noah prodded. "Afraid I'll beat you?"

Instead of answering, she got all the way out of the

car—she was so delightfully easy to bait. "What's your half marathon time?"

It wasn't lost on him that this was the third time she'd asked. He could no longer deflect the question. He tried not to betray any of the chagrin he felt as he said, "Two hours even." And that had been a year ago, the last time he'd run one.

Wendy nodded. Tried and failed to suppress a smile. "You're on."

Which is how he found himself in Wendy's bathroom thinking about her changing in her bedroom across the hall.

She emerged in a loose tank top. It was a little disappointing.

But as she took off down the sidewalk, he realized her grown-up running wear wasn't without its charms. The tank top featured a barely-there racerback, and she wore it over one of those bras that had a bunch of delicate little straps running in an elaborate grid over her back. Her back was lovely. It was a weird body part to find appealing, but... it just was. It was subtly muscular, and he was hypnotized by the way her shoulder blades undulated as she pumped her arms.

He focused on them as he put one leg in front of the other and accelerated to catch up with her—he'd let himself fall behind.

"Keep up, old man!" she yelled, and time folded in on itself. She had always shouted that at him as she sprinted off at the beginning of a run. He had an unsettling sense of déjà vu, of doing this very same thing... what? Almost twenty years ago?

It was spring of his senior year of high school, and he'd been lured out for a run by Wendy after school but before the night shift at the store. Usually he napped in those precious hours. Four night shifts and one weekend day at the store every week plus school had him exhausted. But it was one of those perfect, cold April days when it was just starting to feel like spring was winning the battle with winter. And a run with Wendy always lifted his spirits. Sometimes, it even made him feel like he could just...keep running. Run away from his life and all the endless responsibilities it contained.

Just keep following her bouncing ponytail forever, off into the big wide world.

Except today, despite the fact that the spirit was willing, he *physically* couldn't. Usually they were well-matched. Even though he wasn't running on the school team anymore, he generally managed to keep pace with her. But today, he was exhausted.

The gap between them widened. She didn't notice at first, and he watched her fade into the distance.

Agitation started to claw at him. Not about her beating him, but about...surviving. God. He was *so tired*. How was he going to make it through the rest of the school year? Recently, in moments of exhaustion like this, he'd been starting to panic. Everything was starting to feel so...out of control. Like no matter how hard he worked, he still might not be capable of beating back the forces of chaos that had the power to ruin them.

And then he was going to leave town for college? What the hell had he been *thinking*?

Wendy stopped and looked over her shoulder. He took a deep breath and forced his leaden legs forward. He'd catch up with her, and she'd give him shit. Gloat over outrunning him. He looked forward to it. It would tether him to reality, arrest the panic. It occurred to him that good-naturedly arguing with Wendy was one of the only things he *hadn't* lost when his dad died. He was only sorry he'd had to quit the debate team before she joined. He would have enjoyed making their tendency to spar official.

He was huffing by the time he reached her. But smiling, too. She had somehow, just by standing there with her hands on her hips waiting for him, managed to beat back his impending meltdown. He was ready for her disdain.

It didn't come.

"You're so tired," she said.

What could he do but agree? "Yes."

"You're not sleeping enough." She tilted her head and paused for a beat before adding, "But what can you do? It's not like you have a choice."

The simple statement almost took his breath away. It wasn't that he needed sympathy. He didn't feel sorry for himself. It was just that sometimes it felt like Wendy was the only person who saw him. *Really* saw him. His mother was too lost in her grief and guilt. Jane was...good. She hadn't caused a lick of trouble since their dad died. She worked, too, babysitting and tutoring—as much as he would let her—and she gave him all her money. But she never commented on any of it. They hadn't spoken about their new lot in life.

But Wendy. Smart Wendy. She saw things.

"I *don't* have a choice," he agreed, panting and glad of it because his breathlessness was covering the emotion that would otherwise be weighing down his voice.

"Let's just walk," she said.

And they did.

And she gave him no shit. Just told him about the season's debating theme, which was education. "This week I'm arguing that homework should be banned."

He laughed. "I wish."

"That would make your life a lot easier, wouldn't it?" She was still being uncharacteristically serious. Still *seeing* him.

"Why did I think I could go to college in New York?"

She furrowed her brow. From her point of view the question had come from nowhere. And as a rule, he didn't burden other people—especially not Jane or Wendy—with his worries. But it was like the question was too big to stay contained in his body. Some foolhardy part of him had just blurted it out.

But if she'd been surprised by the non sequitur, she recovered quickly. Kept walking. "Because you got a full scholarship to a great school in a great city."

"But I can't just leave them."

"You can," she said calmly, turning onto a path that cut through a park near their houses. "It's not that far."

"It's not like I can't get just as good an education at the University of Toronto." Now that he'd started voicing the second thoughts that had been plaguing him since he'd accepted the NYU offer, he couldn't seem to stop. "I could live at home, and—"

She wasn't having it. She held up a palm meant to silence him, stopped walking, and turned to face him. "Look. Jane will be fine. I'll make sure of it. She and I have already decided we're going to go to college together, so you don't have to worry about her. I'll be sticking to her like glue."

"But my mother—"

"Is an adult." She leveled a stern look at him, but then her face softened. "And she's not as bad as she used to be."

"You think?" He'd been wondering about that himself. His mom had been interacting with them more.

Coming out of her room to watch *EastEnders* with Jane. She'd even gone on a walk around the block the first nice day of spring. But he hadn't been sure if he'd been reading too much into all that. And there was no one he could talk to about it. No one with whom to triangulate his impressions.

Well, he'd *thought* there was no one. But of course that wasn't right. There was Wendy.

"Yes," she said firmly, and he believed her. Wendy didn't do bullshit.

Her face underwent a further softening. She looked at him and saw his struggles. Quietly acknowledged them. "You're allowed to do something for yourself, Noah."

She was talking about New York, but suddenly, what he wanted to do for himself, here in this park with the birds chirping, was to kiss her.

It was the strangest goddamned thing. It was like some external force had invaded him and stuck this rogue idea in his head. *Kiss Wendy Lou Who.* The girl who saw him.

She must have felt it, too, because her eyes widened and her breath made little puffs of steam in the cold air as she emitted a series of short exhales.

His hand floated up and came to rest on her cheek. It was hot. His skin felt hot all over, too, and he didn't think it was from the running.

"Noah," she whispered.

He thought later that if she had just remained silent, he probably would have done it. But that single word, her familiar voice, jolted him back to his senses. He might be romanticizing Wendy at this moment as capable of seeing into his soul or some shit, but she was still *Wendy*. His little sister's best friend.

What the hell was the *matter* with him?

So, accustomed to doing his duty, Noah retracted his hand, ruthlessly beat back the rising tide of disappointment inside him, and summoned his best big brother voice. "Thanks, Wendy. Knowing you'll be keeping your eye on Jane and my mom will make me feel so much better when I'm gone."

She blinked, clearly in need of a moment to adjust to what had just happened—or not happened.

But then, ever perceptive, she turned and started walking again. He followed, both thankful and disappointed that the...incident had passed unremarked on.

After a few moments, she said, "Only a couple months till school is over. You'll be able to get some rest then, I hope."

"Summer sounds like a dream right now," he agreed, both because it was true but also because he was happy to have something mundane to talk about. "No homework. Just the store. We can go running in the evenings without me falling over dead."

She shot him a sly look—she looked like her usual self again. Once again a mixture of regret and relief swirled through him.

"So maybe by the end of next summer, you'll be able to catch me." And then she took off.

Shaking off the memory, Noah pumped his legs to try to close the gap between them, and this time, in the real and not the daydream world, he had enough energy to do so. He took one last look at Wendy's back before falling into step beside her. Then they jogged side by side at an easy pace for twenty or so minutes until they reached the edge of Riverdale Park. She'd suggested they run to the park and pick up the Don River trail.

"Race you to that tree!" She pointed at an enormous maple about a hundred yards off and sprinted away.

She left him in the dust.

Point to Wendy—both the kid and the grown-up versions of her.

Chapter Five

The text came from Jane just as the front door buzzer rang inside Wendy's condo.

> I'm in your lobby, and I'm invoking the Josh Groban clause.

Wendy tried to swear but she laughed at the same time, so it came out more like a snort. She buzzed Jane up, unlocked the door, and went to the kitchen to turn on the kettle.

The Josh Groban clause. That was not normally a phrase Wendy enjoyed hearing. Wendy and Jane, despite their closeness, did not have the same taste. Never had: back in the day, Jane had been obsessed with the Baby-Sitters Club while Wendy immersed herself in the world of J. R. R. Tolkien. Peter Pan had been their only overlap, really.

She and Jane had an agreement to help manage their present-day divergent taste: Wendy went with Jane to hear the sanitized Pop Ken Doll known as Josh Groban, and Jane went with Wendy to hear the indie bands she favored.

"Hi!" Jane let herself in the front door and kicked off her shoes.

"When and where?" Wendy asked, dropping tea bags into mugs and pouring water over them as she grinned at the sight of her bestie.

Jane sat on one of the stools at Wendy's breakfast bar. "Saturday. Madison Square Garden."

Wendy choked on her first sip of tea. "New York? I'm not going to New York with you to see Josh Groban!" She made a theatrical choking noise to supplement her previous genuine one. But, really: no way. She hadn't seen Noah since his surprise visit six weeks ago, and she was only just starting to get her equilibrium back.

"But—"

Wendy held up a palm. "The Josh Groban clause does not have a provision for air travel!"

Jane made an inarticulate defeated noise and slumped her shoulders.

Aww, shit. Guilt-trip: activated. "Shouldn't you take Cameron anyway?" Wendy needed to start getting used to the idea that she wasn't Jane's main person anymore.

"Cameron hates Josh Groban."

Now *there* was something she could appreciate about Cameron. "And I don't?"

"Of course you do, but unlike Cameron, you're contractually obligated." Jane winked. "Anyway, I have an ulterior motive. I was thinking I might go dress shopping."

"I thought you had a dress." Part of Jane's commitment to a "low-key" wedding was that she'd ordered a simple dress from J Crew.

"I do. It's just that I was talking to Gia the other day,

and she offered to get me in at this super fancy bridal salon where you basically have to be famous to get an appointment. At first I was, like, no, but then I googled it, and oh my *God*, Wendy. You should *see* these dresses. I mean, I know I'm not supposed to want the big, puffy, expensive dress, but…"

Dammit. If this was about the wedding and not just Josh Groban, there was really no way Wendy could in good conscience get out of it. She was supposed to be doing a better job at this whole maid of honor thing, right? Here was a ready-made opportunity. All she had to do was get on a plane and then smile and nod and tell Jane how beautiful she was when really the voluminous dresses she was considering would make her look like a fluffy marshmallow.

She could feel herself weakening.

Jane set her mug down on the bar. "I was thinking this trip might get you a little action, too."

Wendy choked on her tea for the second time. "Excuse me, what?"

"Oh, come on. You've been complaining lately about being in a slump. It's been, what? Six months?"

"Seven and a half months, actually." Not that she was counting. But Jane's point was taken. Things were a little…arid down there.

"You broke up with Christopher, okay, but—"

"We didn't 'break up.'" Wendy made air quotes with her fingers. She didn't like to interrupt her friend, but the correction was necessary. "We were never together."

"Well, you kind of were."

"No. We were fuck buddies. Then he got serious about a woman."

"And that didn't bother you at all?" Jane had never really been down with Wendy's preference toward casual sexual relationships. It wasn't that she didn't approve; she fundamentally didn't understand.

"No," Wendy answered honestly. "It bothered my vagina, maybe, but I *liked* Christopher. I'm glad he's happy."

"God, you're as bad as Gia!"

Their absent friend Gia was known for her devotion to casual sex. "Hey, the modern woman doesn't need a man," Wendy said. And Wendy wasn't as bad as Gia. Not that "bad" was the correct word. Wendy admired Gia's pleasure-seeking ways, but Gia would never go seven and a half months without doing the deed. Wendy wasn't sure how she'd let it go so long, except that, like most lawyers, she worked a million hours a week. Christopher had been a lawyer, too, so late-night liaisons had been easy to arrange.

"Anyway, I don't need to go to New York to get laid." Wendy didn't partake too much in the hard-living life that tended to come with her profession, but it was easy enough to "make friends" when she wanted to. She would replace Christopher when she felt like it. But she took Jane's point—she should probably get on that.

But... An image suddenly pushed its way into her mind—an image of a shirtless Noah Denning smirking at her. And the image had sound.

You should come to New York with Jane next time she visits.

"Oh, I forgot!" Jane hopped off the stool and came back with her bag, from which she produced a package. "My brother sent this to you care of my address."

She dropped the package on the island with a thud. After a one-second delay, there was an identical thud in the pit of Wendy's stomach. The return address was the Office of the New York County District Attorney.

Wendy leaped off her stool like it had burned her.

"It must be your shirt," Jane said. "I told him to leave it here for me to get cleaned, but nope, he insisted on taking it home with him and sending it to his trusted dry cleaner. That's so like him, isn't it? Go way out of his way to make sure something's done right." Jane rolled her eyes, but they gleamed with affection.

"Yes," Wendy said, but it occurred to her that she didn't really know what Noah was like, not anymore. She'd gone running with him when he was last here, but that was the most time she'd spent with him in years. Sixteen-year-old Noah would absolutely have made sure her shirt was taken care of. And modern-day Noah had gone out of his way to do so.

So how to square those versions of him with the one in between? The eighteen-year-old Noah who'd stood her up at the prom? Left her standing there in a dress she'd withdrawn money from her college fund to buy, her face inexpertly painted in newly purchased makeup, the only girl without a corsage because she was the only girl without a date?

Jane had started it all. It had been a joke to begin with, an innocent question lobbed at Tim, a friend of Noah's from the grocery store. It was a mid-May evening, and Wendy and Jane were studying in the Dennings' kitchen as Tim and Noah clattered in, just off a shift.

Well, Wendy was studying; Jane was flipping through *Seventeen* and sighing over a spring formal spread. Wendy *had* been studying, but, as was the case lately, the minute Noah entered a room, her brain turned to mush.

A big ball of mush incapable of thinking about anything beyond the feeling of his hand on her cheek. And as if on cue her cheek—just the one—started burning.

It had been a month since their last run, and she couldn't get over it.

It was just that she'd thought…he'd been about to kiss her? Was that even possible? She still didn't know.

Noah's eyes skittered to Wendy. She'd been staring at him without meaning to. *Crap.* She quickly looked away and forced herself to pay attention to Jane, who was grinning and batting her eyelashes theatrically at Tim.

"Tim, will you take me to the prom?"

Though they ran in different social circles at school, Tim and Noah had become friends at the store. They would often hole up in Noah's room and play video games after a shift. Tim was a rebel of sorts—he had a rock band and he was perpetually on the verge of flunking out. He was a little bit of a legend at their school. And Jane had a crush on him.

It was a mild one though, and it was an open secret—she'd turned it into a bit of a running joke. Tim the brooding bad boy was so different from serious, shy Jane that everyone took Jane's theatrical crushing in the lighthearted spirit in which it was intended.

"Why on earth would I want to do that?" Tim teased.

"Are you *kidding*?" Jane said. "Underclassmen can't go to the prom unless they go with a senior. Think of the social currency that I, a nerdy freshman, would acquire by showing up at the senior prom with *you*."

"Oh, come on," Tim said. "You're not a nerd. You're the coolest girl I know."

Jane burst out laughing. "Then you don't know ninety-nine percent of East York Collegiate."

It was true. Star debater Wendy and comic book nerd Jane weren't getting their heads flushed down toilets or anything, but there was also no way they were getting asked to the prom. For her part, Wendy didn't care. If something wasn't even remotely within your grasp, what was the point of getting worked up about not having it? It was like getting your undies in a bunch because you didn't win the lottery. Why waste the energy?

"Oh my gosh," Jane went on, staring off into space dreamily. "If I showed up at the prom on the arm of East York's resident bad boy, I wouldn't have to worry about *anything* the next three years. Ha!"

Both the guys looked at Wendy, as if for confirmation of what Jane was saying. They were both unplugged from the social reality of school, Noah because he worked so much and Tim because he really *was* East York's resident bad boy and hence had better things to do. She shrugged and nodded. Everything Jane was saying was true.

"Aww, shit." Tim rolled his eyes good-naturedly. "When is it?"

Jane gasped and her eyes grew comically wide. "A week from Saturday."

"Do I have to wear a tux? I'm not wearing a tux. I can get away with that—I'm a bad boy, right?"

"Oh my God! Are you serious?" Jane started jumping up and down, her face awash in happiness. If Tim hadn't been serious, he was now—there was no way anyone could look at that face and not do its owner's bidding.

Tim performed a surrendering shrug. "What the hell? Why not do a good deed before I'm done doing my time at that cesspit of a school?"

Jane hugged Tim, then danced over to her brother and hugged him, too. "You're not going to get all pissy about this, are you, Noah?"

"Nope." He clapped Tim on the back. "It's your grave, dude." The fact that Noah, who was usually so protective of Jane, had given his blessing reinforced just how not a threat

Tim was to Jane, romantically speaking. So it would be a platonic date.

Wendy tried to be happy for her friend. Sure, there was no point in getting your undies in a bunch when you didn't win the lottery. That was still true. But when your best friend won a nice chunk of money playing one of those scratch-off games, it stung.

She forced herself not to look at Noah.

"Eee!" Jane was glowing. "I'm so excited! I can't—"

Wendy could practically see the wheels turning in Jane's head as Jane clamped her mouth shut. She was belatedly realizing that since Wendy wasn't going, she shouldn't be too over the top with her excitement.

Wendy and Jane didn't usually do awkward. They were too deeply embedded in each other's lives for that.

But it turned out there was a first time for everything.

"It's going to be great!" What could Wendy do but recite her lines? "We can go dress shopping tomorrow!"

She must not have been a very convincing actress, though, because Jane's face took on a pained expression and things got even *more* awkward.

"You should take Wendy," Tim said.

Wait. *What?* Was he talking to *Noah*?

"Yes!" Jane said. "That is a brilliant idea! We'll double!"

What was happening?

"I can't." Noah looked at her with apology in his eyes.

Wendy opened her mouth to agree, but no sound came out.

"I work Saturday nights," he added.

"But only until eight," Tim countered. "Wendy can arrive with us, and you can meet us there."

Noah looked like Wendy felt: trapped. But then he seemed to shake himself out of it, and he smiled. It wasn't his usual easy, confident smile, though. It was kind of an awkward, little one, like he was an extraterrestrial trying to master a strange human custom. "All right. Let's do it."

Jane shrieked with joy, picked up her magazine, and started babbling about how amazing Wendy would look in a silver dress she'd seen in it.

Wendy opened her mouth to tell everyone this was a bad idea. But then she shut it. The problem, this time, wasn't that her voice had deserted her. It was that her *scruples* had deserted her. She wanted to go to the stupid prom with Noah. She wanted to get that silver dress and some ridiculously high heels she'd barely be able to walk in, and be seen with a cool senior under a disco ball in the school gym.

But more than all that, she wanted to dance with Noah. When she went running with him, she always felt like there was a bubble around them, a protective shield that temporarily kept out the real world. Inside the bubble they could laugh and talk without the oppression of reality.

Inside the bubble, they could be together.

Dancing, she imagined, would be like that, but more. He would literally have his arms around her. Her heart pounded like they *were* on a run.

"It's not like I ever have time to go to dances anyway," Noah said. "I should probably go to one before I graduate, right?"

Noah's expression was impossible to read. But he formed his face into another smile. Not an awkward one this time but also not one of his signature easy ones. There was...heat in that smile?

Could that be right?

"Anyway, I actually think it will be fun. What do you say, Wendy?"

She felt that hand on her cheek like it had never left.

Could she be brave? Could the wallflower step away from the wall long enough to take what she wanted?

Yes.

So, heart beating like crazy, she smiled back at him. "I say yes."

"Hello?" Jane waved her hand in front of Wendy's face. "Hello? Paging Wendy Defendy. Someone's at the door downstairs."

"What?" Wendy shook her head as the sound of the front door buzzer rang through the apartment. Holy shit, she'd totally tuned out while she'd made that unfortunate walk down bad-memory lane. But she took comfort in the notion that she hadn't made it all the way to the conclusion of the prom disaster. If she ever wrote an autobiography, she would just leave that chapter out. She wasn't that girl anymore. She'd worked hard to not be. She'd picked herself up off that dance floor and changed. Noah had left for college two weeks after the dance, and the next time she'd seen him, she'd become someone else.

"Sorry. I sort of spaced out there for a minute. It's been a long week." She walked over to the buzzer. "Yes?"

"It's Mary."

Wendy buzzed her in. Every once in a while, her aunt stopped in unannounced. It was so delightfully old-school that it always made Wendy happy.

"Wendy." Mary engulfed her in a hug before she even got all the way into the condo. "I was in the neighborhood, and I thought I'd bring you this. I saw it at the church rummage sale and thought of you."

It was an old copy of *Let's Go Czechoslovakia*.

Wendy smiled and refrained from pointing out that Czechoslovakia wasn't a country anymore.

"I don't even know if you're doing Eastern Europe on this trip of yours," Mary said. Even though they didn't have a lot in common, Mary enthusiastically supported Wendy's interests. That meant watching legal dramas on TV and giving her outdated travel guides.

"Jane! What a nice surprise!" It was Jane's turn to get the Mary hug.

The Mary hug was a good thing.

In fact, when Mary released Jane, Wendy went in for another one.

"Oh!" Mary sounded startled, but she wrapped her arms around Wendy again. "Is everything all right?"

"Yes." Wendy's voice was embarrassingly squeaky. Thinking about the prom, which was something she usually avoided doing at all costs, had weakened her defenses. "I'm just glad you're here." They might not have a lot in common, but Wendy could count on Mary. Mary would never abandon her to social mortification and heartbreak. She glanced at Jane. Unlike literally everyone else in Wendy's life, Mary was a constant—she would never change.

"We have a new choir director at church." Her aunt pulled back from the embrace but kept her arms on Wendy's shoulders and examined her face. "He's doing all these modern songs. Half the congregation is up in arms, but I think he's amazing."

"Oh?" Wendy welcomed the small talk. "What do you mean by 'modern songs'?"

"You want to come with me on Sunday and check it out? I heard they're working on a 'mash-up.'" She made quotation marks with her fingers. "I have no idea what that means."

Jane cleared her throat, drawing Wendy's attention. Because they had BFF ESP, Wendy knew Jane was saying,

You can't go to church Sunday because you have a previous engagement with Josh Groban.

When Wendy didn't say anything immediately, Jane said, "Miss Mary, I was just trying to convince Wendy to come to New York with me for a little impromptu weekend getaway."

"Oh, that sounds like much more fun than questionable choral mash-ups!" Mary exclaimed.

Instead of commenting, Wendy poured her aunt a cup of tea. Her gaze landed on the package from Noah. She started ripping it open in order to postpone having to make a decision about New York.

"Airfares are cheap right now," Jane said. "And we can stay with Noah."

Right. Yay. In addition to being tormented by memories of teenage Noah, she'd get all kinds of unwanted exposure to the current-day one.

Inside the package was, as Jane had predicted, her blouse, nestled carefully in a tissue-paper-lined box and restored to its previous pristine state. There was also a note.

Sorry again for the beer shower. Took this to my local wizard of a dry cleaner, then promptly forgot about it, hence the delay. Do you still collect these? —N.

Wendy gasped. Under the blouse was a New York Yankees Pez dispenser. She did use to collect them—though as a lifelong Yankees hater, she never would have collected this particular one. It had been a rare flight of fancy for her as a kid. She'd never told anyone the story behind the collection. The last time she'd been with her father, the day before his fatal heart attack, he'd given her a Pez. Wendy, like nine-year-old girls everywhere, had been drawn in by the Disney princess marketing machine. Her father almost never gave in to her request for treats from the store, but that day he had ruffled her hair and handed over a Princess Jasmine dispenser.

And then, the next day, he died.

She had eaten the candy at his funeral, hiding Jasmine in her pocket and pulling back her head, the little rectangles of candy the perfect size for covert eating. She would pretend to cry—well, she hadn't actually had to pretend—bring a tissue up to her face, and slide a Pez into her mouth.

She'd gone on to collect the rest of the princesses. And it had spiraled from there.

Leave it to Noah to remember that.

"What is that? Oh!" Jane smiled. "You used to collect Pez! I forgot about that! What happened to your collection?" She looked around as if expecting a collection of plastic, head-retracting candy dispensers to suddenly appear in Wendy's condo.

"Oh, they're in a box somewhere." In her storage locker, to be exact. She'd debated getting some kind of shelf or something to display them—grown-ups were allowed to collect quirky things, right?—but in the end she'd decided they were too immature for an adult woman to have. Or at least to advertise that she had considering she hadn't been able to bring herself to actually get rid of them.

"You know what? I think that's a sign!" Jane nodded at the Yankees Pez. "How crazy is it that Noah sends you a New York–themed Pez dude at the exact same time I'm trying to convince you to go there with me? Come on, this is probably your last chance before your big trip."

You should come to New York with Jane next time she visits.

"Listen to Jane," Mary said. "Get out of here for the weekend."

Well, that was it. They were unanimous. Jane, Mary, and the imaginary Noah voice in her head all wanted her to go to New York.

Wendy tore open the package, loaded the dispenser, slid back the player's little plastic baseball cap, and pressed a tart orange candy against her tongue.

Maybe she was crazy. Maybe she'd regret it. But...

"Okay. New York, here we come."

Chapter Six

$\mathscr{N}$oah loitered in the baggage claim area in LaGuardia Friday night, his heart light. It had been a long but productive week at work—jury deliberations on a multi-week trial had concluded, and he'd put away a murderer. Maybe that was an odd thing to inspire light-heartedness, but there was nothing like the successful completion of a trial to give him a satisfying feeling of control and order. And on top of that, his sister was arriving for a visit.

"Noah!" Jane appeared seemingly from nowhere and launched herself at him. "Surprise! Wendy came with me!"

A strange spike of adrenaline made it seem like he suddenly had heat-seeking vision. As he looked over his sister's shoulder at her best friend, who was approaching at a more sedate pace, he somehow became a superhero capable of seeing things regular people couldn't. Like, for example, the little horizontal slice of skin that was barely visible between the top of Wendy's jeans and the hem of her cropped shirt. It disappeared and reappeared as she moved, creating a kind of hypnotic effect. Probably no one else would notice it. So maybe it wasn't heat-seeking vision so much as it was Wendy-seeking vision?

He pulled away from his sister. Wendy drew closer and…shit. He had no idea how he was supposed to greet her. Should he hug her like he had Jane? Shaking her hand seemed way too formal.

And, hello, why was he thinking so hard about this? This was Wendy. Of *course* he should hug her.

She was a little stiff initially, making him fear he had miscalculated, but after a second she softened against him and wrapped her arms loosely around him, returning the embrace. Her breasts brushed against his chest, and God *damn* those breasts. He tried to tell himself that objectively speaking, Wendy had smaller than average breasts. So how was it possible that he was so affected by them? It was just that they seemed so…perfectly proportional to the rest of her. And more than just that, their smallness was part of their appeal. It was hard to make sense of.

Well, it was hard to make sense of with his mind.

Other parts of him were having *no problem* making sense of the whole Wendy thing.

Which, *shit*— He pulled away, grabbing the handle to his sister's roller suitcase and tugging Wendy's duffel bag off her shoulder.

She didn't want to let it go, but he glared at her until she relented and fell into step beside him.

"You should be thanking me," she said.

For giving me a woody? He shot her a bewildered look, because she couldn't know how she had affected him. She couldn't know about the Wendy-seeking vision. *Could she?*

"Because I'm here, you're off the hook for Josh Groban duty." She cracked up. He'd noticed when he was in Toronto for the photo shoot that she had developed a sort of signature laugh. She would throw back her head and...cackle. That was really the only word for it. It was like she was so delighted by what she was saying, she couldn't contain herself. Like cursing, she hadn't done that when she was a girl. He didn't quite know what to make of the laughing, swearing, grown-up Wendy.

"Although maybe I'm making too much of an assumption here," she went on. "Maybe you actually love Josh Groban. I'm just thinking about your unnatural devotion to Nirvana back in the day and guessing that a fluffy-haired Sinatra wannabe isn't really your jam."

It was his turn to laugh, a big, genuine laugh, and it felt good. "Hey, Cobain was a certified genius. Way better than your precious Neko Case." He had forgotten how they used to battle it out for the stereo after school—at least until they had to join forces and unite against Jane, who had always wanted to listen to Mandy Moore.

Wendy opened her mouth, surely to escalate the argument about whose long-ago musical taste was better, but he cut her off. "Wendy Lou Who, despite your perplexing devotion to sensitive singer-songwriters, your underlying assertion regarding my position on Josh Groban is correct. So, yes, I *should* thank you. You are a goddamned *saint* for taking on Groban duty. Not only will I reimburse you for your ticket, I'll take you two out wherever you want to go for dinner tomorrow before the show. Hell, I'll take you out tonight, too. What's your pleasure?"

"Oh, and Kurt Cobain *wasn't* a sensitive singer-songwriter?"

He was trying to formulate his rebuttal—even though she was kind of right—when Jane said, "*My* pleasure is to hole up at your apartment with a Big Mac Extra Value Meal and finish chapter twelve." Jane was working on book eight of her Clouded Cave series, and she'd been complaining about what a slog this volume was. "I told my agent to give me interim deadlines, and I was supposed to email her chapters eight through twelve by *yesterday*."

The way she wailed "yesterday" made Noah smile. He found Wendy's gaze, and they shared a knowing look. It shouldn't have been surprising that they were so in tune—Wendy knew his sister as well as he did.

"*Jane.*" Wendy stopped in her tracks and turned to face her friend. "We're in New York City to buy a magical fairy princess wedding dress and to see your favorite talentless man-child singer! You're not going to stay in and write! Or eat McDonald's! *God.*"

Noah was in complete agreement. "Listen to Wendy. She was always the smart one." He dodged Jane's mock-outraged punch. "There are so many things we could do tonight. We could see a show, hit some galleries—or there's an exhibition at the library on the history of the book." God knew his sister loved libraries.

"Listen, you guys. I know it's dumb, but I'm not going to be able to relax until this is done. If I don't finish this chapter, it's going to *ruin* Josh Groban! If you just let me do this tonight, I *promise* I'll be the world's best tourist and bride-to-be the rest of the weekend." Jane started walking toward the exit as if to signal the end of the discussion. Noah and Wendy had no choice but to follow her. She waved her hand at them as they caught up, the way a society lady would dismiss a servant. "You two can go out, though. In fact, I insist. I'll get this done way faster if you're not underfoot. You guys are both crazy I-heart-New-Yorkers—you can have a little urban hipster geek-out."

Noah looked at Wendy. He could suddenly imagine lots of worse ways to spend a Friday night.

—ᔐ

"Wow!" Wendy exclaimed as the taxi pulled up in front of Noah's building.

Noah grinned. Her curiosity had been piqued ever since the taxi turned north on 678. "Do you live in the *Bronx*?" she'd demanded, and when he'd assured her no, just really, really far up Manhattan, she'd said, "Hmm," and raised her eyebrows slightly, like she was surprised but trying to hide it.

Jane laughed. "Noah lives in this, like, Tudor castle in Manhattan. Have I never told you that?"

"Not a castle," Noah said. "Just a co-op." But he did love his building and his neighborhood. Hudson Heights felt to him like a hidden oasis in the city, and the enormous Hudson View Gardens co-op complex was its gem. He glanced at Wendy. "So you've been to New York a bunch of times?"

"You probably don't realize how much Wendy has turned into a major travel monster," Jane said. "I swear, she's always jetting off somewhere."

He hadn't known that. Like the swearing and the signature laugh, that didn't jibe with his memory of the teenage Wendy.

"Well, not *always*," Wendy said. "But I do like to travel. When I can't get off big chunks of time from work, which I often can't—it's hard when you're a litigator, which I'm sure you know—I tend to hit nearby big cities for long weekends. New York is a short, easy flight from Toronto."

"You've probably never been this far north in Manhattan, though." Most tourists didn't venture as far as his neck of the woods.

"I've been to the Cloisters," she said with a hint of superiority, naming the museum that was indeed half a dozen blocks north of him. Wendy had to be good at *everything*, didn't she? Even tourism.

A few minutes later, his sister was *ooh*ing and *aah*ing over the view of the courtyard and private garden his apartment had—as she did every time she visited. He was trying not to smirk as he watched Wendy press her lips together and take in the living room that opened onto a small nook he used as an office. It was a lot of square footage for Manhattan. He didn't bother telling her that the neighborhood was actually pretty affordable—or at least it had been back when he bought. You didn't become a public prosecutor to get rich, but with this apartment, he could put up a good front.

"I'll change the sheets on my bed," he said. "That way each of you can take a bedroom, and I'll sleep on the sofa."

"We can share the guest bed." Jane dumped her computer case on his desk. "We totally sprung Wendy on you."

"Hey, she's doing Josh Groban duty. She deserves a bed."

"You have two bedrooms?" Wendy's tone was a little too carefully neutral.

"Yup." Noah was still working on suppressing the smirk that was threatening. Which was dumb because even though they were always competing, it wasn't like having a bigger apartment than Wendy equated to any kind of moral superiority.

Wendy strolled over to the window to take in the view. "Your plants are all dead." Well, maybe not to take in the view but to criticize his horticultural failings.

"Yeah." His ex Clarissa had brought them over. They were part of the slow drip of her stuff that had accumulated at his place and had ultimately led to their relationship-ending "are we moving in together or not?" reckoning. She hadn't taken the plants with her when she left, but thanks to his negligence, they were now as gone as she was, a pathetic metaphor for his inability to ever pull the trigger and settle down permanently with a woman.

It was odd, though, when he thought about it. He kept the rest of his apartment in perfect order. He was usually pretty good with responsibility. The dead plants were kind of an anomaly.

Or…they were just plants. They held no symbolic meaning.

"I guess I don't have a green thumb." He grabbed the women's bags. "Let's get you two settled."

He hesitated outside the door to his bedroom, which was the first doorway along the hallway. Rationally, he should put Wendy in the guest room and stick his sister in his room. Not that he had anything to hide, but there was something kind of intimate about having someone sleep in your bed. The logical thing would be to assign it to Jane.

He walked in and dropped Wendy's duffel on his bed.

⸺ᴄ⸱

Noah's bedroom smelled like him. Which meant Noah's bedroom smelled like Christmas trees.

Which was irritating.

Wendy had retreated to Noah's room to get ready for dinner—for her solo dinner with him, the concept of which was freaking her the hell out—but because she was done a bit early, she'd laid down fully clothed on the bed and closed her eyes. She took a lot of deep inhales. Maybe if she did that enough, it would desensitize her. Prevent her from trying to sniff him while they were out.

Jesus. She needed to get a goddamn handle on herself.

She opened her eyes. They landed immediately on a hook on the wall on the other side of the room. His Yankees cap hung on it.

That did not help.

She remembered another time she'd been ambushed by that cap.

Seventeen years ago. The day before Thanksgiving.

It had been Noah's freshman year at NYU. Canadian Thanksgiving fell on a Monday, as it always did, but since the holiday was different from its American counterpart, he didn't have it off. It was just a regular school day for him. So he wasn't coming home.

Which was more than fine by Wendy. She wouldn't be here otherwise, helping Jane make pies for tomorrow. She and Mary and Jane and Jane's mom were planning a feast the next day—Wendy's mom was, as usual, working at the store. Wendy would bring her a plate after the dinner was done.

The doorbell rang. Jane, her arms covered in flour as she readied the counter for rolling out the crusts, said, "Can you get that for me?"

Wendy did as instructed, jogging to the entryway and swinging the heavy oak door open...to reveal Noah.

In a Yankees cap.

"Wendy Lou Who," he drawled. He was wearing the most self-satisfied grin. When she didn't say anything, or move, he added, "Surprise."

She *was* surprised. She was stunned really, unable to speak. But only for a moment. To her relief, surprise receded to make room for...anger?

She hadn't seen him since before the prom last spring—by design. She'd managed to avoid him the two weeks after the dance before school was out and he left for New York—he'd headed there early because he had a summer work-study job.

She'd been a little worried about what it would be like to be in his presence again. Would she be awkward? Nervous? Make a fool of herself in some way she hadn't yet imagined?

No. It turned out, she'd just be *pissed*.

He opened his arms. Like she was just supposed to step into them? Squeal in delight that the great Noah Denning had returned?

No, thanks.

Jane stepped into them, though—she'd come from the kitchen to investigate. "Noah! Oh my God, Noah!"

Adrenaline surging, Wendy turned and walked back to the kitchen. Walked right over to the blob of dough on the floured cutting board and slammed her fist down on it. Listened to Jane shouting for her mom and then to the two of them flipping out over Noah.

"I happened to see a posting on a ride-sharing board for someone making a quick trip," Noah said as they made their way into the kitchen. Wendy wondered if there was any way she could credibly make her way *out* of the kitchen. Instead, she grabbed a rolling pin and started aggressively flattening dough. "So I was able to tag along for the price of gas. I've got to head back tomorrow afternoon, though."

"Whoa! Wendy! That's way too big." Jane came over to where Wendy had indeed rolled out a circle of dough large enough to make a pie for a giant. "That was supposed to be four crusts' worth."

Wendy had to bite her tongue not to snap at Jane. It wasn't Jane she was mad at. She let herself be pushed aside.

"What's up with you, Wendy?" Noah asked as he dumped his backpack on a kitchen chair.

"What's up with that Yankees hat?" she shot back. There was more of an edge to her voice than there had been when she and Noah had sparred in the past. But she didn't mind. She kind of liked it, truth be told. Anger was better than humiliation. Anger was a buffer. It could protect her. Remind her that she wasn't the same person he had hurt so badly last spring.

"I don't know." He took the cap off and threw it on a counter. "I've kind of become a fan."

"How can you be a Yankees fan all of a sudden? You just moved there like five minutes ago."

His expression turned bewildered. Probably because of that edge in her voice. She usually gave as good as she got with him, but she wasn't mean. Historically. But, honestly, that stupid Yankees hat was almost the worst thing about his unexpected arrival. She didn't expect him to be a Blue Jays fan like she was, but he'd never cared about baseball at all, and now he was on the freaking *Yankees* bandwagon? Like any self-respecting Jays fan, Wendy *hated* the Yankees. But apparently, Noah had blithely moved on to a new team, a new city, and a new life.

Noah just blinked.

"What time do you have to leave tomorrow?" his mom asked, the question preempting the awkward silence that had begun to unspool in the kitchen. She looked at Jane. "Can we bump dinner earlier?"

A discussion ensued, the result of which was a decision to move tomorrow's big meal to noon so Noah could attend. Wendy let it all play out, then said, "Mary and I have to serve meals at her church." Which was a total and complete lie. "For the homeless," she added, because who could argue with the homeless?

Noah started to demur, to insist that they leave their plans the way they'd been.

"No, no." Wendy summoned an authoritative, no-nonsense tone. "You three have your noon meal. Then Mary and I will come by later for leftovers and dessert."

To her surprise, everyone agreed without further argument.

Damn. Maybe the whole "become a new person" thing she'd decided to do after the prom was working. Maybe being angry at Noah was working.

Something was working. Because she wasn't that hurt, humiliated girl from last spring anymore. Her anger had somehow deflected her pain. She had become a person who could bend the world to her will.

A person who could be in the world with Noah Denning and remain unaffected.

A knock on the door jolted Wendy from her memories. She wasn't in Jane and Noah's kitchen; she was in Noah's pine-scented bedroom.

"Wendy?" It was Jane. "Noah's ready, but he's too nice to harass you. Luckily I don't have that problem. Are you ready?"

Wendy leaped off the bed. "Yep. Be right there."

She was still a person who could be in the world with Noah Denning and remain unaffected.

Right?

~ ᗏ ~

Wendy hated to admit it, but it was actually better that Jane had stayed home.

"It's actually better that Jane isn't here," Noah said, and Wendy barked a laugh.

"What?" He smiled even as his brow furrowed in confusion.

"Nothing. I was just thinking the same thing. She would hate this." Noah had taken her to a little Cajun place in his neighborhood, and they were sitting at the bar sharing a bunch of dishes including grilled oysters and an odd but delightful Creole-seasoned osso buco. "Oysters and bone marrow—neither of those are really in your sister's wheelhouse."

"Big Macs they are not."

"But delicious they are." Wendy had been working a ton lately, so it had been a long time since she'd had a really superb meal. And the restaurant was charming. It was dark but candlelit, and there was a pleasant background din that made her feel satisfyingly cozy with Noah at the center of a crowd.

Which was kind of a problem. Because she was supposed to remain unaffected. She wasn't sure *satisfyingly cozy* was a phrase she could safely associate with Noah Denning. Usually, in a situation like this, she'd be braced for battle, relying on the stream of anger inside she had tapped into years ago to fuel her.

The problem was everything was just so *delicious*. And two glasses of wine had mellowed her right out. They hadn't even argued about anything all evening.

She sneaked a glance at him, studying his face in the warm, flickering candlelight as she tried to figure out why. She'd only had to see him a handful of times in the past seventeen years, and even then she'd avoided actually *looking* at him as much as she could. In some ways, he didn't look that different than he used to. He had the same dark-brown hair, though it was short now. He'd worn it down to his collar and tucked behind his ears in high school. The intelligent greenish-brown eyes were the same, though there were a few lines around them these days. He had been wearing a suit when he picked them up at the airport, having just come from work, she assumed. It had been impeccably tailored, slim, and light gray, and she'd had to bite her lip when she caught sight of him. But it turned out he filled out casual clothes just as well—he'd changed into jeans and a burgundy T-shirt that should have been nothing special, and yet...

Stop it. So she was temporarily running low on anger. Okay. But that didn't mean she needed to sit here and catalog his gorgeousness like she was a teenager again.

It must be the wine. That was the only reason she could think of that she felt so...agreeable.

"Hey, Noah."

A man wearing chef's whites and a big grin came up behind them. He clapped Noah on the shoulder.

"Wendy Liu," Noah said, "this is my friend Bennett Buchanan. He owns the place, and he lives in my building, too. Wendy's an old friend from Toronto."

"Hi, Wendy." Bennett turned a big grin on her and shook her hand.

"Everything is so delicious," she said truthfully. "I'm going to dream about this sausage when I'm back home." The restaurant was called Boudin, named after the iconic New Orleans sausage.

Bennett nodded at the array of plates before them. "I'm glad Noah finally found a dining companion with some taste."

"Hey!" Noah protested. "Don't defame Clarissa. She might not have had an adventurous palate, but she was all right."

Ugh. Thinking of Noah in this circle of candlelight with someone else made Wendy strangely uncomfortable.

Bennett must have mistaken her discomfort for confusion, because he explained, "Clarissa is Noah's most recent ex."

"Most recent?" She tried for a teasing tone. "Do you have a collection?"

"He's a serial monogamist, this one," Bennett said. "Dates a woman for *years* sometimes. I keep expecting him to pop the question to one of them one of these days, but he never does."

"He probably works too much."

"For sure, he does. Feels personally responsible for putting away every criminal in Manhattan. Which turns out to be surprisingly time consuming."

"Hello. I'm right here. I can hear you guys."

Wendy ignored Noah. She was enjoying this little psychoanalytical foray into his dating habits. It was certainly better than all the psychoanalytical forays she'd been doing on *herself* lately. But she also understood about the long hours of a legal career, so she had to defend Noah. "It's hard to be in law and not work too much. I suffer from that problem myself."

"No time for love for you either?" Bennett asked.

"I'm sure I could make the time if it was a priority."

"Aww," Bennett teased. "Who doesn't want love?"

Wendy shrugged. "Why buy the cow when you can get the milk for free?"

"Excuse me, *what*?"

She turned to face Noah, whose eyebrows had hit the ceiling. "*What* what?"

"Don't turn the question back on me," Noah said.

"Don't ask disingenuous questions, then. Maybe your problem is that you should stop with the long-term dating and start..." She made a vague hand-fluttering gesture.

"Ha!" Bennett threw back his head and laughed. "Good luck with that. Noah's *way* too uptight for casual sex."

"Oh, like you're any better," Noah said to Bennett.

"Well, my reasons don't stem from being a control freak."

"What does that mean?" Noah said, just as Wendy was about to ask the same thing. This was getting interesting.

Bennett held up his hands. "I was just teasing. You're the kind of person who likes to be in control of a situation. There's nothing wrong with that."

Noah didn't respond beyond rolling his eyes. He put his hands on the bar and swiveled in his stool to face Wendy. "So, what? You just sleep your way through Toronto? Is that what you're saying?"

"I don't *sleep* my way through Toronto. *God.* And even if I did, it wouldn't be any of your business. I'm just saying that not everyone believes in happily ever after, so why waste your time—and your prime—in long-term relationships that are almost certainly doomed to fail when you could be..." She raised her eyebrows and made the same vague hand-fluttering gesture.

"Could be what?"

"Oh, come off it." He knew what she meant.

"No, really. What does this"—he copied her gesture—"mean?"

"It means meaningless fucking. Is that what you want to hear?"

He must not have thought she'd take the bait, because he blinked rapidly. At least she had shut him up. She couldn't help but laugh.

"*Anyway*," Bennett said. Wendy had kind of forgotten that he was there. And now it was awkward. "The point regarding Clarissa is that she and Noah are doing the Gwyneth Paltrow–style conscious uncoupling, stay-friends-with-your-ex thing, so he defends her"—Bennett rolled his eyes—"but she had no taste."

It was just like Noah to stay friends with his exes. Wendy imagined a harem of beautiful, accomplished ex-girlfriends of Noah Denning. Women he was once sleeping with on a totally not-casual basis.

"I can forgive pretty much anything," Bennett went on, "except people who willingly choose bad food over good food. Clarissa once had the nerve to ask me if we had any fat-free half-and-half. I do this exquisite New Orleans–style coffee and chicory mixture, and she wants to pour liquid chemicals in it?"

"Fat-free half-and-half?" Wendy echoed, genuinely disgusted. "Is that actually a thing? How do they even do that? Isn't fat the whole point of cream?"

"I like her," Bennett said to Noah. "Hold on to her."

Wendy was pretty sure Noah was about to object, to explain that Wendy was only a friend, and of his sister's at that, but Bennett was no longer paying attention—he was signaling the bartender.

"What are you two drinking?"

"The Grenache," Noah said.

"Which is *excellent*." It was a magical anger-diffusing elixir, too, but she didn't say that part. The harem of ex-girlfriends aside, she was feeling all warm and loose, the way she always did while traveling, when she got away from her daily grind. It was strange to have company, though. Usually the travel warm-fuzzies were a solo experience.

"Wendy, you are a woman of exquisite taste," Bennett declared. "Another round for my friends on the house," he said to the young guy behind the bar.

Noah looked at his watch. "We can't. We're headed down to walk the High Line, and it closes at eleven."

Wendy almost suggested they forget the High Line and just keep sitting here in this warm circle of candlelight drinking wine and talking about what good taste she had, but that would be stupid. When Noah had asked her what she'd wanted to do, she hadn't hesitated. She wanted to visit the High Line, which was a park built on an old elevated rail line. It was the one of the few New York things she hadn't done.

"Well, then, another round for my friends *to go*." Bennett winked at them, and before Wendy knew it they had been disgorged onto the street with a pair of travel mugs full of eighty-dollar-a-bottle wine.

They got on the subway at 181st Street, and Noah said, "It's a long ride, so we should sit." He gestured to a seat and waited until she was settled before lowering himself next to her. Their thighs touched. She pulled away slightly. Then regretted it. Then scolded herself for regretting it. Then went back to regretting it.

"What's the deal with you, Noah Denning?" The magical wine was making her chatty, too, apparently.

"What do you mean?"

I mean why are you so appealing? Why can't you hate your exes like everyone else?

Why can't you be the jerk I remember you being?

He was looking at her funny. Right. She hadn't answered his question. "You live in, as your sister says, a castle in Manhattan, and you're friends with magical chefs who give you wine to go? You grew up pretty good, my friend."

"Well, as it relates to the castle, my big secret is that it's actually pretty affordable. We public servants don't roll in the bucks like you private firm types."

That was true. That divide was part of why Wendy did so much pro bono defense work. Why she argued about rats in front of the Landlord and Tenant Board.

"I lived in the dorms at NYU," Noah went on. "After I graduated, I had this stupid youthful snobbery about Manhattan versus the outer boroughs." He rolled his eyes. "I was determined to stay on the island, and the only place I could afford was way uptown. I lived in this shitty little one-room apartment." He shrugged. "I sort of fell in love with the neighborhood, though."

It was easy to see why. Everything about Noah's life, from his roomy apartment in an enchanting co-op to the vital street life of his neighborhood, was appealing. He was charmed. Just like he had been in high school.

Actually, that wasn't fair. Wendy knew better than to say Noah led a charmed life. He'd been dealt quite the blow when his dad died. But despite all that, he managed to move through the world with a grace that Wendy had always envied—and, if she was being honest with herself, been attracted to.

"Functionally, it's no different from being in, for example, Brooklyn," Noah said. "The commute is a slog—it's probably longer, actually. But I don't know, I like being holed up way at the top of the city." He stretched and sighed like a happy cat. "But it is going to take us a while, so get cozy."

Cozy. There was that damn word again.

Chapter Seven

$\mathcal{I}$t was nearly dark by the time they ascended the steps to the High Line at Gansevoort and Washington.

"How many times *have* you been to New York?" Noah asked, taking a sip of his illicit wine as they started walking. Wendy had proven knowledgeable about the subway system and had seemed to know exactly where to go to access the park.

She shrugged. "I don't know. Maybe eight? Nine?"

"You should have looked me up." He pitched the statement carefully so it didn't sound like he was miffed or hurt or something stupid like that. But seriously. His sister's best friend, the girl who'd practically lived in their house growing up, his long-ago running buddy, had been in his city that many times, and she'd never bothered to drop him a line? Wasn't that a little odd? "I would have been good for a meal or two. Or a run."

Wendy cleared her throat. "I guess I just never thought of it."

Well. That stung. As much as he didn't want it to.

"Anyway, I always travel alone, so I get into this mode where I'm kind of living in my own head—keeping company with myself, that sort of thing."

"Where's the farthest you've been?"

"Well, geographically, Australia. But in terms of remoteness, I'd have to go with Uganda." She laughed, remembering that trip. "Uganda was kind of a disaster, actually. I had this idea I should expand my horizons and do a safari. It turns out I'm terrified of animals when they're not behind bars. So now I just embrace my limitations and stick to cities."

He had to admit, he was impressed. Other than being friends with Jane, Wendy had always been a loner. He'd never been sure if that was by choice or by default. As a girl, she'd been quiet, serious, and shy with outsiders. He had learned recently, though, that she no longer possessed those qualities—witness her astonishing "why buy the cow?" comment at the restaurant, which he still wasn't over. Still, there was some core aspect of her, a *Wendy-ness*, that remained unchanged.

But whether she was still a loner or not was something quite apart from traveling alone. And places like Uganda, too. Wasn't there a guerilla resistance there? He refrained from quizzing her about the safety precautions he sincerely hoped she'd taken. Because, as he'd been so viscerally reminded by his body's reaction to her recently, she was *not* his honorary little sister anymore.

"What's the appeal of all that travel?" He could appreciate a vacation as much as the next person—in theory anyway. He personally never took them aside from the odd trip home to see his mom and sister. But he had been a devoted reader of *National Geographic* as a kid.

"I don't know." She started slowly, like she was trying to articulate a feeling she had never had to put into words before. "The world is so big. Full of amazing places that are nothing like Toronto. Full of possibilities." She tilted her head as if she were considering her own answer. As if she were finding it lacking somehow.

"Most people would agree with that statement, but most people wouldn't translate that into actually getting off their asses and going to Uganda." He wasn't sure why he was pressing her. Her explanation had been reasonable, but he couldn't shake the fact that there was something more she wasn't saying.

"It's hard to explain. It's a bit of a compulsion, I'll admit. I feel it as a responsibility, almost. An imperative. I imagine it's like the way some people collect things, like stamps or, I don't know, vintage records. I feel a certain kind of pressure—it's self-imposed, I know, but there's a completist impulse."

He was nodding. "Yeah, but why travel particularly? Why *not* vintage records? Or why not stick to Pez dispensers?"

⎯⎯℘

Because I'm always running away from heartbreak.

Because I'm making sure that I'll always be able to leave.

And you're the one who made me this way.

As the answers to Noah's question—the real answers—popped into Wendy's head, tears gathered in her eyes. She was body-slammed the way you can only be when you're confronted with a harsh, unexpected truth. It *was* the truth, though. It was all true.

She'd started the travel thing as a way to avoid Noah when he came home for visits. She'd been *literally* running away.

And what had she been running from? Noah and all the pain he had caused. It wasn't that she regretted any of it. She'd come to love travel for its own sake, but how much of that was because it gave her power? Agency. She felt her most invincible when she was tromping through a foreign city alone. Like no one could hurt her. Travel reinforced the knowledge that she'd never be passively left behind again.

Theoretically. She didn't really have any people left to leave her. Her parents were dead. Jane was getting married.

Mary, though. She had Aunt Mary.

She gulped back the unshed tears and searched for something diversionary to say, stuffing the astonishing and unwelcome truth bomb down for examination another day.

She pointed at an apartment building that was tucked up against the rail-right-of-way that was the park. "Like, think about those people. What is their story? Don't you want to know?" There. That was true. She did always wonder about life in the places she visited.

"Their story is that they're wealthy yuppies who bought into that building years before they built this park, and they regret choosing that particular unit now that a parade of humanity passes by their living room every day."

She chuckled at his analysis. "Sure, but that's just an example. The city is full of stories. The *world* is full of stories. Don't you want to know them?"

"Man, you do have it bad." He bumped his shoulder against hers as they walked. It was an affectionate but meaningless gesture. Exactly the sort of thing you'd do when you were teasing your little sister's friend.

So why did it send shivers down her spine?

She took a slug of her wine, wanting to recapture that warm, buzzy feeling from before, as dangerous as that probably was. "Anyway, I'm planning a trip around the world, so maybe that will get it out of my system. I'll have seen it all!"

"A trip around the world," he echoed. "You hear the phrase, but is that a real thing?"

"Sort of. You can actually book a so-called 'trip around the world' with a tour company. They have itineraries that range from a few months to years. But I'm doing it on my own. Six months, thirty-one countries."

He whistled. "Wow. When is this going down?"

"September. About a month after the wedding—I'm taking a leave from the firm."

"So you're just going to pick up and leave your life behind?"

"Pretty much." It wasn't like she had anyone to tell her not to. It wasn't like anyone would really even notice her absence.

Okay, that wasn't fair. Jane and Elise and Gia would notice. Jane was even going to meet her a few times in a few different places over the course of the trip, saying that she simply could not go six months without seeing Wendy. And Wendy had planned things so she could overlap with Gia during Fashion Week in Milan.

And Mary would notice, as would her colleagues. Wendy's assistant was already dreading being assigned to another lawyer.

So there. She had a full life populated with people who would miss her. She was just going to take a break from it for a while.

That was a thing people did. Normal people, not just people who were running from their pasts.

Right?

~~~

"Enough about my travel bug," Wendy said emphatically, stopping near a fountain.

Fair enough. Noah wasn't sure why he'd been questioning her so intently. It was just that doing something like that, up and leaving your life behind, just putting your job and your responsibilities on hold for six months, was beyond his imagining. What would it be like to wake up in the morning in a strange place, with no agenda? No commitments. Alone.

But maybe she wasn't waking up alone. After all, as she'd so vehemently declared in the bar, she was the casual sex type now, right?

He had a sudden image of Wendy waking up in some Mediterranean villa, untangling herself from a handsome, charming Italian lothario. She'd throw open the shutters and the sun would come pouring in. She'd declare her need for coffee, and Mr. Italy would say some shit like, "Later, bellissima," and pull her back to bed.

Goddammit.

"Too bad it's not deep enough to throw a penny in and make a wish." Still gazing at the fountain, Wendy ran a strappy black sandal over the sheen of water that ran over black stones. Her toenails were painted cherry red.

"You don't seem like the wish-making type," he said.

"What is *that* supposed to mean?"

Whoa. He'd offended her. He didn't remember Wendy being so quick to anger. Yes, they'd always competed against each other, but it had never had a genuinely mean edge to it—not that he remembered, anyway. But there had been a few times lately where he'd felt like she was out-of-proportion mad—at him in particular. "I only meant that you seem more like the hard-work type, not the stand-around-and-wait-for-wishes-to-come-true type." Or, you know, the jet-off-to-the-Mediterranean-to-be-loved-up-by-handsome-Italian-strangers type.

She smirked. "Oh. Okay. I'll accept that interpretation."

He chuckled, that flare-up of anger diffused, and they walked in silence for a while, taking in the greenery of the linear park.

"How's work?" she asked as they approached West 17th, where the park widened into an amphitheater of sorts.

Work was a topic he could deal with. Talking about work was much more his wheelhouse than talking about trips around the world. "Busy. We've had a couple people leave and they haven't been replaced yet, so the caseload is brutal these days."

"Do you ever think about going to the private sector?" She smiled and answered her own question. "No."

He raised his eyebrows. She'd answered correctly, but how had she known?

"You're pretty much in the perfect job. You've always had an impulse to help people, I think. And you were never afraid of hard work or clocking long hours."

"You noticed that?"

"Well, you pretty much worked full-time in high school."

"Not by choice, though." He glanced down at her. He rarely talked about those days. In fact, the last time he'd spoken openly about how ground down he'd been back then had probably been with Wendy, on that run that day he couldn't keep up with her.

"I know," she said quietly. "Bennett and I were teasing you about being overly responsible, but you did what you had to do back then."

Well, shit. Of course he knew his mom and sister appreciated how hard he had worked. But he had always tried to downplay it. When teachers asked about the bags under his eyes or his tendency to fall asleep in class, he would laugh it off and vow to cut back on his hours. But he hadn't. He *couldn't*.

He hadn't been looking for glory. He still wasn't. But somehow, all these years later, to know that Wendy, who back then had felt like the only person who really saw him, still remembered the sacrifices he'd made...Well, it was stupidly gratifying.

He cleared his throat. "I guess it just became a habit—the long hours, I mean. So I suppose law was a natural place to end up."

"I would have thought you'd go for corporate law, though. A more lucrative subfield than being a public prosecutor, given your obsession with taking care of Jane and your mom."

"My *obsession*?" That was taking it too far. He'd had a responsibility. He still did. That wasn't the same as an obsession.

"Poor choice of word, but you know what I mean."

He did know, that was the thing. "I thought about it." He might as well tell her the truth. "I even interned at an M&A firm. It was fine, but..."

"But what?" she prompted.

"There was a series of high-profile sexual assaults in the city at that time. They arrested a suspect and charged him. It was all over the news. I followed the trial, as did most New Yorkers. At one point, the lead prosecutor was featured in *New York* magazine. They did an interview with him, asking why he'd gone into law, and why he'd been so dogged with that case in particular. He said, 'I have a mother. I have two daughters. I have a sister. I have a responsibility to make sure they can walk through the world feeling safe. *Every-one* should be able to walk through the world feeling safe.' Or something like that." It wasn't "something like that," though—that had been the exact quote. It was burned into his consciousness.

"So you widened your protector thing from your family to the public." Wendy wasn't looking at him as she spoke; she was nodding and looking up at the dark-blue, starless city sky.

"Okay, *what*?"

"That outweighed the desire to make shitloads of money to send home, is what I'm thinking."

"I do well enough," he said, suddenly defensive. Sure, he could be making much more in corporate law, but he was fine. He had a good life. There was nothing wrong with wanting to help people.

"So what about Cameron?" She startled him out of his thoughts with the sudden shift in topic.

It took a moment for him to extricate his mind from the past. "Cameron? What about him?"

"Do you ever get the feeling that he and Jane are kind of a…weird match?"

Whoa. "What does *that* mean?"

"Okay, that came out kind of wrong."

"Kind of? I never pegged you as a snob, Wendy. Cameron may not have a lot of money, but—"

"That's not what I mean!" she protested. Then she made a vague noise of frustration and walked away.

The sight of her marching away ignited a spark of annoyance in his chest. She thought she could drop that cryptic remark about Cameron into conversation and then just take off, hips swaying beneath her fitted dress?

His inner litigator awakened, he jogged to catch up with

her as she reached the entrance to the Chelsea Thicket, a narrow passageway through a miniature forest. He had the momentary, absurd thought that he had been transported into a fairy tale, and that he was following a magical creature of unknown allegiance into a forest that might or might not contain the seeds of his doom.

"Explain yourself." He fell into step beside her and put his hand on her forearm to stop her from going any farther.

She shrugged off his hand. "Don't get your undies in a bunch. I just worry sometimes that they're moving too fast. That they're too different."

"Evidence?"

"Cameron is rough. Jane is refined."

He set his travel mug on the ground, put his hands on his hips, and tried to stare her down, like he would a hostile witness in court. She was unmoved. She just gazed back up at him, her raised eyebrows telegraphing the degree to which she was unimpressed by him.

As annoyed as he was, he couldn't help but admire her backbone, the way she gave as good as she got. He could imagine her in court, the fearsome warrior. But he knew all about courtroom image, about how winning was at least partly a function of projecting confidence and an unwavering belief in one's argument, so he wasn't going to let her see any of that admiration. Instead, he moved on to oral arguments. "*Wendy.* My sister is a lot of things. I love her more than anyone else in this world. But she is currently sitting in my apartment eating a Big Mac Extra Value Meal. Jane is *not* what you would call refined. Why don't we just drop this little charade and you say what you really mean?"

Something happened then. The fearsome litigator flinched. It surprised the hell out of him.

And just like that, all the tension created by their argument disappeared like a battery losing its charge all at once.

"Don't listen to me." She huffed a little sigh, and if he wasn't mistaken, it was tinged with self-disgust. "I don't know what I'm talking about. I'm just..."

He waited a beat. She seemed to be struggling with some internal demon all of a sudden. In fact, she'd been kind of off all evening. Nothing overt, but just...not her usual bantery self. Quieter. More contemplative. But then prone to quick, sharp spikes of anger.

He put his hand back on her arm. He probably shouldn't have, given that she'd just shrugged off the same touch, but he couldn't not. She was like a magnet.

She looked down at his hand, and the fact that she didn't do anything to try to dislodge it felt like a huge victory.

"You're just what?" he prompted.

She raised her eyes to meet his and said, "I'm just jealous." Gobsmacked, he sucked in a breath. Reflexively tightened his grip on her arm. "I'm afraid of losing Jane. I don't have that many people left."

He was having trouble getting in step with the new direction this conversation had taken. Jesus Christ, if she did this in court, this kind of startling redirection, she was probably unstoppable.

Except he was pretty sure this wasn't a tactic. He could see the disquiet in her eyes. The vulnerability. This wasn't a "startling redirection." It was brutal honesty. His heart wrenched in protest. It didn't want to see Wendy Lou Who hurting like this.

"Wendy, sweetheart. Jane loves you. That's never going to change."

"But it's not going to be the same."

She was probably right. He had the utmost faith in his

sister's devotion to Wendy, but of course the addition of a husband was going to change the dynamics of their long-standing friendship. It was natural to be wary of it. And she was right about people leaving her. Not on purpose, of course, but her parents were dead and she'd been an only child. She was alone in a way that other people were not.

He wanted to comfort her, but Wendy wasn't the kind of woman who appreciated empty platitudes, so he said nothing, merely dipped his head in acknowledgement of the truth as she saw it.

"Anyone with half a brain can see how happy Cameron makes her." Wendy's voice had gone scratchy. At the same time his heart ached for her, it was impossible not to be...affected by that voice. It was confusing. *She* was confusing.

"Any problems I have with this wedding are on me," she went on. "I don't want Jane to know about them. Can we just forget what I said?"

"Of course." He slid his hand farther down her arm. He'd intended a sort of brisk, buoying rub before he let her go, but he got snagged at her wrist. Her pulse was beating out of control.

It was like her erratic heartbeat was contagious, because it was getting harder to breathe. He sought out her throat with his gaze, suddenly compelled to study it for visible evidence of the pulse he was feeling.

But something happened to his eyes. They slid over her graceful neck, and they kept going lower. She was wearing one of those dresses that managed to seem both casual and formal at the same time. A plain black wraparound style that closed like a robe, one side over the other, leaving exposed a long, thin triangle of bare skin. Wendy didn't really have cleavage in the traditional sense. There was no deep V where breast met breast. There was, instead, a gentle sloping of flesh.

It made him crazy.

He wanted to put his mouth on that slope. To follow it to its peak.

It was wildly inappropriate given how much she was hurting right now.

And more to the point he didn't *do* this—he didn't do casual. And he *certainly* didn't do casual with *Wendy*. There was no universe in which Noah Denning was going to be the "milk" Wendy Lou Who got for free.

Goddamn. What was the matter with him?

He closed his eyes a moment.

Which was why he was taken utterly by surprise when she grabbed his T-shirt and pulled him toward her. Hard enough to startle his eyes open so he could catch the sight of her travel mug clattering to the ground and rolling into the trees. Hard enough that he stumbled forward.

Not hard enough, his inner litigator forced himself to enter into the record, that anyone could reasonably say she "grabbed him and kissed him," though that had clearly been her intent. She had grabbed him, yes, but for *her* to kiss *him* was physically impossible; the height differential between them was too great.

So he had a choice, in that instant, as he teetered between shock and understanding.

He chose to kiss her.

Despite his previous angst over his attraction to her, it wasn't a tough decision, ultimately. All he had to do was *not stop himself*. All he had to do was allow himself to keep moving forward in space.

He let himself be pulled until she was flush against him. They didn't match up—there was none of that romance novel stuff about them fitting together like their bodies were made for each other. Instead of her breasts being crushed against his chest, they were crushed against his upper belly. The point of her chin slotted into the soft spot just below his sternum.

She'd gotten him as far as she could, and now it was his turn. So he bent over and, without ceremony, put his mouth on hers.

For a moment, it was a civilized kiss, contained and only slightly investigative as his arms came around her.

But just for a moment.

Because when she let loose a little sigh and twined her arms around his neck, it lit off a string of fireworks inside him. He parted her lips with his tongue. When she started moving her head around, like she was trying to deepen the kiss but wasn't quite succeeding, he grunted his displeasure. He wanted her to *be still*. So he took his hands from her waist and pressed his palms to her cheeks, tilted her head back a bit farther and feasted on her. Her restlessness quieted and for a moment, as their tongues tangled, it was enough. Pleasure radiated through him.

But all too soon, she was on the move again, exerting pressure on his neck with her arms and bobbing up and down on her toes.

"Stop moving," he growled, tearing his mouth from hers only long enough to deliver his directive.

She did not obey. No, that would be too easy. Wendy was a lot of things, but pliant wasn't one of them. No, she just tightened her hold on his neck, gave a little hop and—

Oh. *Oh.*

Now that he understood what she'd been trying to do, he was all in. His arms understood before his brain did, moving to catch her under her bottom and bring her to him. In one fell swoop, she had corrected their height differential—or at least the lower body part of it—wrapping her legs around him so his cock was pressed right against her center.

He took a step, looking over her shoulder for a hard surface he could use to brace them. There was nothing. They were surrounded by trees, but they were bullshit, miniature New York City trees, so he couldn't even back her up against one of them.

Well, fuck, he didn't care. He'd just stand there forever holding her, letting her grind herself on him. So he planted his feet and without even consciously meaning to, gave a little thrust.

She gasped and let her head fall back, which provided him with an extreme close-up of the slope of breast he'd been admiring before. He was just about to lower his mouth to the gentle gradient when a loud throat-clearing noise penetrated his consciousness.

"Dudes, maybe get a room?"

"*Shit.*" Wendy peeled her legs off him so fast he almost fell over from the sudden disequilibrium.

Right. They were in a public park. It was late, but it was the middle of the summer and they were in New York City, where a person was never alone. He had anchored his feet for their epic make-out session right in the center of the path, effectively blocking anyone from getting past.

Wendy slid down his body and buried her face in his chest, presumably embarrassed.

"Sorry," he mumbled to the passersby as he steered Wendy to one side of the path and used his body to shield her from view.

Wendy. Wendy Lou Who. Jane's best friend. The girl he'd taken under his protection and watched grow up.

The woman who lived in another country. The woman who was taking off on a trip around the world.

As if any of that mattered anyway, because she was also, as she'd told him mere hours ago, uninterested in making time in her life for love.

Not that this was love.

God, no.

This was... Wendy.

Fucking hell.

They remained still for a moment. He didn't know how to disengage. How to be in this new world they had created. This was why he didn't really do casual hookups. There was no way to escape this horrible, oppressive awkwardness. The panicky feeling that chaos was about to descend. That he'd let himself get so out of control that he'd acted against his own interests.

They were back in that same position they'd started in, with their bodies flush against each other, except the heat had gone, the interruption having functioned as a metaphorical cold shower. Her chin was back resting on that tender spot below his sternum, but this time, there was something slightly menacing about the proximity. If she wanted to, she could retract her head and slam her chin into that spot, knock the breath right out of him, and leave him gasping in pain, defenseless.

But he should say something. About the kiss. About what she'd revealed before the kiss about her wedding-related fears. He couldn't just... not acknowledge these things.

While he was trying to get his brain and his mouth to co-operate, she stepped back. Paused. Then took another step. Looked around. Her gaze landed on his fallen mug. She kept looking, as if she was trying to locate her own, but it was nowhere in sight. So she walked over to his, took the top off, tilted her head back, and chugged. He watched her throat undulate. When she was done, she used the back of her hand to wipe her mouth.

"Okay, Noah, listen."

"Wendy, I—"

"I know you're freaking out—"

"I'm not freaking out," he said reflexively. But he totally was.

"Okay." She held up a palm. "Whatever. The point is, we're done with..." She waved her hand back and forth between them. "This." Then she raised her eyebrows as if she were daring him to contradict her. "Correct?"

"Yes," he said quickly, glad for the reprieve. They were most definitely done making out. But he should still acknowledge what she'd said earlier, about Jane, right? Reassure her?

Except she didn't seem to need it. She was back to her usual unsinkable self.

"This"—she kept doing the waving thing—"was a mistake. This was some kind of bizarre New York vacation aberration thing." She narrowed her eyes. "What happens in New York stays in New York, right?"

He was coming back to himself, too, as the forces of chaos receded. On the one hand, it felt wrong to just pretend the whole thing had never happened, but on the other, shouldn't he just follow her lead?

Some sort of bizarre New York vacation aberration thing.

And he was glad to be off the hook. He *was*. He just needed his body to catch up with that fact. "Yes. Absolutely. I don't..." He mimicked her motion from earlier, waving his hand back and forth between them. "I don't do this."

Her brow furrowed. "You don't do what?"

"I don't, uh, get the milk for free, generally speaking."

Wait. That had come out wrong—all slut-shamey. He had no moral objection to casual sex, it just wasn't his deal. It introduced too many unknown variables. Required him to cede more control than he was comfortable with.

He expected her to get defensive. To yell at him. He would deserve it—after all, he'd lost his mind as much as she had just then.

But she merely shot him a quizzical look. "Why not? Was Bennett right, back at the bar, when he said you're too much of a control freak to sleep around?"

How to explain without making himself seem like an uptight prude? But then, she'd revealed something about herself just now when she'd confessed her fears about Jane's marriage. Maybe he could do the same. "I suppose he was. I just would rather...know what I'm getting into. Have some control over how things are going to unfold. I find that's harder to do when you've just met a person. When you don't yet know if you can trust her."

She nodded, like that accorded with her image of him.

Then she spun on her heel and started speed walking away. "Keep up, old man."

Chapter Eight

How is Josh?

*W*endy eyed the text from Noah as the opening swells of "All I Ask of You" caused everyone in Madison Square Garden—except her—to shriek in ecstasy.

She almost didn't answer. Not answering would be the smart course of action. Because when you *literally threw yourself* at the only man you'd ever allowed to hurt you, what kind of sense did it make to follow that up with some casual texting?

Why don't you ask your sister?

I did. She's ignoring me.

Wendy sighed and looked around.

It kind of looks like Beatlemania 1964 around here, except instead of musical geniuses, everyone's freaking out over a puffy-headed man-child (who, okay, has a surprisingly rich baritone) doing Phantom of the Opera *songs.*

She watched the little bubbles that indicated that Noah was typing. Then they stopped. She ordered herself to put her phone away.

But then the bubbles came back.

Then they went away again for a full thirty seconds.

She threw her head back in frustration. "Arg!"

Jane shot her a questioning glance, and when Wendy mouthed, "Sorry," the glance turned censuring. God forbid she should interrupt all the emoting going on, both onstage and in the audience.

She heaved a sigh that turned into a yawn. Damn, was she exhausted. She and Jane and Noah had spent the day tromping around the city—they'd gone all the way downtown for brunch, then taken a ferry to Greenpoint and shopped and caffeinated their way through Brooklyn. It hadn't been all the walking that had tired her out, though. No, it was the enervating, on-edge feeling proximity to Noah inspired. The supreme weirdness of having him touch her in normal ways, like to steady her as she stepped onto the boat. The infuriating fact that even that kind of casual touch—he did the same steadying thing for his sister, for God's sake—sent her pulse revving like the boat's engine beneath their feet.

There had been no reason for it. He'd acted totally normal all day. In fact, he'd acted totally normal the night

before, on the long cab ride home from the High Line, talking baseball—talking about the stupid Yankees—with the
driver and then placidly bidding her good night as he made
up the sofa for himself.

All day, she'd wanted to shout at him: "Dude, we made
out yesterday!"

But why? She was the one who'd insisted they not talk
about it. All he was doing was heeding her directive.
Clearly, it wasn't eating him up inside—it wasn't even nib-
bling at him—so she would be well served to take a cue
from him and get the hell over it. Yes, she'd dry-humped
her high school crush in public yesterday, but that was yesterday. Today: moving on.

Her phone buzzed in her hand, and she jumped a little.

LOL.

What? It took him five minutes to type LOL? And *LOL*?
From *Noah*? The control-freak Manhattan prosecutor?

But then there was more.

I'm lying in my bed (don't worry, I'm on top of the
duvet so I won't get any cooties on it) watching the
Yankees game, so guess who is having more fun?

P.S. They're playing the Blue Jays.

She groaned audibly. Well, it would have been audible if
not for Josh proclaiming that he can't regret what he did for
love (*you lucky bastard, Josh*). She would much rather be
watching baseball than the concert.

And that's exactly what she needed, Noah rolling around
in the bed she had to sleep in tonight, pollinating it with

even more of that spicy pine scent of his. Noah's only TV was a small one on the dresser in his bedroom, so she couldn't credibly object to him being there, but damn. She was pretty sure a part of her current exhaustion was attributable to the fact that she'd tossed and turned most of last night, going over and over their evening. She had taken comfort in the fact that by morning, the pine had receded. But now he was in there tainting it all over again like a dog marking its territory.

Why does your bed smell like pine?

Huh?

Of course, what she was really asking him was why *he* smelled like pine, but she wasn't about to admit that.

Christmas trees. Your bed smells like Christmas trees.

Christmas trees mixed with sexy man, but she didn't say that part.

I think my aftershave is kind of piney.

You *think*?

Well, it comes in a bottle shaped like a pine tree, so that's probably it.

She snorted. Oh my God, he was so adorably clueless. Another text arrived.

My sister gave me some aftershave when I was

sixteen. She said it was a good generic man
smell, so I just kept buying the same stuff. I never
really thought about it.

Wendy glanced at Jane, who was belting out the words to
some endless song. Something about kissing the day good-
bye (*if only, Josh*) as Noah kept texting.

It's eleven dollars at the drugstore. I should
probably graduate to something else.

No! Wendy felt the objection like a visceral thing, a creature inside her getting to its feet and preparing for battle.

Eh, it's fine.

Anyway, I'll change the sheets before you get
home.

No! The objection-creature took off running, weapons
brandished.

Nah, don't bother. Total waste of water. Anyway, I like pine.

⁓ total waste

After the game was over and Noah had no reason to stick
around in the room that was temporarily Wendy's, he turned
over and smelled his own bed. Several times, in fact, pressing his nose against various spots on the mattress and pil-
lows and sniffing like a goddamned dog. It did kind of smell
like Christmas, but not because it smelled like pine. All
he could smell was a very faint cinnamon aroma. Cloves,

too, maybe, or allspice. Definitely one of those Christmassy spice smells, anyway. It was the smell he associated with the mulled wine served at the office holiday party every year.

He got up and made his way to the dresser to set down the remote, and as he walked, he rubbed his hands vigorously over his cheeks, then smelled them. Nope, still no pine. Weird. He must be immune to his own scent.

Wendy's toiletries were sitting on the dresser in front of the TV. A few travel-size bottles and a small round tin were arranged in a neat line.

He really shouldn't.

He picked up a travel-size bottle that proclaimed itself "medium-weight moisturizer," and took a big sniff.

Nope. Just a barely-there, vaguely "clean" smell.

He moved on to the next bottle, which was sunscreen. And, he discovered, unscented sunscreen at that.

"Aha!" he said into the silence as he picked up the tin. Before even opening it, he could tell he'd discovered the source of the cinnamon scent. He pried the lid off and was hit with a blast of that mulled-wine spiciness. He had no earthly idea what the...item was, though. It was a solid red circular object that appeared to have a cinnamon stick embedded directly in it.

"Noah!"

Fuck. He fumbled the spicy mystery object back into its tin and struggled to close it, his hands made clumsy by the mortifying prospect of being caught going through Wendy's things.

"Noah, dude!"

Ah, it was Bennett. If he hadn't been having a minor panic attack over the prospect of being busted by Wendy as he pawed through her stuff, he would have realized the voice calling his name was a masculine one.

It was also not coming from inside the apartment. He moved to his bedroom window. Bennett was in the habit of coming home after he left the restaurant and trying to talk Noah into grabbing a drink with him. And by "talk," Noah meant "stand in the courtyard three stories below and yell up at Noah's bedroom window." The restaurateur was always hyper after a dinner shift, but, being a reformed bad boy, he avoided the drug- and booze-infested party scene that was endemic to the restaurant industry.

"I'm staying in tonight," he shouted down.

"Just one drink at Birch's," his friend countered, naming the pub at the end of the block they frequented. Noah had spent a good chunk of his New York life on a stool at Birch's nursing a beer while his teetotaler friend sipped iced tea.

"Come up here instead," Noah called. He actually wouldn't mind having a drink with Bennett. He knew he wouldn't sleep until Jane and Wendy were home safe, so some company would take his mind off the cinnamon mystery object. And, more to the point, would take his mind off kissing its owner, which was all he'd been able to think about for the past twenty-four hours. "I have beer, and you can BYO tea."

Bennett signaled his grudging agreement and disappeared into the building. Before Noah went out into the living room to unlock the door, he paused next to his bed and picked up a pillow. One more sniff to see if he could get a whiff of the alleged pine.

All he could smell was her.

His phone buzzed, and so did his heart. He lunged for it, not sure if he did or didn't want it to be a text from Wendy. He'd enjoyed texting with her during the concert—she was witty, and there really was nothing more attractive than an intelligent, witty woman. But Wendy wasn't just your garden-variety intelligent, witty woman. She was Jane's best friend. She was practically family.

And there he went again. He kept having to remind himself that it didn't *matter* that Wendy was Jane's best friend. It wasn't like that was the only thing stopping him. *Wendy herself* was stopping him. She wasn't looking for a relationship. She was leaving on her big trip.

The text wasn't from Wendy, anyway; it was from Jane.

Concert over. We're going out. Don't wait up.

Yeah, nice try, little sis. He smiled as he typed.

You know I'm going to wait up. But have fun.

It was a good thing Bennett was on his way up. Noah might have a few hours to kill.

Just go to sleep. I'll come home in a cab, I promise. I'll have Wendy put me directly in it.

Wait. What?

Won't Wendy be coming home with you?

She didn't answer for a long time. He went into the kitchen and grabbed a beer from the fridge, staring at his phone the whole while. Finally, Jane's reply came.

Doubtful. Seems like she's going to the boneyard.

He dropped the beer bottle. It didn't break, just rolled until it hit the edge of the stove.

Excuse me?

Bumping uglies?

Doing the horizontal tango?

Getting some stank on the hang down?

Oh my God. Noah closed his eyes against the onslaught
of texted euphemisms. Having a young-adult novelist for a
sister had its downsides, one of which was that she spent
way too much time with *Urban Dictionary*.

When he opened his eyes, it was to yet another unwelcome message.

Oh, my innocent brother. Do you need it explained to you? Wendy is going to find a man to
have sex with.

Noah opened his mouth wide to stretch his jaw, which
had locked. He considered his reply. Because "LIKE HELL
SHE IS" probably wasn't going to achieve his goal.

I know, you idiot. Wendy just doesn't seem like the type.

Which was a lie. Maybe the old Wendy, the one he remembered from years ago, wouldn't have been the type. But
modern-day Wendy most decidedly was. She'd told him as
much herself.

Ha. Ha ha ha. Wendy is exactly the type. It's actually her main goal for the evening. She says it's
been too long and she's getting jumpy as a re-

sult. Says her judgement about men is off. So I'm
supposed to vet her choice, make sure he's not
an ax murderer masquerading as a New Yorker,
and then I'll come home.

Her *judgement about men was off*? Why did that piss
Noah off so monumentally? It certainly hadn't seemed *off*
when she was climbing him like a tree last night. He cracked
his knuckles.

Where are you?

In a cab.

Yes, but where are you GOING?

When there wasn't an immediate reply, Noah carried the
phone with him into the living room and put his shoes on.

To some bar in the Lower East Side.

What's it called?

Okay, down boy. I appreciate your concern, but
I'm thirty-two years old. Do I have a curfew?

Dammit, Jane, just tell me the name of the bar.

There was a knocking at his door. Noah moved to answer
it just as the return text came.

Some place called Yellow.

"Whoa," Bennett said when Noah yanked the door open with enough force to cause it to crash against the wall in his entryway.

"Change of plans." Noah held out his hands to stop Bennett from entering his apartment. "I'm going out."

⸺ ↶

Wendy had kind of forgotten, during her recent dry spell, how boring so many men were. That was why her friends-with-benefits stint with Christopher had been so nice. He'd been smart and funny. He'd read the news. There'd been no love connection between them, but he'd been fun to talk to—in addition to being fun to do other things with. She hadn't really thought she would miss him once he broke it off. And really, she hadn't—until she'd been reminded, up close and personal, how good she'd had it in the Christopher era.

That's why she preferred long-term casual arrangements with smart men rather than one-night stands. Because most men were *boring*. Finding a decent one-night stand was a lot of work for not a lot of payoff.

"Can I ask you something?" She interrupted the bearded hipster dude who was droning on about the ratio of hops to malt in the beer he was drinking. When the guy got over his obvious shock at having had his monologue cut short, he nodded. "Do you live with your parents?" Because as far as she could tell, neither his job as a barista nor his novel-in-progress that was an ironic meditation on postmodern consumer culture in an era of identity politics was going to pay New York rent.

He turned red enough that it was discernable in the dim light of the bar.

Right. She tipped her head back and drained the remaining quarter of her beer in one go. "Look at that. Looks like I need to nip out for a refill."

And to find another prospect. She'd told Jane she didn't need to come to New York to get laid, but it turned out that after everything that had gone down with Noah, she *definitely* needed to get laid. Tonight.

She had a point to prove to herself.

There was only so much self-revelation a girl could take, and last night's detonation had her wigged out. After her texting interlude with Noah, she'd spent the rest of the concert thinking about him. Not that that was unusual these days, but she'd really let it sink in how much Noah Denning had, simply by not showing up that night, made her into the woman she was.

She'd tried to take back her own power that night at the dance, but was it possible that she hadn't succeeded at all? That by making him into a monster in her head, she'd stayed as under his spell as she'd always been?

"Hurry back." The aspiring novelist grinned at her.

"Will do," she lied as she headed to the bar. God, at least the downtown Toronto law party scene, dull as it was, was populated by *financially independent* boring men.

She was young, single, reasonably attractive, and *not* looking for love. So why was this so hard?

All of a sudden, a Josh Groban song filled the room. Jesus Christ, it was like the universe was aligned against her. Was it a sign? And if so, of what?

As she waited for her beer, she scanned the room for Jane and found her huddled over an old-school jukebox with her new best friend, a librarian in the New York Public Library system. They'd struck up a conversation right when Wendy and Jane arrived, but once they'd started yammering about diversity as a guiding principle in collection development, Wendy had headed out into the crowd to hunt.

So Josh was Jane's doing. He wasn't a sign from the universe.

She paid for her drink, turned around—and crashed smack dab into someone and spilled her beer all over him.

And that someone was Noah Denning.

Whose shirt was now drenched.

"We have to stop meeting like this." His eyes flicked down to his beautifully tailored, probably super expensive, off-white button-down—which was now covered in wide rivers of Guinness—and then back up to meet her gaze.

She should probably apologize, but she wanted to hit him. She wanted to *pummel* him, actually, to pound her fists against his chest and kick his shins with her stiletto heel.

Well. Last night she'd been thinking about how her anger at him had disappeared. Clearly that had only been temporary.

She had no particular reason to be angry at him right now, though. Beyond, of course, the usual: he'd broken her heart. And added to that the cherry on top that apparently her entire adult personality was his doing.

But she had nothing *specific* to be angry with him about. Nothing that would stand up in court.

"What are you doing here?" she asked.

"I'm cock-blocking you." He smiled as if he'd announced he was here to give her a present.

Okay, *there* was a cause for her anger, a bit delayed, but hey, retroactive justification worked for her.

"*Excuse me?*" She invested those two words with all the icy haughtiness she could muster. Because how dare he? Just because Mr. Control Freak Conscious Uncoupling didn't deign to do one-night stands didn't mean he had any jurisdiction over her. It was none of his goddamned business who she did or didn't sleep with.

"But probably there's some other name for it when you're doing it to a woman." Noah spoke mildly, still wearing that nonchalant smile. "Pussy blocking, maybe?"

Wendy gasped. It wasn't like she was a prude. The girls had been right when they'd told Noah at the photo shoot that she had developed a potty mouth. You hang out with hard-bitten lawyers for enough years and it sort of changes you. Or changes your vocabulary, at least. But to hear Noah saying those words…well, it messed with her head.

He flagged down the bartender. "I'll ask my sister. She's a walking *Urban Dictionary*." He glanced at the empty glass Wendy was still holding, then down at his ruined shirt. "Two pints of Guinness, please. And a towel."

Wendy had no idea what to say. Which was not a position she was accustomed to—or appreciated—being in.

Noah paid the bartender, pivoted to face her, and held out one of the drinks.

"You know what, Noah? Fuck you." There. She'd found her tongue.

Completely unruffled—*maddeningly* unruffled—he leaned against the bar and surveyed the room. "I have to say, I think I *would* be a better prospect than most of these guys." His gaze made a complete, unhurried circuit of the room before settling on her. "When it comes to fucking, I mean."

She gasped again—*goddammit*. She hated that he knew he'd gotten to her. But hearing Mr. I-Don't-Do-Casual talking so nonchalantly about "fucking" was doing something to her. She put on her courtroom face and ordered herself to stop gasping even if she had to stop breathing to do so.

His eyes danced. Apparently, this was all very amusing to him. "I'm just saying, the pickings seem pretty slim here."

"There are tons of guys here." Damn, she wished she'd hung in there with the barista-slash-novelist. At least then when Mr. Ego here made his grand entrance, he'd have been greeted by the sight of her talking to another guy.

"Yeah, if you're into excessive facial hair and retro ironic T-shirts." He wrinkled his nose. "How are we not in Brooklyn right now?" Seeming to realize that she wasn't going to take the beer he'd ordered for her, he set it on the bar behind him. "And I bet this crowd isn't winning any awards for its conversation skills. I bet it's all community gardens and craft beer." He scoffed. "Give me a Guinness any day."

She agreed with that last part. Actually, she agreed with all the parts. He'd hit on exactly her objections to the guys who'd shown interest in her this evening, but of course she wasn't about to let him know that. "You're forgetting that conversation skills are not the most important attributes in this context."

"Point taken. But beards?" His gaze fell to her crotch. "Ouch."

There was no mistaking his meaning. He didn't look away, either, and he must have secretly been a comic book character with heat-vision or something, because suddenly she was wet between her legs. God, the idea that he would assume a hypothetical bearded hookup would go there. He hadn't been kidding about not being the casual sex type. He had no idea how hookup culture worked.

Well, hell, if he was going to come in here and get all aggressive, she could dish it right back. She picked up her beer from the bar and only when she'd taken a nice long drink did she say, carefully pitching her voice to project a nonchalance she did not feel, "Your observation is irrelevant. In my experience, a guy you pick up in a bar is not going to go down on you the first time you fuck him. In fact, *no* guy is going to go down on you the first time you fuck him."

She was actively trying to ruffle his feathers. She was sick of being the only one gasping in shock here. But damn him, was he made of stone? Because he kept lounging against the bar nodding like he was considering her argument, as calm as he would be in a low-stakes, unremarkable trial. Then he shrugged and said, "Well, that's a missed opportunity for them, then, isn't it?"

Her face heated. She thought he was done and started to turn, preparing to leave—because why stand around torturing herself with this weird, charged conversation any longer?—but then he said, "It also proves my point."

Was this guy ever going to knock it off? "Which is?"

"That I'm a better prospect—when it comes to fucking— than these hipsters." He sneered a little as he once again surveyed the room. When his gaze returned to her, he licked his lips. He actually licked his lips.

All right, enough. She was just going to call him on it. She set her beer down again on the bar and got right in his face. Or, right in his neck, because even with her heels, that was as far as she came. She was undaunted, though; she was used to confronting tall guys who'd overdosed on machismo. Hell, that practically described her entire professional existence. "Noah Denning, are you propositioning me?"

"No."

He answered so quickly and with such decisiveness that she felt like he'd slapped her.

Or, you know, like he'd stood her up at the prom.

The shame was the same. It was *exactly* the same.

"I was speaking hypothetically. Because this"—he waved his hand back and forth between them, mimicking exactly the motion she'd used last night—"is done. Some sort of bizarre New York vacation aberration thing? Remember?"

"Oh, I remember." She remembered everything. "You just sounded for a minute there like maybe you'd reconsidered your whole prudish stance on cows and milk."

She was trying to bait him, but it didn't work. "Nope. I'm just here to check on my sister." He scanned the crowd. "You know, on account of my *obsession* with taking care of her."

Wendy took a little bit of comfort in the way he referenced what she'd said about him last night. It was, at least, confirmation that some of her words had gotten to him. "She's dancing with a librarian." She pointed at the other end of the bar where Jane and her new bestie had moved on from Josh and were bopping around to "Uptown Girl."

"A librarian?" Noah looked equal parts amused and confused.

"Yeah. You know, *that's* the kind of guy I always imagined Jane would end up with. Someone bookish."

"We've been over this." His voice took on a menacing tone.

"Yeah, yeah. I know." She did. She needed to stop beating this dead horse.

Noah's gaze returned to his sister, and at that same moment Jane looked up. What would it be like to have a sibling you were so connected to? What would it be like to have *anyone* you were so connected to?

Upon recognizing her brother, Jane smiled and waved. Then she grabbed the librarian's arm and started towing him toward the bar. A second guy, who'd been standing nearby on the dance floor, followed them. Although the librarian was nothing to sneeze at, Guy #2 was Fine-with-a-capital-

F. He was so gorgeous, in fact, that Wendy would even say nice things about his novel-in-progress if it meant she could get in his pants. Maybe she'd finally found her prince for a night.

More important, maybe she could hit on him in full view of Noah. She whistled a little, just loud enough for Noah to notice. When he raised his eyebrows questioningly at her, she said, "I would listen to *that* guy talk about craft beer and community gardens all night long."

His retort was cut off by Jane's arrival. She stepped right into his arms for a hug. "Hello, brother-mine! Have you come to collect me because I missed curfew?"

Noah rolled his eyes, but he didn't deny it.

Jane turned to her man-posse. "This is my brother, Noah. Noah, this is Jake. He's a librarian, and we've been having quite the chat about young-adult literature."

Jake stuck out his hand. "I'm a big fan of your sister's books."

Wendy entertained a momentary fantasy where Jane was still single and the two of them could pick these guys up. Jane could go home with Jake, and Wendy could go home with Jake's hot friend. But of course Jane would probably ruin things by falling in love with Jake and expecting Wendy to do the same with Jake's friend. She would want them to get married and buy adjoining houses or something.

"This," said Jane, gesturing to Wendy's fantasy man, "is Jake's husband, Julio."

Right. Of course.

Wendy could *feel* Noah smirking as he greeted the men.

Jane put an arm around Wendy and squeezed. "Jake, you met Wendy earlier. Julio, this is my best friend Wendy I was telling you about. She's the maid of honor in my wedding."

"Oh, she could *totally* pull off tartan," Julio said, not acknowledging Wendy other than to let his eyes scan her up and down like she was a horse at auction.

"Julio is a costume designer for Broadway shows," Jane said excitedly. "We were talking about the wedding—he had the idea that we could incorporate Cameron's heritage by having the bridesmaids wear tartan dresses."

"Cameron's from Thunder Bay," Wendy said, because it was all she could think to say, given that she was still reeling from the fact that her fantasy one-night stand not only wasn't straight, he was, apparently, redesigning her bridesmaid dress.

"It's a great idea." Jane pulled away from Wendy and made a dismissive gesture in Julio's direction. "But the wedding is going to be really low-key. The girls already have their dresses. I'm totally not one of those high-maintenance brides."

"Honey, you can be as high-maintenance as you like," Julio said. "It's your *wedding*."

Jane got a moony look on her face, and Wendy got a sick feeling in her stomach.

Noah looked at his watch. "Well, shall we, ladies?"

"We shall." Jane let loose a big yawn, and Wendy gave up. There was no point in sticking around. Sometimes the only thing you could do was lose your case and move on to the next one. Time to go home—like, all the way home to Toronto. Just one more day to get through, and tomorrow she and Jane were slated for Jane's dress appointment, so she wouldn't have to deal with Noah, who was planning to go into the office even though it was Sunday. She could do this.

Wendy could feel Noah watching her while Jane said good-bye to her new friends and procured their address so she could invite them to her low-key wedding. Because low-key weddings always involve guests you met once in a bar in another city.

When she was done, Noah gestured for Jane to precede him, but he didn't take his eyes off Wendy. Once Jane had started cutting a path through the crowded bar, he repeated the gesture. Wendy, as much as she wished she could flee to the airport and get on a plane home right now, stepped ahead of him.

As she did so, he leaned down and whispered in her ear. "See. You knew you were going to end up coming home with me tonight."

She didn't bother responding, merely kept following Jane through the crowd as if she hadn't heard him. As if her whole body hadn't ignited at his words.

She felt oddly like they had faced off in court and he'd won the day. She hated that feeling. But Wendy was fair. She was clear-eyed. There was nothing she could do, at least for now, but concede.

Point to Noah Denning.

Chapter Nine

$\mathcal{N}$oah did not go into the office on Sunday.

When Wendy emerged from her bedroom, aka the Christmas tree–scented torture chamber, it was after nine, so she assumed he'd be long gone—which was why she came out wearing only a T-shirt and underwear.

"Well, now I get to see the bottom half."

She screamed.

He was sitting in the living room commenting wryly from over the top of a newspaper. She'd walked right past him on her way to the kitchen.

"Ack!" Jane hustled over to Wendy and performed the same ineffectual airplane-arms shielding thing she'd done when Noah walked in on Wendy changing her shirt at the photo session in the spring. "I'm sorry! I should have warned you he was here!"

Wendy, tugging the hem of her T-shirt down to cover her butt, composed herself and made the same reply she had back then. "No worries. It's only Noah."

It was a lie then, and it was a lie now.

"I talked him into coming to the bridal salon with us," Jane said.

"What happened to your workaholic ways?" Wendy called over her shoulder as she headed back to the bedroom.

"I rethought my priorities. How often do you get to go wedding dress shopping with your little sister?" Noah said as Wendy reemerged from the bedroom fully dressed.

"Well, you never know," Jane joked. "This Cameron thing might just be a phase."

Noah's gaze whipped to Wendy's, and her face heated. He didn't say anything, though, and she appreciated the hell out of that.

"Nah," Wendy said, talking to Jane but looking at Noah. "I'm pretty sure Cameron's the real deal."

Noah smiled at her. It was sort of like the smiles he used to give her after her softball games—a proud parental smile. Which, as embarrassing as it was, made sense. He knew what it had cost for her to say that.

But there was also something else in that smile, something she couldn't quite identify. Something that made her uncomfortable. It was almost like he could see inside her.

But that was impossible.

Right?

⁓

Maybe this hadn't been a good idea. Maybe the correct number of times a man should accompany his little sister wedding dress shopping was actually zero. Because as far as Noah could tell, he was adding no value to this excursion. He was just sitting on a big poufy pink chair in a room that he could only describe as an antechamber while Jane tried on approximately one million wedding dresses.

And, ignorant as he was about such matters, he'd had no idea how long it took to put one of those things on—or how many helpers it required. Each new dress required a small army of overly Botoxed women in Chanel suits to carry it into the fitting room, and, from the sound of things, to hoist it onto Jane.

And worse, all the dresses kind of looked the same to him. They looked good, to be fair, but he wasn't seeing as much difference between them as Jane seemed to.

The only thing that was saving him from going out of his skull with boredom was Words With Friends.

Words With Friends with Wendy, to be precise.

H-E-L-P she spelled from inside the dressing room. She was in there with Jane and the Chanel army, so she wasn't taking a turn very often, but he was staring at his phone like he was waiting for the secrets of the universe to be revealed.

Then came a message from the app's chat feature.

That was actually a message from beyond the grave. I have been smothered by tulle.

He didn't know what tulle was, but he cracked up anyway.

But it was also, you will have noticed, a triple letter score for the L.

He wouldn't have thought Wendy was an emoji sort of person, but that last message was followed by a face with its tongue sticking out.

He calmly played L-I-N-K-E-D with the same L, rack-ing up a nice chunk of points. A message came immediately in.

Oh, bite me.

He grinned. He had to talk himself out of sending her a big smiley face back.

There really was nothing as fun as sparring with Wendy.

For Wendy and him, sparring was routine. It was their normal. It had been ever since they were kids.

He was beginning to think that where they had gone wrong the other day—even though it had felt so very right at the time—was that they'd stepped out of that routine. They'd been bickering—par for the course for them—when he'd thought she was expressing disapproval over Jane and Cameron's relationship. But then, in a whiplash-inducing shift, she'd told him a pretty big truth about herself, and his instinctive response had been to comfort her. Which was fine—he didn't regret that. But then of course there had been that searing kiss, which he most certainly did regret.

Maybe regretted.

Well, regretted its aftermath anyway.

And then, last night, he'd gone even further off the rails by swooping into that bar and cock-blocking her. Which, in the bright light of day, he had to admit was none of his business. That had been way out of character for him. He wasn't a caveman—usually.

So if he was feeling unsettled about that kiss and its consequences—and happy and calm arguing with her via Words With Friends—surely that signaled a way forward: more sparring. Yes. The way to survive the wedding-enforced proximity in their future was to get things back to normal. Find something to argue—superficially—about. Double down on "normal."

Buoyed, he tuned into the discussion under way in the dressing room. They were talking about something called mermaid dresses.

"Just try it!" Wendy ordered over Jane's insistence that she absolutely, positively didn't want a "mermaid dress."

Several minutes of rustling followed. Then, Jane: "Ohhhh."

"Told you."

They were coming out, so he set down his phone.

"What do you think?" Jane asked as she emerged.

His eyes slid over her without really taking her in and settled on Wendy, who was gazing at Jane and wearing a satisfied look. Clearly, Wendy approved of the dress. He had a momentary thought of disagreeing just to be contrary—in the name of his larger cause of finding something to argue about so as to get things back to normal. But he probably shouldn't do that over something as important as his sister's wedding dress. So he turned his attention back to Jane, who was being helped onto a little platform across from a three-way mirror.

"Wow." She looked *great*. Even he could see that this dress worked better than the previous ones had, though he couldn't articulate why. "I think that's the one."

"It really does show off your hourglass figure, dear," said one of the Chanel ladies.

He got up and went over to Jane. "Let me buy it for you."

"Let *me* buy it for you," Wendy said, and Noah almost cracked up. His assessment was spot on: arguing was their normal. And he hadn't even been trying there.

"Huh?" Jane turned a confused look on both of them. "Neither of you is buying my wedding dress. Honestly, you two are so weird. Haven't you ever watched *Say Yes to the Dress*? This is the part where you're supposed to be getting all emotional over me having found the perfect dress."

She was kidding—he thought.

"Sorry," Wendy said. "You know I'm not really a crier. I just want you to have the best wedding ever."

"*I* want you to have the best wedding ever," Noah countered. It was true. He wasn't even saying that as a counterpoint to Wendy—or at least that wasn't the only reason he was saying it. He wasn't the type to get choked up over dresses, but he wanted her to be happy—happy and safe. It was all he'd ever wanted. And the way he often defaulted to showing that was with cash.

"Well, I appreciate that, but I'm buying my own wedding dress!" Jane put her hands on her hips and looked down at him from her platform like a mother scolding a kid. "Why don't you channel your enthusiasm into something more useful?"

"Like what?" he asked.

"Well, if you really want to help, brother dearest," she said, "you could get involved with planning Cameron's bachelor party. Jay, God bless him, is a little..."

"Uninspired?" Wendy supplied.

Jay was Cameron's brother, and as such, Jane's future brother-in-law. Noah didn't know him that well, but he could see why Wendy would say that. Jay was a great guy, but he didn't make a big impression. He was an accountant. He seemed very straitlaced.

Wendy laughed. "Yeah. He's probably going to repeat his own boring bachelor party." She turned to Noah. "They hung out all night in the same pub he always goes to. There was nothing special about it." She smirked at Jane. "Except

I guess of course that you and Cameron got it on for the first time that night."

"Hey." Noah covered his ears. "I don't need to hear that."

"Yes," Jane said. "Cameron probably doesn't even care, but I kind of do. I want him to have a big, fun party. It's not going to come from Jay. And his other groomsman besides you and Jay is this guy Hector he knows from the army. Hector is...how do I say this? Hector is not the most thoughtful guy in the world."

"I got you." He had this. "One spectacular bachelor party coming up."

"You want Cameron to have a big, fun party, but what about yours?" Wendy asked. "The girls and I have been taking you at your word when you said you wanted a low-key wedding." She glanced at the dress. "Don't take this the wrong way, but that is not a low-key dress. You gotta tell us if you want us to kick it into high gear for the bachelorette."

Jane made a sheepish face. "I kind of want you to kick it into high gear for the bachelorette."

And...there it was. The perfect battleground being handed to him on a platter—the way to undo all the weirdness of this weekend with Wendy. He wanted to laugh in triumph. Instead, he took a step forward, puffed up his chest, and said, "Hey, Wendy, I bet I can throw Cameron a better party than you can throw Jane."

"Oh, really? You? Mr. Serious?" Wendy smirked.

"What does *that* mean?"

"You're not exactly the cut-loose sort."

He took a step forward and folded his arms across his chest. "I am, too."

She stepped forward, too, and arranged her arms in a mirror-image gesture. "All right, Noah Denning. You're on.

Prepare for defeat. And if you're so confident, why don't you put your money where your mouth is?"

"Here we go," Jane muttered.

"With pleasure. What do you have in mind?"

"Guys," Jane said. "I know enough to know that I probably can't stop you from making this stupid bet, but you are *not allowed* to bet big piles of money on it."

Wendy ignored her. "What I have in mind isn't financial." She grinned and let her gaze rake him up and down, sizing him up. "Loser goes to Josh Groban."

"Ha!" Noah let loose a bark of laughter. That was a great stake.

"For life," Wendy added ominously.

Well, shit. Things were getting serious. But he was in. He was so in. He stuck out his hand. "You got yourself a deal."

Chapter Ten

*W*endy was stuck in one of Toronto's famous traffic jams. She was supposed to be at the airport picking up Gia, who was arriving a couple days in advance of the bachelorette party.

Her phone buzzed. She shouldn't have picked it up, but she was at a dead stop. It was Noah.

How's the party planning going?

They'd been texting a bit since they'd made their bet in New York. Doing a bit of trash talking.

I rented out a branch of the freaking Toronto Public Library.

She'd like to see him top that. She picked up the phone again and attached a couple of pictures to her next text.

The invitations were on vintage library cards. The cocktail stirrers are topped with little tiny books.

And the waiters are nerdy, bookish hunks.

She didn't have a photo to go with that last text, but she would take one at the event and make sure he saw it. Ha!

Ooh. A book theme. You really know how to throw a party, Wendy. Maybe I should just give up now. NOT.

Oh shut up. What are YOU doing?

Like I am going to tell you?

Hey! I told you mine.

We never said any of this had to be public.

Well, if our plans aren't public, how do we judge who wins? How can we decide which is the best party if you won't tell me about yours?

There. She'd like to see him argue with that logic.

You may have a point.

HA. SO THERE.

I suggest we let the wedding party vote. Photograph your party, and I'll do the same. When we're all together for the wedding, we'll share the

photos and each of us can describe our party
and try to convince the group to vote for us.

Wendy was all over this idea. Simple math was on her
side. She had the girls, and what Noah was forgetting was
that two of his guys were married to—or about to be married
to—two of her girls. They'd be able to flip either or both Jay
and Cameron. So no problem. She had this in the bag.

You're on.

Then for good measure, she added:

Sucker.

The driver behind her laid on the horn. The jam had broken
up a bit so she hit the gas. A few minutes later, she was
pulling in to the airport's cell phone lot, where people picking up passengers could wait to be summoned. Her phone
buzzed again and she fumbled for it, adrenaline surging, before she remembered that it would almost certainly not be
Noah, but Gia. The person she was waiting for. Jeez.
    It wasn't Gia, though; it was Cameron.

Hey, can you do me a favor? Apparently I'm going to Vegas this weekend. Surprise bachelor
party—Noah just sprang this on me. Jane is supposed to do an author visit on Friday morning at
a school in Peterborough. I know she'll say she
doesn't care, but I don't want her to go alone. It's
a long drive. Any chance you can go with her?

Holy shit. Noah was moving the party to *Vegas*. That *bastard*.

Wendy *thought* she had pulled out all the stops on Jane's party, renting out a historic branch of the library so their favorite book nerd could have the bash of her dreams. But, shit! There was no way her party, no matter how perfectly on-theme and Pinterest-ready it was, could compete with Las Vegas.

Well, okay. This was a curveball, but it wasn't time to award Noah the victory yet, not even remotely.

It was time to fight dirty.

She picked up her phone.

No problem. I'm picking Gia up at the airport right now. We'll get Elise and we'll all go with Jane on Friday morning—start the bachelorette festivities early.

She let her phone sit for a moment, waiting before sending the next text, so it would seem like a casual afterthought.

So, you guys are going to Vegas? When?

Jay and Hector and I are leaving tomorrow. Noah, who was the mastermind of all of this, can't get off work Friday, so he's going to fly in on Saturday and join us.

Is he now? She tapped her fingernails on the phone before replying.

Well, have fun.

Will do. You too. Take care of my girl.

Wendy thought about correcting him. Yes, Jane was Cameron's girl, she would reluctantly acknowledge, but she was also *Wendy's* girl. But before she could decide whether to say anything, a text from Gia arrived saying that she was outside the terminal.

All right. Next step: get Gia on board. Wendy started the car, pulled around, and scanned the arrivals area until she found an effortlessly beautiful glamazon.

"So," she said as Gia got into the car. "Change of plans. We're going to Vegas for the bachelorette."

"We're what?" Gia paused half in and half out, her brow knitting between her striking amber eyes. Seeing Gia after a long stretch apart was sometimes a shock to the system. It shouldn't be possible for a human being to be so pretty. Gia had literally just stepped off a plane from Tokyo, but instead of looking like she'd spent fifteen hours in a metal tube whose main feature was its ability to dehydrate and exhaust mere mortals, the six-foot beauty looked like she'd spent a refreshing morning twirling in the Alps while singing about her favorite things.

"Okay, back up now." Gia sat, made a rewinding motion with her hands, then leaned over to kiss Wendy on the cheek. "Hi!"

Wendy grinned. "Hi."

Their group of four sorted into two pairs of best friends. Jane and Wendy of course went way back to childhood. They'd gone off to university together, signing up to be roommates, and had met Elise that first year. Gia was later to the scene, arriving as a freshman when the rest of them were seniors. Elise had been Gia's resident assistant, and the two of them had formed a fast friendship.

Because Wendy had only overlapped with Gia that one year at school, and because Gia had dropped out after her first year and begun a modeling career that had her jetting all over the world, Gia and Wendy weren't particularly close aside from the foursome. But Wendy sometimes thought if they'd met as fully formed adults, she and Gia, with their penchant for travel and their shared outlooks on life, would be the most natural pairing.

"Okay, now what's this about Vegas?"

"We need to take this party up a notch."

"Is this about the non-low-keyness of this supposedly low-key wedding?"

Wendy barked a laugh. "You noticed that?"

"Jane sent me a picture of the dress. That was not a low-key dress."

"Those were my words exactly. But that's on you. You're the one who got her all hyped up to go to that ridiculous salon."

"Don't lay this shit on me, sister. Jane is going the path of Bridezilla Elise whether we like it or not." Gia sighed. "If I didn't love Jane so much, I'd be like..." She lifted both middle fingers.

The lewd gesture gave Wendy a rush of the warm fuzzies. In fact, she was getting a little teary-eyed at the sight of her bold, fearless friend. Gia did what she wanted— lived large and made no apologies for it. That wasn't all that common when you really thought about it.

"Hey." Gia laid a hand on Wendy's arm. "Is everything okay?"

"Yeah, yeah." Wendy reached into her bag. "Here. I got you a butter tart. I thought you'd be hungry after the flight." Gia had a sweet tooth, and butter tarts were among her favorites. And if her mouth was full, she was less likely to object to Wendy's Vegas plan.

"Thanks. I actually ate on the plane, so I'll save it for later." She shot Wendy a quizzical look. "You sure you're okay? I mean, I'm used to the sight of me bringing people to tears, but…"

"I'm just glad you're here. I could use a break from all this wedding crap. We're the last women standing, you know?"

"You know it." Gia held up her hand for a fist bump. "No ball and chain for me, thank you very much."

"Hear hear," said Wendy, getting her shit together—what a stupid little emotional moment that had been—and pulling away from the curb.

"But seriously, I feel like something's up," Gia said. "Has Jane really gone off the deep end?"

"No, no. She still *thinks* she's doing the 'low-key' thing." Wendy let go of the steering wheel with one hand and made air quotes. "So she can't get too out of control because that will violate her image of herself and create a disturbance in the force. So she's kind of at odds with herself."

"That's tricky. In some ways Elise—God bless her—was easier because at least you knew what you were dealing with."

"I think you might be right." Wendy merged into traffic. "An overt bridezilla at least makes her demands clear."

"Crystal clear." Gia snorted. "Remember the felt?"

"Ha! Yes!" Elise had gone on a last-minute tear before her wedding, forcing the bridesmaids to hand-make paper for place cards, and the process had involved putting felt into blenders. "Yeah, so I get the sense that Jane actually wants more than she's saying—she wants us stuffing felt into blenders, or whatever her nerdy equivalent is—but she doesn't *want* to want it, you know? She doesn't want us to think she's as bad as Elise was."

"So Jane secretly wants a bigger-deal bachelorette party?" Gia asked.

"I think Jane secretly wants a bigger-deal everything, but she's using this coded language. Like, for example, she keeps talking about how 'fun' it would be if the bridesmaids wore tartan dresses."

"You mean like Scottish plaid?"

"Yup. Which, thank God, it's too late to special-order." Gia was a size-two knockout who would look good in a burlap sack so "little black dress versus bullshit tartan" probably wasn't such a big deal for her, but Wendy would look like Little Miss Scotland in a plaid dress. If, you know, Little Miss Scotland was Chinese.

"Wow," said Gia.

"Yeah. So anyway, I'm suddenly thinking that canapés at the library isn't going to cut it."

"What are the boys doing?" Gia asked.

"They're ah, going to Vegas. I just found out. They surprised Cameron with the news today."

"Wendy, you sly girl!" Gia exclaimed. "You want to invade the boys' party. Show them up."

"Well, actually…"

Gia shifted in her seat to face Wendy. "Well, actually *what*?"

"I *may* have made a bet with Jane's brother over who could throw the best party."

Gia cracked up again. "Jane mentioned something about that. So is this Vegas thing about showing Jane a good time or winning your bet?"

Wendy made a guilty face. "Both?"

Gia banged on the dashboard. "Either way, I think it's a great idea. I'm in!"

"Really? I thought I was going to have to do a lot more convincing."

"Hell, a trip to Vegas *and* beating the boys? Sign me up."

"You think Elise will be into it, though?" Wendy asked.

"Are you kidding me? Remember during her own wedding how obsessed she was with invading Jay's bachelor party? What is this if not that on a grand scale?"

Wendy chuckled. "The only problem is that we have fifteen people coming to the library party tomorrow night."

"So we still do that. She gets two parties. Is Noah throwing Cameron two parties?"

That was a very good point. "I like the way you think."

Gia opened the calendar app on her phone. "Okay, how about this? Night at the library tomorrow as planned with the bigger group, then the four of us fly to Vegas Saturday."

"That's perfect, because Noah isn't flying in until Saturday anyway. Apparently he can't get off work, so he's going a day later than the other guys."

"Great. We'll make it a surprise for Jane. We'll time it so we arrive around the same time as Noah. He'll shit his pants."

Wendy cackled. It was all so delightfully evil.

"We stay two nights there, then we fly back Monday," Gia went on. "Instead of spending the weekend listening to Jane subtly lament that the window has closed for tartan, we show her a not-low-key time. What would you call that? A high-key time?"

A higher-key time than Noah was showing Cameron. An idea popped into Wendy's head. "Maybe we could hire a male stripper?"

Gia barked a laugh. "Yes! I think what our girl needs to take her bachelorette from low-key to high-key is a lap dance from a stripper dressed as Elvis!"

"Or one dressed as a librarian—in keeping with the theme."

"Yes!" Gia pumped her fist. "I'm super into this for selfish reasons, too."

"And what would those be?"

"I need to get laid."

"Huh?" The non sequitur gave Wendy pause. "You don't need to go to Vegas to get laid. All you need to do is, like, make eye contact with a human male and crook your finger."

"You know I prefer things to be uncomplicated."

Wendy nodded. "One and done. Two and through." That was Gia's motto—she'd sleep with a guy once, twice in extreme cases. But that was it.

Gia gave an unapologetic shrug. "Uncomplicated is easier in Vegas. No one is looking for lasting love in Vegas."

"What happens in Vegas stays in Vegas," Wendy said. Damn, she loved Gia. Although that phrase reminded her of another, less comfortable one, one that had so recently come from her own lips: *What happens in New York stays in New York.*

Gia pulled out the butter tart and lifted it as if it were a drink. "What happens in Vegas stays in Vegas. Cheers to that."

Wendy thought back to that bar in New York, to Noah taunting her with his suggestive, borderline lewd talk. "Well, you know what? I need to get laid, too. Preferably by a big, hot stranger who's not looking for lasting love."

"Yay!" Gia put away the butter tart and got her phone out. "I'll call Elise."

"Hey, before you do that, where am I taking you?" Wendy was almost at the point where she needed to decide which branch of the highway system to get on. "Elise's, I assume?"

Gia sighed and let her phone drop to her lap. "Yep."

"Don't sound so excited."

"Oh, you know, the aforementioned ball and chain thing.

Third wheel and all that—not that they do it on purpose. I wish I could stay in a hotel, but Elise won't have it. She says I live in hotels, so I'm not allowed to stay in one in Toronto."

"Why don't you stay with me?" It was awkward to ask—Gia always stayed with Elise when she was in town—but Wendy found herself genuinely wanting Gia to say yes.

"Really?"

"Yeah, we can work on the Vegas arrangements after dinner." They had dinner planned with the Toronto crowd. It would be really nice to have Gia over at her place after *that* couples extravaganza. "We'll do some shots after hanging with the marrieds."

"I would love that." Gia rested her hand momentarily on Wendy's forearm. "Thanks."

"Great." Wendy smiled her first genuine smile in a long time as she chose the southern branch of the highway that would take them to her downtown condo. "We single ladies gotta stick together."

⁓

Wendy surprised herself by actually having fun at dinner that night, which was at Elise's house. The entire wedding party was in attendance: Elise and Jay, Jane and Cameron, Wendy, Gia, and Cameron's friend Hector.

Well, the entire wedding party was in attendance save for one person.

"Do you think we should FaceTime my brother?" Jane exclaimed after dinner.

"Nope." Wendy was on her third post-dinner scotch, which probably explained why she had answered what was supposed to have been a rhetorical question—and answered it loudly enough for all eyes to swing to her. "I mean...these things are always awkward."

"What things?" Elise asked.

"Oh, you know, FaceTiming is never the same as having someone with you in person," Wendy said weakly, still sober enough—alas—to be aware of how lame she sounded.

Luckily, Jane didn't seem to register it and was already punching emphatically at her phone. "I'm totally doing it!"

"Leave it to Jane to drunk dial her *brother*," said Cameron with obvious affection in his voice as he slung an arm around her shoulder.

"Hey!" Jane objected, trying—but not too hard—to shake off his arm. "I'm not— *Noah!* Hiiii!!"

"Janie," he said. "What are you doing?"

Gah! His voice. Noah's voice was always compelling, but right now it was all sleepy and gravelly, like Jane had woken him up. Wendy glanced at her watch. It was eleven.

"Having dinner with all the wedding people and missing you! I want to see you!"

Wendy shared a glance with Gia and then with Elise, who'd been brought on board and had enthusiastically endorsed the Vegas plan. Jane would be seeing her brother sooner than she realized.

"What are you doing?" Jane leaned in closer to her phone. "Are you still at *work*?"

"Guilty. I've got a trial starting Tuesday, and since I'm jetting off for Cameron's party the day after tomorrow, I've got to finish prepping now. So that means late nights today and tomorrow."

"Well, I'm tempted to lecture you about work-life balance, but I suspect it will do no good! Say hi and bye to everyone." She lifted her phone and started panning across the room. Wendy looked at her hands and willed the sofa she was sitting on to swallow her whole—it was big and fluffy, so it wasn't that farfetched.

"Wendy Lou Who." She hadn't been looking, but it didn't matter. That damned voice shot straight to her core. They might as well have been back in that stupid hipster bar in New York, with him calmly informing her that he was a better prospect for fucking than any of the guys there. Jane stopped moving the phone. Wendy could hardly keep *not* looking at Noah, so she forced herself to raise her eyes. And there he was, iPhone-size, in a white shirt with the sleeves rolled up and his tie loosened.

"So I heard the cat is out of the bag about my party," he said. "My amazing, classic Vegas party."

"Mm-hmm." Wendy inspected her fingernails as she affected a noncommittal tone. In truth, she was practically bursting. Her evil plot made her so happy.

"I really hope you ladies have fun at the library," he taunted.

"We will." She beamed at him, refusing to take the bait, which she knew would only irritate him more.

"Is this about that stupid bet?" Jane asked.

"What bet?" Cameron asked.

Jane turned to her fiancé. "These two are competing over who can throw the better bachelor or bachelorette party."

Cameron cracked up. "Oh, man. Sorry, Wendy, but I think Vegas beats the library."

Jane swatted him. "You don't know that!" Wendy loved how loyal Jane was, even though she was clearly jealous of the guys' destination shindig.

"Aren't these things subjective anyway?" Jay asked, trying to be diplomatic.

"That's why we're all voting at the end," Gia said.

"Isn't that just going to split us along gender lines?" Elise asked.

Wendy held up her hands as everyone started talking. "Everybody just wait. All we ask is that you withhold judgment and vote honestly at the end." Except Cameron, whom Wendy planned to pressure into voting for Jane's team.

From the phone, Noah guffawed. He couldn't imagine a scenario in which she would top him. She'd show him. She swallowed a laugh and asked him, by way of deflection, "What are you working on?"

"Aggregated cemetery desecration in the first degree."

Whoa. She'd only been asking to get him off the topic of the warring parties, but that was hella interesting. "Wow. You can go a whole career without seeing something like that." She certainly had. "Does first degree require a prior conviction?"

"It does indeed. Dude paints swastikas on gravestones in Jewish cemeteries." There were aghast murmurings from the room. "Got any advice for me, counselor?"

Her brain started whirring. "Other charges?"

"Oh yeah, a veritable cornucopia of them. Third-degree criminal mischief, firearm possession, criminal possession of stolen property, and unlawful fleeing."

She whistled. "They'll try to bargain."

"No doubt, but not until I've lost a shit-ton of sleep preparing for them not to."

She shrugged. "Part of the job."

"What would you ask for?"

"Depends what you have on him."

"Prints. Red spray paint in his house. Surveillance video of his car leaving the scene. That's all a matter of public record. The rest I can't tell you."

"Can he be ID'd in the car?"

"Only circumstantially. We don't have good video."

She shook her head. "What the hell good are these god-damned privacy-invading Big Brother security cameras anyway if they don't get clear shots?"

"Hey! You're not supposed to be on his side!" Jane was delighted by their exchange.

Her outburst reminded Wendy that, oh yeah, they had an audience here. She'd been a little too into talking shop with Noah.

She turned back to the camera. "I don't know New York State law, but I'm thinking I'd offer to plead to the rest if you drop the biggie."

"Wait," Hector, the other groomsman, said. "She's defending that creep?"

"Well, not that particular creep," Elise said. "But she's a defense attorney."

Hector, whom Wendy had met only a handful of times—at the infamous photo shoot, for example—said, "I don't know how you sleep at night."

Here they went. Sometimes Wendy felt like she had to have this conversation at every cocktail party she went to, after the "And what do you do?" questions were asked and answered.

"I sleep just fine," she snapped, too tired to dish out the more patient version of this speech—plus, Hector was sort of a jerk. "In fact, I sleep like a goddamn baby. You know why? Because it's my job to help uphold this little thing we call the right to a fair trial. Section 11 of the Canadian Charter of Rights and Freedoms. Sixth Amendment to the United States Constitution. Hallmark of democracies everywhere."

Hector blinked rapidly. "Even when you know some-one's guilty?"

"I act for my client. If my client tells me he's innocent, he's innocent. My personal feelings don't come into play."

"Wow," Hector said. "I don't know if I could do that."

"Someone has to." Noah spoke from the phone, drawing everyone's attention. "The system depends on it. I've tried a number of cases where I was convinced the defendant was guilty—all the evidence pointed to it—and then the defense would drop some bomb that definitively proved innocence. Am I glad I lost those cases? You'd better believe it."

What the hell? Wendy looked around to see if Noah's impassioned speech in support of her argument was causing anyone else to freak out. Nope, just her. She tried to get the fluttering in her stomach to stop. She wasn't sure why she was so surprised. He'd been to law school. Hell, all it took was a junior high civics class to absorb the lesson of innocent until proven guilty.

"And what about minor possession cases?" Noah went on. "You have any of those recently, Wendy?"

"Yeah. Teenage pothead. Busted at a party. Underage possession—third offense."

"And what happened to him?"

"We pled it down. He did court-ordered rehab followed by a few months of house arrest, and he's going to be doing community service until he's like twenty-five." She smiled at the memory. The judge had given that kid so much community service, he might well have preferred a smaller dose of straight-up jail time. But she was proud of her work on that case. She truly thought that with the oversight of the court and the fact that she'd essentially scared the living crap out of him, the kid had a decent chance to get his life back on track.

"Right," Noah said. "Canada has more liberal drug laws, but in some states here, there's a strict three strikes you're out law on drug possession. They'd take this teenager, lock him up, and throw away the key. Does that seem right?"

"I see your point," Hector said.

"Damn right," Noah said. "Prosecutors get a lot of glory, but good defense lawyers are the unsung heroes of the system. And Wendy's a *great* defense lawyer."

Her cheeks heated. She wasn't sure how he could possibly know that. Yes, she worked at one of Toronto's top firms, which wasn't something you just stumbled into, but…

"Okay!" Gia clapped her hands. "As fascinating as all this legal foreplay is, if it's going to go any further, the two lawyers need to get a room." She motioned to Jane. "Just give her the phone and she can take Noah into Elise's bedroom." She was grinning as she spoke, and everyone else laughed, but *shit*. Their discussion there *had* felt kind of… heated. She loved Noah's mind. Well, she *appreciated* Noah's mind. Talking with someone who thought fast and critically was a pleasure.

An *intellectual* pleasure.

But she didn't need Gia getting the wrong idea, so she smiled and said, "Sorry. Got carried away there."

"You ladies sure know how to throw a party," Cameron teased, grabbing Jane so she fell back onto his lap. She shrieked and struggled to keep the phone upright.

"I hope tomorrow night's bachelorette party is this exciting," Noah said from the phone.

"Oh, shut up." Jane turned the phone around so she could look at her brother. "I think it's pretty clear that you Vegas boys are going to have more fun than we are." She paused, her expression turning wistful, and Wendy, Gia, and Elise shared an amused look. "But we are going to paint this town red! I'm just not sure who's going to bail us out of jail if you all are gone."

"Wendy," came the voice from the phone. "Wendy will bail you out of jail. Actually, Wendy will make sure you don't go to jail in the first place. Stay with Wendy, and you'll be fine."

"I was kidding, you overprotective dork," Jane said.

Wendy knew as much, but the immediate vote of confidence, even in jest, combined with Noah's earlier praise of her abilities, warmed her insides.

Chapter Eleven

$\mathcal{N}$oah was exhausted. He'd pulled near all-nighters Thursday and Friday nights, caught a few hours of sleep in the wee hours of Saturday, then dragged his sorry ass to the airport. Not the most auspicious start for what was supposed to be a weekend of debauchery. Well, semi-debauchery. It wasn't like Cameron was going to do anything crazy with the bride's brother present. Cameron wasn't the type to do anything crazy anyway. The guy knew where his bread was buttered.

Which made Noah a very happy man.

Also an entry in the happy-making department? He was pretty sure he was going to win his bet with Wendy. Yeah, her book-themed party for Jane was cute, but it didn't involve air travel. Vegas was classic. He was going to show Cameron a great time—a chaste, respectful great time—and document the hell out of it.

So: he was happy. But still exhausted. After struggling

to cram his bag into the dollhouse-size overhead bin—and to cram his body into the dollhouse-size seat—he sat back and closed his eyes.

Sleep, blessed sleep. The flight was five hours and fifty-five minutes, and one of Noah's talents was that he could fall asleep instantly and anywhere. He'd developed the skill in high school, when he was working nights at the store. He would literally sleep away his middle-of-the-night "lunch" break at work, not to mention his study periods at school. Now *that* had been true exhaustion. Mixed in with the ever-present worry about his sister and mom, and probably a good measure of unresolved anger at his dad.

He stuck his ear buds in and shook his head as if to physically clear the memories. He hated thinking about those days. Doing so made him feel almost as out of control as he'd felt back then. Like his life was hanging by a thread.

So, sleep. He nestled back into his headrest, and his well-trained body let loose a huge yawn. He could feel himself slipping, surrendering to—

"Noah!"

"Jane?" His eyes flew open and rested on... "Wendy?"

His entire body jolted awake. More than awake. How could Wendy be here, on this plane, on a runway at LaGuardia?

And yet there she was.

And another question, one he'd asked himself many, many times in recent months: how could such a small woman—she actually fit in the goddamn plane—have such a huge presence? How could she light every nerve ending in his body on fire without even saying a word?

"Surprise!"

The word came from Jane; Wendy still hadn't spoken. Noah could recognize his sister's excited, gleeful tone anywhere, but he kept his gaze on Wendy, who looked right past him as she made her way down the aisle. Her face, totally neutral, gave away nothing. She was acting as if it were the most natural thing in the world for them to be on this Vegas-bound plane together.

Goddammit.

"The girls surprised me with a last-minute Vegas party," Jane exclaimed, stopping next to his seat.

Yeah, he got that. Clearly, the two days' notice he'd given Cameron had been too much. Allowed Wendy too much time to marshal her troops.

Wendy had made it farther down the aisle and was out of his sight. He forced himself to pay attention to Jane rather than to turn so he could keep watching Wendy.

"Vegas," he said. "So why are you on my plane here in New York?"

"There were no direct Toronto–Vegas flights left that all four of us could get on," Jane said.

No direct flights his ass.

"Wendy thought it would be a hoot to connect through New York and try to get on *your* plane," said Elise, who was standing behind Jane.

"Did she now?" He really, really wanted to turn around. But he refused to give her the satisfaction.

"So I got your flight info from Jay." Elise did an affectionate shoulder-checking thing with Jane.

"Right." He began mentally dictating a "note to self: murder Jay" memo.

"Would you like me to switch seats with you?" the woman sitting next to him asked Jane.

"That's so nice of you, but it's okay!" Jane smiled over her shoulder at Elise. "I'm gonna sit with my friends. Just pausing to bug my brother for a sec."

"You'd better go, then." Noah made eye contact with Gia, who was in line behind Elise. She shot him a sheepish-bordering-on-sympathetic smile. "You're holding everyone up."

"Oops! Sorry!" Jane blew him a kiss and started moving.

After the women had passed, Noah sat back and tried to be cool. But he didn't even know where they were sitting. Were they two rows back from him? All the way at the back? Which side were they on? Could she see him from where she sat?

It was too much. He gave in and twisted around.

Jane and Elise were getting settled in a few rows up from the back of the plane. Gia was in the row across from them—she was so tall he could spot her easily though she was already seated next to the window. The aisle seat next to her appeared to be empty.

It wasn't, though. He knew it wasn't.

It was just occupied by a short person.

As if she'd felt his attention, the short person in question suddenly leaned around the edge of her seat and stuck her tongue out at him.

He refrained from doing the same but only just. He sighed, turned back to face front, and opened a magazine. He was not going to get any sleep on this flight after all.

Point to Wendy.

—☙—

When the plane landed, Wendy got out her phone and pulled Gia aside. They had two nights in Vegas, and she was damned well going to make the most of it.

And by "make the most of it," she meant "hire the beefiest yet nerdiest stripper she could find." So far, Jane's plans seemed to be limited to manicures, restaurants, and gambling. Which was fine. Wendy was into all that. But all she'd done by moving the party to Vegas was even the playing field. If their party was going to *win*, she needed to take things up a notch.

"She'll be okay with a stripper, right?" She showed Gia her phone, which was open to the website for an establishment called Exotic Boys Incorporated. She wanted to up the ante on the bachelorette festivities, but she didn't want to make Jane truly uncomfortable.

"Oh yeah. I'm sure she'll— Wait." She grabbed the phone. "Wendy! Are these strippers or male prostitutes?"

"Strippers! My God, Gia, I'm trying to put on an epic bachelorette party here, but I'm not a madam!"

Gia scrolled on the phone and then handed it back to Wendy at a page marked "services." There were various "dances" listed in different time increments, but there was also a "deluxe experience" that was a lot more expensive than regular dances.

"Oh my God!" Wendy threw her head back and cackled. "Do you think that's what 'deluxe experience' means? Well, hell, you did say you wanted an uncomplicated Las Vegas hookup, didn't you?"

"Ha! So did you!"

"So should I get us a couple of deluxe experiences?" She was kidding. Yes, she needed to get laid, but not that way.

"Nah. We don't need to pay for it, Wendy. We've got it going on."

"*You* have it going on. I'm not so sure about me."

Gia swatted her. "Well, *I'm* not paying for it. I gotta go get my bag. You make the transaction."

Laughing, Wendy made the call.

"Good afternoon, Exotic Boys Incorporated, Marilyn speaking. How may I help you?"

"Oh!" Wendy wasn't sure what she expected. Press one for a hot fireman; press two for a hot Elvis impersonator? No, but she also hadn't expected an actual human to answer the phone on the first ring, much less one named Marilyn. "Yes, hello. I'm in town for a bachelorette party for my friend, and I'm looking for a dancer."

"Ah," Marilyn said. "You've come to the right place. Are you looking for a party bus or in-room entertainment?"

"Um, in-room entertainment, I'm thinking? Tonight, if possible." Might as well get this party started right.

"That's no problem. Can you give me an idea of what you're looking for? Our most popular dancers at the moment are cop, firefighter, tuxedoed gentleman—"

"I'm not sure we're in the market for the usual cop or firefighter thing. I'm looking for something a little more...cerebral." Ha!

"We have a nice 'hot for teacher' experience. Or we do a Los Alamos package—your dancer will arrive attired in a scientific lab coat and hand out sex toys emblazoned with the phrase 'Caution: nuclear fallout.'"

Wendy cracked up. A person really could order up anything in Vegas, it seemed. "What about a librarian?"

"I'm sure we could pull something together." Wendy could hear the clack of fingernails on a keyboard. "You know what? I have the perfect gentleman in mind. He's a published author, in fact."

"Are you kidding me?" Jane was going to love this. "He sounds perfect."

"What time did you want him to arrive?"

They had dinner at eight with the guys—somehow even though they had only dropped the "we're going to Vegas" bomb on Jane this morning, she'd already arranged a joint dinner. And there would probably be drinks afterward so…"Midnight? Is that too late?"

Marilyn said, "In Vegas, midnight is early. Now, what kind of experience are you looking for?"

"You mean time-wise?" *Or are you asking if I want to hire a rentboy, Marilyn?*

"Time-wise, yes. We book in one-hour increments, but you can also opt to enjoy the company of your dancer for the entire night."

"That would be the, ah, *deluxe experience* I saw on your website?"

"It would be."

"And what does the deluxe package entail, exactly?"

"The standard package includes full nudity and unlimited lap dances, though it is customary to tip for lap dances, even in a private in-room setting. The deluxe package includes additional services negotiated between you and the dancer."

"But if I book the deluxe package, the 'anything else' is sort of, uh, implied?"

"It is."

A silly idea arose. Maybe Wendy *should* actually book the deluxe package. Jane would love that their stripper was an author. She'd want to talk his ear off. Which she could do—after the stripping—if Wendy paid for more time. She could even try to get her hands on his book and they could run it as a "book club." Ha! Instead of the usual bachelorette penis-themed decorations, they could continue the literary theme from last night. And Marilyn had said, "anything else," right? How much would their stripper love it when "anything else" turned out to be "talk about books with the bride." Jane would probably end up inviting him to the wedding like she had the real librarian in that bar in New York.

"The deluxe package sounds *great*, actually."

She rattled off her credit card info for Marilyn and, exceedingly pleased with herself, turned around and—

—crashed smack dab into Noah Denning's chest.

"At least you're not carrying a beer this time." His expression was hard to read, but she thought there might be a little bit of…anger there? Oh, shit. Had he overheard her phone conversation and assumed she was hiring a sex worker for…actual sex-related activities? Instead of, you know, talking-about-books-type activities?

Well, whatever. This was a bachelorette party. She was allowed to hire a stripper. The details were none of his business. For that matter, she was allowed to hire a goddamned prostitute if she wanted. Anyway, she'd been talking really quietly. He would have had to work hard to overhear. He was probably just mad she had crashed the boys' party. As he should be. Ha.

"Shouldn't you be getting your bag?" She nodded at the carousel where the others stood. It had just come to life, and suitcases were being disgorged onto it.

He glanced at a carry-on-size duffel on the floor at his feet. "I'm a light packer."

Wendy looked down at her own carry-on, then back at her friends, who were still waiting for their bags, chatting as they watched the rotating conveyor belt. She waited for Noah to say something. To throw out some zinger or other. Or, if he had in fact heard her ordering "the deluxe package" and had jumped to the obvious—though incorrect—conclusion, to try to put a stop to her plans, like he had that night in the bar in New York.

He said nothing.

Fine. They would just stand here side by side until the bags arrived.

She knew how to withstand scrutiny, to be cool under pressure. She certainly wouldn't think about the feeling of Noah's hungry mouth on hers.

Or his cock pressed against her as she writhed against him like a...like a person who would order up "the deluxe package" in Las Vegas? *Damn it all to hell.*

"I'm not—"

They'd both started speaking at the same time, but he'd beat her by a heartbeat. "*We're* not getting a stripper."

She blinked, taking a moment to absorb the declaration and to adjust to the conversational tone it had been delivered in. She'd been prepared for rage or mockery. Or...something.

Was it possible he simply didn't care that he'd just overheard what had probably sounded like her attempting to hire a male prostitute? And why was that, somehow, more mortifying than the idea that he *did* care and was going to get all up in her face about it like he had in that bar in New York?

"Why not?" she ventured, feeling like she was stepping onto a minefield. "I don't think Jane cares." Jane's official stance on the matter was that what she didn't know wouldn't hurt her, and she'd reportedly told Cameron as much.

"Well, it turns out Cameron does."

Wendy was surprised. Surprised enough to remove her attention from the fascinating baggage-collection scene she'd been staring at and turn to Noah.

Which had been a mistake. Because he was looking at her so intently, she feared his eyes might be capable of burning through her skin. Stopping her heart.

Ugh. She wanted to look away again, but to do so felt like admitting defeat somehow.

"Yeah," Noah went on. "When Jay started planning the bachelor party—before I took over—I said I wasn't doing anything that would directly or indirectly disrespect Jane, and Cameron said, 'And you think I am?' He got quite pissy about it, actually."

"Oh, that doesn't necessarily mean no stripper." Wendy waved a hand dismissively. That made more sense. It was cute that that's how Noah had interpreted Cameron's statement, though. "I wouldn't assume Cameron thinks a stripper would be disrespectful."

"Ah." He nodded. "So that's why he went on to specify *no strippers*, I suppose."

What? Damn. Okay, surprising point to... *Cameron* there. Cameron who wasn't even in the... game? Or whatever this was she was doing with Noah.

"That's probably also why," Noah went on, "he told me he didn't care what the single guys in attendance did, but that we needed to keep it to ourselves. I believe his direct quote was 'You, Noah, can have a three-day orgy for all I care, but I don't want to know about it.'"

Wendy cleared her throat, still not willing to look away even though she had no idea why. The words "Noah" and "three-day orgy" in the same sentence could not be doing wonders for her appearance, dignity-wise. Her face flamed, and her scalp prickled so painfully she feared her hair might actually start falling out before his eyes.

Well, shit. She was officially crushing on Noah Denning. Again.

Except this was different. This wasn't some adolescent starry-eyed crush. She didn't do that anymore. This was lust. Which, though inconvenient, wasn't the end of the world.

At least, she consoled herself, he couldn't see what was happening between her legs. He couldn't see the slick of moisture that had gathered there as a bunch of images and concepts—Vegas, the "deluxe package," Noah, *three-day orgy*—swirled in her mind.

Or maybe he could. Because as if on cue, his eyes dropped. Slid, really, down her body. She'd been dressed for flying, so she was wearing jeans, a T-shirt, and a pair of Keds—not exactly siren material. But it didn't seem to matter, because when his gaze cycled back up and found hers again, his eyes burned as surely as did her skin. There was something in that searing gaze.

A warning.

She just wasn't sure exactly what about.

But she stared back at him defiantly anyway. Because it seemed that now they were having a staring contest, and she didn't intend to lose.

"Hey, you light packers, we're all ready to go!"

Jane's voice came floating over. Surely it was okay to look away from Noah now. It wasn't ceding if their...thing had been interrupted by someone else.

Right?

She had no idea who had won that round.

⎯⎯⎯⎯

Where the hell was Wendy?

The guys, who were staying at the Paris hotel, had gone to collect the girls, who were staying at New York, New York, for dinner, and everyone had gathered in Jane and Wendy's room for a glass of wine before they left. The guys had been as surprised as Noah had by the appearance of the women in Vegas, but none of them seemed to mind having their party crashed. Cameron and Jane were all lovey-dovey, and Elise and Jay were talking about playing checkers later, which almost seemed to him like some kind of foreplay.

Wendy was nowhere in sight, even though this was her and Jane's room. Noah had had to restrain himself from asking where she was. Had to tamp down the spike of... what? Anger? Panic? The spike of *something* that came from the notion that perhaps she was out enjoying the "deluxe package" he'd heard her order earlier. But that was ridiculous, if for no other reason than he'd quite clearly heard her say midnight, and it was only seven thirty.

He told himself to calm the fuck down. He couldn't even be sure what he'd heard meant what he feared it did. Really, why would those four women be hiring a prostitute? Jane certainly wasn't going to be, uh, partaking of those services. Neither was Elise. Normally, he'd think that any "deluxe package" being ordered was for Gia, who, God bless her, was an unapologetic party girl. But before he'd overheard the actual transaction, he'd heard Gia and Wendy talking about wanting to hook up while in Vegas. Gia had *expressly* told Wendy she didn't want to, uh, hire out for the task.

Which left Wendy.

There was no other interpretation.

And wasn't it just like her? She had a low tolerance for bullshit. She was young, single, and in Sin City.

But also? No fucking way. He might have been out of line last month when he'd prevented Wendy from picking up a guy in that bar in New York, but this was different. This wasn't a one-night stand based on mutual attraction. This was a financial transaction.

And, honestly, it mystified him. Yes, Wendy was no-nonsense. Practical. But she was also gorgeous. Smart. The whole package. If she wanted, she could have a lineup of guys willing to do her bidding, whether that was show her a good time for a night or prostrate themselves at her feet for a lifetime.

But anyway, it didn't matter. It wasn't a mystery that needed solving, because it *wasn't happening*. He was going to call in all his retroactive overprotective pseudo big brother chips, and Wendy was going to find her "girls gone wild" party crashed by more than one guy tonight. The clock would strike midnight, and just like Cinderella, Wendy's fantasy would disappear like a smashed pumpkin.

And this had *nothing* to do with their little war.

Wendy—the real one, not the imaginary one he'd been picturing in all kinds of unsavory scenarios—emerged from the bathroom wearing a short red dress. It knocked all his plotting right out of his head.

The dress had one sleeve that reminded him of a wide-strapped tank top, and then the neckline did this diagonal sort of thing, leaving her other shoulder bare. As a result, one of her collarbones was covered, and one was exposed.

The asymmetry of that was making him a little crazy. Certain things come in pairs. Shoes. Gloves.

Breasts.

And, apparently, collarbones.

He wanted to drag down the bodice of the one side and expose her left collarbone.

"Wine?"

He had no idea how long Gia had been standing next to him offering a glass of wine.

"Sure, thanks." He cleared his throat and surveyed the room as he took a sip. Gia and Elise wore black, and Jane wore dark green. They were made up for a night on the town. Gia and Jane had pouffed their hair up, and Elise wore hers piled on top of her head. Wendy, by contrast, wore hers in a simple high ponytail—the better to show off that damned solitary collarbone, he supposed. But instead of a hair elastic, the pony was somehow magically secured by a coil of her own hair. Her face was bare except for dramatically darkened lashes and a slick of red gloss on her lips.

She looked like a prom queen, like an effortlessly beautiful girl ruling over her court of lesser princesses. Next to Wendy, the others looked fussy. Like they'd tried too hard, whereas Wendy had just pulled her stunner of a dress out of her carry-on, maybe sharpened her one collarbone, and called it done.

"Everything okay, brother-mine?" Jane asked, and Noah blinked rapidly as he nodded. Could you lie with a nonverbal gesture? Because with a sudden thud in his stomach, he realized that was what he was doing. He could no longer deny what was happening here. Could no longer chalk up what had happened in New York to momentary insanity. To "some kind of bizarre New York vacation aberration thing," to use Wendy's terminology.

Because why else was he losing his mind over the goddamned "deluxe package"?

He was officially lusting after his little sister's best friend. Over prickly, complicated, not-interested-in-buying-the-milk Wendy Lou Who, who was planning to get it on with a stripper tonight.

God*damn* it. This was a huge fucking problem.

"You know what they say!" Elise trilled, making a funny face at Hector as Noah forced himself to tune in to the conversation around him. "What happens in Vegas stays in Vegas!"

"Hey, you don't need to tell me," Hector said, and Noah rolled his eyes. He hadn't been exaggerating when he'd told Wendy about Cameron's rules for the weekend. Not that Hector needed Cameron's blessing, but he seemed to have taken the "go ahead and have an orgy, but don't tell me about it" as an imperative.

Still, it was gross to tell the women about his plans, wasn't it, Noah wondered as Hector outlined his aim to "get with" a showgirl. Wendy was, apparently, planning to sleep with a gigolo tonight, but you didn't hear *her* bragging about it.

Oh, Christ. How was he so fucked up that he was simultaneously blowing a gasket over Wendy hiring this guy and proud of the way she was comporting herself while doing so?

"Not a prostitute," Hector clarified. Noah couldn't help but look at Wendy, who was examining her fingernails. "A showgirl. Like in the movie."

"The movie?" Jane asked. "You mean *Meet Me in Las Vegas*?"

Hector looked at Jane blankly.

"*Diamonds Are Forever*?" Gia suggested.

"Nope," Hector said. "*Showgirls*."

Cameron put his head in his hands. Noah wasn't really sure how upstanding Cameron had collected such a Neanderthal of a friend. But the women laughed.

"You go for it, Hector." Jane patted his back affectionately.

"Yeah." Elise looked intently at her husband, Jay. "There's something about Las Vegas, isn't there? Like, a 'when in Rome' sort of vibe? I mean, we *are* in Sin City, right?"

Hmm.

An astonishing idea landed fully formed in Noah's mind. Maybe his huge fucking problem wasn't so huge. Maybe it wasn't even a problem. Wendy wanted to get laid in a no-strings sort of way. And…

What happens in Vegas…

He looked at Wendy again. At Wendy's goddamned collarbone.

No. He was being irrational. There was a reason he steered clear of casual sex, namely that he didn't like losing control—Bennett had been right with his armchair diagnosis. And that was with women who weren't Wendy. Wendy specifically added a whole layer of complication he didn't need. So he was just going to have to suffer through unrequited lust and focus on his mission: derail the deluxe package.

Her phone rang and she jumped. He did, too, not because of the phone per se, but because he'd been so attuned to her, his body was like a mirror of hers. She jumped; he jumped.

"I'm sorry, I have to take this," she murmured as she slipped through the door that linked Jane and Wendy's room with the one next door, which he assumed belonged to Elise and Gia.

He waited ten seconds, then got up and walked to the dresser where the wine bottle was resting, on the pretext of pouring himself another glass. The conversation had moved from movies about showgirls to actual shows that could be seen in Vegas, and while everyone else seemed interested in a classic revue featuring the aforementioned showgirls, Jane, God bless her, was trying to get someone to go see Celine Dion with her.

He slipped through the connecting door.

The adjoining room was dark, which he hadn't expected. He stood still, straining his ears. He did not hear her. He saw no cell phone glow. The only light in the room was a sliver coming from its main door. She'd flipped the latch so she could leave the room but still get back in. He moved toward the light and tried to remind himself that he wasn't dying.

Even if Wendy slept with a sex worker in Vegas, he wouldn't die. His lungs would continue to expand and contract. His heart would continue to beat.

Probably.

He could finally hear her. She was standing in the hall talking on the phone.

"And what about music?"

He moved as close to the slit in the door as he dared.

She giggled.

He *hated* that.

"Her favorite musician is actually Josh Groban, but I don't know if that's really the best music for the, um...evening."

Then she laughed again, harder, the signature Wendy cackle.

Goddammit.

"That sounds amazing. Thank you!"

Then another pause. He could hear the sound of tapping—maybe her fingernails against the metal door frame.

"Right. Yes. About that..." She was a little breathless.

Fuck. He wanted to punch the wall. The only reason he didn't was that this conversation was all theoretical. Because Wendy was *not* sleeping with this guy. He didn't care if that made him a presumptuous asshole; it *wasn't happening*.

"That sounds great, Gunnar."

Gunnar? The stripper-slash-prostitute was named *Gunnar*?

Something happened in his head then, a sort of rushing sound, except "rushing" was too mild a word. It was more like a tsunami. Rage and confusion swirled around inside him. He had to lean back against the wall and take a few breaths.

When he was able, a moment later, to clear the blurry gray spots from his vision and tune back in, she was wrapping up the conversation.

"Okay, then!" she trilled. "We'll see you at midnight!"

Yes, Wendy, we'll see you at midnight, and you'd better be ready. Because you thought we were having a good-natured little battle over whose party was cooler? Not anymore.

Now it's war.

Chapter Twelve

The girls were drunk. Well, Jane, Elise, and Gia were drunk. Wendy herself was stone-cold sober. Somebody had to take responsibility for this no-longer-low-key bachelorette party. She glanced at her watch. Eleven thirty. They were at the Coyote Ugly bar in their hotel—it had been hard to pry the girls from the guys and herd them back to the hotel after dinner, so she considered it a triumph that they were even back in the hotel, knocking back kamikazes and cheering on the house dancers as they gyrated and performed their elaborate routines on top of the bar.

In all her travels, Wendy had never darkened the door of a Coyote Ugly—not the original one in the real New York or any of the dozens of franchises elsewhere. She could see now that her judgment had been sound. "Oh no, you don't." She grabbed Elise just as she was about to climb on the bar at the invitation of one of the dancers.

"Oh, come on!" Jane said. "She should go!"

"Come with me, Jane!" Elise exclaimed. "Let the single ladies stay here and be sticks in the mud."

"Look." Wendy let go of Elise and lifted her hand into the air—but she used the other one to grab Jane, who seemed like she was considering Elise's suggestion. "I'm not trying to be a stick in the mud. Go dance—for sure. But on the bar? You're both drunk off your asses."

Jane wrenched herself from Wendy's grip but stumbled a bit in the process. "Whoa."

"See?" Wendy raised her eyebrows. "You'll fall to your death if you get up there."

Jane, undecided, turned to Gia, who'd been watching the whole exchange in silent amusement. "Gia, you're the tie-breaker. Good idea or bad idea?"

Gia did not hesitate. "Bad idea. Why don't you hit the jukebox instead and see if they have any Josh Groban?"

Jane clapped her hands, delighted by the diversion, and skipped off, pulling Elise along with her.

"This place is the worst," Gia said.

Wendy raised her club soda in a toast of agreement. "I'm surprised Hector isn't here."

"Ha!" Gia barked a laugh.

Wendy thought again how the one good thing that had come out of this wedding was the deeper kinship she'd discovered with Gia. Something about being in solidarity with Gia in the eye of the party storm emboldened Wendy. "Let me ask you a question. Do you think Cameron is right for Jane?"

She regretted the question the moment it was out, because Gia's face scrunched up in confusion that soon morphed into concern. Maybe even pity. Wendy could handle pretty much anything, but not pity.

"Oh, sweetie." Gia knew *exactly* where Wendy's irrational question had come from.

"You saw the way he rebuffed her at Elise's rehearsal dinner," Wendy said, reflexively still attempting to argue her case. "He broke her heart."

"Right, but you weren't there when we had the big confrontation with him later that night, when he showed his true colors."

"So everyone keeps telling me. But I wasn't there because I was busy trying to spackle Jane's shattered heart back together enough that she could get through Elise's wedding!"

She would never forget that night in the motel down the road from the wedding-site B&B where everyone else was staying, holding Jane while she cried because Cameron had publicly rejected her. Wendy's heart had broken by proxy that night.

Wendy knew what it felt like to put on a party dress and stand alone under the lights while humiliation subsumed you.

"Well, trust me," Gia said. "He rebuffed her because he thought he was saving her from him. Yes, it was shitty and idiotic, but he suffered as much as she did that night. Maybe more."

"Are you forgetting that Jane started spending time with Cameron because he was such a menace that Elise assigned her to babysit him? I mean, we had *meetings* about what a menace he was."

"Oh my God! Yes! I'd forgotten about that!" Gia laughed, clearly delighted by the memory. "That's hilarious. That will make a good wedding toast."

Jesus Christ. What was the matter with her? Embarrassment flooded Wendy. Shame, too. She ducked, praying the lights in the bar were dim enough that Gia couldn't see her pink cheeks. Why couldn't she get on board—*really* get on board—with this wedding?

"Hey." Gia edged into her space but thankfully didn't force her into eye contact. She merely placed a hand on Wendy's arm. "Jane's just getting married. She's still gonna be your best friend."

"I *know*," Wendy said, too sharply.

"You guys." Jane crashed into their space, and Wendy was seized with the momentary terror that she'd overheard them, but she clearly hadn't, because she was holding Elise by the hand—Elise who was sobbing.

"Honey!" Gia held out her arms. "What's wrong?"

Baby, Jane mouthed at them from behind Elise.

Oh boy. Wendy felt like a jerk, but she glanced at her watch. She didn't want them to miss Gunnar. Elise sometimes had these...episodes, and they could last a long time. She was infertile, thanks to a pretty bad case of endometriosis, but she wanted a baby.

"Someone put 'Sweet Child O' Mine' on," Elise said through her tears.

Wendy and Jane exchanged a confused look. Guns N' Roses had prompted a baby breakdown?

"She always thought it would make an excellent lullaby," Gia explained. "It's kind of a trigger."

"Maybe you should give some more thought to adoption?" Wendy said gently. Elise had always dismissed the idea, but if the baby fever was so bad that 1980s hair metal songs were making her cry, she should reconsider.

"Or surrogacy." Jane patted Elise's stomach. "Grab an egg and do some laboratory magic. Any of us would carry it for you."

Wendy met Gia's eyes. She was pretty sure the look they exchanged meant they did not consider themselves part of "any of us" in this case.

"Aww, you guys." Elise initiated a group hug, and when

she pulled away, she wasn't crying anymore. "I'm sorry. That song always does it to me, and the fact that I'm drunk doesn't help. Anyway, no, no babies by any method. If it was up to me, I might consider it, but you know that's Jay's deal breaker." It was true. Elise and Jay's initial courtship had involved some drama in that Elise had assumed no one would ever want to marry her because of her inability to conceive. It had turned out to be a huge mark in her favor— Jay most decidedly did not want children.

"Honestly, a baby is probably the only thing that would ever cause us real problems," Elise said. "The only thing that would ever come between us." She laughed, but it wasn't genuine. "So it's for the best."

"Still," Wendy said. "I'm sorry." Elise's sadness was palpable, and it was hard to witness.

Elise shrugged. "What do they say? You can't always get what you want."

Wasn't that the truth?

"Part of growing up is accepting that, I think," Elise said.

Everyone kind of nodded in agreement, but a touch of awkwardness descended—until Gia clapped her hands together and said, "You know what this party needs?"

"What?" Jane asked.

"A stripper." Gia winked at Wendy as the other two started shrieking.

⌣

Twenty-four hours ago, if Noah had been instructed to enumerate the lucky breaks he'd had in his life, it would have been a short though heartfelt list. The scholarship he'd gotten to NYU. His job, which allowed him to do important, fulfilling work even if maybe he did flirt with the workaholism that everyone was always accusing him of. Having Jane for a sister. Well, she'd be number one on the list.

And a more recent addition: how easy it had been to steal a key to Wendy and Jane's room earlier, when they'd been having pre-dinner drinks. When he'd slipped back into the room after overhearing Wendy's plotting, he'd just picked it up off the dresser.

One more thing that he was going to add to that list this evening?

The fact that Gunnar the Stripper Librarian showed up before the women did.

"Hey," he said, pulling open the door to reveal a massive wall of man. There was no other way to describe the dude. Noah considered himself not bad in the body department, but this guy was a younger, less bald version of the Rock.

He was also wearing a skintight, short-sleeved white button-down shirt that strained over his enormous biceps, a red bow tie, and horn-rimmed glasses. In one hand he carried a duffel bag, in the other a stack of books tied together with a leather strap of the sort you saw in old-fashioned movies.

Gunnar looked down at his phone. "I'm sorry. I must have the wrong room."

"Not at all." Noah swung the door open. "The ladies will be here momentarily. Come right in. We're all so looking forward to your...performance." *Which is all that's happening tonight, buddy.*

"Ah." Gunnar flashed Noah a knowing smile and winked. "The more the merrier."

Noah had to hand it to the guy. He was the consummate professional. If by "consummate professional" you meant "equal opportunity flirt." Once he realized that Noah was staying, and jumped to the obvious conclusion, it was like he'd flipped a switch that turned on the full force of his charm.

For example, he brushed more closely against Noah than was necessary when passing through the door. Paused a little too long with a twinkle in his eye. Flicked Noah's biceps, which, though not nearly as massive as Gunnar's, were respectably defined, and murmured, "Nice."

Damn, this guy was good.

"So, Gunnar," he asked, as his guest started moving furniture around in the room's sitting area. "Is this your full-time gig?"

"Kind of." He pushed a side table against a wall and began adding chairs next to the sofa in order to create more seating. "I got into advocacy for sex workers a couple years ago and ended up writing a book on the topic. Now I'm in law school."

"Really?"

The smooth façade dropped as Gunnar's lip curled a little. "Really," he said, with just a touch of defensiveness in his tone.

Aww, shit. "I didn't mean to sound like a jerk. It's just a coincidence—I'm a lawyer, too."

That perked Gunnar up. "Cool! What kind of law?"

"Criminal prosecution. I'm a New York County ADA."

"Now don't get any *Pretty Woman*–type ideas here." Gunnar started setting up some small speakers. "I'm not one of these hard-done-by people stripping and tricking to make my way through school. I'm always going to be a sex worker. I'm just doing the law thing so I can be an advocate for the sex industry. Like, on the side."

Noah chuckled. "You have to respect a man who knows what he wants." It was true. "You probably make a lot more money than you would in most fields of law."

It was Gunnar's turn to chuckle. "You know it. ADA. You probably aren't doing it for the money."

"I'm in it for other reasons."

"And those are?"

"I want to protect people." He was surprised at how readily the answer came to his lips. He had never given much conscious thought to the motivations behind his career choices—that is, until he and Wendy had talked about it that night in New York when she had accused him of transferring his protective streak from his family to his job. But it was true—as usual, she'd seen him in a way no one else did.

"Why?" Gunnar asked.

"What do you mean?"

"You want to protect people. That's noble. But *why* do you want to protect people?"

Well, shit. He didn't have an answer for that. Other than "It's what I do." Anyway, what was this? Stripping with a side of psychoanalysis? "And why do *you* do it?" Noah asked by way of deflection. "Why are you into...stripping?"

"You can say it, you know."

"Say what?"

"Prostitution. You guys ordered the deluxe package. No reason to be shy about it."

"Well, *I* didn't order it."

Right. Gunnar looked down at his phone. "Wendy Liu did." He grinned. "Never had a request quite like this one before."

Oh, *shit*. He was going to throw up. He was actually going to be physically ill.

But fine. That's why he was here. To cock-block Wendy. Again.

"Hey, you okay?" Noah felt himself being pushed into a chair. "Sit down. Take a breath."

"What is this?" Noah asked. The chair he was sitting in had not come with the room. It was a sort of fancy folding chair.

"The lap dance chair. We need one without arms. Most of the hotels on the Strip have desk chairs with arms, so I come prepared."

"You're a regular Boy Scout."

Gunnar waggled his eyebrows. "Wanna try it out?"

He resisted the urge to explain that it wasn't like that—not that there was anything wrong with "that." He was here purely for . . . other purposes. But he settled for "I'm pretty sure that's not in the Boy Scout handbook."

"Oh, come on." Gunnar rotated his hips suggestively. "You're forgetting about the lap dancing badge."

—☙—

"Where is the damn thing?" Wendy rifled through her purse as they all stood outside her room. "Jane, I can't find my key."

"Oh, I have mine!" Jane mimicked Wendy's searching motion, digging around in her handbag. "I thought I did, anyway . . . Dang, it's in the pocket of the jeans I was wearing earlier. Well, I'll go down to the front desk and get a new one made."

"No!" Everyone turned to look at Wendy. That had come out too vehemently. She was just oddly on edge for some reason. "You can't miss the arrival of Gunnar!"

"The stripper is named Gunnar?" Elise asked, cracking up.

Gia produced a key and used it to open her own room. "That's what adjoining doors are for, my friends. We left it open, I'm pretty sure."

Right. Wendy tried to calm her nerves as she followed everyone in. She had an odd sense of foreboding, which was stupid. All that was going to happen was some innocent stripping followed by the "deluxe package" literary salon starring published authors Jane and Gunnar.

"I have to pee so bad!" Jane disappeared into the bathroom. "Don't start without me!"

Wendy searched Gia's face for any sign of the dread that was settling in her own gut. There was none—just a conspiratorial grin.

Gia moved toward the adjoining door. She had only just gotten her head through when she pulled it back abruptly and slammed the door.

"Noah is in there."

"What?"

"And he is not alone."

"Gunnar's already there?" Elise asked.

Gia nodded. "And I'm pretty sure the two of them are talking about lap dances. Is that possible?"

What the fucking hell?

Goddamn him. So, clearly he *had* overheard her call in baggage claim this morning.

Wendy had been hoping the increasingly pervasive sense of sadness and foreboding overtaking her would disappear. Maybe she should have been more specific with that wish, though, because although the dread had disappeared, it had been replaced by rage.

White-hot, blind rage.

White-hot, blind, *paralyzing* rage.

"Did I hear you say *my brother* is over there?" Jane came out of the bathroom.

Gia nodded and looked like she was trying not to laugh.

"All right," Jane said. "He has now officially gone too far on this whole party competition thing." She pushed through the adjoining door, and Elise and Gia followed.

Wendy, though, was pinned to her spot. Unable to move. The paralyzing part of her rage was…paralyzing. Apparently her anger had done a number on her vocabulary, too.

Well, shit. The only way to play this was to own it. Clearly, Noah had heard her hire the stripper. He may or may not have assumed that the stripper was going to provide…additional services. But either way, it was none of his goddamn business. She took a deep breath and slipped through the door.

He was already looking at her.

And he wasn't pleased with what he saw. His mouth pressed into a tight line, and a vein bulged on his temple.

"Noah!" Jane said after she was done shaking hands with the stripper—who knew strippers were so mannerly? "What are *you* doing here?"

He removed his gaze from Wendy and organized his features into a less menacing arrangement before turning to his sister. "I overheard some plotting"—his gaze flickered back to Wendy—"and I decided to crash the party."

"Are you kidding me? I know you're super invested in this whole older brother chaperone thing, but you can't crash my bachelorette party!" Jane pointed at the door. "At least not *this* part of it," she added in an urgent whisper.

He smirked. "I think I already *have* crashed your party."

"Okay, okay." Jane rolled her eyes. "Good job. A-plus. I didn't realize this bet of yours"—she looked between Wendy and Noah—"involved sabotage, but with you two, I should have figured."

Wendy was speechless. And that never happened. And Jane was right. This was some grade-A sabotage, even if it made her mad as hell. Not only was she going to have to award a point to Noah, she was going to have to award like a thousand of them.

Jane walked over to Noah and beckoned Wendy to join them. "I need a moment with the two of you." Wendy tried to think of reasons she could credibly refuse to join her friend's little confab but, coming up with nothing, walked to her doom while Elise, Gia, and Gunnar opened a bottle of wine on the other side of the room.

Jane motioned them even closer so they formed a little huddle. "Okay, first of all, Noah, you are *leaving*." Before he could say anything, she added, "But before you do, let me ask you both something. Do you think this"—she hitched her head toward the party that was gearing up— "is okay?"

"Of course it's okay," Wendy snapped, belatedly realizing that her answer had come out way too brusquely. "You said Cameron could get a stripper."

"I know, but I don't think he's going to." Jane glanced at her brother with a questioning look.

"He's not," Noah confirmed. "He's not going to care if you do, though," he added, startling the hell out of Wendy. That was about the last thing she expected Mr. Morality Police to say. "It's all harmless fun, isn't it?" That last question came with a pointed look at Wendy.

"And it's not like he *owns* you, Jane," Wendy said, ignoring Noah's scrutiny. "Sheesh."

Jane shot Wendy a bewildered look. "I know that," she said, her confusion starting to look a little like hurt, which made Wendy feel like a monster. "I just...God, I just love him so much. I would never want to do anything to hurt him."

"Ah, Janie." Noah mock punched his sister. "Two things. One: you know I don't want to hear about that mushy stuff. But, two: I *promise* he's not going to care, but if you want absolution in advance, why don't you just ask him? Text him right now. I guarantee he'll tell you to have a good time."

Jane mock punched her brother back. "That is an excellent idea." She pulled out her phone and started typing. A few seconds later, she grinned and turned pink.

"What did he say?" Wendy asked, half hoping Cameron would pull the plug on the whole thing. Because that strange, heavy sadness was still with her.

"He said..." She glanced at her brother and then made a show of turning the phone so he couldn't see it but Wendy could.

Have fun. Then get your pretty ass in a cab and come over here. I'm about to kick Jay out of the room—he can bunk with Hector and Noah. Text me when you're on the way, and I'll meet you in the lobby.

Wendy's throat started to ache. Before Jane lowered the phone, another text from her fiancé arrived.

In fact, no, I don't want you alone in a cab so late. I'm coming to get you. I'll wait in the lobby of your hotel. Take your time getting all wound up for me...and then we'll go back to my room together.

It was followed by a string of eggplant and peach emojis and then a bunch of the nail polish ones, which was probably some lovers' inside joke.

Wendy's eyes started to water. It hurt to see such a display of...what? Chivalry leavened with the perfect amount of filth? God, the way he had exerted such a fierce possessiveness, yet left Jane free to do her own thing, to have her own fun. Well…it wasn't what she had expected from Cameron.

And she was jealous.

Totally, utterly, mortifyingly jealous.

"Okay!" Jane did a little twirl and made her way over to Gunnar, who had already started his music. "Let's get this party started." She checked her watch. "Because I have twenty, thirty minutes tops."

So much for the deluxe package.

"You have somewhere more exciting to be?" Gia asked.

Jane laughed. "I actually do. Cam is kicking his brother out of the room, and I'm going to stay there tonight."

Wendy couldn't take it anymore. She was going to cry.

So she made her way over to Gia and whispered in her ear. "I've got to go to the lobby for a bit to settle up our accounts with the company that's providing the evening's entertainment."

Gia nodded and didn't notice when, instead of going out the main door, Wendy slipped through the adjoining door to the other room.

Nobody noticed.

Which, although that had been her aim, was pretty much par for the course.

Chapter Thirteen

*W*endy sank into the bath in Gia and Elise's room and let loose a big sigh. Yes, it was kind of weird that she was taking a bath shortly after midnight when there was a stripper—a stripper *she* had hired—doing his thing in the adjoining room. It was just that when she'd fled, a jumble of shitty emotions cresting in her chest, she'd been breathless, determined not to cry. She'd come into the bathroom in Gia and Elise's empty room and suddenly, on top of the sadness and anger that had been warring in her chest, she was…ashamed. Ashamed for shit-talking Cameron. Ashamed of wishing Jane wasn't getting married. Ashamed that she was jealous over it. Ashamed of the stupid, juvenile bet with Noah that had inspired her to bring the bachelorette party to Vegas in the first place.

So, after staring at herself in the mirror in disgust for a few minutes, she'd impulsively decided to get in the bath. She wasn't going to go back next door—her poor heart couldn't take it. She wasn't naive enough to think she could just wash off her shame, but, somehow, the idea of undressing, of immersing her body in water as hot as she could stand, had seemed like an oddly logical next move.

The problem was the bath *didn't* clear away the crud. It just reminded her why she wasn't normally a bath person. All baths did was provide a comfy setting for brooding.

She tried to resist, but she was already feeling so low. So vulnerable.

So she just let her mind go there. She'd been so excited. So stupidly excited.

New dress, new shoes, new haircut. New makeup, purchased not from the drugstore, but from the Clinique counter at the Bay. New underwear even, pretty underwear, including a lacy push-up bra, though she knew Noah would never see that part of her outfit. She'd spent six hundred bucks, all told, which she'd taken from her college fund without her mom's knowledge.

Wendy felt the stares of her classmates as she entered the made-over school with Jane and Tim. She steeled herself. It was inevitable, given that she was arriving alone.

"My date is meeting me here later," she whispered to Mr. Piper, the math teacher manning the registration desk. It wasn't against the rules to go stag to the prom, but as a single underclassman, she needed to be with someone older.

"Who's your date, Wendy?" Mr. Piper asked. Luckily, he knew her from her advanced track math class.

"Noah Denning."

She'd been trying to keep her voice low, but she must not have succeeded, because the female half of the couple in line behind them burst out laughing.

Wendy's face ignited. Tim started to say something, but

Mr. Piper, who was looking down at a clipboard, said, "Yes. Okay, here you are," and waved them in.

The theme this year was Out of This World, and the main entryway had been totally transformed. It was hung with thousands of tiny lights, including some grouped into a Milky Way, and couples were being herded under a big arch made up of the planets of the solar system, in order to pose for photos.

"Be in our picture," Jane said as they approached the front of the line.

"No, you go ahead!" There was no way Wendy was crashing Jane's portrait. When Jane seemed like she was going to argue some more, Wendy turned an entreating look on Tim, who must have heard her silent plea, because he hustled Jane under the arch and made quick work of the photo, so Wendy only had to stand awkwardly on the sidelines waiting for a couple minutes.

They felt like hours, though. She held her head high, aware of the stares of everyone in line behind Jane and Tim. "I'm waiting for my date," she wanted to say, because it was true, but there was no need to be so loud about it. Her point would be made sweeter when Noah Denning arrived and took her arm. She hoped they could come back and get their picture taken when he did. This was a night she was going to want to remember.

And not only because she had *a* date.

Because it was Noah.

Because maybe, if she was very brave—or very lucky, she couldn't decide which—whatever had almost happened between them last month on that run would happen again.

Maybe more than that would happen.

The stares became more overt once they made their way into the gym, where the dance itself was being held. Her reward—and her classmates' comeuppance—was coming, though, so she could hold out.

Which she kept telling herself as she shooed Jane and Tim out onto the dance floor. They'd been insisting on staying with her, but that only made it worse. She didn't need a babysitter.

Then the whispers started. Well, they weren't really whispers in the sense that most of them were designed for her to hear, snarky comments about the girl who'd come to the dance alone.

But she could stand the discomfort, because he was coming. So she stood there, sweating but holding it together as the gossip grew louder and more vicious.

Until a teacher came over and found Jane to pass along a message from Noah that he *wasn't* coming.

"What?" She wasn't sure why she was asking that. Jane had whispered the news, but Wendy had heard her just fine.

"Apparently he's staying on for the overnight shift at the store." Jane placed her hand over her heart. "I'm so sorry, Wendy."

"He probably didn't feel like he could turn it down," Tim said. "If you do back-to-back shifts, you get double-time for the second one."

"Oh my God." Jane rolled her eyes. "I know he works so hard for a reason, but *honestly*. If there was ever a shift to turn down, this was it."

All Wendy could do was blink—which hurt because her eyeballs were dry. Everything was dry: her throat, her mouth. Her heart, which felt like scorched desert earth, run though with a network of cracks. It felt like the cracks kept continuing, radiating out through her body and into the gym itself, splitting open the floor so she was marooned on an island, hot and thirsty and alone.

She thought, suddenly, about that dumb Princess Jasmine Pez dispenser her dad had given her the day before he died. The situation was different, but the feeling was the same. Of being blindsided. Deliriously happy and then . . . alone.

She shook her head. She was being ridiculous. It *wasn't* the same thing. Her dad had *died*. He hadn't left her on purpose.

Unlike Noah, who had.

Self-delusion was not Wendy's thing. If there was any dignity to be salvaged in this situation, it was in the knowledge that she wasn't lying to herself. The truth was that although Noah probably cared about her in his way, it was because she was Jane's best friend. Because she was around. They went running because she was *there*, always there, in his house, the girl in need of a surrogate family. He came to the occasional softball game because he felt guilty that she was always the only kid on the team with no one in the audience. But she wasn't important enough for him to turn down a shift at the store.

So he'd put his hand on her cheek. Big freaking deal. She'd been deluded if she'd been reading something into that. The truth was Noah didn't see her as a romantic interest, and he never would.

Facing the truth was hard, but it gave you a way forward. A way to start mending your heart. She took a deep breath and tried to imagine water raining down on all those cracks in her heart. Filling them in, or at least disguising them enough that the terrain could be traversed.

"Let's just go home." Jane looked at Tim and hitched her head toward the coat check.

"No." Wendy spoke sharply enough that it stopped Tim in his tracks. "Why would I want to go home?"

She could hear the mania in her tone, but it was better

than not saying anything, than cowering silently and being led out of the dance like a silly child who had been stupid enough to get her hopes up. She *did* want to go home. She wanted to wash the paint off her face, curl up in her bed, and cry. But she had to stay, at least long enough to show all these bastards that she didn't care about being abandoned by Noah Denning. To show that she was in on the joke. Wendy Liu thought Noah Denning would go to the prom with her? Ha, ha, ha, *hilarious*!

She didn't know if she was allowed to stay here without a senior date, but she sure as hell was going to try.

Jane looked unconvinced. The DJ cued up some horrid Coldplay ballad. "Tim," Wendy said. "Dance with me?"

"You bet."

Normally, she would ask Jane if she minded lending out her date, but she needed to *move*, so she grabbed his arm and towed him toward the center of the floor, where they could get lost in the crowd.

"I'm sorry, Wendy."

She shrugged as he pulled her into a loose embrace. "No big deal."

"Noah works so much, I'm not actually sure how that place is going to survive without him next month."

"Next month?" It was late May. She would have assumed Noah would work as much as possible over the summer.

"Yeah, he's leaving for New York the day after graduation."

"He is?"

"He got some work-study job or something. Had the option to start early. It pays more than the store."

"But..." *I thought we were going running this summer.*

But why would she think that? Hadn't she just forced herself to face the truth? If Noah wasn't going to turn down a shift to come to the freaking prom with her, he certainly wasn't going to turn down a job because he'd promised to go *running* with her.

She took another deep breath and kept concentrating on the mental image of water rushing into the chasms in her heart. Icy-cold water that was, paradoxically, healing.

And she decided something right then and there: she was *done* putting herself in situations where people could hurt her. Leave her.

She was *never* going to let anyone do this to her again.

"Anyway," Tim went on as he looked around at the other couples, "I'm sure he didn't realize how awkward his bailing was going to make things for you. Jesus Christ, is this a public school or a cult?" Wendy shaped her mouth into the smile that was required. "Next time I see him, I'm going to murder him on your behalf."

She looked at the dots of lights swirling around the floor, then up at their source, the disco ball. It was silver, like her dress. All jagged edges and impervious surfaces. That was a better pattern than the network of cracks she'd been imagining. She imagined herself made of mirrors, hard and shiny and impermeable.

Because from now on, that's what she was.

"Eh." She let a shoulder rise and fall. "Don't waste your energy. It's only Noah."

She said it like she meant it.

Wendy jumped when a noise reached through her consciousness—and across seventeen years—and yanked her back to the present. She cocked her ear, but she heard nothing. She must have imagined it. Which was fine. She'd take any excuse, even nonexistent noises, to get her out of her head.

She was disgusted with herself. The prom had been almost twenty years ago. It was *not* worth this much mental energy. See? This was why baths sucked.

Honestly. If someone else had been telling the story, she'd have been tempted to say, big deal. You got your heart broken. You were humiliated. It happens all the time. Welcome to the human race.

But it wasn't just humiliation that had made the experience so formative, she could see as she looked back from her grown-up vantage point. It was the sense that she'd failed herself. That she'd been so utterly taken in by all the trappings of the prom. That she'd compromised her pride. That she'd allowed herself to get her hopes up. The pain of that night wasn't even really about Noah—it was about her and what she was made of.

Noah Denning hadn't broken her heart.

She had *let* her heart be broken.

But at least that had been the last time. She hadn't put herself in that position again, not even when Noah called her the next day and apologized. She'd brushed that off as her pride demanded, and it hadn't even been that hard. Because she'd transformed herself under the disco ball, into something strong and unbreakable.

⸺৹

Noah watched Wendy leave. She said something to Gia and then slipped next door without anyone else noticing.

Except him. He noticed.

The logical thing for him to do now was to follow his sister's orders and leave. He had won this evening's battle—or at least the first part of it. He had successfully crashed the party, which everyone seemed to think had been his sole aim. He still needed to stick around to make sure no "deluxe packages" were consumed, but he could just as easily do that by lurking outside to make sure Gunnar left when the dancing was over. He wasn't in a homophobic panic over the idea of watching another guy get naked, but he also didn't need to see his sister get a lap dance—he totally took Jane's point there. He would let the women have their fun.

But...what if Wendy went back through the adjoining door and then, after the show, stayed there with Gunnar? If Jane was going to stay with Cameron, that meant Wendy had her own room.

Shit.

Why had she left, anyway? Didn't she want to see the show?

A possible answer to that question exploded in his consciousness like a bomb. Had she gone next door to get ready to sleep with Gunnar?

Jesus fucking Christ.

"Noah!" his sister called. He was sitting on the bed closest to the bathroom, manically jiggling his legs as he imagined Wendy putting on makeup next door. Or, God help him, getting condoms or something. "Why are you still here? I mean, I love you, but...leave!"

"I'm going!"

He got up, but instead of leaving, he made his way over to the adjoining door. It was unlocked from this side. What were the chances she had left it unlocked on hers? Very slowly, so as not to attract attention from either side, he tried the handle. Nope. Locked.

He should take that as a sign. If he stood right outside and listened through the door, he'd be able to hear when the show was over and...what the post-show plans were. He didn't need to bust in on Wendy to find out what she was up to.

But...fuck it. He was going to do it anyway.

He picked up a purse he recognized as Elise's, rummaged through it, emerged triumphant with a key card, called, "Bye!" to the party, and hightailed it out of the room.

He paused outside her door, half afraid of what he might find. Arguably, it was better not to know, but he was beyond that. Some unfamiliar, primal part of him *had* to know what she was doing.

His hands were shaking so badly, the first attempt at unlocking her door didn't work. He paused for a moment after the red light blinked at him, waiting for it to reset. Waiting for his heart, which was thumping wildly for some unknown reason, to reset.

This was what he'd felt like that night at the bar in New York. Like Wendy was about to sleep with some random guy and it was going to kill him.

And what was the saying? *Over my dead body.*

It was possible that it was actually going to happen. Because if Wendy thought she was going to sleep with Gunnar tonight, she was going to have to get through him first.

—ⱺ

Wendy hit the drain with her toe when she heard the door click open. So maybe she hadn't been hearing things a bit ago—that was definitely the sound of someone entering with a key card. "Is that you, Gia?" she called. "I'm in the bath."

She was met with silence.

"Gia? Elise? I'm sorry I bailed. I'm borrowing your room. I just...needed a moment."

A moment in the bath. Because I love baths so much.

More silence.

Maybe Gia or Elise had popped in to get something and had already gone? Or—shit—maybe someone had called hotel security on them. Maybe the girls had been making too much noise, and the party had been shut down. That wouldn't be good for her chances with the bet. Although maybe there was a way she could spin it: *our party was so fabulous that it got busted.*

Only one way to find out. She was past done with this stupid bath anyway. She pushed up out of the water and felt her way to the towel rack. She'd forgotten to turn on the fan, and the bathroom was all steamed up.

Wrapping the towel around her, she pushed open the door, her skin pebbling at the blast of cold air in the room in contrast to the overheated bathroom and her eyes blinking to adjust from darkness to light. "Gia? Is that you? I know it's weird that I'm—"

Noah. Noah was there—*right there*, two feet away from her. And he was *pissed.*

"What the hell are you doing?" he growled.

"The better question is what are *you* doing? I'm taking a bath! You can't just barge in here!" She started to brush past him, but then realized that since she wasn't in her room, she had nowhere to go. There was no refuge, except maybe back in the bathroom where her clothes were, but to return to her steamy cocoon seemed like it would signal a retreat. She didn't know what was happening here, but she knew instinctively that "retreat" was not the message she wanted to send.

So she stopped just outside the bathroom door, unsure of what to do but unwilling to show it. She tried to summon some anger to match his. He couldn't just let himself into the room like this. It was an arrogant, entitled thing to do. But her brain didn't seem to be cooperating. It was drink-

ing in the sight of him, his sleeves rolled up over his lean
forearms. Thinking about those forearms under her ass as he
held her up that night on the High Line, held her up so she
could wrap her legs around him.

Stop. She wasn't playing this right. She wasn't playing
this right *at all*, because her aborted mission to pass him
meant she'd ended up even closer to him than when she
emerged from the bathroom. His chest was a mere six inches
from her face.

No, it was even closer. Because he puffed it up like he
was a cartoon character preparing for a confrontation. "You
hired a *prostitute*? What the hell, Wendy?"

She gasped, but then bit her lip to make herself stop mid-
inhale. Gasping, like retreating, was not a good look for her
right now.

"Oh, don't act so surprised. I heard you ordering the
deluxe package. And later, getting all giggly with him on the
phone."

She had to get away from him. She couldn't stand here
with their torsos practically touching. So she took a big step
back. It wasn't a retreat if you planned it, right? She was just
taking a moment to run through her options.

She considered telling him the truth, that in keeping with
the literary theme of the bachelorette weekend, she'd actually hired Gunnar to talk about books with Jane after the
stripping portion of the evening. But why? What the hell
business of his was it if she wanted to sleep with a rentboy?

"Huh, Wendy?" he taunted, taking a step toward her, as if
rejecting her previous attempt to put some distance between
them. "What are you doing over here by yourself when your
'deluxe package' is over there?"

"I told you. I'm taking a bath," she said haughtily.

"And why are you taking a bath?" he needled.

"Why don't you just say what you really mean?" she snapped. "Ask what you really want to ask." She wanted to make him say it. Make him hear how unreasonable he was being. God, the thought that he truly believed she would hire a prostitute...

Worse, that she would *need* to.

But she had been the only girl at the prom without a date, hadn't she? Maybe he still thought of her as *that* girl. The one he'd been able to leave behind without a second thought.

"What do I really want to ask?" he prodded.

"You want to know if I'm going to fuck the stripper," she snapped, hoping enough anger would smother her mortification.

"No, I don't," he said, suddenly, strangely calm. "Because you're *not* fucking the stripper."

"Jesus Christ, Noah. Of course I'm not. Give me some credit. I ordered the deluxe package as a *joke*. Gunnar and Jane were supposed to talk about books."

Something happened to Noah then. On the surface of things, it looked like he deflated a bit: the exaggerated cartoon chest underwent a slow de-puffing. But the impression it gave wasn't one of defeat. It seemed more like...relief?

"Not that it's any of your business," she added, even though the snarky postscript made her sound like a petulant child. She retucked the top of her towel to tighten it, which drew his attention to the...top-of-the-towel area.

"In some ways, that's kind of a waste." His voice had completely shed its confrontational quality and gone a little gravelly. "All that anticipation. All those pheromones zinging around. A few drinks."

"I'm completely sober." Though suddenly, inexplicably, she wished she wasn't. The looseness, the confidence that alcohol could bring would not be unwelcome right now. Because then she could kick him out. Or . . . something.

No, not "something." Because when she'd asked him at the bar in New York, when he'd been getting all pissy and aggressive, if he was propositioning her, he'd said no. Had walked away from everything he'd been implying. And no matter how much she was lusting after him, she was *done* letting Noah Denning hurt her.

She lifted her chin and pushed past him, leaving the comforting steam of the bathroom and marching into the center of the cool, too bright room.

He followed her. "Completely sober, huh? Good. Sober is better."

"Better for what?" Now that she was out here, she didn't know what to do. She hitched her towel up higher. "Better for kicking your ass out of this room?" Because, there, that's what she should do.

"Better because tomorrow you'll remember everything."

"Remember what? What a presumptuous prick you are?"

"Remember everything I'm going to do to you. Because remember how I'm your best prospect when it comes to meaningless fucking? I was better than those assholes in New York, and I'm better than Gunnar."

She gasped again—*goddammit*. Gasped like a stupid naive girl, which was *not* what she was. Fuck him and his mind games. Fuck his ability to get her all riled up with a single sentence.

Wendy was not a girl who gasped. Not someone who stood by while a man said suggestive things to her that he had no intention of acting on—especially the only man she'd ever allowed to hurt her. He was just being mean now, taunting her like this. So, once again, *fuck him*. She was calling his bluff. She'd show Mr. I Don't Do Casual Sex what he was missing.

She dropped her towel.

And *he* gasped.

She laughed, a surge of triumph making her bold. Well, bold*er*. She was already standing naked in front of Noah Denning. She thought suddenly about how people sometimes talk about feeling, in moments of stress or confrontation, like other people could see through their clothing, see them naked and exposed. Wendy felt the reverse. Like even though it was totally illogical, that underneath her skin, there was a sparkly silver dress, and that Noah could see it. And that by seeing it, he was seeing something much more intimate and private than her naked body. She had to protect that dress, and the girl who had worn it.

So she had to keep mouthing off. "I don't need a stripper to get off. I don't need you. I don't need anyone. I can take care of myself."

And hell, she just might, once he finally left. She was horny, which only made her madder. She hated the power he had over her, all these years later, even after she'd done everything she could think of to take some for herself.

But, whatever. This was only lust. An animalistic response. She was bigger than her desire.

She started to turn away, but he touched her arm as she moved past him. "I know you don't *need* anyone, Wendy. But don't you ever *want* anyone?"

She shivered, and he rubbed his hand up and down on her arm, like he was trying to warm her up. She looked down at her bare feet next to his big Chelsea boots. He didn't know that she wasn't cold. That she was, in fact, on fire. If she was shaking, it was rage. Or that stupid ever-present lust. Or some goddamned combination of the two—opposing forces that kept her pinned in place.

The hand that had been rubbing vigorously up and down her arm slowed. Came to a full stop on her shoulder. Then slowly, slowly, it started to make its way up along the side of her neck until it came to rest on her cheek. She wanted to look away, but she would not allow herself. No, she forced herself to put away the memory of that silver dress and to meet his gaze, strong and unashamed.

His eyes burned, but it didn't seem like there was any anger remaining behind the heat she saw in them. And his hand, in contrast to all their fighting words, was so gentle on her cheek.

His hand on her cheek. It was happening again.

Except it *wasn't*. She was an adult this time, an adult who knew what she wanted. Who knew how to *take* what she wanted without getting her heart mixed up in things.

So she leaned into his touch. Just a little.

It was enough to shift everything.

He leaned down, not slow, not fast, but with even, clear intent. She lifted her mouth to meet his, but she'd miscalculated apparently because— Oh! He was going for her neck. No, her collarbones. He pressed an open mouth against the right side and groaned a bit as he did so. The moment his lips made contact with her skin, she surrendered.

The only regret she had left niggling at her was the idea that *he* was going to end up regretting what was about to happen. Noah Denning didn't sleep around. This was not who he was.

But right now, logic was not strong enough to penetrate the fog of desire that had overtaken her. So she stood on her tiptoes to give him better access. The one hand remained on her cheek, but the other snaked around her, pulling her flush against his chest. She wanted to press even harder against him, to rub herself shamelessly against him like a cat, to use his body to hitch herself up and around him the way she had in New York. But every part of her felt tender, too soft, against his fully clothed body. His crisp white button-down was stiff against her oversensitive nipples. His belt buckle pressed into the vulnerable flesh of her belly.

So she reached for the buckle and started undoing it. He jerked a little, startled, but recovered quickly and, catching up to what she was doing, let go of her with both hands— she had to bite her lip so as not to howl in protest—and yanked his shirt from his jeans. She worked on the belt while he undid his shirt buttons. It should have been awkward, but all it did was make her burn hotter, make her more desperate to get his skin against hers.

He stumbled trying to get his shoes off, and by the time he righted himself and managed to get his pants and boxers off she was shaking even harder than before.

He was magnificent. Not that she was surprised, but...*my God*. There were the muscles she'd seen glimpses of during costume changes after their various wardrobe malfunctions, but they were everywhere. Not enormous, but *there*. Making themselves known in a cascade that went from sculpted shoulders to defined abs to...well, the man had a marvelous cock. Of course he did. Pink and symmetrical and pleasingly though not intimidatingly large, it bobbed between them like an upside-down divining rod.

He opened his mouth like he was going to say something. Talking was a bad idea. It had the potential to derail everything. So she reached up and clamped one of her hands over his mouth and said, preemptively, "Shut up."

And, hallelujah, it worked. He peeled the hand off his mouth and sat on the bed, pulling her along with him, grabbing one of her thighs as she came and arranging her on his lap so she was straddling him. It was the perfect position for them, going a ways toward ameliorating their height difference.

And they kissed. Oh, they kissed. She wasn't sure if minutes passed or hours as they feasted on each other, battling with their tongues as surely as they had earlier with their words. He stroked deep into her mouth, wringing low moans from her that came from somewhere way down in her core. Hell, they felt like they came directly from her clit, like it was commanding her to vocalize what he was doing to her body.

And she was humping him like a goddamned teenager in heat, rocking her hips back and forth. But she couldn't get close enough, couldn't get enough pressure, enough friction, *enough Noah*.

And then he touched her breasts, and she lost her mind. How was it possible he hadn't touched her breasts before now? They'd been glued to his chest as she ground on him, his arms banded around her torso like he was afraid she'd escape, so that was why, but, oh God, when he did... the rush of sensation, of electricity to her nipples nearly undid her.

"Wendy," he whisper-moaned, and it startled her. He so rarely called her just "Wendy" without the "Lou Who" attached to it.

She had to get him inside her. "Do you have any condoms?" she asked.

"No."

She wrenched herself off his lap, relishing the wordless, growly protest he made, stalked over to Gia's bag, and started rummaging through it. Clothes, makeup, magazines—everything she would expect Gia to have except... "She *must* have some condoms."

She ran to the bathroom and tried both girls' toiletries bags, even though she knew Elise, with her endometriosis, didn't bother with birth control.

"Wendy," he said again. "Wendy." He was getting closer—his voice was louder on the second incantation of her name. He appeared in the dim bathroom—she hadn't turned on the overhead light and had been conducting her rummaging by the ambient light from the main room—and he looked so...carnal. Like she was made of dust and wishes, and he was all flesh and muscle and man. Like she was a shadow of a person, and he was an actual person. "We don't need condoms."

"Yes, we do!" she protested. "I'm not on birth control, and..." Shit. They couldn't detour here to have the whole STI conversation, because that would be it. Noah would be reminded that he didn't do casual sex, much less with her, and that would be the end.

"That's not what I mean." He took her hand and led her back into the dark, into the corporeal world, grounding her with his heat. Gently, he pushed her to sit on the bed and kept pushing until she was flat on her back. Then he covered her with his body and kissed her again, deeply. She was about to protest that they couldn't just roll around naked and make out indefinitely or surely her head would explode, but then his hand brushed lightly between her legs, and he moved his lips to her neck, nuzzling there for a minute. Then, as he whispered, "No guy is going to go down on you the first time you fuck him, huh?" he moved down her body, fast, before she even had time to process what he'd said.

"Oh my God!" she exclaimed as he licked her clit, firmly and decisively.

And it was like that lick had been an initial claim staked, a declaration of intent, because he backed right off. Her hands flew to his hair. She wanted to keep him there. Well, she wanted to actively shove his face back between her legs, but she wasn't that bold. So she rested her hands gently on his scalp, loving the feel of his hair. How was it possible that she'd grown up with Noah Denning but never touched his hair?

He licked his lips and shot her a wicked grin before gently dropping kisses all along her seam. They were light, teasing kisses, and they were wonderful. And terrible, because she wanted so much more. She squirmed, trying to maneuver herself into a better position, but he clamped his hands on her thighs, immobilizing her against the bed. She cried out, half in protest, half in encouragement, because as he did so, he licked deeper into her, humming his pleasure.

"Oh my God, Noah," she panted, both reveling in and resisting the state of arousal she was trapped in. She wasn't going to be able to come like this—she needed more direct pressure on her clit for that—but the torture, the limbo, was so unbearably, exquisitely delicious.

"What?" He lifted his face off her body. "I'm just trying to meet your expectations." He tried to affect a casual expression but could not hide his grin. "And no condoms, so…"

"Uhhhh," she moaned. And, once again, it was half frustration, half pleasure. That was the way it was with him, she was learning.

"Oh, but am I *not* meeting them?" he teased. "You'd better tell me what you want. Do you want to talk about craft beer?"

She pressed on the back of his head. God help her, she *pressed on the back of his head.*

"What?" He lowered his head and licked her lazily, but way too low. "I'm not sure I got that." Another leisurely lick, higher, but still not quite where she wanted him. Where she *needed* him. "Didn't your friends say that grown-up Wendy has a potty mouth? I think I'd like to hear from grown-up Wendy." Then, damn him, he pulled away entirely and sat back on his haunches, regarding her like he was a sculptor and she his creation.

"I want you to lick my clit," she said, her voice all scratchy. "Like you did at the beginning. I want you to lick it and suck it until I come."

A slow smile blossomed. "That," he drawled, "will be my pleasure."

And then he did exactly what she asked, followed her instructions to the letter, licking her like an ice cream cone he was afraid was going to melt if he didn't work fast enough. And when she was moaning and writhing, he seemed to know just when to fasten his mouth around her and suck. It was only a second before she was shuddering and shaking, rocked by the most intense orgasm she'd had in a long time. Maybe ever.

He'd knocked her out. Nothing was working quite as it should. Her vision was hazy, her ears were full of the sound of her own heartbeat, and her brain . . . well, her brain had gotten off the train a few stations ago.

Which was why it took her a few minutes to catch up to the fact that while she'd been leveled by a shattering orgasm, he was still hard. Of course he was—he'd been single-mindedly focusing on her, implementing his peculiar mix of torture and pleasure.

While she was blissed out, he'd sat up on his knees and he was jacking himself with one hand, staring at her the whole time. "Let me," she said, resting her hand over his. When he let go, she started sliding her hand up and down, trying to mimic his pace. Her hands were smaller than his, and the tips of her fingers didn't reach the tip of her thumb as she pumped. She wondered if the smaller surface area of her grip versus his would be a disappointment.

"Oh my God, *Wendy*," he said, as if he had heard her unarticulated insecurities and was discarding them, and that was followed by a series of noises she could only describe as a cross between a grunt and a moan. They were the sexiest noises she had ever heard. So she tightened her grip a little and increased her pace slightly. His eyes rolled up to the ceiling, and he closed them for a moment.

When he opened them, they focused immediately on her face, and he started coming, painting her chest with ribbons of come.

She wanted to writhe around and rub it into her skin like a stupid cliché of a porn star, as if that would somehow amount to a claim staked: *this jizz is* mine.

What the hell?

He flopped down next to her, so they were lying side by side on their backs.

She was lying naked with Noah Denning in a hotel room in Las Vegas.

And they were on Gia's bed, which was...Well, having gotten it on with Noah was bad enough, but somehow, the idea that she'd done it in her friend's bed made everything seem extra weird.

"How did you even get in here?" As soon as it was out of her mouth, she regretted it. "How did you even get in here?" was probably not high on the list of things a woman should say to a man who had just rocked her world with his face between her legs.

Thankfully, he chuckled. "You girls need to learn to be a little more vigilant about your keys."

"That doesn't give you the right to just—"

The door opened.

The door opened.

Of course it did. This wasn't her room, after all. Why shouldn't its occupants return at will?

"Wendy! Are you in here?" called Gia. "The adjoining door is locked! Gunnar's getting ready for his finale. He wants to talk to you about the weird-ass literary deluxe package you booked and—"

There was nowhere to go. Nowhere to hide. Barely time for Noah to whip the covers up and over both of them before Gia's jaw hit the floor.

"Oh my God!"

At least it wasn't Jane. "Gia, if you can just—"

"Oh my *God*!" Gia was blinking extremely rapidly.

"Gia, this isn't—"

"I'm going to go back over there." Gia was still opening and closing her eyes rapidly, as if enough blinks would cleanse her eyeballs of the horror she'd just witnessed. After a few seconds of that, she turned her attention to Wendy and contemplated her in silence for a few heartbeats before saying, "I suggest you get dressed and come over and try to act normal so Jane doesn't find out you slept with her brother." She paused and let her gaze roam over them for a few moments. "Unless this is a . . . real thing. Something you're prepared to come out about."

"No," Wendy said quickly, even as some small part of her brain posed the question: *Why* can't *it be a real thing?*

She quashed that part of her brain. The most important thing was that she'd answered Gia's question before Noah could.

Because she had to be the one who set the parameters this time. Yes, they'd just slept together, but that's all it had been.

She wasn't getting abandoned again, left standing under the lights alone.

Chapter Fourteen

*I*f Wendy and Noah are getting it on, you know what that means, Gia. You need to hook up with Hector."

Elise dropped her one-sentence bomb over breakfast the next day, and it was hard to say who objected more, Wendy or Gia.

"I am not 'getting it on' with Noah!" Wendy said at the same time that Gia made a loud, vague noise of protest. They were sitting on stools at the counter in an old-school diner, and both women swiveled to face Elise, who was seated between them.

Wendy still couldn't believe Gia had told Elise, though if she had wanted what had happened with Noah to be a secret, she shouldn't have banged him in her friends' room. They had, by some miracle, agreed that no one should tell Jane, so Wendy supposed it wasn't the end of the world.

Well, it wasn't the end of the world that Elise knew that she'd slept with Noah.

The *actual* sleeping with Noah part?

The jury was still out.

Though she supposed she hadn't slept with him, technically. In an old-school penis-in-vagina sort of way.

Oh, who was she kidding? It had been the best sex of her life.

She'd had the best sex of her life with her best friend's brother, the boy who'd hurt her so badly. The first and last man to break her heart.

And she wanted to do it again.

Okay, yeah, jury deliberations complete: it was the end of the fucking world.

Last night, Wendy had managed to get her shit together sufficiently and quickly enough to attend the end of the Gunnar Show. And it turned out the money she'd spent on the deluxe package had been a total waste because Jane had, as planned, hightailed it downstairs to meet Cameron as soon as Gunnar had completed his final gyration. Gunnar had offered to "talk about books" with Wendy—and he'd winked exaggeratedly as he did so—but she'd declined.

"You're not getting it on with Noah?" Gia sipped her coffee placidly. "Hmm. So I guess the reason I caught you guys naked in my bed was because you *weren't* getting it on."

"Okay, yes." As much as Wendy wanted to, she could not deny reality. "But not *get* it on. *Got* it on. Singular past tense."

"So everyone got it on last night except you," Elise said to Gia as she attacked her omelet. "That's an unusual twist."

In last night's evolving game of musical beds, Cam's brother, Jay, once he was booted out of Cam's room because Jane was there, decided to get his own room rather than bunk in with Noah and Hector. Which meant Elise had followed in Jane's footsteps and decamped to her husband's room at the Paris hotel. So much for competing bachelor and bachelorette parties. These parties were totally, irredeemably commingled.

"You don't know that I didn't get lucky last night." Gia pushed the pieces of a waffle she'd cut but not eaten around her plate.

"Are you kidding me? You would have told me by now. You would have texted me after the fact," Elise said with obvious affection in her voice. "Or maybe even *during* the fact."

Wendy was glad to hear that marriage hadn't made Elise off-limits for late night post-hookup texts from her best friend. She had assumed that once one half of a friendship was married, that dynamic would change.

Gia made a noncommittal noise and shuffled her food around her plate some more, but the grin she was trying to suppress said that Elise was correct.

"Well, tonight you need to pick up Hector," Elise said. "It completes the set. You can't argue with fate."

"Completes the set?" Gia echoed. "I have no idea what that means."

"You know. Then everyone in the wedding party is hooking up with someone else in the wedding party."

"I am *not* hooking up with Noah," said Wendy at the same time that Gia said, "I am *not* hooking up with Hector."

Elise ignored Wendy. "Oh, come on," she said to Gia. "You're not that picky."

Whoa. Gia shot Elise a withering look. Elise almost certainly hadn't meant anything by the remark, but, damn, it had come out pretty slut-shamey.

"What's wrong with Hector? For a night, I mean?" Elise went on, oblivious to her friend's irritation. "You have that 'one and done' rule anyway. It's not like you have to *date* him."

"There are two things wrong with Hector."

Elise looked startled, either at the odd specificity of Gia's answer or at the sharp tone in which it was delivered.

"One: he knows who I am."

"You're a model," Elise said.

"Yeah, but I'm not a *super*model. I'm not a model-slash-actress. I'm not in Taylor Swift's squad. I'm not trying to move into lifestyle—you will never see me goop-ing."

Gia was always making those distinctions. She actively avoided the spotlight.

"I'm not on social media," she went on. "I can walk down the street and not be recognized."

"Right," Elise said. "I know all that. But I don't see what that has to do with Hector."

"Hector knows me. He mentioned he'd seen me in the *Sports Illustrated* swimsuit issue a couple years ago."

"So? The *Sports Illustrated* swimsuit issue is a huge deal."

"Yes, but I wasn't one of the headliners. They always have a few big-name, legitimately famous people, and then the rest of us are just sitting there getting sand in our butt cracks. A guy who has gone to the trouble of finding out my name..." She trailed off and curled her lip in disgust.

"Okaaay." Elise looked unconvinced.

On the surface, Wendy could see how people might have trouble understanding Gia's logic—she was a model who didn't want people to see her modeling? But Wendy got it. She didn't want a man who wanted her *because* she was a model. "You said two problems with Hector," Wendy prompted, hoping to ease the tension-filled exchange. "What's the second one?"

"I'm not going to complete your 'set,' Elise," Gia said. "Hector could have the brain of Bill Gates and the body of Chris Hemsworth, and I wouldn't go near him on principle." Then she shot Wendy a look. "Someone has to be the last woman standing."

Wendy felt it like a knife to her gut.

"Hey, girls!" Jane appeared behind their stools, looking impossibly bright-eyed after a night of drinking, strippers, and who-knew-what with Cameron. She smiled at them all, but when her gaze landed on Wendy, she blew her a kiss, the same greeting the two of them had shared for more than twenty years.

Wendy lifted her palm to pantomime plucking the kiss out of the air, and, traitor that she was, pressed the palm to her heart. She'd never slept with a guy and not told Jane. That knife that Gia's comment had stuck into her gut slid in deeper...

"My brother is going to come shopping with us, okay? He'll be here in a sec."

...and twisted.

─ ୬

Sunday morning the guys slept in, but Noah hauled himself out of bed for a day of shopping and sightseeing with the women. He wasn't really sure why. He could try to rationalize it as being about his "who can throw the best party" thing with Wendy—like trailing along after them would somehow mess up their fun.

But that was bullshit. The truth was he'd heard his sister and her friends talking about it yesterday, and this morning he'd "happened" to wander over to Cam's room just as Jane was leaving to meet her friends. After looking at him funny, his sister had asked if he wanted to come, and he'd jumped at the chance like a puppy being taken on an unexpected walk by a beloved master.

And that master wasn't Jane.

As evidenced by the fact that he couldn't stop watching Wendy.

Watching Wendy drink coffee. Watching Wendy buy fancy lotion. Watching Wendy and the girls laugh at inside jokes. Watching Wendy take in the fountains at the Bellagio.

Watching Wendy act completely fucking normal. Like last night had been no big deal. Like he hadn't had his face between her legs eight hours ago.

But this was fine. He could deal with Wendy's indifference. Wendy's indifference was *good*. It wasn't like they were ever going to become a couple.

He just...wouldn't have minded a sign that last night had affected her, even a little. That she was struggling with the embers of the inferno that had so recently engulfed them. Because he sure as hell was.

But apparently it had been a case of slam, bam, thank you, sir. But what had he expected? She'd outright *told* him, that night at the bar in New York, that she wasn't looking for a relationship.

So he stomped on those embers. Poured water over them until they were merely a steaming pile of ash. Melodramatic, but, shit, he needed to be ruthless. Like Wendy was.

The problem was he couldn't seem to find his footing. Couldn't get back to normal with her. He'd had plenty of opportunities to argue with her or to pay for things—to get things back to their version of normal, in other words—but he couldn't summon the necessary fight. He just drifted around...watching her.

This was why he avoided casual sex. It so often came with all these confusing emotions. You didn't know where you stood. You had no control over how things were going to go.

After shopping, he was taking a much-needed pre-dinner breather when Jane came by his room. Hector was out, so she flopped on Noah's bed and proceeded to carry on a conversation while he shaved in the bathroom.

"You know, you don't have to follow me around all the time," she said.

"*You're* the one in *my* room."

"You know what I mean. You invaded the party last night, and today, you crashed our shopping."

"You invited me along!"

"Yeah, because you were *already right there*."

"Eh, the guys were planning to be at the tables all day. Not really my scene." That much was true. A man didn't grow up so close to the edge of financial ruin only to throw away his money gambling. Of course, he couldn't tell her that the real reason he'd been stuck to her so intensely since they got to town wasn't actually *her*.

"Anyway, I'm not talking about today. Or not *only* today. I'm thirty-two years old, Noah. You don't have to take care of me anymore."

He wanted to feign confusion, but once again, he knew what she meant. Finished with the shave, he rinsed his face and stared at himself in the mirror. His sister was a capable adult. He knew that, with his mind, anyway. He headed out of the bathroom. "I just..." What? He had no idea what he wanted to say. Everything was all muddled in his mind.

"You can't let go of the idea that you have to take care of Mom and me," she said.

He couldn't deny it. It maybe didn't explain his particular brand of intensity today, but it was true in a general sense.

She scooted over to one side of the bed and patted the other. He went reluctantly, feeling like he was walking a plank to his death rather than sinking into a fluffy, feathery bed. He braced himself against the headboard for the lecture he was due.

"Do you know that I always felt like Dad's death was my fault?"

What? That was not what he had expected.

"That's *ridiculous*." He was speaking too sharply. He gentled his voice. "He drove drunk. He wrapped his car around a tree."

"I know." Her eyes filled with tears. But then she proceeded to spin a shocking tale, telling him about how she always looked after their dad, cleaning up when he was sick, talking him out of driving.

About how she had secretly started reading books for kids whose parents were alcoholics.

About how, after learning from one of them that it wasn't her job to parent her parent, she got angry.

"So one day, I stopped. I decided I was done taking care of him, done trying to hide the worst of it from Mom." She swallowed. "The day he died, I knew he was drunk. He was going out to buy more beer. I usually talked him out of doing that by pretending I needed help with my homework, or, if that didn't work and he was bound and determined, I called him a cab. That day, I just didn't call one. I yelled at him. I told him he was an embarrassment and he should just go to bed. Then I went to my room and put on headphones." Her voice broke. "I saw how bad he was, and I turned away."

He had seen none of this. *None.* The revelation felt so dramatic, she might as well have punched him. His heart broke at the thought of his sister, so young—she'd been eleven when their dad died—taking such a burden onto her small shoulders.

His response to his dad's alcoholism had been to be out of the house as much as possible, to load his schedule with after-school and evening activities. Which of course had only made things worse for Jane, he saw now. He'd left his little sister to deal with the day-to-day fallout of their father's addiction.

"It wasn't your fault," he croaked, willing her watery eyes not to overflow, because then he'd lose it, too. "He was never going to stop. He was going to kill himself one way or another. It was just a question of when and how. You *can't* think it's your fault."

"I don't, anymore." She smiled like she was remembering something nice. "Though that's been a more recent revelation."

The look on her face made him ask, "And does this revelation have anything to do with Cameron?"

"Let's just say he's made me see a lot of things differently." Her smile grew. "Anyway, my point is not to trot out this whole 'poor Jane' sob story. The point is what happened after Dad died."

"What happened after Dad died?" he echoed, feeling stupid asking the question, because he'd been there. But obviously, he hadn't *really* been there, not in any way that mattered.

"I became the model kid. You became the parent—you had to grow up way too soon—and to compensate, I became the model kid."

"What do you mean?"

"Why do you think I never gave you or Mom any trouble? Like, not even once?"

His mind skittered over the past. Jane had never dated. Never got mixed up in drinking or drugs. Got good grades. Didn't go to parties. Her social life had consisted mainly of sleepovers with Wendy.

"Because you were a good kid?" She *had* been. It had been in her nature...he'd thought.

"Yeah, I was. Because I was terrified to be anything else."

"Oh my God." Having it all laid out like this, he realized how weird it was for someone to go through their entire youth without a single rebellion. "I didn't see..."

Yeah, there was a hell of a lot he hadn't seen, wasn't there?

"I know," she said. "Because that's how I wanted it. I didn't want to make your life any harder than it had to be."

"I'm sorry," he said, his voice finally cracking, unable to withstand the onslaught.

She scooted closer to him and wrapped her arms around him. "There's nothing to be sorry for. You didn't do anything wrong. You did everything *right*. You took care of us. Do you know how grateful I am to you for that? We survived because of you. I mean, Mom was lost those first few years. God, Noah, if it hadn't been for you, I don't know what would have happened. They may have taken us away from her, I suppose."

He nodded against her head and hugged her tighter. That had always been his worst fear, the family being separated.

She pulled away and looked him directly in the eye. "My point is that I was trying not to rock the boat, but somewhere along the way, I *became* the person I was pretending to be.

I actually *became* this cautious, risk-averse, guarded person. Like, for real."

He blinked rapidly. Her eyes, the same brownish-green as his, did the same thing.

She sniffed and smiled. "But I figured out that I don't have to be that person anymore. The threat I was reacting to is long past. The threat *we* were reacting to is long past."

Her use of the word *we* wasn't lost on him. She wasn't just talking about herself here.

"I will always love you, Noah," she went on, "and I'll always want you in my life. You're my *brother*." The way she said *brother* imbued the word with all the meaning he felt, too—she was his sister, but because of what they'd been through together, she also felt like his fellow soldier. "But you don't have to worry about me anymore. I promise, if I need help with something, I'll tell you."

"I'm not sure I can just turn it off—worrying about you," he admitted. It was like his early years had hardwired his brain. "But I'll stop sending you money," he said, trying to leaven the situation with a little humor.

"Good," she said. "But also...I just wish you could let up on yourself a little."

"What does *that* mean?"

"I figured out that I don't have to keep being the person Dad's death made me into, right? You don't have to either. I think you're on autopilot just as much as I was. You work all the time, for one thing."

"I like my job."

"I know, and that's great, but it's like it's an imperative for you more than a job. And it's not just that. You have to be in control of everything all the time. The sending me money is a symptom of it, just like the workaholism." He started to protest, but she held up a hand. "I'm not criticizing. I get it. You had to stay in such control for so long to keep us afloat. But you don't have to anymore. You can let up on the gas a little. Have some fun."

Holy shit. Was she...*right*? Bennett had said a variation on the same thing, that night in his restaurant with Wendy. Had outright called him a control freak. Noah had always thought there was nothing wrong with being a perfectionist. With being dedicated to a certain way of doing things, whether those things were work or relationships. But if all the people closest to him were coming to the same conclusion, maybe that conclusion was worth considering.

"Have some fun," he echoed. "I don't...I don't really know how to do that."

Not in the way she meant, anyway. He had fun hanging out with Bennett. Going running. Or at least he thought he had. But none of that had been as much fun as—

"Ha! I'm new at this, too. But, hey, for once you're not in a long-term relationship, so maybe go out and get drunk and meet a nice young lady who's interested in a little 'what happens in Vegas stays in Vegas' action?"

—as that.

Already took care of that one, Jane.

He got up and walked to the window so she wouldn't see his face, which felt like it was on fire. His brain was burning, too, feverishly churning through the astonishing new information she'd dumped into it.

Jane was still chuckling at the apparent ludicrousness of her suggestion that he find someone to hook up with. "Seriously, though, just let yourself relax a bit. Follow your interests."

"I do follow my interests." But of course that was a hollow protest, because as this whole conversation had highlighted, what were his interests? Beyond running, putting away criminals, and, to use Wendy's word for it, "obsessing" over his sister?

Jane swatted him on the shoulder—she always saw through him. "Maybe you should start by *getting* some interests. What about traveling? Remember that big map you had on the wall in your bedroom when you were little? You'd read a book about a country, then stick a pin in that country. Maybe you should actually go see some of them. Take a cue from Wendy."

He had totally forgotten about that. He *had* been captivated by the rest of the world when he was young—he'd had the *National Geographic* subscription and everything.

There was a lot he'd forgotten about who he used to be. It had all been swept aside, in service of survival.

"Eh," he said, trying to inject some levity into the conversation, because, honestly, he couldn't take any more. "I also used to skateboard. Remember that? Putting in some time at the skate park would be a hell of a lot cheaper than becoming a jet-setter."

Jane rolled her eyes, but she smiled as she rolled off the bed and said, "Good talk, brother-mine." She snapped her fingers. "Now put your shoes on. It's almost time to go. And speaking of world travelers, Wendy picked tonight's restaurant, and she never leads me astray in that department." She walked over to the window and did that thing women do when they've been crying in makeup, swiping her fingers below her eyes. "I *love* Wendy, and not just because she picks the best restaurants. Damn, this wedding is making me all emotional, but, seriously, don't you just *love* Wendy?"

A noncommittal murmur was all Noah could muster as Jane's earlier words echoed through his brain. *Maybe you should start by* getting *some interests.*

He was pretty sure that by "start getting some interests,"

Jane didn't intend for one of those interests to be her best friend.

As she grabbed her purse, he said, "One more thing."

"Yes?"

"I'm kind of pissed you never told me any of the stuff about how you were feeling. I thought we told each other everything." God, listen to him. He sounded like a junior high girl in a spat with a friend. But he couldn't help feeling a little betrayed. "Everything important, anyway."

"We do!" she protested. "I'm just a little...late with this one." Then, seeming to realize he was serious, she sobered and said, "I'm sorry." But it wasn't long before she was back in mischievous little-sister mode. She raised her right hand. "I, Jane Denning, do solemnly swear that from here on out my brother and I will tell each other *everything*." She threw her head back and laughed. "You're going to live to regret this."

─────ᘒ

Maybe he could get into fine dining, Noah thought as he tried to slow his rate of inhalation of the most incredible steak he'd ever tasted. Fine dining was an "interest," right?

"I'm sorry this place only has one Michelin star, but getting a table at the better places takes literally months," Wendy said as they all tucked into their main dishes.

Noah had been pretty sure that the lobster cocktail he had ordered to start with—on Wendy's recommendation—was not going to be topped, but, yeah, as incredible as it had been, one bite of his flatiron had topped it.

As soon as the bite was safely swallowed, he laughed. "You're *sorry* you took us to this place?"

She shot him a look he couldn't decode. "Where would you have taken us if you'd been in charge, Noah?"

"Nowhere this good." But then he belatedly realized that she'd been baiting him, trying to pick a fight. Probably attempting to get things between them back to normal—he had been in that position himself. In fact, that's the whole reason they were both here in Vegas, with their competing parties.

Great job on the whole "getting back to normal" front.

"Anyway, *I* didn't take us to this place," Wendy said to the table. "I just recommended it. We only got in because Gia's agent made some calls."

After they toasted their resident semi-famous person, Jane said, "Wendy claims it's easy to find good fancy restaurants. She says the greater culinary triumph is in finding holes in the wall with great food." His sister shot her best friend an affectionate look. "She still talks about the frog porridge she had in Singapore!" Jane went on. "Isn't that the grossest thing you've ever heard?"

Singapore. Was it safe to travel there alone? He had no idea.

Wendy looked up from her plate. Her eyes found his immediately. So now probably wasn't the best time to get out his phone and google the aforementioned question.

Dinner passed like that—with Noah watching Wendy, and Wendy occasionally catching him doing it. Noah felt like he was perpetually two steps behind everyone else, like his brain was moving at half its normal speed.

It also wasn't helping matters that she was wearing another dress that managed to be effortlessly beautiful. It was totally different from yesterday's dress, but the effect was the same—turning him into a drooling idiot. Instead of the vivid red from yesterday, this one was a subdued ivory. A swingy minidress, it was sleeveless and high-necked, but the top part was made of mesh or something similar. It allowed a hint of what lay beneath, but only a hint. The outline of collarbones but not the overt display of them.

What the hell was *up* with him and collarbones lately?

He sighed and tried to focus on his steak. It was going to be a long dinner.

Chapter Fifteen

*W*endy wasn't a game player. Usually.

She didn't do things like manipulate a situation so she could be alone with a guy she was lusting over. Usually.

But no matter how much she was trying to hide it, and no matter how fucked up it was, she wanted to sleep with Noah again.

The problem was she didn't see how she could get him alone without a little manipulation.

When dinner broke up, it was nearly eleven thirty and everyone was tired. Both the girls and the boys had had late nights yesterday. As they stood in a circle in the lobby of the Venetian, people started proclaiming that they were going to call it a night. Elise and Jane were headed to Paris with their respective men. Gia, however, wanted to go out.

"Come on!" she wheedled, making puppy-dog eyes at Wendy. Then, lowering her voice, she whispered in her ear, "Don't leave me alone with Hector!"

"Sorry, Gia, I'm done. I'm going to head back to the hotel."

Normally, Wendy would have womaned up and kept Gia company, but she was wagering on another scenario. If Gia went out, and if Elise and Jane stayed at Paris, that would leave Wendy to head back to New York, which was on the southern end of the Strip, by herself, something Noah would never—

"I'll walk you back to your hotel, Wendy," Noah said.

—allow. Ha. Once the surrogate big brother, always the surrogate big brother.

Or something.

Really, she had to stop thinking of him in those terms, even if she wasn't successful in talking Mr. Control into letting loose one more time.

"We're on the Vegas Strip, Noah," she said, reciting the next line in her script of manipulation. "I'll be fine. There are a million people out there." And now he was thinking of a million different harms that could befall her in Sin City on the twenty-minute walk back to her hotel.

"Let's go," he said, as if her objection wasn't even worth the effort it would have taken to dismiss. She tried not to smirk as he pressed his hand against her lower back and started propelling her through a replica of St. Mark's Square. She didn't bother pointing out that since the Paris hotel was actually on their way, if on the other side of the wide Las Vegas Boulevard, they might as well walk part of the way with the others.

No, her mind was set. Her mind might be making a big mistake, but it was set on that mistake.

And she wasn't kidding herself. What she was about to do was wrong. It was the difference between first and second degree murder: premeditation. It was one thing to get carried away in the moment, quite another to *plan* for the moment.

What she *hadn't* planned for, though, was *getting* to that moment. In her imaginings, the successful culmination of this evening involved some very hot sex. Some hot *meaningless* sex. Some "get the boy out of your system" sex.

It did not involve Noah keeping his hand pressed against her lower back, the way guys always did in movies to show they cared about a girl.

It did not involve him grabbing her hand and pulling her back when she stepped off the curb slightly prematurely as the light was changing from red to green.

Wendy had traveled the world. By herself. She didn't need anyone to take care of her.

More to the point, she didn't *want* anyone to take care of her.

No, the real truth was that she didn't want to *enjoy* being taken care of.

Goddammit.

Well, she would just have to turn that part of her brain off. She could do that.

"I suppose you've been to Venice. The real one, I mean." Noah waved his free hand at the hotel complex behind them. She thought back to the fake St. Mark's Square with its fake clouds painted on the ceiling and its fake gondolas gliding under its fake bridges.

"I have." And that was a perfect example of what she'd just been thinking. She'd been to Italy twice, alone, and without any knowledge of the language. She'd deflected pickpockets and Casanovas alike with no help from anyone.

"You must be rolling your eyes at all this Vegas stuff—Venice, Paris, ancient Egypt. Probably all places you've been."

"Well, I haven't been to *ancient* Egypt," she teased.

He chuckled. "Touché."

"I know what you mean about Vegas, but I'm not sure I agree. Everyone talks about how fake Las Vegas is, but to my mind, that's part of its charm. It's not pretending to be something it's not, not really. It revels in its artificiality."

"There's no self-delusion," he said.

"Exactly." She swiveled her head to look at him as they walked. He was regarding her curiously.

"You're not a fan of self-delusion, are you, Wendy Lou Who?"

She was not. "Self-delusion is for the weak."

Usually.

Weakness was not something she could generally afford. Other people, maybe, people with big families and best friends who weren't getting married. People with support networks.

He laughed, though she hadn't been kidding.

"Let's get a cab," she said, hailing one even as she spoke. Talking too much wasn't a good idea. Better to get there quickly and get on with it.

He looked down at her feet. "Sure. Those shoes look killer."

She followed his gaze. She was wearing her standard four-inch black stilettos, her favorite pair that could go from work to evening with ease. They did hurt her feet, but some things in life hurt. "Oh, no, I'm used to these. These are my court shoes."

He was still looking at her feet. Suddenly, her feet *really* hurt, burned in fact, like she'd been outside in the freezing cold and come in to an overheated house. Then his gaze started to move, a slow elevator working its way up her body, bringing with it that same dangerous heat.

When he finally met her eyes, he said, "I suppose pain is for the weak, too?"

She had to clear her throat to ensure that what came out sounded clear, strong. "Something like that."

A few minutes later, they were disembarking from the cab, and before she could lose her nerve—this premeditation shit was terrifying—she hopped out of her side and took off, trusting he would follow. Noah wasn't going to be satisfied until he'd seen her safely to her room.

She burst through the doors and made a beeline for the part of the lobby next to the gambling floor.

And there was that goddamned hand again. She needed to get that hand off her. Well, she needed to get that hand *on* her, but under the correct circumstances.

So she sped up, shaking off his touch.

"Hey," he said. "Everything okay?"

She had to pivot out of his way, do an undignified little half pirouette in the name of self-preservation. Then she speed-walked toward the stupid fake neighborhood section of the hotel. There was a mini Times Square and fake cobblestone streets lined with fake brownstones, complete with fake fire escapes.

There was even a fake manhole cover emitting fake steam.

Perfect.

She stopped suddenly, standing nearly on top of the manhole cover, and turned to face him. "Where are we?

His brow furrowed. He was probably worried about her sanity. She couldn't disagree there. She had, after all, just made a little speech inside her head about self-delusion being for pansy-asses, and here she was about to embark on the mother of all delusions.

"We're in Vegas."

"No." She did a Vanna White thing with her hands, gesturing around to encompass their immediate surroundings. "Where are we?"

"Uh, New York?"

"Correct. And what do we say about New York?"

He was still looking at her like the men in white coats would be appearing any moment. "It's the city that never sleeps?"

"No."

"If you can make it here, you can make it anywhere?"

"No." She stamped her foot in frustration. "What do *we* say about New York?" She changed the direction of her Vanna-White-ing and gestured from her chest to him and back again, the same way she had that night on the High Line.

She saw the precise moment he got it. Bewilderment was replaced, briefly, by astonishment, which was in turn supplanted by, if she wasn't mistaken, pure, unadulterated lust. He tamped that down pretty fast, too, though, got his shit together and said, with a remarkable lack of inflection, "I see. And if the court will allow it, we're also in Vegas, and you know what they say about Vegas?"

Well, wasn't that a nice little bit of window dressing for her argument? Noah wasn't a brilliant legal mind for nothing. She bit back a smile. She was trying to project confidence bordering on entitlement, not "OMG, I'm so thrilled you just agreed to have meaningless sex with me again!"

"What happens in Vegas stays in Vegas," he said, answering his own question. "So the way I see it, that's like an extra layer of protection." He was clearly suppressing his own smile as he raised his eyebrows suggestively.

"Speaking of protection..." Her face heated. Gah. She could outright proposition him but she couldn't manage the necessary logistical discussion? What was the matter with her? She wasn't shy about these sorts of things. Usually. But hadn't she just been thinking that she didn't go in for self-delusion, either? It was a night of firsts, apparently, and right now, to utter the word "condom" felt like she might as well shout, "I want you to fuck me."

But, hell, Wendy had learned that the only way to deal with things that were scary or uncomfortable was to embrace them head on. Afraid of traveling alone in a place you don't speak the language? Book a goddamn ticket. Facing off against a legendary prosecutor in front of an unsympathetic judge? Get a freaking manicure, put on your court shoes, and slay.

So she just said it. "I want you to fuck me this time, so we're gonna need a condom."

Something sparked in his eyes. Good, upstanding, responsible Noah liked that idea. So she added, "Condoms. Plural."

"I'm on it," he said quickly. Gratifyingly quickly. "Go upstairs. I'll come to you soon."

—⌒○⌒—

Noah had had a lot of sex in his life.

Okay, maybe not *a lot*. The handful of one-night stands he'd had in his youth, before he'd decided they weren't for him, had ended awkwardly at best. One had led to a harrowing pregnancy scare.

It just wasn't worth it, to his mind. Wasn't worth the risk, the loss of control.

But he did okay. He dated. He'd had several girlfriends over the years. His relationships usually followed the same progression—he would meet someone he was attracted to, indulge in a little flirtation, go on some dates, and before he knew it, he had a girlfriend.

It worked for him not least because in his opinion, the most attractive part of a woman was her mind. What could he say? He went for smarts, and you couldn't always get a sense of a person in one night. He wasn't immune to beauty, but he liked his beauty to come with brains.

The only problem with his tendency toward serial monogamy was that at some point, it had to end. Like with Clarissa wanting to move in together. It had made sense on paper, but he just...couldn't do it.

He never could.

He shook his head as he entered the gift shop in the casino. No need to stroll back over his entire romantic history. It wasn't relevant to what was about to happen.

Which was that he was going to have casual sex with Wendy.

Wendy certainly wasn't going to demand a commitment from him. She had made that abundantly clear by inventing that weird New York loophole. So in a way, it was the perfect arrangement. It was like a one-night stand, but not. Because he knew Wendy. She was undeniably gorgeous, but she was also smart as hell. Thinking about the gentle slope of her breasts—and about her goddamned collarbones, for fuck's sake—got him hard. But so did thinking of her demolishing a witness in court. Pushing the tolerance of a judge with objections that skirted the edge of reasonableness.

"Will that be all?" the woman at the cash register asked, barely looking up from her phone as she scanned the box.

"Yes." There was a display of random items on one corner of the counter, a mixture of essentials like Advil and travel toiletries, but also silly things like souvenir shot glasses and...His eye snagged on something. "Actually, no." He impulsively grabbed the item in question. "This, too, please."

Five minutes later, he paused outside Wendy's door. Last time he'd been outside a hotel room containing Wendy, he'd been consumed with anger, ready to blow. But then there she'd been, in a towel, equally angry, lashing out at him, a worthy adversary.

And then she'd dropped that towel and demolished him.

He had no idea what to expect this time. Wendy was clearly an assertive woman. She did what she wanted. He liked that. A lot. So he wouldn't be surprised to find her in the bath again. Or in a towel. Or totally naked.

The latch was propping the door open, so he knocked lightly, then slipped into the dark room.

His fantasies had gotten away from him, because she was standing at the window fully clothed.

She turned at the sound of him entering, and his heart did a strange thump. The room was dark, but the curtains were open, so she was bathed in the ambient light of Sin City.

He knew with his mind that Wendy was tough. That her size belied her strength.

She was a small, self-contained, self-sufficient universe of one.

But from this vantage point, she looked young. He imagined she looked sad, though of course that was ridiculous. It was too dark to see anything that would have suggested that. Still, he could sense her. He knew truths about her, somehow, without having to see them with his eyes.

She was cold. She was vulnerable.

"Noah."

Her voice, strong and sure across the darkness, jarred him. He must have been mistaken about that last thing, because there was nothing vulnerable in the way she said his name.

He dropped his purchases on the desk and moved toward her, stopping short, unsure how to proceed. Last time, he had been fueled by anger, which had, at the sight of her dropping her towel, ignited into lust. There had been no premeditation, no second-guessing, just pure, mindless instinct. There hadn't been room for anything else.

This time, there was room.

There was still lust. He was pretty sure he was now conditioned for life, like Pavlov's dog, to salivate at the sight of Wendy. But there was also all this... space that needed to be crossed to get to her. A whole gaping chasm, in fact, that had the potential to flood with awkwardness, nerves, second thoughts. There was room for cooler heads to prevail, for one or both of them to think too hard, or worse, to verbalize why this was a big mistake.

"Stop thinking, Noah."

He almost laughed but managed to hold it at a grin as she took a step toward him, eyebrows raised. It was such a funny juxtaposition. Here he was all tied up in knots over what was about to happen. Wendy, by contrast, did not seem to be having that problem.

"You know what?" she said. "Most people enjoy this. You could, too, if you lightened up a little."

What was it about everyone telling him to lighten up all of a sudden?

But she was right, at least about the situation immediately at hand. So, taking her directive literally, he moved toward the desk lamp. He wanted to see her. If they had to be in a fake New York-within-Las Vegas fantasyland to make it okay to sleep together—which he wasn't questioning, because they pretty much did—he wanted to see everything.

So, yeah, enough with the introspection bullshit.

He switched on the light.

She smiled. "Take off your clothes."

So he did what the lady told him to: he took off his clothes.

He paused, shirtless, to relish the slight intake of breath that resulted. But she tamped that shit right down, pressing her mouth into a thin line like an elementary school teacher about to lose her temper, and let her gaze flicker down his body. It was a "get on with it" gaze, and he wasn't about to disobey.

It wasn't lost on him, as he kicked off his pants, that her command flipped their positions from last night. When she'd dropped her towel, she'd been naked, and he'd been fully clothed. But he was, strangely and inexplicably, cool with their current situation. The weird thing about Wendy was that there was no script. With all those girlfriends from his past, they had settled quickly into established roles. Someone initiated. Someone called the shots. Usually him, which was fine. Sexy, generally. And that's how things had played out last night with Wendy. He'd been obsessed with going down on her, because he remembered her assertion from New York—the real New York—that no guy would do that the first time, and had been determined to prove her wrong. So he'd gotten bossy.

But maybe this whole giving up control thing had something to recommend it, because fuck, right now he had no earthly idea what was going to happen and he was amazingly okay with that.

She stalked over to him, pressed her palms against his chest, and walked him back toward the bed. She shoved him, hard, and he fell back, bouncing a bit on the mattress as he landed, but the rebound was absorbed by her body as she climbed up him.

And oh, God, the uncertainty, the ceding control, had been more than worth it. They stared at each other for a long moment, and, when he couldn't stand it anymore, when he feared his heart might jackhammer out of his chest, he threaded his hands through her hair, pulled her head down, and kissed her.

She made a noise that started out desperate but then slid into something closer to relief. She sounded like a woman who had been waiting a very long time and was finally getting what she needed. He loved that. His *dick* loved that. He pressed the pads of his fingers harder against her scalp and swept his tongue through her mouth, which was soft and hot as it moved against his. She undulated her hips, grinding herself against his erection. The silky material of her dress was slippery, too smooth. Not what he wanted, not even close. So, leaving one hand on her head and continuing to work over her mouth, he used his other hand to tug the fabric up. But then, *fuck*, she was wearing tights, and they were in the way.

Skin. He needed skin. "Who wears tights in the summer in Vegas?"

"It's cold in these stupid hotels," she shot back, and he loved that even now, she was arguing with him.

"Get these off," he growled, burrowing his hand under the waistband and grabbing her ass, which, he knew with the sliver of rationality that remained in his mind, probably made it harder for her to do what he'd asked.

But she managed, squirming and swearing, to work the tights to her knees, and then to free one leg completely. He was impatient, and one leg was enough. Growling, he flipped them and bent to kiss her again, her mouth swallowing the groan that ripped from his throat when she wrapped her legs around him. She'd done that last night, too, and last month, in the real New York, and he fucking *loved* it. He wanted her to climb all over him, to cling to him like ivy choking a building. And when she rocked her hips against him—hard—he had to press his mouth against her bare shoulder and bite down to keep from blowing his load right then and there.

He didn't bite hard, just rested his teeth, really, but she moaned so loudly, he did it again.

"You like that, do you?" he said, and did it again, actually biting a little this time.

She bucked wildly against him. "Where are the goddamned condoms, Noah?" she gasped, her voice raspy and needy.

"On the desk," he managed, grunting as he moved off her to retrieve them. But somehow, she was out from under him so fast that she beat him to the desk and was ripping the packet open by the time he reached her.

He'd assumed they'd get the condom and go back to the bed, but he'd thought wrong. She positioned the condom at the tip of his dick, her breath growing shallow. Her hand slid down his length as she unrolled it, and he hissed at the contact. He let his head fall back momentarily, needing to stare at the ceiling to reset himself, to rein in his lust.

Which was why, when he righted his head, he was totally, utterly gobsmacked by the sight of her bent over the desk.

"What are you doing, Wendy?" he said, though of course he knew what she was doing. *Shit.* He squeezed the base of his dick and took a deep breath. His attempt to slow himself down was undone by the very sight of her, though. She'd positioned her hips right at the edge of the desk and her torso was pressed flat against its surface. Her feet didn't hit the floor. Her legs dangled, one of them still entangled in her tights. The skirt of her dress was flipped up.

Then she lifted herself up on her elbows, twisted around, and found his gaze. And, *oh, fuck*, those needy brown eyes imploring him, while her lower body was bare to him.

"What are you waiting for?" she asked again.

"Nothing," he said, because that was the correct answer, the answer they both wanted.

He took a step forward and sent a hand down to check that she was ready. "Oh God," he bit out, shoving the skirt of her dress up as high as it would go. Wendy was so wet, his hand came away coated. And he fucking loved it. It made him want to roar.

She reached around and grabbed his retracting arm and pulled on it while she glanced meaningfully at his dick, clearly communicating her desire that he get on with things.

She wasn't strong enough to halt his retreat, though, unless he chose to follow her cue.

He would—of course he would—but not quite yet. Because although it took every ounce of his strength to hold back from burying himself in her, he was beginning to understand that part of what made the attraction between them so explosive was the fact that it was tinged with confrontation. It had been there from the start—arguing in the park in New York, and then, later, outright war.

At this moment, it turned out that *not* giving Wendy exactly what she wanted was pretty much the sexiest thing in the universe.

So he moved toward her, covering her back with his body and nestling his dick against her ass, but that was all he did. She thrust her hips back and moaned in frustration, but he did not oblige her. Instead, he repeated his motion of earlier, dragging the fingers of one hand through her hot, slick folds, eliciting another aggrieved moan.

There was a mirror above the desk. He could see his reflection in it, but not hers, because she was lying flat on the desk, below the bottom edge of the mirror. He used his other arm on her shoulder to lever her torso up enough that she could see them, too. Once he'd established eye contact in the mirror, he stuck the fingers that had been inside her into his mouth.

"Mmmm," he groaned, and when he had licked them clean, added, "you taste so fucking good."

And it was true.

That was the funny thing about them together. There was only truth between them, always had been. They had often been at odds, both as kids and more recently, but he had never lied to her.

Which was why when he said, with the taste of her still on his lips, "You are gorgeous," he meant it. Fuck, she looked like his every fantasy come to life, with her long black hair messed up from his hands tangling in it, mascara smudges bracketing eyes heavy with desire.

So he finally gave her what she wanted, using one hand to guide himself inside her. He gave himself what *he* wanted, too, which was to see her collarbones. He used a finger from his other hand to work into the mesh panel of her dress. Once he'd made a sufficient hole, he yanked.

When it worked, when the mesh tore, leaving those perfect, symmetrical collarbones bared to his gaze, he felt like the fucking champion of the world.

And when she said his name in a desperate whisper that was half entreaty, half affirmation, he was undone. He pressed one palm, open as wide as it could go, loosely over her neck so that he could feel the ridges of her collarbones—*his* collarbones, they felt like—and slammed into her again and again, relishing the slap of flesh on flesh.

Her torso started sinking, unable to remain upright

against the force of his thrusting. The desk moved, too, with every stroke, banging against the wall in time with the grunts that were coming from somewhere deep in his chest. The room service menu fell to the floor, and the phone's receiver clattered off its cradle.

He used his last sliver of control, to slide his free hand around and cup it over her sex. He angled the base of his palm over her clit. His arm hurt as he kept up the punishing pace, trapped as it was between her body and the edge of the desk, but if that was the price of her pleasure, he welcomed the pain.

As he barreled toward the cliff, he began to fear that he was going to get there before she did. "What do you need?" he said, not letting up.

She shook her head like she couldn't find the words and ground herself harder on his hand. "Just don't stop."

"I'm not going to stop," he said gruffly, pressing his fingertips harder on her collarbones. He was close, though. He could feel the storm in his body concentrating, coalescing. But they didn't lie to each other, so he added, "I'm going to come harder than I ever have, inside you. But I'm not going to stop with this"—he ground his palm harder over her sex—"until you're screaming."

And then she did just that. It was followed by the spasming of her inner muscles around him, and he gave a few more ruthless thrusts, banging the desk so hard against the wall that the mirror shook, and then he detonated.

Chapter Sixteen

Holy fuck.

This had been a mistake.

Wendy stayed where she was, draped over the desk with Noah draped over *her* while she pondered what she'd done.

She'd thought she could compartmentalize. That she could have sex with Noah in the present, and not let all the emotion attached to teenage Noah infect things.

She had been wrong. She felt...off. Shaken up. But, okay, she wasn't past the point of no return here. It wasn't like she was *in love* with him. She could fix this.

They stayed like that for a long time, panting in the silent, brightly lit room, Noah still inside Wendy's body.

When Noah heaved a sated sigh and pulled out, she wanted to scream from the injustice of it, like a kid who doesn't want her birthday party to end.

But it had to end.

She allowed herself an extra moment while she listened

to him dealing with the condom, heaving a deep sigh even as she remained prostrate on the surface of the desk. Eventually, she was going to have to get up and face what came next. And there was no way that what came next wasn't going to be at least a little awkward. If there was a protocol for having the best sex of your life with the only man who'd ever broken your heart and then somehow getting him speedily and smoothly out of your hotel room, she was not privy to it.

Procrastinating, she stretched, letting her arms slide out in front of her and fanning them to the sides, like she was making a snow angel from on her belly instead of her back.

One hand closed around something hard. "What is this?" Still not quite able to muster the strength to heave her body off the table, she remained prone as she retracted her hand, object enclosed in it, bringing her eye to eye with...

Pez Elvis.

She bolted upright as if the table were made of fire.

"Oh, I saw that in the store where I bought the condoms, and I wanted to...give you something," Noah said, like it was no big deal. He chuckled in a way that might have bordered on self-deprecating. "Something besides condoms."

Oh, *shit*. She *was* past the point of no return.

She burst into tears.

Which of course brought him to her side in a flash.

Damn him. Damn him to hell. Why did he have to be so fucking thoughtful all the time?

Because he was a thoughtful, kind person. That was the terrible truth. He always had been, and he was now. The part in the middle, where he stood her up at the dance? It had been an aberration.

Fuck.

She loved him.

But he could never love her back. He couldn't all those years ago, and he couldn't today.

The truth was like an awful, clawing beast inside her, fighting to get out. All she could do was cry, and let it. Then maybe she'd be able to get up, to put herself back together. To become smooth and un-hurtable again.

"Oh, shit, Wendy, I'm sorry." Noah's voice was heavy with regret. He laid his hands gently on her back, so terribly gently. "That was too much." Then the hands disappeared, and she cried even harder, their loss the final burden, the one that made the collective weight she was carrying heavier than she could bear. Instinctively, she took a step toward him, her body wanting those hands back regardless of what a bad idea it was.

But they were otherwise engaged, scraping across his scalp angrily, almost pulling his own hair. "God," he bit out. "I'm an idiot. I knew this was a mistake."

"No," she said, through tears she couldn't get to stop. But at least they were silent tears; she wasn't audibly sobbing anymore, just leaking from her eyeballs. She couldn't blame him this time. "It's not that. This was..." She trailed off, making a weak version of the Vanna White gesture that had accompanied her declarations earlier this evening. It was one thing to have the best sex of your life, quite another to say it out loud. She was glad her dress hadn't come off, glad the rip he'd made in it hadn't exposed her breasts. She smoothed the dress down. "This was good," she finished softly, then bent over—ostensibly to put her tights back on but really so she'd have an excuse not to look at him.

"What is it, then?" he asked quietly.

She stayed bent over, even though she knew she couldn't hide from him indefinitely. She needed a moment to...put on her armor.

"Please, tell me what's wrong."

I'm in love with you, that's what's wrong.

She stood up, met his eyes, and opened her palm. "You got me a Pez."

He smiled uncertainly. "Which I would not have done if I'd known it was going to make you cry."

And you don't love me back. I tried to harden myself against you all those years ago, but it's all happening again.

"It was more just...that you remembered."

"Did the Yankees one I mailed you make you cry, too?"

He was teasing, so she tried to form her lips into a smile. "No." But it had inspired her to make that fateful trip to New York—the real New York. The trip that had started all of this.

I'm right back where I started.

But again, it wasn't his fault. "I'm just...a bit over-whelmed by the fact that you remembered something so insignificant as the fact that I used to collect Pez." She was aware that this explanation had, again, fallen short. Women didn't burst into post-sex sobbing because someone remembered something about their former hobbies.

Normal women didn't, anyway.

"Of course I remembered." He furrowed his brow. "I remember everything."

Her defenses were down because she'd slept with him. That goddamned Elvis Pez had unhinged her. Because the next thing that came out of her mouth was: "Do you remember standing me up at the prom?"

—❧

He did remember, that was the thing. Not in the sense that he stayed up nights thinking about it—but of course he remembered. He'd been strangely, sharply, surprisingly disappointed when he'd had to call the school that night to pass on a message that he wasn't coming. And not just because he felt bad about leaving Wendy dateless, but because he'd *wanted* to go. Which, he'd told himself at the time, was ridiculous. It was a school dance. A bunch of streamers and balloons in the gym, a lot of bad music being spun by a sub-par DJ, everyone sweating in ill-fitting formalwear.

But he'd wanted to see what Wendy was wearing. Wanted to dance with her. He'd wondered if it would be as much fun as running with her.

But, as he'd always done in those days, he'd set aside what he wanted in favor of what needed to be done.

"They offered me a double shift at the store," he said slowly, sending himself back to that evening. The plan had been that after his normal shift ended, he'd go meet Jane, Tim, and Wendy at the school. He had a rental tux stashed in his car and had been planning to ninja a corsage together from the store's floral section. But then two of the night stockers had called in sick and the manager had offered him not only double but triple time to stay on for the overnight shift. He hadn't even hesitated. It wasn't like it was an actual date.

"You said it was fine." He hated the defensiveness that had crept into his tone. He'd called her to apologize the next day, and she'd brushed it off. Hell, she hadn't even really wanted to go to the dance in the first place. He and Jane had had to talk her into it.

"It *was* fine." Wendy turned and looked at herself in the mirror. She paused for a moment, then started wiping away the mascara smears under her eyes.

It's fine. Those had been her exact words, in fact, when they'd spoken on the phone about it. He had taken them at face value. Wendy had always been mature. And she was

practically part of his family back then—one of the few
outsiders who knew how tight things were. So when she'd
said she understood that he had to take the extra shift, she'd
understood. She'd waved away his apology and then...

And then he had hardly seen her for seventeen years. He
remembered thinking it was odd that she hadn't come to
the good-bye party Jane threw him a couple weeks after the
dance. And then, when he came home to visit, she'd rarely
been in town. The few times she had, they hadn't gone on a
single run. His interactions with her had been limited to din-
ners with Jane or church with her aunt Mary. In fact, he'd
probably only seen her half a dozen times in the seventeen
years since he graduated.

Holy shit.

Okay, he needed to be rational here. He was giving himself too much power in this story. If he went over every
person he knew and tried to figure out which of them were
likely to be carrying around a hidden seventeen-year-old
wound, Wendy wouldn't even make the top ten. Hell, the
top hundred. Wendy was smart and efficient and self-aware.
She didn't *do* shit like that.

But then why had she suddenly brought this up?

"Did I..." *Arg.* He ran his hands through his hair, which
wasn't a habit he had generally, but he feared that before
the night was over, he would manage to tear off his scalp.
"Wendy, was me not showing up at that dance a bigger deal
than I thought it was?"

She shook her head, with her back still to him. She
seemed to be done fixing her appearance, but she kept looking in the mirror. He tried to catch her eye, but her attention
was fixated on herself. "You needed the extra shift. You did
what you had to do. You didn't need to worry about hurting
some kid's feelings."

She sounded like she was reciting lines from a play, and not very convincingly.

"But I did, didn't I?" All the evidence supported that conclusion. He wasn't one for running from his mistakes. He couldn't make it right retrospectively, but he could, at least, own his mistakes. "I *did* hurt you."

She didn't deny it, which, for Wendy, his worthy adversary, the woman who always had a snappy defense, was saying volumes. God, what an idiot he'd been not to see it. He'd let himself stand up a shy wallflower of a girl for a couple hundred bucks? Yeah, things had been tight back then, but not taking that extra shift wasn't going to put them out on the street. It hadn't even been about the money, really. By that point, he'd basically been on autopilot. Work? Yes. That was just what he did back then. Work was the one variable he could control.

"I was..." He searched for the words to explain. "Back then, I was consumed with not dropping the ball. I was single-minded about what I regarded as my responsibilities."

As soon as the words were out of his mouth he realized they were still true. That's what Jane had been trying to get him to see this afternoon. *You're on autopilot just as much as I was,* she'd said. *Let up on the gas a little.*

"I know." Wendy was still talking to herself in the mirror, but at least she'd stopped crying. "You protected Jane, and by extension, me, since I was always around."

"I tried to." And he had. It had been the imperative burning in his chest, powering him through those impossible years.

She finally met his gaze, allowing him to see her eyes, though only the reflection of them in the mirror. "It wasn't that I didn't appreciate your protection. I did. And I do even more now, in retrospect."

"I sense a 'but' coming."

She turned around. Somehow, the sight of her real eyes, not merely the reflections of them, sliced through him like a sharp stick, clearing away decades of cobwebs that had prevented him from seeing the world clearly.

"But protection wasn't all I wanted from you."

Oh my God. He prided himself on having taken care of his sister and her friend, on being attuned to what was happening to the girls, to their unmet needs.

Apparently he'd had huge fucking blinders on when it came to Wendy, though.

He hardly dared to ask the next question, but it needed to be done. His throat was so dry, it came out barely audible. "What did you want?"

"Besides not to be humiliated at the prom?" She didn't say it in an accusing way. There was nothing in her tone but defeat. And, God, that wasn't right. Not from his Wendy Lou Who. His mind conjured an image of her all dressed up, standing under the disco ball in the school gym...alone.

This was why she'd been so angry at him. The wedding had forced her to spend time with him in a way she hadn't since they were kids. And she was still mad. The flashes of anger he'd seen from her, the ones that had seemed out of proportion, uniquely targeted at him—they all made sense now.

There was a knock at the door.

Neither of them acknowledged it. They remained where they were, Wendy having recovered her composure, her face completely blank. He, on the other hand, was not composed. Far from it. His chest hurt, and he feared his spine might actually buckle under the weight of the epic error he'd made so many years ago.

The knock became a pounding. "Wendy!"

That broke their stalemate, because they both knew that voice.

"Wendy, open up! I can't find my key! It's an emergency."

Noah could tell from his sister's tone that it wasn't a wedding-related emergency, but a real one.

Fuck. Instinctively, he started toward the door, but he stopped himself. He was not supposed to be here.

And if he *was* going to be in his sister's best friend's hotel room at one in the morning, he was not supposed to be naked.

Wendy jolted into action, calling, "Hang on a sec! Be right there!" Then she whirled, grabbed his hand, pulled him to standing, and whispered, "I hate to turn this into a bad Hollywood rom-com, but you are going to have to hide in the shower."

"But—" His sister was in trouble. She needed help. He couldn't hide in the shower.

"Listen to me, Noah," she hissed. "You can eavesdrop from in there. Whatever it is, I will take care of it. If you're needed, I'll figure out a way to get rid of her, and *then* you can find her and do your goddamned white knight thing."

He hesitated.

Then she said, "Please. Please don't do this to me."

And there it was again, that vulnerability he thought he'd caught a glimpse of when he'd first walked into the room and seen her looking out the window. There she was, the girl inside, the girl who didn't want to be humiliated by him. Correction: the girl inside who didn't want to be humiliated by him *again*.

So he hid in the bathroom. Left the door open a crack and actually got into the shower and closed the curtain like he *was* in some kind of stupid romantic comedy. Except he was pretty sure that when the heroes in romantic comedies hid naked in the bathroom, they didn't feel like they had been run over by a truck.

His clothes sailed in through the crack in the door. He'd forgotten them, but Wendy must have gathered them.

He heard the sound of her unlocking the door, which was saying something because the blood in his head was like a raging river.

"Wendy!" His sister was breathless, her voice high. She took a deep breath, audible even to him in the next room. Then, her name again, but this time he had to strain to hear it. The second "Wendy" was said with a hitch in Jane's voice that almost made him bust out of the bathroom, but he forced himself to be still.

"It's your aunt. She's been in a car accident."

There was a kind of indeterminate shuffling sound, then a *thud* he hoped to God wasn't Wendy falling. He waited for her to say something—anything. To make any sound at all. But there was only more from his sister. "Someone from the church called me. They've been trying to reach you, but apparently your phone is off?"

Then it came: the wail. Wendy making a sound of utter defeat.

He'd been imagining something horrible having happened to his sister. But this. This was just as bad.

He grabbed his pants and started jamming his legs into them. He had to get out there, damn the consequences.

─ে৯

Wendy had experience being blindsided. No matter how prepared you were for a trial, it sometimes happened. A surprise witness, a bombshell piece of evidence your client didn't tell you about.

But that was different. This wasn't her job. This was her *aunt*. The last family member she had.

She pushed off the wall she'd crashed back against and grabbed Jane's arm. "What did they say? Where is she?"

"She's at Sunnybrook Hospital." Jane's voice was heavy. "They're trying to get her stable enough to do surgery. They don't know much more, other than she got hit by a car while she was crossing Warden Avenue."

"Who is *they*?" Wendy asked.

"I spoke to someone named Leticia who works in the church office. Your aunt had a program from a church service in her pocket, so the cops contacted the church. Leticia said when they couldn't reach you, they tracked down one of the partners at your firm, who told them you were here for my bachelorette weekend. He called your assistant, who gave them my number."

The amount of detective work required. The number of people who had to be woken in the middle of the night. All because she was off indulging herself. Suddenly, she understood how Noah felt, like escaping one's responsibilities was simply too big a risk.

Still, Wendy was accustomed to being blindsided. Even if this particular blow was bigger, sharper, deeper than any she'd encountered before, she knew what to do. Keep her mind calm and agile. Quickly consider her options. Ruthlessly throw away anything that wasn't going to help her in this moment. Make a decision.

"I need to get to the airport," she said, shaking her head against the hug Jane was trying to inflict on her. If Jane touched her, Wendy would succumb to the terror that was lapping at the edge of her consciousness. She needed to keep that terror away. "I didn't answer my phone because

I can't find it anywhere. Can you go see if I left it at the restaurant?"

A noise came from the bathroom. Damn Noah. What was he doing in there? She shuffled a few steps back toward the bathroom door, as if her presence would provide any kind of meaningful barrier between the siblings.

"Are you sure? I can call Elise or Gia and send them for the phone."

The door handle was turning. Shit.

Wendy shook her head as she reached for the door handle from her side, though she knew that if he wanted to come out, she wasn't capable of stopping him. "I have all kinds of sensitive work stuff on that phone, and I trust you more than anyone." She didn't even have time to feel bad about how ruthlessly she was manipulating Jane. She wanted to fall into her best friend's arms; instead, she had to send her away by lying.

So she could murder her brother.

Jane nodded. "I'll call the room with news one way or the other." Then she blew Wendy a kiss.

Wendy pantomimed catching it and pressing it to her chest, but only because it was the quickest way to get rid of her friend. Really, though, there was no point in pressing the kiss to her chest, because there wasn't a heart inside there to receive it, at least not one that was in working order.

The door hadn't even fully shut behind Jane when Noah emerged from the bathroom. He'd put his pants on but was still shirtless, and he had a determined look in his eye. He was going to try to comfort her, or worse, do that *and* try to address what had been unspooling between them before Jane had arrived. God, she'd basically admitted her teenage crush on him. Why? Why would she *do* that? It had absolutely no bearing on their grown-up selves, on their contemporary lives.

He wrapped his arms around her and just said her name. "Wendy."

No. She couldn't do this. She couldn't get close enough to him to let him hurt her again. So, summoning her last bit of strength, she pushed on his chest. Hard.

He let go of her, but he tried to grab one of her hands.

She was surprised to find she was still gripping the Elvis Pez dispenser with all her might. It was inside plastic-and-cardboard packaging, and she'd been holding on to it so tightly, the edge of the cardboard had cut into her palm, leaving a deep groove. Her hand hurt like hell, actually, but she'd only just realized it.

She opened her palm fully, letting Elvis fall to the ground, and held both hands out to Noah like stop signs. "Don't."

"Wendy, I'm not—"

"*Don't*," she said again, louder, making a jerky motion with her hands, which were still raised. Whatever it was, she couldn't hear it. "Just go."

He tried to reach for her again, *damn him*, and she twisted out of the way of his incoming arms. He made a frustrated noise. "I can't just leave you when—"

"Stop!" She actually yelled this time. It worked; he stopped. "If you care about me *at all*, you will leave now and forget"—she gestured vaguely behind her—"this. What happens in fake New York stays in fake New York, remember?"

He took a step back. Good. She'd beaten him back.

"Can I at least take you to the airport?"

"No. Your sister can take me to the airport. But in order for that to happen, you have to leave so I can call her and tell her I found my phone under the bed." God, she sounded like a cold-hearted bitch.

She shook her head. It didn't matter how she sounded. Nothing mattered except getting back to Toronto.

"Please, Noah." Normally she would hate for him to see her weak, but she tried to infuse her voice with all the desperation she felt. "If you care about me at all, please leave."

He looked at her for a long time but eventually pulled his shirt over his head. "All right then. Good-bye for now. But I'm calling you tomorrow."

He slipped out the door. When she tried to close it behind him, it snagged on Elvis.

She bent down to retrieve him, and, for the second time that night, a Pez dispenser made her cry.

Chapter Seventeen

Would you like to pray together?"

Reverend William Long, from Aunt Mary's church, sat down next to Wendy in the surgical waiting room.

"Sure." Because really, why the hell not?

Wendy had already offered the God she was pretty sure she didn't believe in everything she could think of in exchange for sparing Mary's life. She'd work less. She'd stop traveling and move in with Mary. She'd take a cue from Noah and stop having casual sex. She'd bargained everything she could think of, but she hadn't tried straight-up praying.

Wendy had always been secretly dismissive of what she saw as her aunt's simplistic devotion to an organization that basically subscribed to the notion that a man in the sky was in charge of what happened to humanity. But regardless of whether any of it was actually true, she'd been bolstered by the outpouring of love and support for her aunt—and by extension, for her—in the thirty-six hours since she'd been back from Vegas.

And this Reverend Bill—he'd told her to call him that—was not a bad guy. She had seen him at church, of course, preaching sermons. But in person he was cooler than she would have expected. He was an interesting mixture of kind and efficient, and he didn't flinch when she baited him. For example, she could say things like, "What actually *is* praying, anyway? Is it just asking for what you want? Like a shopping list?"

He chuckled. "I like to think of it more as asking for what you *need*."

"I need my aunt to not die," Wendy said without hesitation.

"Why?" he asked gently. "Everyone dies."

Wendy rolled her eyes. She didn't care if she was being rude. "I suppose this is the part where you tell me that if it's time for God to take her, it's her time. Well, eff that." She congratulated herself on not using the real curse word there. It was what she'd been screaming in her head. "It's *not* her time."

"Do you perhaps mean it's not *your* time? That you're not ready for your aunt to die?"

"That's exactly what I mean."

All Wendy could think was about how often her aunt invited her to church. Wendy usually went with her on Christmas Eve and Easter Sunday—or the odd one-off Sunday when Noah was in town and insisted on going. But that happened once every couple of years, tops. Would it have killed her to show up every now and then on a random Sunday, because it was important to her aunt and her aunt was all she had left? God, Noah was more thoughtful about church with Mary than Wendy was.

Wendy hadn't cried yet. Not since she'd picked up that stupid Elvis Pez from the floor of her hotel room back in Vegas. Somehow, she'd gotten through the seemingly endless flight home without crying. She'd sat at her aunt's bedside in the ICU, holding Mary's limp, IV-pierced hand, without crying. She'd conferred with doctors, listened to diagnoses of brain swelling and cracked vertebrae, and phrases like "too soon to tell," and "possible paralysis," and "surgery will tell us a lot." She'd talked to cops, doing her best to answer questions so they could decide whether to lay charges against the driver who'd struck her aunt.

All this she had done without crying.

She'd thought maybe she was out of tears, that maybe her night with Noah had sucked them all out of her.

But, no, it turned out that a simple "Do you perhaps mean it's not *your* time?" was what finally did the trick.

The toxic mixture of shame and fear was too much. She was ashamed of not spending more time with her aunt, who was, after all, as much an orphan as Wendy was. But also afraid. Gripped with stone-cold terror. She'd gotten herself all twisted into knots over the idea of Jane "leaving her" when she got married, when all along she should have been paying more attention to the one person who never, ever would—or so she'd thought.

"Wendy. Wendy, sweetie, don't cry."

It was Cameron, who'd come from the cafeteria bearing coffee. Cameron, who had been at her side literally nonstop since they got back from Vegas. He and Jane had arrived back in Toronto a few hours after Wendy and had come directly to the hospital and spent that first day with her, but eventually Wendy had talked Jane into going home to get some sleep, pointing out that there wasn't anything to do or know until after this morning's surgery.

But Cameron, damn him. She hadn't been able to shake him.

Reverend Bill passed her a box of tissues and murmured something about leaving for a while. Wendy nodded her thanks, secretly relieved that she was off the hook with the whole praying thing.

"Don't you have to work?" she asked as Cameron set down the coffees he was carrying. He sat next to her, slung one of his stupid, giant, beefy arms over her shoulder, and side-hugged her.

"Nope."

"Don't you have school?"

"Nope."

He was lying. Cameron worked full-time and went to school part-time, so there was no way he didn't need to be in one of those places at nine in the morning on a weekday.

"Hey…" He gave her a little squeeze with the arm that rested on her shoulders before retracting it. It seemed like he was going to say more, but then he closed his mouth.

"What?"

"Well, I was going to say, 'It's going to be okay.' But we don't actually know that, and you're not the kind of person who appreciates platitudes."

She nodded. That had been perceptive of him.

"But I will tell you this. No matter what happens, you're not going to be alone in this."

"I appreciate that, Cameron, I really do, but I kind of am. Mary's my last surviving family member."

"No," he said—more sharply than was called for, she thought. "I've got your back, Wendy, whether you like it or not. It's the way things work now."

"How do you figure that?"

"Easy. You're Jane's person. Jane's my person. There-
fore, you're stuck with me. Simple logic."

"What do you mean I'm Jane's person?"

"I don't know." He looked away, embarrassed. "You're,
like, her soul mate or some shit. I don't know. Girl bonds.
You tell me."

Wendy couldn't help but smile through her tears at his
caveman-esque attempt at expressing his emotions. "I'm
pretty sure *you're* Jane's person, Cameron."

He shrugged. "I should be so lucky. Anyway, I'm newer
to the scene, so I'm gonna have to go with you."

"You really love her, don't you?"

He paused for a moment before answering. "I really,
really do."

A sob rose through Wendy's chest, and she didn't even
try to hide it. Just let the next one come as Jane's fiancé's
supersize, surprisingly comforting arms snaked around her
again.

"Yep," said Cameron with a resigned cheeriness in his
tone. "Whether you like it or not, I've got your back now."

And damn if that didn't make her cry even harder.

Chapter Eighteen

*N*oah paused outside Mary's hospital room in Toronto. He was prepared for anything. Well, he was prepared for two possibilities, really. One would be rage. He'd seen flashes of anger from Wendy since the spring, and now that he knew where it came from, he was of the opinion that he deserved it.

God, he'd spent the past five days going over and over what had happened, both in the hotel room and all those years ago at the prom that wasn't. He'd had two bombshells dropped on him that last day in Vegas—Jane's confession about feeling responsible for their father's death and then arranging her subsequent life so she wouldn't be a burden on him, and Wendy's astonishing revelation.

He'd wanted only to do right by both girls back then. Instead, he'd made a hash of everything.

So, yes, he had earned Wendy's anger.

But his money was on the second option he'd braced himself for: indifference.

He was mostly convinced that he would open that door, and he'd get…nothing. She, having exorcised her feelings toward him—the bad ones *and* any residual lust-related ones—would raise her head and look at him blankly. Like she didn't know him at all.

Indifference was what he expected based on the radio silence he'd had from her since Vegas, anyway. When his first few calls had gone to voicemail, he'd started texting her. He'd tried apologizing again for the dance. And for that last night in Vegas—though something in him rebelled at apologizing for such spectacular sex. He'd tried asking after her aunt. He'd tried asking after *her*. He'd even sent her a link to a "What kind of Pez dispenser are you?" Buzzfeed quiz. She never replied.

Jane had kept him filled in on Mary's progress, of course, so he knew she was out of the woods. He knew, broadly, what was happening.

But he didn't know what was *happening*.

So, yeah, he was ready for anything. Armored. Indifference, rage, whatever—bring it on. He just needed to *know*.

He pushed open the door.

And had to correct himself. He'd been ready for anything…except delight.

"Noah?" She looked up, her tone incredulous. A parade of emotions passed over her gorgeous face—bewilderment and trepidation, mostly, but there was definitely some delight in there, too, before she tamped it down.

She was lying next to her aunt watching TV, both of them smooshed against each other on the single hospital bed.

He tried to breathe, but nothing happened.

She scrambled to her feet.

"What are you doing here?"

"I, ah . . . I'm here for the wedding." That was true. Partly. He couldn't say *I'm here because you won't text me back*.

"But I thought you weren't coming until the day before."

She wasn't going to let him off the hook, was she? Of course not—this was Wendy. "I decided to come early."

"What about work?"

He shrugged, trying to telegraph a casualness he did not feel. "I brought some work with me. Handed off to colleagues the stuff that required my physical presence." She had no idea how unprecedented that was. Or maybe she did—Wendy had always seen him in a way other people hadn't.

"Jane must be so thrilled."

"I suppose she will be." He hadn't thought that far ahead. Had just been sitting in his apartment last night, all restless and jumpy. The usual calmness that working brought, the sense of control it conferred on him, was nowhere in evidence. He couldn't keep his mind on anything—was unable to lose himself in work like he usually could. All he could do was scroll through those eleven sent texts, going back over them to obsessively check the "read" stamp on them, when he'd thought, *Fuck it. I'm getting on a plane.*

"Jane doesn't know you're here?"

"I came here first." That didn't really answer her question, but he was still suffused with the overwhelming feeling that he didn't know what was *happening*. He didn't know what he was supposed to *do*.

He hated that feeling.

"Is that Noah?" said Mary.

Well, shit, there was another thing he'd gotten wrong. Clearly, the first thing he was supposed to do was to pay attention to the patient. He could worry about the rest later.

"Miss Mary." He walked over and smiled down at her.

She looked so small, and not in the way that Wendy was small. Wendy was small but big, which probably made no sense to anyone besides him. Her aunt, though, was small and frail; dwarfed by the machinery around her and lost in a too-big hospital gown, she almost looked like she could slip away and no one would notice. He bowed his head a little and said, "I'm here for my sister's wedding, but I came early to see you."

"You were always such a good boy."

I tried to be! he wanted to shout. But he just looked at Wendy, who was...smiling? What the hell was going on here? Being at war with Wendy was, comparatively speaking, much easier than this.

"My sister tells me you're doing well," he said to Mary. "What's the prognosis?"

Wendy answered for her aunt, her smile widening into a full-fledged grin. "The prognosis is *great*."

─────ഗ⁓

"What happened to you?" Noah asked as he held the door for Wendy at the diner she'd suggested they decamp to for lunch.

She shot Noah a bewildered look, and, yes, maybe that wasn't the right way to ask the question, but damn, it was like Wendy had taken happy pills. It was disconcerting as hell.

Wait. "Did they give you antidepressants?" That might have happened, right? If she'd been consumed with grief? "Is that why you're so chipper?"

"Ha!" She did her cackling thing, and it warmed his insides even as it continued to throw him off his game. "Nope!"

She didn't say any more until they'd been shown to their seats. She disappeared for a minute behind the menu, and he wondered if she was avoiding him, but then she lowered it abruptly and said, "I'm so sorry I didn't text. I kept meaning to, but things have been so...insane. I'd get one from you, and I'd think, oh, I'll text him back later when I can sit down and actually think about it. Then, the moment I wasn't needed at the hospital, I'd go home and fall dead asleep."

"No problem." He was kind of lying. No, he was *totally* lying. Her lack of a response had not only not been "no problem," it had made him insane enough to bail on work and impulsively get on a plane to come check on her.

But she was...fine. Not in need of any comfort or solidarity from him.

"Anyway, it's better in person."

"What is?"

"The apology I'm going to make."

Huh?

"I'll have a tuna melt now and two pieces of lemon meringue pie to go," Wendy said to the server, who had arrived to collect their orders.

"That's a really...specific order," he said.

"Gia's arriving tonight. She has a freakish fondness for lemon meringue."

Noah stumbled his way through ordering a sandwich, and when the server left, Wendy looked him straight in the eye and said, "I'm sorry I laid all that shit on you in Las Vegas."

"You didn't 'lay any shit' on me."

She ignored him and just kept talking. "I'm also sorry I basically sexually assaulted you."

"Hang on, now. You did *not* sexually assault me." And also: *he* certainly wasn't sorry about it, whatever she was going to call it.

"I knew you weren't into getting the milk for free, so to speak, but I pushed it anyway. That was shitty of me."

"It's really okay. I'm the one who should be apologizing." He just didn't quite know how to do it. If only he'd *known* back then how she'd felt.

"I'm assuming the whole 'What happens in fake New York stays in fake New York' clause still applies?" She looked down and fiddled with her silverware, the first indication that she was at all unsettled. "About everything that got, uh, said and done there?"

He blinked. She was going way too fast here. "If we want it to."

She blew out a breath and grinned sheepishly. "Well, that's a relief."

Noah had said "we." If *we* want it to. She'd obviously heard "you." If *you* want it to.

Him? He had no freaking idea what he wanted.

"And I know it's asking a lot, but I'd really prefer to keep what happened between us from Jane. I don't want to make what is supposed to be the happiest time of her life any more about me than I already have."

"Sure thing." He was in total agreement there. He couldn't help adding, "It was fun, though."

"Ha! So you admit that there's something to be said for meaningless fucking!"

"God, do you have to call it that?"

"No, I don't *have* to call it that. I just enjoy taunting you." She grinned. "What would you call it?"

"Casual sex?"

His answer had come out more like a question because it didn't really describe what had gone down in that hotel room in Vegas. There had been nothing casual about it.

He shook his head. Of *course* that's what it had been.

Jesus. Even if he'd wanted it to be something more, it was completely impractical. They were enmeshed in satisfying careers in different countries. She was leaving for her trip around the world.

And of course there was the fact that attempting a relationship with his sister's best friend was a supremely unwise idea. When it ended, as all his relationships eventually did, how would they possibly untangle it?

"Meaningless fucking. Casual sex. Whatever you call it, it *cannot* happen again," she said. "Just so we're clear."

Crystal clear. Also clear? That he was a little more disappointed than he should have been. But he nodded and said, "Some sort of bizarre fake-New-York-in-Vegas vacation aberration thing."

She burst out laughing at his twist on the excuse they'd been feeding each other. "We should start a band and call it Vacation Aberration."

He let himself smile with her, let her happiness chase away that niggle of disappointment. "You still haven't told me what's with this whole Happy Wendy thing?" If they were being direct, which it seemed they were, he was just going to ask.

"Happy Wendy." She smiled, as if to demonstrate that she deserved the moniker. She looked thoughtful for a moment, then said, "I talked to the priest from Mary's church. Like, really talked."

He choked on a sip of his water. He had an image of her earnestly confessing her sins. And of doing so using her signature forthrightness and colorful language. He couldn't help it; he cracked up.

"I'm serious!" Wendy swatted his forearm. "You know how they say a brush with death can make you change your ways?"

He nodded and turned serious. She clearly wasn't kidding about this.

"Turns out it works secondhand, too." The waitress arrived with their food, and Wendy murmured her thanks, but she didn't make any move to eat, just kept regarding him curiously from across the table. "That last day in Vegas, and that first day back in Toronto, before I knew my aunt was going to be okay...those were the two worst days of my life."

He wanted to lodge a protest, to point out that one of those days had also contained the best sex of his life, but it was not the time for that. This was not about him.

"Like, who had I become?" she went on. "I had my undies all in a bunch over the idea of losing Jane because she was getting married. I was trying to take that out on Cameron, to construct some kind of bullshit argument in my head for why he's not good enough for her. But to what end? It's not like I was ever going to stand up and object to the wedding, so what was the *point* of all that?" She sighed and rested her chin on her hands. "And then *you*."

His heart sped up. He wasn't sure why.

"I'm so worked up about this wedding that I have to start fighting with you? I mean, yes, we've always sort of done that, but *Noah*, I brought Jane's bachelorette party to Vegas not for *her*, but because I wanted to show you up." He opened his mouth to say something reassuring, but she wasn't done. "I've been carrying this stupid grudge for *years*. Because of something that happened at the *high school prom*. How screwed up is that?"

"About that..." She still hadn't let him apologize.

But she wasn't done. "And it took my almost losing Mary—losing everything—to realize what an asshole I was being."

"You're not an *asshole*." She was being way too hard on herself. Everything she said she'd done—carried a grudge against him all these years, had reservations about Jane getting married—made a certain kind of sense, if you knew where she was coming from. And he did.

She ignored him, still intent on her speech. "After Mary's surgery, Reverend Bill and I were standing outside her room, and you could see her through the window in the door. She hadn't woken up yet. I said to him, 'I can't lose her.' He said—he's like this weird philosophical dude; he's always saying these maddeningly vague things that seem kind of trite initially but kind of sneak up on you with their profundity. He said, 'Sometimes it's better to focus on what you have rather than what you don't have or are in danger of losing.'"

He nodded. He couldn't argue with that perspective.

"And, honestly, Noah, it was like he'd hit me over the head with this super deep, profound truth. If I was a religious person, I would call it a revelation. Everything suddenly looked different. I still had my aunt. She was going to be okay. She's going to face a huge amount of rehab, but she's going to be okay. And I have Jane, the best friend a person could want. And I have *Cameron*. Ha!"

He raised his eyebrows.

"Who turns out to be kind of a mensch."

"You had a revelation sparked by an Anglican priest, and now you're calling Cameron a mensch. How ecumenical of you."

She chuckled. "Yeah, so I've lost stuff, is the point. I've lost people. But I also *have* people. I always have." She made a punching motion like she was trying to affectionately jab his shoulder, but she couldn't reach it across the table, so she switched to pointing at him. "I had a pretty good substitute big brother back in the day, for example."

"Except I messed up back in the day."

"Once. You messed up once. But not even really, because I never *told* you that you messed up. You didn't know how important that stupid dance was for me."

"I am sorry," he said. "I wish I could go back and be there for you."

"All things considered, you were there for me. No, not all things considered. *Overwhelmingly.* You were overwhelmingly there for me."

Well, shit. Why did his eyes suddenly itch? He wanted to ask her to elaborate on the sense she'd given him, in Vegas, that she'd had a crush on him as a kid. But this was her revelation. He didn't need to insert himself. Also, he wasn't sure if his voice would work, so instead of opening his mouth to talk, he opened it to shove some fries into it.

"Anyway," she went on, "I just turned everything inside out. I'm appreciating what I have now, rather than what I don't. So that's where Happy Wendy comes from."

He cleared his throat. "Maybe you should start a gratitude journal." Joking was easy. Joking would get them back on more comfortable ground. "Subscribe to Oprah's magazine. Put up some posters of aphorisms. You know, like with sunsets and kittens?"

"Hey now, I wouldn't go that far."

"Good. Because while I'm glad you've had this, uh, big insight, I gotta say, I think I kind of miss Prickly Wendy. Combative Wendy." It was true. In some ways, he'd never felt more alive than when he was sparring with Wendy, in person or via text. It was like everything he loved about his job transferred over to . . . a ridiculously attractive, intelligent woman. "I'm not sure I know how to interact with you if we're not arguing over something."

"Oh, don't worry. I'm sure all this agreeableness is just temporary overcompensation." She did the Wendy cackle. "The pendulum will no doubt settle somewhere in the middle of Happy Wendy and Prickly Wendy."

⸺Ꮹ

"I'm going to have to give up either Thailand or Hong Kong," Wendy said to Gia over curry and a pile of maps and calendars that evening in Wendy's apartment.

Wendy's travel plans had been modified by her aunt's accident. She was still going to take six months off work, but instead of continuously traveling, she'd decided to make twelve trips of two weeks each, and on each trip, she'd hit two countries. Then she'd come home and hang out with Mary for two weeks before starting the cycle over again.

"Why are you so calm?" Gia asked. "I would expect you to be freaking out over this disruption. You've been planning this trip for so long. It was your big thing."

Wendy shrugged. "Yeah, but you know what else turns out to be my big thing? Not having my aunt dead."

Gia lifted her glass of water. "Cheers to that."

"Mary actually tried to convince me to go as planned. She has this squadron of people from her church to help her while she's in rehab, so I'm kind of redundant. But I turned out to be strangely fine with changing my plans. Anyway, I think this will be fun. I've always tried to, like, collect places as I traveled. I've never spent a week in a single place. It will be kind of cool to get to know places differently, to really get the rhythm of them, you know? And, fuck me because this is going to sound like a Hallmark movie or something, but I'm looking forward just as much to hanging out with my aunt. Like, really getting to know her in a way I haven't so far." She lifted her own glass, which was filled with Guinness. "Liu spinsters unite."

"Hey, don't say that!"

"Why not? I'm not married. I have no plans to get married."

"I have no plans to get married either." Gia raised her glass again as if to punctuate the point. "But 'spinster' implies, like, dust and cobwebs." She made a vague gesture at her body. "Ain't nothing getting dusty here."

"Yeah, I need to get a new Christopher," Wendy said, because that's what she was supposed to say. In truth, despite her big speech in the diner, the idea of sleeping with anyone but Noah anytime soon made her feel sick to her stomach. And wasn't *that* an unwelcome development?

"A new fuck buddy, eh? Don't you ever want to, like, cuddle afterward?"

What the hell? Wendy thought Gia was the one who understood. "Do *you*?"

"No, ma'am! Just checking."

Wendy was strangely relieved. "No, I want to talk about case law afterward, maybe, though. That's why Christopher was so ideal."

"What about Noah? You guys can talk law pretty, uh, heatedly."

Wendy had ordered a bunch of Indian food and was halfway through her plate, but Gia hadn't started hers. She deflected the Noah question by saying, "How come you're not eating?" Or drinking either, now that she thought about it—Gia had opted for water, saying she was dehydrated from her flight.

Gia looked down at the plate and pursed her lips for a

moment before saying, "I'm not really hungry. I ate on the plane."

Wendy refrained from pointing out that no one ate on planes anymore and watched Gia scoop up a forkful of the stewy chicken and lift it to her mouth. But she ate it like ice cream, letting her mouth slide over the bite and lap up some of the sauce without actually fully transferring any actual food into her mouth.

"Gia, are you turning into a model with an eating disorder? Do we need to sit you down and have you watch some after-school specials?" Wendy was kidding. Kind of. Because now that she thought about it, Gia hadn't eaten much in Vegas either.

Gia laughed. "Oh my God, no." Then she took a regular-size bite of the curry. "Anyway, as for the Europe portion of the trip, don't stress if Milan doesn't make the cut."

"Oh, Milan is making the cut." Wendy was ridiculously excited about hanging with Gia in Milan, actually. "I'm pairing it with Vienna, so if you want to come with me there, too, you're totally welcome. A week in Milan, then a week in Vienna."

"Awesome. I don't have all my bookings yet, but if you come in that week we talked about, at most I'll have one or two more days of work before I'm free."

"Done." Wendy made a note in her calendar.

"But back to *Noah*," Gia said.

Dammit. Wendy thought she'd deflected sufficiently that Noah had been forgotten. Forgotten by Gia. Wendy, of course, wasn't capable of forgetting Noah for even a day. She'd meant everything she'd said at lunch. She was sorry she'd spent so long being angry at him. She was glad to have him as a friend. But...God, she wanted him. When he'd appeared in Mary's hospital room, she'd been so *happy*.

She *loved* him. The thought was still as astonishing as it had been the night she first had it in Vegas. Even more astonishing? The follow-up question she'd been pondering. If she'd been in love with Noah when she was a kid, and if she was in love with Noah now, did that mean she'd been in love with Noah for *seventeen years*?

She couldn't just turn that off.

Yet. But she'd have to learn to. Because she couldn't just go through life *feeling* all this shit about someone who could never love her back.

"Hello? Earth to Wendy."

Crap. She also couldn't tell Gia any of this. "Sorry, I spaced out for a minute there."

"Were you thinking about *Noah*?" Gia teased.

The buzzer signifying a visitor went off. Yes! Saved by the buzzer! Wendy hopped to answer it. "Yes?"

"It's Noah."

Well, shit. She wasn't going to catch a break, was she? She sighed. "Come on up."

"Wendy and Noah, sitting in a tree ..." Gia sang.

"What are you?" Wendy rolled her eyes. "Twelve?"

"K-I-S-S-I-N-G," Gia finished, then stuck her tongue out at Wendy.

"I rest my case. I told you, it was just a weird Vegas thing." A weird fake New-York-in-Vegas thing, actually, but Gia didn't need to know about that.

"Hey," he said when she opened her door to let him in. "You left your pie at the diner." He handed her a box.

"Ahhh!" Wendy brought the box over to the island she and Gia had been seated at and popped the top open. "This is a whole pie, though!" She turned to Gia. "I'd just ordered two slices."

Noah followed her. "Well, I'm told there is a model in

town with some serious lemon meringue love." He winked at Gia. "Hi, Gia."

"Hi, *Noah*." Gia stressed his name as she got up and retrieved three plates from Wendy's cupboard. "And this way, you can have a piece, too, you clever boy." Then she said, "Oh, crap. I have to run out. I have a spread in the new *Vogue*, and I promised my agent I'd buy a bunch of copies for tear sheets for my portfolio. I totally forgot."

"But…" Wendy had been about to call bullshit. There was no way Gia had a spread in *Vogue*. A spread in *Vogue* was huge. Wendy would know if Gia had a spread in *Vogue*. Wouldn't she?

Well, shit. She wasn't exactly winning any friend of the year awards lately. Maybe she *wouldn't* know. She certainly hadn't asked Gia anything about her career lately. "But why can't your agent get his own—"

"I'll just run to the corner!" Gia trilled. "Back soon." She grabbed her phone from the counter. "Soon-*ish*."

"But—"

It was no use. Gia was out the door, leaving Wendy face-to-face with Noah Denning and a lemon meringue pie.

Noah settled himself at Wendy's kitchen island. "How'd the afternoon go for Mary?"

"Really well." Wendy rummaged in the cutlery drawer. "They're talking about moving her to a rehab place next week. She knew Gia was coming to town today, so she chased me off for the evening."

"That's good." Wendy could use a little down time. God, what a couple of weeks she'd had, with their battling Vegas parties and her aunt's accident. Not to mention…well, him.

He was torn between an urge to laugh and a powerful impulse to do something stupid, like hug her.

"Pie?" Wendy got out a knife. "And/or curry? I also have Guinness." She wrinkled her nose. "Lemon pie, curry, and Guinness. Three delicious things that are, together, an abomination."

"Mmm. Lemon meringue pie and Guinness. I don't know. I'm kind of feeling it."

She slid the knife and plates over to him. "You slice, and I'll get the beer."

She did, and then she started cleaning up dinner, moving around the small kitchen and putting things to rights. She paused at one point, frowning at a plate full of some kind of curry before scraping it back into a takeout box. Then she stepped up onto a footstool to put something back in a cupboard. His first impulse was to get up and help her, but he squashed it. She wouldn't want his help. And this way, he could check out her butt. Just because there was going to be nothing more between them didn't mean he couldn't admire her from afar.

She was wearing a pair of leggings and a Toronto Blue Jays T-shirt. Her feet were bare, and her hair was pulled back into a messy bun on the top of her head. He realized that, running aside, he hadn't seen her in anything so casual since they were teenagers. Even when they'd been in New York, or at the photo shoot in Jane's yard, Wendy's "casual" look had been polished, pulled together. And of course, there had been the going-out looks in Vegas, featuring the infamous collarbone-concealing dresses.

She did casual well, too, not that he was surprised. He shifted on his seat. "I'm sorry I ruined your dress."

She stepped off the stool and turned to face him. "What?"

"Your dress. That white dress. In Vegas." She reddened

as she realized what he was talking about. "I seem to be two-for-two on ruining your clothes. If you want to give it to me, I'll take it to my guy at home and mail it back."

"We're not talking about that," she said, her color still high. "*Remember?*"

"Ah, yes." He used the side of his fork to cut a bite of pie. "What happens in fake New York stays in fake New York. It's just that—"

"Noah, what part of 'I don't want to talk about it' do you not understand?"

"Look, we slept together," he said, persisting for some reason he couldn't quite name. "It's a little weird."

"It's *a lot* weird. And the only way to make it *not* weird is to *stop talking about it*."

Right. He would stop pushing. He wasn't that much of a dick. "You know what's a good way to not talk?" He surveyed the apartment, which was immaculately ordered and impeccably decorated in a sort of modern style that managed to be spare but not cold. He did not see a TV.

"What?"

He glanced meaningfully at her chest. Well, not at her chest, but at her T-shirt. Could he help it if looking at her T-shirt also required him to look at her chest? "Jays versus Orioles, seven o'clock on TSN."

"And bookish Jane doesn't have cable." She did the Wendy cackle thing, and for some reason, it triggered a pooling of warmth in his chest.

"It appears neither do you." He let his gaze pass over the living room again, looking for a cabinet or something that might be used to obscure a television. "Unless you're hiding a giant man-cave down that hall?" he asked hopefully.

"I am not hiding a giant man-cave. But I do have a tiny den with a big-ass TV in it."

"I knew you wouldn't let me down, Wendy Lou Who."

She rolled her eyes, picked up both beers, and set off down the hallway. "Bring the pie."

A minute later, they were ensconced on a piece of furniture that was larger than a chair but smaller than a loveseat. It was like a chair on steroids. She hadn't been kidding; the room was tiny. There was just enough room for the monster chair, the TV, and a rickety rocking chair in one corner.

The mega-chair had a matching mega-ottoman. Wendy took a stack of books off it and extended her legs out, recliner-style. He followed suit and sighed in contentment as she flipped to the game.

"Yes!" she said, taking stock of the score—they were at the top of the second inning, and the Jays were up 1–0.

Noah was indifferent about the outcome of the game. Despite Toronto being his hometown, he wasn't a Jays fan— he hadn't gotten into baseball until after he'd moved away, and this game wouldn't have any bearing on the fate of his Yankees. But damn, he *was* a fan of watching Wendy be a Jays fan. She was knowledgeable about the game and the politics of the league, and she was *into it*, punching her fist into the air in excitement and hanging her head in dismay depending on what was happening. It was kind of like watching the game with a guy.

Except not. Because when he watched a game with Bennett, he generally wasn't painfully aware of every inch of his own body. His skin didn't feel prickly when Bennett was nearby. His mind didn't keep slipping away from the game and back to a hotel room in Vegas a week ago.

"Be right back!" She popped up as if she could hear his dirty thoughts and disappeared down the hall. When she came back, she was holding two fresh beers and had a quilt tucked under her arm. "Hold these." She handed him the

beers and arranged the quilt over her legs. "I'm freezing."
She took one of the beers back with one hand and held up
the edge of the quilt with the other. "Want some?"

"Sure." He scooted toward her. In their wrangling to balance the beers and arrange the quilt, his hand brushed the
top of her foot. "Holy shit, you weren't kidding. Is this a
foot or an icicle?"

She laughed. "The AC in this building is intense. There
usually isn't any intermediary state between boiling and
freezing."

He'd only grazed her foot. It had been an accident. He
should have pulled away. When a woman told you she
wanted to forget her sexual past with you, the correct response to incidental contact with her was to pull away.

He clasped his hand fully around her foot. When she
didn't react negatively, he squeezed it. She moaned a little,
and it went straight to his dick.

"I should get socks," she said, but she didn't move.

So he set his beer down on the side table and grabbed her
other leg. Put one hand on each foot. They were both cold
to the touch. He wanted, suddenly, more than he could remember ever having wanted anything, to hear another one
of those low moans. So he squeezed again, both feet this
time. Her shoulders physically lowered as she closed her
eyes. But no moan. Then an uptick of sound from the TV
drew her attention. A Blue Jay had hit a triple with one runner on base. He squeezed again, harder this time.

"Uhhhh."

There it was.

"Jays up and a human foot-warmer." She sighed. "Is this
heaven?"

He tucked the one foot under his thigh to keep it warming
and wrapped both hands around the other and began mas-

saging, his chest heavy with...something he couldn't explain.

It wasn't a sexual thing, not exactly.

But there was something so profoundly companionable about warming Wendy's feet while they watched baseball.

"Hey! Are you watching the..."

It was Gia. They hadn't heard her come in.

But they'd both heard her trail off awkwardly.

Wendy yanked her feet from Noah's grasp and bolted to an upright seated position.

He'd totally forgotten about Gia, as, apparently, had Wendy.

"Baseball!" Wendy said, too loudly. "We're watching the baseball game." She slid as far away from him as it was possible to get. "Want to join us?"

"Nope." Gia grinned. "I'm going to bed with a piece of pie."

Chapter Nineteen

FIVE DAYS BEFORE THE WEDDING

*I*t turned out that the closer they got to the wedding, the less "low-key" things became. For example: the last-minute fitting for new dresses for the bridesmaids.

"I just think this is going to be so much better, because it's a nod to Cam's heritage." Jane tilted her head as she took in the sight of Wendy, Gia, and Elise, who were crammed into Jane's tiny kitchen trying on new dresses Jane had ordered. Jane hadn't been able to find actual tartan dresses that would arrive soon enough—thank God—but she'd ordered plain navy sheaths and was having tartan sashes made. Nobody pointed out that Cameron's Scottish-named father—himself a third-generation Canadian—had never been involved in his kid's life, so functionally speaking, Jane's husband-to-be wasn't any more Scottish than the rest of them.

"Totally." Gia tugged at the hem of her dress. The dresses were meant to fall to mid-thigh, but the glama-zon's barely covered her butt. Wendy's, of course, came to her knees. "We're gonna need some alterations, though."

Though Wendy would have preferred sticking with the little black dresses Jane had originally planned on, these weren't bad. Much better than the purple things Elise had insisted on for her wedding. And the girls with their plaid sashes had it *way* better than the guys, who had been moved from suits to kilts.

Wendy had not been able to stop thinking about Noah in a kilt since Jane had proclaimed the switch.

"Alterations will be no problem," Jane said. "The tailor who's making the sashes will do them rush. Can you all meet me there tomorrow at ten? Then we can try them on with the sashes, too. I know that's kind of awkward timing, but it was the first opening she had."

Wendy made a mental note to call her assistant and get her to move things around. She'd kept her schedule as light as possible this week anyway. Between her aunt and the "low-key" bride, she'd assumed she'd be in demand outside the office.

"Hey, look at all the pretty ladies."

Well, damn. It was Noah, emerging from Jane's office, which doubled as the guest room. He wasn't in a kilt, but he *was* wearing plaid, in the form of pajama bottoms. But perhaps more notable was what he was not wearing: a shirt. He was all sleep-disheveled, running his hands through his hair, which stuck up at odd angles, and yawning. It struck Wendy that although she'd slept with him twice, she'd never actually *slept* with him, so she'd never seen him first thing in the morning.

It turned out he was just straight-up delicious first thing in the morning.

Gia performed an exaggerated wolf-whistle.

Elise laughed and said, "Maybe you should have the groomsmen wear the kilts on bottom and nothing on the top, Jane. Like the cover of a romance novel."

Jane rolled her eyes. "Go put on a shirt, Noah."

He obeyed his sister, but not before spearing Wendy with an intense look. Was he waiting for her to weigh in on his appearance like the others had? Because that was not going to happen, even if she had been able to pick up her jaw enough to muster a coherent sentence.

Slipping back into the office and reappearing a moment later pulling a T-shirt over his head, he said, "Mighty early for a dress fitting, isn't it?"

"The new dresses came in last night, and we needed to make sure they were going to work," Jane said. "And Wendy and Elise have to work today."

"Sorry if we woke you up," Elise said.

"S'okay. I'm headed out for a run anyway." He yawned again as he walked over to the coffeepot.

Wendy couldn't look away from his mouth. It was surreal to think about how that mouth had been all over her body, and pretty recently, too. It had whispered dirty nothings into her ears, and it had traveled down and tortured her clit.

Damn.

"Wendy, you gotta go." It was Jane, grabbing her arm and shaking her out of her lust-fueled daze. "You have a meeting at nine, right? That's why we're all here so early."

"Right." God, she had to stop mooning over Noah.

"Who's going to the subway?" While Wendy was busy fantasizing about Noah's mouth, he had laced on running shoes. "I'll walk you that far."

"I have my car," Elise said. "I'm dropping Gia at the gym. We can swing by your office, too, Wendy."

"That's okay," Wendy said quickly. Too quickly, apparently, because Gia shot her a look. "It's out of your way." Which was true, but also not something Wendy would normally have concerned herself with if an alternative to the overcrowded rush-hour subway presented itself.

"All right, Wendy Lou Who, let's go," Noah said.

She moved toward the door but turned back when Jane cleared her throat. Oh, right. She kissed her fingertips and blew the kiss to Jane, who caught it and pressed it to her chest, but Jane laughed as she did so. "I'm not sure a too-big bridesmaid dress is really the right look for the Monday morning meeting with the partners."

It was true. The weekly nine a.m. meeting of the firm's partners and senior associates was the one thing on Wendy's calendar this week that was immovable, and it had been the reason their dress fitting session took place so early.

Noah smiled. "Go change. I'll wait for you."

She sighed. Noah Denning was turning her brain to mush.

Chapter Twenty

*N*oah was feeling his mid-thirties. He'd always been a runner, from when he was a kid on the cross country team. Even in the hard years after his dad died, he'd managed to find one or two opportunities a month to go running with Wendy. But he no longer ran as long or as often as he used to. A knee injury he'd shrugged off in his youth dogged him more and more the older he got, and he always regretted it if he didn't get enough rest between long runs. He'd taken up weight lifting to compensate, because vanity required him to look decent in his court suits.

All of which was to say that there was no reasonable explanation why, on the Thursday before the wedding, he was setting off on his fourth run in four days, this one—God help him—a twelve-mile one. He would pay for this tomorrow. He'd probably have to limp down the aisle come Saturday.

"Keep up, old man!"

Actually, there was an explanation, just not a *reasonable*

one. Her name was Wendy, and she was bouncing along ahead of him at a punishing clip along a trail that wound through one of the city's ravines.

While walking her to the subway after the dress fittings at Jane's, on his way to go running, the talk had turned to *her* favorite routes. Which had led to him suggesting a joint run the next day. Hey, he'd said, they couldn't sleep together anymore, but there was no law against running together was there? They'd had fun doing just that last time he'd been in town. She had done the Wendy cackle and agreed.

So they'd run eight miles the next day.

And then five yesterday—what Wendy called a "light" day.

Which had led to him suggesting another one today. Of course, he'd been thinking more like two miles for today—light days were more his wheelhouse—but no, Wendy's regime called for twelve. So here he was.

He'd lost his mind, basically.

But it was a nice way to go, with a view of her ponytail bobbing ahead of him as she began the climb out of the ravine, her lean legs, exposed by a pair of hot pink shorts, pumping twice as hard as his longer ones.

He wasn't sure he could blame the fact that he was way more out of breath than she was solely on his advanced age.

"Only one more mile once we get back to street level," she announced as they turned onto a sidewalk that would take them out of the ravine onto a regular city street. She slowed down, looked over her shoulder at him, and said, "Race you to the top!"

And she was off, blazing up the hill.

There was no way he could catch her. He didn't *want* to catch her, really. He was quite happy chugging along behind her, enjoying the view. In fact, he realized with a start, he was quite happy generally.

Which was kind of unprecedented.

It wasn't that he was *unhappy* generally, but this expansiveness in his chest, this overwhelming feeling of contentment? This was new. It was like a runner's high, but more.

Surely it had to do with Jane. She was getting married to the love of her life, and that shit was contagious.

But that didn't feel like enough of a reason.

Wendy was getting farther and farther away as she powered up the hill. Well, she was just going to have to wait. He was done. He slowed to a walk.

But then someone else appeared up there with her. A guy—a young one dressed in a baggy T-shirt and jeans about seventeen sizes too big. He took a step toward Wendy. Wendy took a compensating step back. The guy said something—Noah was too far away to hear. Wendy gave him the finger and started jogging away.

The guy followed.

Fuck that.

Suddenly Noah found his inner sprinter. He tore up the hill and caught up with them. Wendy was jogging on the sidewalk, and the kid was coasting alongside her on a skateboard.

"What's going on?" he asked gruffly, putting himself between the two of them. Wendy stopped, and Noah rested a hand on her back.

"What's going on is this gentleman would like me to suck his dick. I would like him to fuck right off. So we're at a bit of an impasse."

I'm going to hurt him.

The thought was equal parts surprising and violent. Noah

worked in the justice system. He *believed* in the justice system. He didn't do vigilante shit.

Nevertheless, he lunged for the guy.

"Noah!" Wendy called.

"Okay, okay, I'm fucking right off," the dude said, skating away before Noah could touch him.

"What the hell was that, Noah?" Wendy asked.

"What?"

"That caveman shit. I thought for a minute there you were actually going to hit him."

"I was," Noah said, still kind of amazed at himself. This possessive, angry stuff wasn't him—normally.

"Dude, that was just your garden variety street harassment. It sucks, but it happens all the time. I had it under control."

Holy fuck, suddenly he *did* know what was happening. Why he had gone so uncharacteristically alpha-dog just now. Why he'd been so inexplicably happy just before that. Why everything about Wendy lately had been so *confusing*. The mystery suddenly snapped into focus inside his head, and the force of his conclusion nearly knocked him off his feet.

He was in love with Wendy.

He laughed out loud. It was suddenly so fucking obvious. Their ever-present banter. His next-level protectiveness when it came to her. His obsession with her *collarbones*, for fuck's sake.

And *this* was what had been missing in all his other relationships. Why he could never pull the trigger and propose, or move in with a woman. They weren't Wendy.

Holy shit. *He was in love with Wendy.*

What's more, he was pretty sure he had always been in love with Wendy.

Which, paradoxically, was maybe the reason he hadn't

realized it? He was always telling himself that Wendy was like another sister to him, but that wasn't really true. It hadn't been true back then, either. Yes, he'd felt protective of her, but...in a different way than he'd felt protective of Jane.

And *that's* why he had been so strangely disappointed when he'd agreed to the extra shift that night of the prom. He had lost so many things when his father died—his carefree childhood, his extracurriculars, his running, his social life.

But had he also lost the possibility of something with Wendy? Of that fondness he'd always felt for her blossoming into something more?

His skin started to prickle all over.

She was looking at him funny, her hands on her hips.

Well, shit. He had no idea what to do about this revelation. She didn't want to be with him, not in any way that meant anything. And even if she did, they didn't live in the same place. She was about to flit off on her trip.

So he did the only thing he could do in that moment, which was to start running again. She fell into place beside him. Turned to him and smiled as they settled into a leisurely pace. He smiled back. Even though he had no fucking idea what to do, even though his little come-to-Jesus moment had pretty much exploded his head, he was still happy. Stupidly, feeblemindedly happy just to be with her.

As they did their final mile, everything looked different to him. The sky was extra blue. Graffiti on the side of a building extra interesting. A busker playing a violin extra talented.

Jesus Christ. He almost felt like bursting into song. Was this what being in love was like—being in a musical?

"That's it." Looking at her sports watch, Wendy slowed

to a walk. She pressed some buttons and said, "Not my best time."

"Eh, I was slowing you down."

"True." She smirked up at him. "I'm going to walk from here and get a giant-ass sandwich for dinner on my way home. So I'll see you tomorrow? Or you want to take a rest day?"

"I'll walk you home," he said automatically.

Her eyes rolled skyward. "Noah. You left for college seventeen years ago. That means I've spent almost two decades walking places by myself."

He couldn't argue with her logic, but he also couldn't argue with his, which was that as long as he was around, there was no need for her to walk anywhere alone. That was true regardless of his feelings about her. But really, he wasn't ready to say good-bye yet. He wanted to keep testing out these startling new feelings. See if being with her might *actually* make him burst into song. So he said, "Maybe I want a giant-ass sandwich, too. I'm so hungry, I could gnaw my own leg off."

It was true, suddenly, and it got more true as she told him about the Italian sandwich shop she frequented. "I'm telling you, you have never had a better veal parm."

Her hair was a mess—more of it had come out of her ponytail during their aggressive run than had stayed in—and her skin was pink and sweaty.

"Oh my God, the mozzarella is so fresh, and they tear up these monster basil leaves and layer them in."

She was smiling and gesturing dramatically as she described the sandwich. Inexplicably, despite the post-run dishevelment, she looked as beautiful as she had in Vegas, in those killer dresses.

"What?" she said.

Shit. He'd been spaced out there, thinking about her messy yet gorgeous hair. "I'm sorry. What?"

"You're looking at me really funny."

"I am? I guess I must be, uh, fantasizing about that veal parm."

She shook her head. "Weirdo."

He caught sight of a sign on a restaurant they were coming up on. It was not her Italian place. But for a second it sort of seemed like it wasn't an accident, that they were about to pass a restaurant with that particular name.

Did he dare?

If she agreed, it would only complicate things unnecessarily. Make life harder in the long run. Because he had no plan. It wasn't like he could *do* anything with his newfound revelation. Wendy was never going to love him back. If he'd ever had a chance with her, it had come and gone seventeen years ago. Grown-up Wendy didn't do relationships. She'd told him that outright.

But anyway, she would almost certainly not say yes. Aside from his own secret...yearnings (Jesus Christ, he had *secret yearnings*), there were a million reasons why what he was about to suggest was a terrible idea, and Wendy would no doubt spend the rest of the walk to her preferred restaurant enumerating them. She would shoot him down, and that would be that. She would be *right*. And he would go back to Jane's and take the world's longest Epsom salts bath. Right after he took the world's coldest shower.

So better to just leave it alone.

Which was why it made no sense that he stopped in front of his target and said, "Or we could go here."

She looked up and read the sign. "New Yorker Deli. I've never eaten here. I think it's pretty much your basic knock-off of a New York..."

He watched comprehension kick in. She opened her mouth all the way, like she was stretching her jaw, then closed it and pulled her bottom lip under her top teeth, scraping it in a way that made him want to replace her teeth with his.

"Jane doesn't have to know," he said, as if that was the only, or even the primary, reason why what he was suggesting was a Very Bad Idea.

"I don't think this is wise." She was, of course, correct. He was about to agree, but she kept talking. "What are we going to do, go in there, order a lox bagel, and then get it on in the bathroom?"

The litigator in him saw an opening—she was wavering. The decent man in him didn't take it. "You're right. Anyway, veal parm sounds much better than lox on a bagel. I don't know what came over me."

He did know, though. *You. You came over me.*

Her eyes darted around, like she had been expecting a fight and didn't quite trust the notion that he wasn't going to press her.

He smiled and took her hand. Which was a stupid, pointless thing to do. It wasn't going to get him into her pants— or her hot pink shorts. It wasn't going to alleviate any of those goddamned secret yearnings. It had nothing to do with his mission to see her home safely. It didn't *achieve* anything.

It just felt good.

Damn, it felt good.

Even with all the uncertainty between them, all the *impossibility*, there was something amazing about the simple act of walking down the street on a summer evening when the sun was just beginning to set, holding hands with a pretty girl who could run circles around you.

To his great surprise, she didn't pull away. Maybe she felt it, too.

And eff him if he didn't then start swinging her hand, like they *were* in a goddamn musical.

They were halfway down the block when she stopped. "Or..." She did the lip-scraping thing again. "We could get takeout." When he didn't answer right away—he was trying to gauge if she meant what he thought she did—she added, "From the New York place. We could get food there, bring it to my place, and it would be kind of like..."

"It would be kind of like a little bit of New York in your apartment." He spun them around and towed her back up the street faster than was probably seemly. He was going to hell, but he didn't care. He pulled a couple of twenties out of the pocket in his running shorts and handed them to her. "I'll have what you're having—and I'll get us a taxi."

⁓

A person had to have pretty well-developed denial skills to justify what was about to happen, Wendy thought as they rode the elevator up to her condo in silence.

Which, apparently, she did.

It was just that when the opportunity to sleep with Noah one more time presented itself, she could not walk away. Even though she knew it wouldn't be good for her heart. He was just so delicious, sweaty from the run and worked up from that charged confrontation with that skateboarder.

So certain other parts had told her brain to take a hike. Noah had the bag from the New Yorker Deli in one of his hands. In his other, he held one of hers. After she'd come out of the restaurant with a couple of grilled Reubens and a tub of potato salad, he had a taxi waiting. They could have walked—her place wasn't that much farther—but there seemed to be an unspoken haste to the proceedings, like they needed to rush before their suspended disbelief on the whole New York illusion came crashing down. Or her brain got back from its hike.

The most astonishing thing was, after they got out of the cab, he took her hand again. Earlier, she could maybe chalk up the hand holding to an odd runner's high. Their run had been such fun, and the evening so lovely, it had felt natural to let him grab her hand. Well, not natural—this was still *Noah*, after all—but somehow an organic extension of the evening.

But now? There was no reason to hold hands. They'd basically just negotiated the fact that they were going to have casual sex again, which was about as far from hand-holding, aw-shucks romance as you could get.

But there it was, his big, warm, stupid hand engulfing hers as soon as she slid out of the taxi. Like they were a normal couple arriving home with takeout.

And, *holy shit*, now he was lifting their entwined hands to his mouth so he could kiss her wrist without letting go of her hand.

What the *hell*? Even though she could admit to herself that her emotions were hopelessly tangled up in what was about to happen, she needed *him* to keep things compartmentalized. It was too confusing otherwise. Too potentially heartbreaking.

The elevator dinged for her floor. She moved to exit, pulling against his grip in a "drop my hand" sort of way, but he didn't let go. He didn't even seem to notice. They reached her door. Okay, this was the moment. She needed both her hands to unzip the hidden pocket in her running shorts and extract her key. So she tugged on her trapped hand, eyebrows raised.

He *still* didn't let go, just gazed at her with his eyes twinkling, like he was thinking about a secret joke. She managed, awkwardly, to get the door open one-handed and lead him inside.

"You want to eat..." How could she put this delicately? Well, there really wasn't a way, so screw delicacy. "You want to eat first?"

"I do not." Still holding her hand, he used it to pull her against his chest. "You don't like holding hands, do you?"

She ignored the question as she tried to squirm out of his grasp, though she wasn't sure why, as that was counter-intuitive to the spirit of this encounter. She succeeded only in twisting in his arms, so she was facing away from him, her back to his front. "What happened to gnawing your own leg off?" She gave an ineffectual yank, which only caused him to band his free arm around her torso.

"I find I'd rather gnaw something else." He lowered his head to the back of her neck and lightly scraped his teeth against her skin.

Goosebumps rose, quick and sure, over her entire body, and she shuddered. He must have been distracted by her re-action because she managed to wrench herself out of his grasp. She turned, facing him with her hands in front of her face like they were opponents sparring in a boxing ring.

"No," she said, seized with the inexplicable desire to be contrary just for the sake of it, like she needed to disavow the obvious signs of pleasure he could no doubt read on her body. "To answer your previous question, I don't like hold-ing hands."

"What's wrong with holding hands?"

"It's not called for in this context."

He let loose a big guffaw as he took a step closer. "In this *context*? What, pray tell, is this context?"

He was coming closer, so she moved back to compensate. "Well, you know…" God, did she have to spell it out? If they had to invent elaborate rules about only having sex in New York, the whole point of that sex was that it wasn't *relationship* sex. It wasn't *hand-holding* sex.

He was trying not to laugh, and not really succeeding, judging by the snort that escaped. Fine. She *would* spell it out for him. Maybe that would sober him up. "Meaningless fucking—you know, your favorite phrase? That thing you don't like to do? That is the context."

He nodded, his face a parody of seriousness as he kept advancing on her. "Ah. I see. So hand holding in the context of meaningless fucking offends your sense of order."

That was exactly right. But she wasn't going to give him the satisfaction of agreeing so easily. Also, it *was* kind of funny when stated like that. She pressed her lips together. If she wasn't going to agree with him, she *certainly* wasn't going to laugh.

Grinning, he lunged for her. She was still holding her hands out as if to ward him off, but he moved so fast, he managed to grab them and lace his fingers through hers.

"Ooh, I got you now! Double hand hold!"

She struggled laughingly, but in truth his hands had some kind of magic power. He might as well have grabbed her boobs, or gone straight for the prize, because she'd gone tight and achy all over.

"Oh no!" he taunted. "Are you not going to have meaningless sex with me now that I'm holding both your hands?" He propelled her down the hall as he spoke, him walking forward and her walking backward.

"Shut up," she said, no longer trying to hide the fact that she was cracking up.

"Ooh. *Shut up.* What a profound and articulate argument!

You must be a really good lawyer. I bet 'shut up' wows them in court."

In keeping with the whole "profound and articulate" thing, Wendy stuck out her tongue at him.

"Hold your horses." Just as they were about to pass her bathroom, he stopped, pivoted, and steered her inside. When he let go of one of her hands to flip on the shower, it was more of a disappointment than it should have been. "It's entirely possible that you, after running twelve miles at breakneck pace, smell like rainbows and lollipops. I, however, do not."

She stood on her tiptoes and planted her nose as high as she could reach on his body, which was just above his sternum. He smelled like sweaty Christmas trees. She didn't hate it. But... "Point taken." She tugged her other hand out of his grasp—finally!—and pulled off her tank top. The bra was more of a problem. Removing a sports bra was not a dignified maneuver at the best of times. And now, with an audience? And with nipples that had grown almost painfully hard because of his proximity? She turned her back to him, crossed her arms over her chest, grabbed the hem on both sides, and started wrestling with the damned thing.

"I think you need to work on your striptease skills."

His voice was so deadpan, she couldn't help letting loose a peal of laughter. "Hey! Have *you* ever tried to take off a sweaty sports bra?"

It was weird, all this laughing and bantering. Their previous encounters had been dead serious. Dead sexy, but also dead serious. She wouldn't have thought that Noah did silly. More than that, she wouldn't have thought that silly could go so well with sexy.

"There's a first time for everything." He batted her hands out of the way and started to work the fabric up her torso.

The bra had not been designed to lure him. It was made out of one of those wicking fabrics, and it was damp with sweat. How mundane. How *not* sexy.

And yet.

There was something exquisitely intimate about what he was doing.

"Lift your arms." His voice was lower than before, having shed its teasing tone, and oh, *that voice*.

She obeyed, and he worked the bra up over her arms and off. His hands made their way back to the sides of her torso, rubbing the indentations he found there, soothing them with a warm, firm touch.

She sighed, a big, relieved one that was out before she could control it. It was just that it felt so *good*. It shouldn't be possible to store tension in the sides of your torso.

And yet.

His palms still resting on her sides, just under her breasts, he swung his fingers up and pressed them into the muscles under her shoulder blades where she *definitely* stored tension.

She hissed out a breath that was part pain, part relief.

"Damn, Wendy," he rasped, his hands moving up to massage the tough ridges that connected her shoulders to her neck. "I think you need to work on your relaxation skills, too. These are like bricks."

She tried to think of a witty rejoinder, but in addition to softening the tissue of her shoulders, the steady pressure of his strong hands had softened her brain.

So she just stood there and let him soften her.

"Get in," he said after a minute, dropping his hands from her shoulders and tapping her on the butt. "Take off your shorts and get in the shower, and there's more where that came from."

A part of her wanted to not obey, just on the principle of the thing. To sass him. Because that's what they did. She was comfortable with a perpetual state of semi-confrontation. Not so much with easy acquiescence.

And yet.

She took off her shorts and got in the shower.

Chapter Twenty-One

·

ot *damn.*

Noah needed a moment to collect himself, so he paused outside the shower after stripping. His chest was strangely heavy, which was odd, considering that he'd spent much of the past few minutes either trying not to laugh or failing at trying not to laugh.

She was right. Their situation did not call for hand holding. Or shoulder massages. Or flirtatious joking.

But he couldn't help himself. She was so easy to rile.

And, simultaneously, so in need of comfort.

And so impossibly sexy.

Also there was the part where he was in love with her.

It was a confusing combination. Too many physical and emotional responses were roiling through his body at the same time, some of them contradictory, all of them powerful.

"Hello?"

Her voice jolted him.

"Am I doing this by myself? Because if so, I'll just get a move on washing my hair."

Instead of answering, he stepped into the shower. She turned, drenched, her hair a black curtain plastered to her head. Her gaze flickered down his body, then back up. She smiled.

"Where's the shampoo?" He looked around but did not see any bottles.

"Oh, I use a shampoo bar."

"A shampoo what?"

She picked up what looked like a regular bar of soap. "Shampoo in solid format. Lasts longer, contains less toxic junk." She rubbed the bar between her hands, then brought the resulting lather and the bar itself up to her head and started rubbing.

"Hey, now, that's my job." He took the bar from her and—ah! He knew this bar. It was round and red and chunky. He brought it to his nose, inhaled, and laughed. The cinnamon mystery object decoded at last!

She furrowed her brow. "What's so funny?"

"Nothing. I like this smell."

The brow unfurrowed. It was like watching her usual expression in reverse. "I know! It's the perfect not-too-girly scent. It's kind of cranberry-ish, kind of spicy-ish."

"Kind of Wendy-ish."

The furrow came back. He ignored it, put his hands on her shoulders to spin her around, and mimicked her movements with the bar, creating a good lather on her head before setting it on the shower caddy.

She was so . . . wary. He'd seen flashes of vulnerability in her in recent days, but they'd just been little hints, papered over before he could fully take them in. Had she always been like this? He thought not, but he was questioning now how much he had really seen back when they were kids. Both Wendy and Jane had dropped bombs on him in Vegas, and he was still struggling to reconcile what they'd said with the women they'd become.

He dragged the pads of his fingers across her scalp, and she moaned like she had before when he was rubbing her shoulders.

"You and Jane had that Dead Dads Club, remember? You'd say it like it was a joke, but I think I'm correct in believing that it actually brought you both comfort?"

She tried to turn her body to face him—that *had* been a non sequitur, he supposed—but he brought his hands back down to her shoulders to show her he wanted her to stay in place. He needed the answer to the question, but he wasn't sure he could bear it if she was looking at him with her skeptical litigator face while she spoke.

"We did." Her tone was tinged with suspicion. "And you're not wrong. Jane was the only one who really got how much my dad's death affected me."

"How did it affect you?" He'd missed everything that his sister had been going through back then, so he almost certainly had no idea what Wendy's deal was, either.

There was a long silence, and he thought she wasn't going to answer. If she didn't do holding hands, she probably wasn't about to spill her guts on long-buried grief, either. But then, to his surprise, she said, "It changed everything."

Realizing that he was standing there with his hands still in her hair, he resumed massaging her scalp. "What does that mean?" he asked softly.

Another long pause, then a sigh, a big one, like she was surrendering to something. "Well, I was nine. I still needed a dad."

He nodded, though she couldn't see it.

"But beyond that, it meant my mom had to be at the store all the time. We did okay, but the margins were low. She couldn't afford to pay someone to take over his shifts, and the store was open eight to eleven, seven days a week. When we moved closer to the store, the idea, in theory anyway, was that I could more easily hang out there, but my mom didn't really want me there. She was happy for me to just be at your house all the time." She paused and huffed a small laugh. "You know how some parents desperately want their kids to take over the family business? Mine did not. She wanted me to become a doctor or a lawyer, so she was always shooing me to your house to study. I know she did that because she loved me, and she wanted me to have a good life, but..."

"In a way, you lost both parents when your dad died." He moved his fingers from her scalp and lathered up the length of her hair. He didn't really know how to wash long hair—he'd never done this with a girlfriend before—but he wanted to prolong the activity as a way of keeping the conversation going.

"Yes." Her voice was almost inaudible over the noise of the falling water. "In a way."

And then she'd thought she was going to lose Jane. And her aunt. His throat tightened as he was flooded with emotion. Not pity. Wendy wasn't the kind of person who inspired pity. It was sympathy, yes, but it was leavened with a big dose of respect. Awe, even. At Wendy, and at Jane. The Dead Dads Club.

The Lost Girls.

The girls who'd had to harden themselves to survive.

"But you and Jane did, too," she said. She was right. Their mom had lost her mind after their dad's accident. The depression she'd retreated into had taken a decade to lift. She'd never worked outside the house, but after the accident, she'd barely *left* the house.

He cleared his throat to break up the chunk that had lodged there. "Jane told me that she blamed herself for our dad's death."

"I know she did," she said softly. "She told me that after all the drama at Elise's wedding."

"Did she tell you she changed everything about herself after that? That her whole life became about trying to be good, to keep her head down and never cause me any trouble? And that she stayed that way the rest of her life, kind of by default? Until she . . ."

"Met Cameron," Wendy finished, sadness in her voice. "No, she didn't tell me that, but I'm not surprised. She actually *became* the good girl she was trying so hard to impersonate." She was silent for such a long time that Noah thought she was done talking. He kept shampooing. But then she spoke again. "Things can happen that calcify you. Actually change the kind of person you are."

He paused, his fingers tangled in her hair. "Did that happen to you?"

She shrugged, and the movement of her shoulders drew his attention. He could probably not credibly continue with her hair anymore. He pushed it aside and started massaging her neck.

"How could it not?" she finally said.

Noah hated to think of Wendy as calcified. But that thought was pushed aside by a more astonishing one. Had that happened to *him*? Was that what Jane had been trying to tell him in Vegas?

"How come I wasn't in that club? The Dead Dads Club?" The question burst out of him before he could stop it.

She did turn then. He didn't try to stop her this time. She wrapped her arms around him, pressed her cheek against his chest, and squeezed. "You should have been."

And just like him with her earlier, she wasn't offering him pity, just a deep, empathetic solidarity.

Then she said it again, louder and with more feeling. "You totally should have been."

⁓

Wendy was a lobster being slowly boiled to death in a pot, the temperature rising so gradually she was oblivious to her impending demise. It was the only way to explain how she'd gone from proclaiming that hand holding didn't mix with meaningless fucking to hugging Noah in the shower after they'd spilled their guts about their goddamn childhood traumas.

It was also the only way she could explain why, after standing there in silence for a few minutes, letting the water rain down on them, she let him wash her body. He was tender and unhurried as he slicked her with soap. It wasn't sexual, but it wasn't not sexual, either, even though that made no sense. He gave each part of her the same degree of careful attention, letting his hands slide up her back and then down her front. He didn't stop at her breasts, but he didn't skim over them, either. Her nipples puckered in his hands as he kneaded, and she hitched a breath.

He covered every inch of her with soap, including the bottoms of her feet—he placed her arms on his back for balance as he crouched and patted her calves to get her to lift her feet one at a time. When he was done lathering her, he switched the water from the rain-style showerhead to the detachable one, and started rinsing her. The suggestiveness, the playfulness of earlier was gone, but there was something insanely erotic about being the object of such focused attention.

When he finished rinsing her body, he turned her again so she was facing away from him, pressed his hand lightly against her forehead to get her to tip her head back, and said, low and raspy, "Close your eyes."

She did, and he rinsed her hair, using his fingers to separate the strands as he moved the showerhead back and forth. When he was done, he put the nozzle back and changed the setting back to the rain head. Then he pushed her gently to the back of the shower and stepped under the spray. Quickly, with much less care than he'd shown her, he soaped his own body. He didn't switch the soap out for the shampoo bar, just continued on up to his head with the soap. She should probably offer to wash him, to swap roles. But there was something about watching him, about the difference between how attentive he had been with her and how careless he was being with himself, that was strangely, strongly compelling.

She had thought maybe they'd have sex in the shower. But no, he merely turned off the water when he was done and opened the curtain. She stepped out, grabbed her towel, and got one for him from under the vanity. They dried off in silence.

Then he led her to her bedroom and started making love to her.

There was no other way to describe it. Wendy valued linguistic precision, which was why she'd referred earlier to the "meaningless fucking" she had expected the evening to bring. It was probably also why her friends had labeled her a potty mouth. Maybe they were right, but she believed in calling things what they were.

Her previous couplings with Noah had been hot, athletic, even a little bit rough.

This was none of those things. No, that wasn't right—it was *one* of those things: hot.

As he laid her back on her bed, he started again with the slow worship of her body, but this time instead of a bar of soap, he used his mouth. And his hands. He used long, firm strokes, almost like he was still trying to give her a massage, running his hands up from her knees to her hips and back down again, while his mouth moved over her inner thighs.

"Oh my God," she breathed. She almost couldn't take it, this slow-burning torture.

"Mmm." She didn't know if he was agreeing or trying to soothe her.

She reached for his head, putting her hands in his hair, needing to anchor herself to something, but he shook them off, moving up her body and transferring his intensive ministrations to her breasts. He stroked, kneaded, kissed, licked, and sucked, and she just about lost her damned mind.

It went on and on. Her body was languid and limp as he spread slow, smoldering fire through her. Every time she mustered enough strength to try to touch him, he batted her away, sometimes shushing her in the process, though she hadn't said a word.

They were silent, in fact, aside from the moaning noises she was making—the noises she couldn't stop making as the torment ratcheted up and up and up.

When the noises turned more frustrated, he came farther up her body, covering her mouth with a kiss he seemed to mean to be soothing, but it only made things worse. Better. Both. His tongue swept against hers, with the same gentle but firm pressure he'd been using on her body, again and again.

She couldn't stand it anymore. The clichéd way to describe such an extreme degree of sexual arousal was to say she felt like she was ready to combust, to burst into flames. But it was more like an unraveling, like he was pulling her soul slowly out of her body. She wanted to ask him to fuck her. To *finally* fuck her. But the words seemed too strong for what was happening. Or not strong enough, she wasn't sure.

So she tried to say it another way, one that came less easy but felt more true. "Please." That got his attention. He lifted his head and looked at her with concern etched across his features. "Please, now? I can't wait anymore."

He closed his eyes, almost like continuing to look at her was too hard. But when he opened them, he smiled. They'd been doing a lot of smiling today. Smiling and laughing. But this was different. This was part relief, part surprise... and all gorgeous. It lit up his whole face.

She wrapped her legs around his waist, as she had done at some point every time they'd been intimate together. It was beginning to feel like that was where her legs belonged.

He exhaled a shaky breath, like he was surrendering a great burden, and took his cock in hand—God she loved the sight of that, of his strong hand holding his beautiful cock. Nudging her entrance with it, she lifted her hips off the bed to meet him.

"Oh!" she breathed when he finally, finally entered her, relishing the little burn as he slid past her body's initial resistance. He pressed down on her clit with a thumb as he did so, and she saw stars.

But then he stopped. Went totally still. Instinctively, she tightened her grip on him, with both arms and legs.

"Condom," he bit out. "We forgot a condom."

They couldn't stop. *She* couldn't stop. She shook her head violently and her hips bucked off the bed, knowing, in a way her brain did not, that she couldn't lose him. "It's okay," she whispered. "It's not the right time for anything to happen—my period is due any day now."

"Fuck," he bit out, the curse giving way to a groan as he slid back home.

She let out a shaky exhale, relief and lust swamping her at the same time.

He made love to her the way he had done everything that evening—slow and steady and relentlessly. He covered every part of her body with his. His impossibly deep kisses were a drug as he worked her breasts, enveloping them entirely with his hands. His hips ground into her slow and dirty, and at the end of every stroke, when he was buried in her seemingly as deep as he could go, he kept grinding, getting a little deeper. Because he was lying on top of her, every stroke put pressure on her mound, and she was close, so close.

On a groan, he stopped kissing her, pulled back, and looked into her eyes. He kept up with everything else—the lazy, torturous grind of his hips, the steady sweep of his hands on her breast, but he did it all while staring at her. He stared so intently it was like he was daring her to look away, like he was extending a thread between them, weaving a web to catch her in.

She felt her climax cresting all through her body, in her arms and belly, and between her legs, of course. "Oh," she gasped as she came and came and came. Still she stared at him, trying and failing to read what was in his face.

As if to thwart her efforts, suddenly his face contorted, like he was in terrible pain. "Wendy," he said quietly, with such heaviness in his voice he almost sounded sad. Then, with a groan that seemed obscenely loud given how hushed and almost reverential their lovemaking had been, he pulled out. He was already coming, and he spent on her stomach.

He was already coming. Meaning some of it was inside her.

Jesus freaking Christ, what was the *matter* with her?

Panic started to swirl through her body, almost as powerful as her orgasm had been.

Wendy had never understood people who got pregnant "by accident." Those failure rates associated with condoms? They didn't apply to her. Wendy used condoms correctly, and she used them religiously. She'd never been too caught up, too drunk, too *anything*, not to stop long enough for her partner to sheath himself. It was a first principle.

She could only tell herself that since her period was set to arrive tomorrow or the next day, she almost certainly wasn't ovulating. And she was clean, and she would bet the farm Noah was, too. So it was fine.

Probably.

But, honestly, she was disgusted with herself. The idea of being carried away by passion to such an extent that you *abandoned* a principle like that? It was—

"What was that?" Noah rolled off her, grabbed some tissues from the box on her bedside table, and started cleaning her up.

"What was what?" There was a *thunk* and, already on edge, she jumped. She knew that *thunk*. It was the sound of Gia dropping her enormous handbag on the counter in the kitchen.

Not only had Wendy not used a condom, she'd totally forgotten she had a houseguest.

"Oh my God." She banged her head on the headboard a few times. "We have to stop doing this." Rolling away from his ministrations, she scrambled out of bed. "Just once, I would like to have sex without Gia arriving immediately after the deed is done. Is that too much to ask?"

"Wendy? You home?" She heard the clack of Gia's high heels on the hardwood floor.

Apparently, it was.

She ran to the door, opened it a crack, and said, "I am! I'll be out in a minute."

She turned back to Noah. He was back to his joking ways, lounging naked in her bed and doing a poor job of suppressing laughter.

Well, okay. She could deal with jokey Noah better than serious, intense, *lovemaking* Noah.

She put her hands on her hips. "You're lucky I live on the twelfth floor, or I'd make you climb out the window."

"Eh." He stretched but otherwise made no move to get out of her bed. "It's only Gia. She's already on to us."

"You're not going to be so blasé when I come back with your gross sweaty running clothes and make you get dressed so you can leave."

───ᐟᐟ───

Short of keeping Noah locked in her bedroom indefinitely, there was no way to hide what had happened. So Wendy got dressed, retrieved Noah's clothes, and threw them into the bedroom, leaving him to his own devices while she went to face her fate.

"You go for a run?" Gia asked when Wendy, her hair still damp, appeared in the kitchen.

"Yep." Wendy braced herself.

"I should take up running." Gia was in the process of opening a bottle of wine. "Instead, I'm going to drink, because I just came from Jane's house."

Wendy heard the door to her bedroom open, and her face heated.

"Hmm. I was at Jane's house, and Jane's *brother* is at *your* house." Gia splashed some wine into a glass and whispered, "How *interesting*." Then she raised her voice and said, in a singsong tone, "Hi, Noah!"

"Hi, Gia." He was the picture of composed nonchalance, strolling through her living room in his running clothes like it was the most natural thing in the world.

Gia held up her bottle of Cabernet. "You want some wine?"

Noah opened his mouth, and Wendy was pretty sure he was about to accept, so she sent him a death glare. But, truthfully, part of her—some dangerous, unhinged part of her—wanted him to stay. Wanted to kick back and have a glass of wine with one of her best friends and her...what? *Her what?* That was the problem. He could never be what she wanted him to be.

"No, thanks," he said, clearly having got the message. "I, ah, should be going." He looked at her as if he wanted her to confirm that he'd spoken his line correctly.

She turned the volume up on the death glare.

He let himself out, giving her a stupid little salute before he disappeared.

Gia poured a comically large glass of wine and slid it across the kitchen island to Wendy, her eyebrows lodged high on her forehead.

Wendy took a long, undignified chug, then said, "So what's up with Jane that's driving you to drink?"

"What's up with Jane's *brother* that's driving *you* to drink?"

"We went running," she tried, even though she knew deflection was futile.

Gia gazed down the hallway. "In your bedroom?"

Wendy sighed. "Okay. I admit that Noah is turning out to be…a problem. But he's going home in a few days, and that will be that. Anyway, that"—she gestured back to her bedroom—"*was* that. Done. Finished. So please don't tell Jane." She hated asking that. She hated that she'd put herself in a position where she *had* to ask that. She and Jane didn't keep secrets from each other.

They hadn't, anyway, not historically. They did now, thanks to her.

Gia took a sip of her wine and regarded Wendy thoughtfully over the rim of her glass. "What if you could have whatever you wanted?"

Wendy blinked, taking a moment to adjust to the strange, vague question. She had been expecting the Inquisition. Or a guilt trip about going behind Jane's back. She deserved both. "Nobody can have whatever they want."

"Yeah, but what *if*? Humor me."

"Okay, um…I'd wave my wand and make my aunt immediately better—no rehab required—and I'd make partner at the firm."

"That's not what I'm talking about, and you know it."

Annoyance flared in Wendy's chest. That jet-setting Gia thought she could just parachute in and start getting pushy about Wendy's love life—or lack of it—was kind of irritating. "It doesn't even matter. He lives in New York."

"Which you visit on the reg. And, dude, I think you just answered my question with that protest."

"Gia. It's just sex." She was lying. Because whatever had happened earlier, in her room, had not been just sex. Goddamn Noah.

"It *was* just sex," she declared in an attempt to make herself believe it. "Past tense."

"Really? Because from my vantage point, things look a little different. He's rubbing your feet while you're watching baseball. You're off every night going running with him. Every time you guys start talking about law, the pheromones get so thick the rest of us have to go outside for some fresh air."

"Gia, stop. You can't—"

"No, *you* stop." Gia held up a hand to punctate her command. "Why are you so determined to be unhappy? I mean, I know your dad died. You raised yourself. Or Noah raised you—*whatever*."

"You can't just dismiss my whole life history!"

"Maybe *you* should think about dismissing it. Because that seems like a better option than letting it paralyze you."

Wendy's retort was cut off by the fact that all the breath had left her body. Blinking rapidly, she thought back to her conversation with Noah in the shower. What had she said to him? Sometimes things happen that calcify you. That change who you are. She had never thought of that as a bad thing, per se, just a fact. Of course, her father's death had been sad. She wasn't *glad* it happened. But it, and its aftermath, had made her into the driven, accomplished woman she was. She did good work. She had great friends.

That was enough.

Wasn't it?

Horrible, mortifying tears gathered in the corners of her eyes. She refused to let them fall, though, so she pressed her lips together and swallowed hard.

"Oh, sweetie." Gia's voice had lost its edge. She slid her arm across the island and grabbed Wendy's hand. "I'm sorry. I don't mean to be a bitch. I just want you to be happy, and sometimes I think you need a little push. So don't answer my question out loud, but think about it. But not just with your current lawyer brain. Think about it with your whole self, the kid who lost her parents *and* the modern-day, independent, kick-ass lawyer." She paused, then posed her question again. "What if you could have whatever you wanted?"

I'd have Noah. Wendy didn't hesitate. She wasn't sure who answered the question, though. The girl standing alone under the disco ball in the school gym? The woman who'd run all around the globe, initially because she was trying to avoid the boy who'd broken her heart and later because it gave her the power she craved? Because it reassured her she always had the power to leave?

What if she *could* really have him? Why had she never let herself even contemplate that possibility?

She picked up her wine and drained the rest of it.

"Jane is driving me to drink," Gia said, clearly attuned to the fact that Wendy needed the conversation to move on, "because now she has this idea that at the rehearsal tomorrow, it would be really 'fun' if we handed out notecards and everyone wrote down their advice for the newlyweds. Which is fine. I have no problem with that. But I also have no advice. And she asked me to give a speech explaining this to everyone and kicking it off with my own advice."

Wendy snorted. The idea of Gia, of all people, expounding on the best practices of settled, monogamous life, was genuinely funny.

"Right?" Gia refilled Wendy's glass. "I tried to get her to ask Elise—or you." Wendy started to protest, but Gia kept talking over her. "Don't worry. She didn't go for it. I think she thinks I feel left out. You're the maid of honor, and Elise, with her designer's eye, has been involved in choosing flowers and invitations and all that. I was trying to assure her that I didn't feel left out, but..."

"You can't protest too much," Wendy said.

"Which is why I'm giving a speech tomorrow night about how to be good at marriage." She snorted.

Wendy lifted her glass. "Well, then, I'd say we're both equally fucked." It was her way of acknowledging she'd heard what Gia had said.

She'd heard it. She just didn't know what the hell she was going to do about it.

Chapter Twenty-Two

Good morning!"

Noah had barely opened his eyes and had only half emerged from his room when his freakishly chipper sister accosted him. At least she had coffee—which she shoved into his hand as she guided him to her kitchen table. His muscles were destroyed from yesterday's exertions—and he didn't just mean running.

"Don't yell at me, but I printed out some info I thought you might be interested in."

He groaned without even knowing what she meant by "some info." In another life, Jane would have been a librarian—in one sense, Wendy had been right on with Gunnar the stripper librarian. Jane was always looking things up, printing things out, passing along links.

He tried to focus his eyes on the first paper in the stack, but his mind was stuck on another version of this morning, one he had been turning over in his mind. One he was having trouble letting go of.

It was an alternative reality, one in which he woke up in Wendy's apartment.

In Wendy's bed.

A reality in which he didn't have to get up and slink out in dirty clothes. No, he'd have some clean clothes there— maybe she'd give him a drawer.

Maybe he wouldn't have to leave at all. They could make brunch together after a run. Then, later, if her feet were cold—

Wait. What the *hell* was he doing? He wasn't the sort of person who got caught up in romantic daydreams. And daydreams about *rubbing a woman's feet*, for God's sake?

No, he was the opposite of that person. He was the one who was always bailing when these sorts of domestic fantasies became too real. The guy who couldn't propose. Couldn't move in with a woman.

And anyway, for the thousandth time, *Wendy didn't want a relationship*.

"Hello? Earth to Noah?"

"Sorry." He shook his head to try to clear the image of a curtain of black hair fanned out over a white pillowcase. "So what's this?" He started shuffling through the papers. They were blog posts and advice about how US-trained lawyers could qualify to practice in Canada. He rolled his eyes. "The US and Canada are different countries, Jane. They have different legal systems. Even if I wanted to, I can't just decide to practice here."

"Just hear me out!" She held up a hand to forestall the additional protest she must have known was coming. "I know it's not easy. But according to my research—"

"Where is this coming from?" Jane had nagged him

about a lot of things over the years, but moving home wasn't one of them.

"It's coming from our conversation in Vegas, partly."

"What do you mean?"

"Well, like, I finally have my shit together." Noah still felt terrible that he'd never realized that her shit *wasn't* together. "And it sort of seems like Mom is starting to as well. She even has a boyfriend."

It was true. He'd been to his mom's place twice since he'd been to town, and he'd been pleasantly surprised to find her bright-eyed and talkative. His mom had spent so long living under the shadow of her late husband—his erratic behavior while he was alive, and the deprivation his death left behind in their family—that Noah had assumed that was just the way she was now. He suddenly thought back to something Wendy had said yesterday, in the shower, about how some things happen that calcify you. That had certainly happened to his mom—or so he'd thought. But apparently not permanently, because at her house the other day, she'd been talking happily about a school she volunteered at and a guy she was dating.

"Mom and I are less work now," Jane said. He started to object, but she cut him off. "Don't pretend you don't know what I mean. My point is, I think it would be easier for us to...be a family now. We talked about you having some fun, and you said you didn't know how. I was thinking I could, like, help you. You could move back, take some time off to study to qualify here, and, I don't know...hang out." Jane had grown sheepish, embarrassed. She wasn't looking at him as she spoke. His heart twisted. "I know I'm being selfish, but I miss you."

"I miss you, too, Janie." He got up, tugged her to her feet, and hugged her.

After a moment, she pulled away and made a dismissive gesture. "Anyway, I know it's crazy. You can say no after the wedding. For now, just humor me and tell me you'll think about it."

There was no way he could just up and leave New York. His job. His entire life. But he wasn't going to get into that with Jane the day before her wedding, so he just picked up his mug and said, "I can't think about anything until I've had coffee."

⌒

That afternoon, as Wendy was getting ready for the rehearsal dinner, she started to panic again about the fact that she and Noah had had unprotected sex.

Not that the panic part was novel. She'd pretty much been in low-grade terror mode since her "chat" with Gia. She hadn't been able to sleep last night. She'd been going over and over every moment between her and Noah, from the filthy to the flirty to the tender, asking herself what it would mean if Gia was right. She'd just been reflexively assuming that Noah wouldn't want an actual relationship with her. He'd rejected her once before, so that was it, right?

But did she really know that?

What if she *could* have everything she wanted?

The prospect was scary as hell.

But then, as if her brain wasn't satisfied panicking about one thing, it started snagging on everything else. She called her aunt in the rehab center twice to make sure everything was okay. She'd been visiting Mary every day, but because of wedding obligations today and tomorrow, she would be going two days without seeing her.

She even started fretting about what to wear to the rehearsal, which wasn't like her. She had a well-edited wardrobe full of clothes she liked and felt confident in. She should have been able to pull anything out, do some makeup, throw on her all-purpose black stilettos, and be good to go. That's what she'd done in Vegas.

But instead, she found herself transported into a teen movie where she tried on and discarded dress after dress. To add to the effect, Gia eventually came in, plopped down on her bed, and started issuing pronouncements.

"No," she said about a loose, raw silk number in burnt orange. "Too avant-garde." She grinned. "And by 'avant-garde,' I mean 'shaped like a potato sack.'"

Wendy considered booting Gia from the room. She didn't need a peanut gallery, especially not one whose entire membership was made up of a high-fashion model. But instead she changed into a navy dress she sometimes wore to work.

"Nope. Too conservative. Also the same color as tomorrow's actual bridesmaids' dresses."

Wendy shot Gia a look. "Are the fashion police going to arrest me?"

Gia made a face and disappeared into Wendy's closet. She came out with a gray cocktail dress, a swingy number Wendy had bought for a formal work party a couple of years ago but ended up deciding wasn't really her. She'd never worn it. She'd meant to return it but something had inspired her to hold on to it even though she'd been pretty sure it would never see the light of day.

"Is that too dressy, though?" she asked.

"It's perfect," Gia proclaimed, even though she herself was wearing something that looked remarkably like the potato sack she had so recently been disparaging. Wendy supposed that if you were a six-foot-tall glamazon, you could get away with potato sacks.

So, after wasting way too much mental energy on what to wear, Wendy rushed through a hair and makeup routine. They had to hurry downstairs and grab a cab so as not to be late. Jane's "key" had, of late, swung as far from "low" as it was possible to be, and Wendy didn't want to rock the boat by showing up late.

Once her dress worries were gone—or at least made obsolete by the fact that it was too late to change—she started fretting about what was going on in her uterus. Or fallopian tubes. Or whatever.

She had talked herself into believing there was no chance she could be pregnant. And, really, there *wasn't*. She'd looked at her calendar, and her period was due today. So she was in the clear. *Right?*

"What the hell is up your butt?" Gia nudged Wendy as the cab pulled away from her building.

Wendy's default was to deny, but Gia already knew she'd slept with Noah again, and she could use some advice.

"Noah and I didn't use a condom," she whispered. "And I'm freaking out that I might be pregnant. But my period is due like any second, so I should be fine, right?"

Gia sucked in a breath. Wendy had wanted Gia to reassure her, to wave off her fears. Instead, she said, "Probably. But if I were you, I'd be popping the morning-after pill."

"The morning-after pill?"

"Emergency contraception? Prevents fertilization?"

Wendy knew what the morning-after pill was. She was just repeating after Gia like a dumbstruck idiot because... well, because she *was* a dumbstruck idiot. Never in a million years had she thought of herself as the kind of person who would need emergency contraception.

She put her head in her hands.

"Ah, sweetie." Gia had been saying that a lot lately. "Do we need to stop at a pharmacy?"

Without lifting her head, Wendy nodded. "Jane's going to be annoyed, though. It's going to make us late."

Gia patted her hand. "Better than *you* being late—ha!"

—⟨⟩

The restaurant was chaos when they arrived.

"There you are!" Jane hurried over to Wendy and Gia. "I think I invited too many people!"

Jane and Cameron had rented out a little Italian place near Jane's house for the rehearsal dinner. It had great food and a fun, cozy vibe.

It was also packed with people. They stood shoulder to shoulder at the small bar and milled around the café tables that studded the space.

Wendy surveyed the crowd. "How many people *did* you invite?" She'd been expecting the usual rehearsal dinner suspects—the wedding party, Jane and Noah's mom, Cameron's mom, and that was pretty much it. You know, low-key.

"Hi!" Elise bounded over to them. She leaned in to embrace them both—one arm around Wendy and the other around Gia—and whispered, "Help me roofie her drink."

"Oh my *God*," Jane wailed as she looked at the stuffed room. "They *told* me that fifty would be too much of a squeeze. But did I listen?" She turned back to the girls, looking truly stricken. "I just thought since the wedding is so, you know..." Wendy forced herself not to look at Gia.

"Low-key. I mean, it's at an amusement park. So I thought maybe people would enjoy a fancy dinner the night before." She heaved a defeated sigh.

"And they will." Wendy took a step forward and grabbed Jane's hand. "Don't panic. What was the plan? Do the rehearsal outside and then eat?"

Jane nodded. "We were going to let people have drinks while we were out back doing a quick run-through, and then come in and eat."

"Okay," Wendy said. "There are tables out back, right? So we'll just let people be a little tight in here while we do the rehearsal really quick, and then we can disperse some of the guests outside for the meal."

"You don't think it's better to have everyone together for the dinner? I wasn't going to seat anyone outside."

"Nah." Gia picked up on Wendy's mission to calm Jane. "That's what's cool about a funky place like this. You can keep the restaurant feel. We can do the toasts at the beginning, with everyone standing—it'll be cozy, but we can be brief—and then we can move to our tables. If we can get maybe a quarter of the guests seated outside, it will ease the pressure in here."

Jane's shoulders inched down as she appeared to relax a bit.

"I'll go do a count of the seating out back," Elise said, "and let the staff know what we're thinking."

They all snapped into gear, Elise to make the alternative seating arrangements, Gia to round up the wedding party and officiant, and Wendy to go to the bar to top up Jane's drink.

"Hey."

She felt him and heard him at the same time. Maybe she could have stood one or the other, on its own, but his low voice, the way it stretched to include Jane and Wendy but no farther, plus the steady pressure of his palm on the small of her back. It was too much. It set her blood moving. Without greeting him, she glanced over her shoulder to see if he was touching Jane in any way. He was not.

Just her.

"You feeling better?" he asked his sister.

"Yes. Wendy saved the day."

"Of course she did." He flashed her a smile. She would have expected it to be at least partly teasing, but it wasn't. It projected only calm certainty. Faith in her.

What if you could have everything you want?

She turned to him and smiled. "You look good, Noah." He really, really did. The man could fill out a suit like no one's business. This one was blue, but brighter than the conservative navy that would be acceptable in court.

He looked startled. *Ha.* Whatever he'd been expecting from her, it wasn't a smile and a compliment.

"I'm told we're to head outside." He held out both arms. Wendy took one, and Jane the other.

What if you could have everything you want?

What if, instead of watching Jane and Noah with jealousy, feeling like no matter how genuinely they welcomed her, she'd always be a little bit of an outsider, she suddenly...wasn't?

What if she could have the man she loved?

She took a deep breath of the heavy summer air when they got outside. She needed to steady herself.

"You okay, Wendy Lou Who?"

"Yep." It was a lie. Wendy was profoundly not okay. But she had a wedding rehearsal to get through, so there was nothing to do but soldier on. Put on her court face.

"All right," the officiant called, raising her voice to get

everyone's attention, "bridesmaids and groomsmen, pair up, please, and we'll do a quick run-through of the ceremony."

Wendy looked around for her partner Jay, who was Cameron's brother and best man—and, of course, Elise's husband.

"Pass her over, dude." Jay and Elise had arrived at their side and Jay was joking with Noah. She hadn't realized she was still clutching Noah's arm. Right. She dropped it. A little too reluctantly.

"Trade you," Noah said. Elise was his partner in the wedding, and he took her arm.

Wendy scanned the crowd for Gia, who was paired with the dreaded Hector. Her friend caught her eye and made a quick gagging motion behind Hector's back.

"We'll go through the ceremony as well as the scripted stuff that will happen at the reception," the officiant explained. "It shouldn't take long, either tonight or when we're really doing it tomorrow. Jane and Cameron want their guests to be free to run around the amusement park, so they've kept the formal parts of the evening to a minimum."

Really, all the girls' jokes about it not being particularly low-key aside, this was the perfect wedding for Jane, the pop culture nerd who had recently discovered her inner thrill seeker. And the perfect groom, too, though it had taken Wendy a while to see it. Cameron had his arm casually slung over Jane's shoulder. He was a bit rough around the edges, yes, but there was something about his posture that exemplified everything about their relationship. He was protective but not possessive. His arm, which she knew was covered with tattoos under his suit, rested lightly, both literally and metaphorically.

"And then I'll ask the crowd if anyone objects to this union," said the officiant when Wendy tuned back in.

Her face heated. She had *never* been going to do that, but the prompt made her retroactively embarrassed over all the mental energy she had expended trying to argue—to herself mostly, but also to Noah—against Cameron. From her current vantage point, she could see how obviously all her issues had been just that—*her* issues.

"And then I'll pronounce you husband and wife," the officiant said. "And tell you to kiss."

"You should practice that now!" Gia exclaimed, and everyone laughed as the bridal couple obliged.

The officiant guided them through the recession, and then they gathered around while she went over how they would enter the reception. "And that's pretty much it. Short and sweet."

"Low-key," Jane said, and Wendy bit the insides of her cheeks and made eye contact with Elise and then Gia in turn.

"You're all dismissed from your official duties this evening," the officiant said. "Enjoy the party."

Elise made her way over to Wendy, leaving Noah chatting with the officiant. Gia tagged along, too, making a face of exaggerated relief as she left Hector behind. Elise pinched a bit of Wendy's voluminous skirt between her thumb and forefinger. "By the way, I love this dress on you."

"Isn't it so perfect on her?" Gia said.

"I don't think I've ever seen you in silver," Elise said. "It totally suits you."

Silver? Wendy looked down at herself. "It's gray, though, isn't it?"

"Too shiny to be gray," Elise said.

"Totally silver," Gia agreed.

Oh my God. Wendy was at a fancy party in a silver dress. Maybe that was why, after she'd bought the dress, she'd never seemed to find an occasion to wear it. Had she been subconsciously rejecting it? She would never buy a silver dress. Not knowingly, anyway.

She started to panic. Well, no, she *kept* panicking. Because that's pretty much what she'd been doing since the whole unprotected sex incident.

And...suddenly *panic* wasn't the right word. *Terror* was what she was feeling right now.

Because she realized that she'd left the fucking morning-after pill in the cab. The pill they'd made a point to stop for on the way.

But okay. Okay. It was a two-minute walk to Queen Street. There would be pharmacies there. She just had to slip out, and she'd go buy another one.

And anyway, she was *not* pregnant. It was just insurance.

She took a deep breath. It was going to be okay. She was a successful, responsible, independent adult who had made a mistake. She hardened herself. She could handle this.

"Wendy. Wait."

—⟨⟩

Wendy was leaving?

Noah had been talking to the officiant, but he had one eye on Wendy. He wasn't sure why, just that it was sort of impossible not to watch her when she was in the vicinity.

She was probably just going inside to check on something. He tried to pay attention to what the officiant was saying, but...something was wrong with Wendy. Her face was scrunched up as if in pain—and he couldn't let that stand. So he excused himself and went after her.

"Wendy. Wait."

She stopped in the little hallway that connected the patio

with the restaurant. She was wearing a silver dress with a short swingy skirt. As she turned, both the skirt and her long hair flew out behind her. The sight of her took his breath away.

"What?" she said, all annoyed and short, and he almost laughed. That was the cure for his heart-eyes-emoji gasping.

"What's wrong?" Because whatever else was or wasn't happening between them, he knew her. Something was wrong.

"Nothing."

"Bullshit." Something was wrong, and he intended to find out what it was.

She rolled her eyes. "I had a pill I needed to take, and I just realized I left it in the taxi on the way over here."

Okay, this was a surmountable problem. She'd forgotten her allergy meds or something. He was slightly annoyed that he hadn't known she had allergies—or whatever—but a pill was a tangible thing he could retrieve. "Let me take you home to get another one."

"No, no. I don't have another one. It was..."

"It was what?" A pit opened in his stomach. Was there something seriously wrong with her? *Jesus Christ.*

"It was a morning-after pill."

"A *what*?" He staggered backward. He actually staggered. His legs were no longer capable of holding him up.

"Morning-after pill. Emergency contraception."

"I know what it *is.*" But *holy fucking Christ.* "I thought you said you weren't...you know, in a fertile part of your cycle."

Argh. That had not come out right. He did not object to the rightness or wrongness of her claim about what part of her goddamned menstrual cycle she was on.

He objected to her taking the pill.

He objected to her taking the pill.

Holy, holy, holy fuck.

He, Mister "I Can't Propose," did not want some extremely hypothetical child of his and Wendy's to...what? Not implant? Not fertilize? He didn't even know how the fuck morning-after pills worked, only that *he did not want her taking one.* The only other time he'd had a pregnancy scare that had *not* been his reaction. In fact, that time, he would have broken into the goddamn pharmacy and *stolen* a morning-after pill if he'd needed to. Hell, that time had pretty much cemented his decision not to sleep around casually. That's how much he hadn't wanted an unintended pregnancy.

This was...not like that.

Holy fuck.

"There's nothing to worry about," she said. "I was just going to...make sure." She pinched the bridge of her nose. "Look, we broke the 'only in New York or fake New York' rule pretty badly last night. I just want to make sure that...there are no consequences."

What he wanted to say next was *Don't take the pill! We'll figure everything out, but don't take the pill!*

"Move to New York!" he blurted instead. "Move in with me. You'll be able to get a job. The best firms in the city will fall all over themselves to get you. I have connections—"

She sighed and pushed herself off the wall. "Noah. I'm not pregnant. I'm just paranoid."

"I know. I know." Why was that so...disappointing? "But even if you're not, I want..."

What? What did he want?

"What? What do you want?"

Even in the midst of his turmoil, he couldn't help but admire her razor-sharp intelligence as she plucked his very thoughts from his head. She wasn't letting him off the hook. She never would.

She looked at him for a long moment as he floundered. Finally, she said, "Because we slept together a few times, you're freaking out."

"I'm not freaking out." But that was a lie. He *was* freaking out. Just not in the way she meant. He wasn't freaking out because they'd slept together a few times. He was freaking out at the possibility that they might never do it again.

"You have this obsessive, protective impulse, and you can't just let it be." She started talking faster as annoyance crept into her tone. "It has to *mean* something so you're trying to *make* it mean something retroactively, and your version of that is I give up everything—my career, my friends, my aunt—and move to New York? No, thanks. Yes, I had a crush on you back in the day, but I'm not that girl anymore. I went out and made myself a life. I worked hard for my life. I earned it."

"I'm just…" God. What? *What?* Why couldn't he make sense? "I just need you to pause for one minute. I need to catch up. It feels like we were just in New York fighting because you were trying to convince me that Jane and Cameron were all wrong for each other, and now…" *Now I'm in love with you.*

Maybe he should just say it. Lay out all his cards. She wouldn't want to hear it, he was pretty sure, but what did he have to lose at this point?

A movement in the periphery caught his attention.

Oh, shit.

"Jane," he whispered. The only way this whole conversation could be worse was if his *sister had overheard all of it*.

"You guys are sleeping together?" Jane said, confusion written across her face. Then she swung her gaze to Wendy, and confusion was replaced by hurt. "And you don't like Cameron?"

Chapter Twenty-Three

$\mathcal{W}$endy felt like bugs were crawling all over her skin.

Noah was being completely irrational. He thought she might be pregnant. He was exactly the sort of man who would step up in this situation. All those girl-friends he couldn't commit to? She would bet partner-ship at the firm that none of them had had a pregnancy scare.

And this wasn't a pregnancy scare. She *wasn't* pregnant. She was just, as she'd said, making sure.

But besides that, his solution was *abandon your hard-won life and move into mine*? Typical Noah, trying to con-trol everything.

She refused to be controlled.

She'd been asking herself all evening what life would be like if she could have what she wanted. This exchange made it clear that she couldn't. He didn't love her. He was will-ing to move in with her—or to "let" her move in with him.

But for what? To co-parent? Perhaps with some meaningless fucking on the side?

No. Wendy might be new to this love thing—or at least new to recognizing it as such—but she knew enough to understand that she couldn't settle for anything less than the real thing.

She might be alone under the disco ball, but at least it was her goddamned disco ball.

But then, Jane. Jane had heard them.

The bugs multiplied. They swarmed her insides—her stomach, her lungs. Her heart.

"You don't like Cameron?" Her voice was so *small*. So defeated.

"No." Wendy moved toward Jane, but Jane held out her hands to signal she wanted no contact. "I mean, I *do* like Cameron..." Wendy's voice caught. "Now. Anyway, it was never about that. I was afraid to lose you. I was an *idiot*." A tear started to fall. She swiped it away angrily.

Without acknowledging anything Wendy had said, Jane turned to her brother. "Noah," she said, her voice gaining some confidence. Some indignation. "How could you sleep with Wendy without telling me?" She swung back to include Wendy in her next accusatory question. "Were you two just going to keep this from me forever?"

It was a fair question.

Wendy had no answer. No answer other than *I lost my mind, but it's okay because I'm leaving soon. I'm running. It's all scheduled.*

I'm leaving.

That was the solution. As much as she'd had a little epiphany about the reasons she traveled so much, the fact remained that her methods had never failed her. Teenage Wendy had been stuck, but grown-up Wendy was not. She could always leave.

So that's what she did.

She turned around and walked swiftly up the corridor. By the time she reached the end of it, she was running.

She heard them mobilizing behind her. The sounds of her friends conferring.

Heard Noah say, "What do I do?"

Heard Gia answering him. "Wait," she said. "You wait."

Wendy ran faster.

—✐—

Noah waited.

He went to the bar and got a Guinness, as if he were a normal man. Not one who'd just had his heart ripped out and handed to him.

The restaurant had a row of stools against a small wooden counter that looked out the front windows. Miraculously, it was empty—the rest of the crowd was focused on the interior of the restaurant and the open bar in back.

There wasn't even enough time for his head to stop spinning before someone slid in beside him.

"Noah."

He sighed. He loved her, but this was not what he needed right now. "Hi, Mom."

She didn't say anything, which he supposed he should be thankful for. She just clinked her glass of soda water against his beer and patted his arm.

Eventually, he asked, "Are you happy, Mom?" He had never asked her anything remotely like that before, but suddenly he needed to know. His big love revelation yesterday had made him think about happiness—about what it was, about how to get it. About whether it was even possible for someone like him.

She didn't answer for a long time. He thought she wasn't going to.

"I think I am."

He would have laughed, had his entire fucking world not just imploded. "You *think*?"

"Well, you know, I don't have that much practice with it. I'm not totally confident I would recognize it." She glanced at him. "I think you know what I mean."

He did. Life had been unpleasant when their father was alive. He had no doubt his parents had loved each other once, but his father's addiction had ultimately grown bigger than that love. Grown bigger than all of them.

"Jane snapped out of it," she said, and he didn't have to ask what she meant by "it." "She met Cameron, and it was like a veil was lifted. And it wasn't even as simple as 'Cameron made her happy.' I think Cameron helped her decide to be happy."

He nodded. That was a good way of describing it.

"For me, it was more gradual. I hadn't really thought about it in happy-unhappy terms until you asked me just now. But yes. Having a boyfriend has been fun. I'm not sure he's the love of my life, but we have a good time. I joined a hiking group, and I volunteer at the school. I'm pretty sure all that is stuff that a happy person does?"

"I think so." Her words brought him a small measure of comfort.

"But you," she said, her voice growing sad. "I'm sorry I asked so much of you when you were young."

"You didn't ask anything," he started to protest, but she cut him off.

"I didn't have to. I just disappeared and let you take up the slack." Her voice was heavy with emotion. "You had to grow up too fast. You skipped a lot of important stuff."

Like the prom.

Where had that absurd thought come from? Even if he allowed her argument, she wasn't talking about high school dances.

"Yeah, you skipped a lot of important stuff because you were taking care of us, but for the love of God, you've got to stop doing it."

It was Jane speaking, though, not his mom.

"Move over." She shoved him not gently on the shoulder.

He moved, and she squeezed between them, standing between their stools. "So, Mom, it turns out Wendy and Noah have been getting it on."

"I heard."

Noah put his head in his hands. He knew there was going to have to be some sort of reckoning with Jane, but did it have to be now, in the middle of her rehearsal dinner? Did his *mother* have to be involved?

"I can't say I'm surprised," his mom added.

What?

"Me either," Jane said. "I mean, I *was* surprised, but when I stopped and thought about it for a minute, it made total sense. They're perfect for each other."

What planet were these women on?

Jane turned to him. "I'm going to ask you a question. Since you've been lying to me for weeks, I think I'm owed an honest answer."

He refrained from pointing out that he hadn't lied, per se. He'd merely neglected to mention a few things. That was a distinction that might have flown in court, but it wasn't going to work with his sister. "Okay."

"Could you love Wendy?"

I already do. I always have.

He didn't verbalize what was in his heart, though, because life wasn't that simple. Instead, he said, "Love is never the problem."

"What does *that* mean?"

"It means there's a pattern with me. I start dating someone, and it's fine. It's fun. There's…affection, or whatever." He didn't bother saying that he'd never experienced anything close to the depth of feeling he had for Wendy. "But then, at some point, when things start to get more serious, I just…can't do it. It starts feeling like too much responsibility, I guess."

He braced himself for derision. To his surprise, Jane and his mother both looked at him with sympathy.

"I'm going to say two things," Jane said. "They contradict each other, but somehow, they're both true. Bear with me, okay?" He nodded. "The first is that you've *always* taken responsibility for Wendy. Because she was my best friend. Because she needed it. Because she was a Lost Girl, too. But Wendy isn't someone you have to deliberate over *adding* to your list of responsibilities. She's already on it. She's already in your care, whether you like it or not."

The truth of it was a punch to the gut. It was obvious. It *should* have been obvious. He was still processing the simple yet profound truth of what she'd said, when Jane hit him with more.

"The second thing is that, even though you won't—or can't—see it this way, you *don't* have to be responsible for Wendy. She's fine. She's an adult. You can trust her to make her own decisions and to deal with the consequences of her actions. If she loves you, don't push her away because you're afraid of what you might feel later. I mean, there might be a million other reasons to push her away, but that's not one of them."

"No," his mother said gently. "I think that's not quite

right." Both siblings swung to look at their mother. "There aren't a million reasons to push her away. There's really only one, and that would be if you simply don't love her."

He did love her. He loved her so much.

Jane smiled. "I stand corrected." She lowered her head to rest on Mom's shoulder for a moment, and Mom gave her an affectionate squeeze. "Anyway, the point is, I know it's scary. I mean, *I know*. But what the last year has taught me is that sometimes you just have to give up trying to control everything and start trusting your heart."

Then Jane popped up off her stool. "Now I gotta go get this dinner moving. I have to go see Wendy as soon as I can get out of here."

"You're not angry at Wendy?" he asked. "Or me?"

She shrugged. "I'm not gonna lie. This whole situation is a little weird. I'm hurt that you guys didn't tell me what was going on. And I'm annoyed that Wendy was apparently secretly hiding this hang-up about me getting married. But I understand where it comes from."

"Where does it come from?"

"It comes from being a Lost Girl. And that's the reason I'm not angry, not really. Wendy and I, we're the Lost Girls."

"I've got to go over there," he said. "Do you think she went home?"

Jane held up a palm. "Hang on. This is where you get Wendy's best friend Jane and not sister Jane." She shook a finger at him. "You'd better not go over there unless you have something definitive to say to her."

"Define definitive."

"You were all wild-eyed and creepy back there. And just now, when I asked you if you could love Wendy, you said, 'Love is never the problem.' That doesn't sound very definitive to me."

He started to object, but actually, she was right. He had asked Wendy to move in with him in New York as a response to the notion that she might be pregnant. And he hadn't really even asked—it had been more like an order. What he had not said was anything about love. About what was in his heart. Wendy deserved to hear that. So he needed a plan—something other than ordering her to up and merge her life with his because she might be knocked up.

"I call dibs," Jane said. "*I'm* going over to Wendy's soon as I can get out of here, and you…" Jane pressed a hand against his chest. "You figure out what the hell you want before you do any more damage."

—⌒⌐

History was repeating itself, Wendy thought as she buzzed Elise up to her apartment. Repeating itself with inversions. Here she was, fleeing a wedding rehearsal with a broken heart. At Elise's wedding, it had been Jane fleeing. Wendy had comforted her. Now it was Jane's wedding and Elise was comforting Wendy. It would have been funny if it wasn't so sad.

"Hey, sweetie." Elise stepped inside.

"You drew the short straw, I guess," Wendy tried to joke.

Elise didn't bite. "Nope. That scene had become decidedly *not* low-key. I'd rather be here."

Wendy laughed. And cried a little, too. And walked into Elise's arms when she held them open.

"The guys at the rehearsal were bellyaching about missing a Jays game. Is there one on? You wanna watch?"

That made Wendy cry harder. Elise hated sports. She was the type of person who thought there were goalies in a baseball game.

Elise led Wendy to her den, pushed her down on the couch, and covered her with the same quilt she and Noah had snuggled under only days ago. "Hang tight. I'm gonna go order us a pizza."

Ninety minutes later, stuffed with pizza and garlic bread yet somehow still hollow inside, Wendy watched listlessly as Elise fidgeted. Then her phone vibrated and she stood suddenly. "I'll be right back." Wendy didn't bother pointing out that there were two outs, loaded bases, and it was the bottom of the ninth. Elise hadn't been paying attention anyway—she'd spent most of the game on her phone. But hey, Wendy didn't mind. She was glad to have the company, glad Elise wasn't forcing her to talk, though she suspected her reprieve would not last beyond the end of the game.

"Wendy."

Or apparently it wasn't even going to last that long. An adrenaline spike pushed Wendy out of her slumped position. "Jane. Jane, I..." What? What could she say? It's not like she hadn't known she would have to talk to Jane at some point, assuming Jane wasn't going to just ghost on her, but...Her mind churned, trying to settle on the right words.

Well, there was always the truth. She turned off the TV. "I'm sorry."

Jane sat on the other chair in the room, the old family rocking chair. Normally she'd have shoved Wendy over and shared the oversize TV chair with her. It stung that she didn't.

"So you don't like Cameron."

"That's not true." Wendy cringed. She was going for honesty here, right? It was the only thing that might allow her to make amends. "Anymore." Jane started to speak, but Wendy talked over her. She had to get it out. "I didn't think he was right for you initially. But that, and me not liking him, had nothing to do with him, really, or even you. I see that now. I'm just sorry it took a near tragedy for me to get my head out of my ass and really let myself see him. Let myself see how good he is. How good you are together."

"You said at the restaurant you were afraid to lose me."

Wendy nodded, miserable. "I felt like I'd already lost so much. Other than Mary, you were the only person I had left. I know it makes no sense, but I sort of felt, irrationally, like he was taking you from me."

"I don't think you know how much it hurts me..." Jane's voice cracked. She struggled to continue. "To hear that you think you could ever lose me. I mean, *you're* the one taking off for six months."

Wendy blinked, stunned at the pain in Jane's voice. "But...you'll be a newlywed. You won't have time for me, so it's perfect timing for this trip."

Jane pressed her lips together and stared at Wendy for a long time. Then she said, "Are you insane? Why do you think I'm rearranging my publishing schedule so I can jet off and join you at various points on this stupid trip? Do you know that I had to ask for an extension on the book so I can come to Bangkok? Do you think I care about stupid Bangkok? I mean, you're still giving me shit for eating McDonald's in New York. Do you think I want to go to freaking *Thailand*?"

Wendy, who had thought she was out of tears, started crying again, which started Jane crying. Then Jane got up, belatedly smooshed in next to Wendy, and put her arms around her. "Nothing lasts forever," Jane whispered. "I can't promise that nothing will change once I'm married, but you're not getting rid of me that easily."

Which made Wendy cry even harder.

They just sat like that for a minute or so, letting themselves cry, until Jane said, "We never did this kind of drama when we were teenagers."

Wendy couldn't help but chuckle through her tears. "We were either freakishly mature or else emotionally stunted."

"I'm going to have to go with emotionally stunted."

Wendy sighed. "Yeah." Then, because she couldn't imagine a time when she'd ever not be compelled to keep apologizing, she said, "I really am sorry about all the Cameron stuff. I just . . . lost my mind for a while."

"I know." Jane pulled away and looked at Wendy. "Is that your defense when it comes to my brother, too?"

Wendy buried her head in her hands. "Basically." That wasn't even remotely all of the truth, but what was the point in explaining the complicated evolution of her feelings for Noah? He didn't return them, not in any way that involved her and not some imaginary responsibility she represented. Analyzing the situation would only put Jane in an awkward place. She couldn't provide the usual best friend shoulder to cry on in these circumstances, and Wendy would never ask her to.

"I admit I was shocked," Jane said. "Hurt that you were carrying on behind my back. But the more I thought about it, the more I realized it wasn't about me. And the more logical it seemed. I don't know why I never saw it before, but you two are kind of perfect for each other."

"It doesn't matter, though, does it? My feelings are irrelevant. It takes two. And he doesn't want *me*. Not really. He doesn't love me. He just said all that back there because he thought I might be pregnant—you know Noah and responsibility."

Jane nodded and rolled her eyes at the same time. "My brother, despite being so smart, can be kind of slow on the uptake sometimes."

Wendy grabbed her best friend's hand. "I don't deserve to ask you this, but please can we not talk about Noah?" She had to be ruthless with herself. To pick herself up and start walking through the pain. Because that was the only way out. And anything that was going to slow her down, she didn't want. Maybe all her travel had been for the wrong reasons, had been an overcorrection, but she couldn't help but think that the underlying impulse had been correct. She could choose how to feel.

"You got it," Jane said. She picked up the remote and turned the TV back on. The game was over. Jane started flipping. "Oh, look! *Sex and the City*." Sure enough, the four lead characters were sitting around having brunch. "That's totally the four of us, don't you think?"

Wendy chuckled. "Which one am I?"

"Oh, you're totally Miranda." Jane cuddled up next to Wendy. "And I'm Carrie, and we're best friends."

And that wasn't nothing, Wendy reminded herself. When her heartbreak healed—if it healed and didn't just become a big lump of scar tissue she had to learn to live with—she'd still have Jane and the girls.

Jane's phone buzzed.

Wendy caught a glimpse of a really long text as Jane picked up her phone. "You should get going," she said. As tempting as it was to cocoon in here with Jane forever, surely she had stuff to get done. "You're getting married tomorrow!"

A slow smile blossomed on Jane's face. It was probably a sext from Cameron she was reading. Then she cleared her throat and looked up, suddenly all businesslike. "I am getting married tomorrow. And I do have…something I need to do yet tonight." She smirked, but then she looked up in what seemed like alarm. "You'll still be in the wedding, right? You don't have to do anything but show up, right before the ceremony."

"Are you kidding me? Of course. You're not getting rid of me that easily. Where else am I going to wear that tartan sash?"

"I know it will be hard. You know that I, of all people, know how hard it will be." Jane was referring to her big declaration of love to Cameron at Elise's rehearsal dinner that had been rebuffed.

"It is kind of shocking how history is repeating itself, isn't it?" Wendy said.

"I don't know. I don't think it's that shocking. We always did everything together. We're the Lost Girls."

Right. Wendy didn't point out that since Jane was about to marry the love of her life, she probably couldn't call herself "lost" anymore. Even though Wendy understood now that she wasn't going to "lose" Jane, things *were* going to be different.

Jane blew Wendy a kiss, and Wendy plucked it out of the air and pressed it against her broken heart.

Chapter Twenty-Four

THE WEDDING DAY

As Jane had predicted, the wedding was going to be hard.

But maybe not quite as hard as Wendy had expected, thanks to Gia and Elise, who were doing a bang-up job keeping the heartbroken maid of honor distracted.

"Maybe this wedding *is* actually pretty low-key," Gia said as the three of them queued up for a ride. "I mean, how many weddings have you been to where you get to go on a roller coaster an hour before the ceremony?" Part of Jane and Cameron's courtship a year ago had involved crazy—for Jane, anyway—stunts, and the couple counted this amusement park as a special place.

"Are you sure Jane doesn't need us for anything?" Wendy suspected her friends had been dispatched with instructions from the bride to babysit her. She sure as hell appreciated not having to see Noah any more than necessary, but she didn't want to make life any harder for Jane. She'd done enough of that lately.

Gia looked at her watch and then at Elise. "Not yet."

Two rides later, Wendy was being herded toward the area of the park where the wedding would take place. There would be a short ceremony outside, followed by a reception inside a pod that looked like a geodesic dome.

Wendy started to panic. "Jane said I could swoop in just before the ceremony started." And that wasn't for another thirty minutes. "It's too early." She stopped walking. Literally dug her heels in.

"Yeah, but we have to get changed and stuff." Elise took Wendy's arm. "Jane wants us to be ready to go."

"You're just gonna have to woman up, Wendy." Gia grabbed hold of Wendy's other arm.

Her friends had to tug her harder than was probably seemly to get her moving. But, crap, they were right. Jane had cut Wendy a lot of slack about the logistics of the day. Anyway, it wasn't like she hadn't been part of some terrifying trials in her day. So she put on her court face and put one foot in front of the other.

And kept doing it until she hit the door of the reception pod. It was too early for the guests to have arrived, but she spotted some of the guys milling around outside—not Noah, thank God. They were wearing kilts. They looked good. Damn, now she was going to have to spend the evening looking at Noah in a kilt. Just to rub salt into her wound, and—

"Oh!" Elise exclaimed, looking at her phone. "Gia, Jane needs us!" She spoke artificially loudly.

Wendy narrowed her eyes.

"Right!" Gia chirped. "Wendy, we'll meet you inside in a second. Go ahead and start getting changed. Our bags and dresses are all in there."

Something was definitely going on, but before Wendy

could ask what it was, Gia opened the door to the pod and literally shoved her inside.

"Ow!"

She turned, intending to go back outside and see why her friends were being so weird but stopped when her gaze snagged on the...Empire State Building?

Huh?

The room was lined with fabric backdrops, the kind you would see in plays, with scenery painted on them. One contained a bunch of iconic New York City skyscrapers, another the Statue of Liberty.

What the everloving hell?

She performed a slow rotation, her mind trying to make sense of the scene even as her heart started skipping out of control.

There was the Brooklyn Bridge and Times Square.

She kept turning, as if by doing so she would somehow be able to make sense of the situation. The pod was otherwise set up for a wedding reception, studded with floral-bedecked tables and fabric-draped chairs.

She appeared to be alone, so she walked toward the center of the space in order to take it all in.

It was like Jane had gone off her rocker and decided to set her bogus Scottish wedding in—

"Fake New York."

She gasped as Noah stepped out from behind one of the backdrops. If she'd thought her heart was out of control before, she'd had no idea. There he was, in a navy kilt and white shirt like some kind of *Outlander* fantasy come to life. He was her friend, her champion, her protector. *Almost* everything she wanted him to be.

"I made a mess of things yesterday," he said. "I led with responsibility instead of desire."

What? What was he *talking* about?

"It's because I'm used to thinking of life in terms of duty. I'm used to asking myself, 'What are my responsibilities?' Not 'What do I want?'" He huffed an incredulous laugh. "It still sounds strange, saying that. What do I want?"

She took a step toward him, but he waved her off. It was strange, talking from such a distance—she in the center of the room, he at the edge, with the snow of a Rockefeller Center Christmas behind him. He seemed to need to say his piece without her getting in his way. So she tried to calm her clattering heart enough that it wouldn't drown him out.

"What I want, it turns out, is you. Not because you might be pregnant, but—"

"I'm not pregnant." She couldn't keep herself from interrupting him. He deserved to know. "I got my period this morning."

"Well, that's disappointing."

"*Excuse* me?"

—ᴄᴈ

Noah laughed. Nothing about their current situation was laughable, but he couldn't help it. He'd come so far from the trigger-shy boyfriend of yore. It turned out he'd just never had the right woman by his side.

"Yeah, so when I contemplate the question of what my desires are, what I actually *want*, my head just fills up with…you." He had to make her see. "Not because you might be pregnant, but because you're *you*. Because no one has ever argued with me like you have. Or outrun me like you have. Or…*gutted* me like you have. So I'm as surprised as you are, but yeah, I'm fucking *disappointed* that you're not pregnant."

"But—"

He held up a hand. He had to get this out. She could object when he was done.

"But whether you're pregnant or not is neither here nor there. I got it wrong last night when I made it seem like that was what I was reacting to. I mean, what I said was true. I *do* want you to be with me, but you were right. I was asking you to give up everything while I did the same thing I always do."

"Which is?"

"Live my same old tightly controlled life." He took a deep breath. "The thing about my life is that it doesn't scare me. I know what's coming. I'm comfortable."

"That's not nothing. You worked hard for that."

That was part of what he loved about Wendy. She understood. "But it's not enough anymore. Once I figured out what I actually wanted—which, by the way, in case it's not clear, let me say one more time, is *you*—I thought, how can I get that? Under what circumstances can I have what I want?" He lifted his hands, gesturing around the room. "So here we are."

He saw the moment understanding dawned. "Fake New York," she whispered.

"Yes. Jane and Cameron helped me get all this together last night. I rented these things at a theater supply store, but I'll buy them if need be. I'll carry them around with me wherever we go if that's what it takes." He realized then that he'd neglected to say one essential thing. "Because I love you. I was too chickenshit to say that part last night. But I love you. Not because I'm supposed to. Because I *do*. I always have."

"How can you just—"

He had to interrupt her again, because words were not

enough for Wendy Lou Who. You couldn't just say "I'm sorry I left you at the dance," you had to actually *not leave her at the fucking dance*. He had to *show* her he meant what he was saying.

"I'm quitting my job," he said quickly. "I'm moving back here. You shouldn't take that as pressure, because I'm doing it for lots of reasons, my mom and Jane among them." That was the truth. Maybe not the whole truth, but it was *a* truth, and as much as he wanted Wendy, he wanted her to be free to choose him.

"I want to *be* with them, not just take care of them from afar," he added. "I'm taking some time off to study to qualify to practice law here."

"How much time are you taking off?" Her voice had gone all scratchy.

"I was thinking six months. I can spend that time any number of ways. I can wait for you while you're on your trip—if you want me to."

"What are the other options?"

Okay, here he went. The Hail Mary pass. The most terrifying thing he could imagine: just up and leaving his life. "I can go with you. If you want me to."

"You would do that? What about your mom and Jane? What about what you just said about being with them?"

"Well, I'm not going to lie. The prospect of just...fucking off for half a year is kind of terrifying. But I think that's exactly why I should do it. I want to be with you more than I want to...feel in control."

"Noah—" She was trying to talk, but her voice had cracked.

He swallowed the lump forming in his own throat. "This two weeks on, two weeks off thing sounds about perfect to me. I'm gonna have to give my family some time to get used to me, right?" He gestured behind his head. "And I'll haul this goddamn fake New York backdrop anywhere you like—to Timbuktu—if it makes a difference. If it lets you…" He cleared his throat. "If it lets you be with me."

"Noah—"

"But there's also a third option," he said, because he had to get it all out. Lay his case fully before the jury. "I can let you go. I can just let you go. It will kill me, but I'll do it if that's what you want. You'll go back to being Jane's best friend."

She shook her head. Seemed unable to speak.

He strode over and took her hands. "Maybe the past *didn't* calcify us, like you said. Maybe we're more supple than we thought. Maybe we can bend without breaking. Become something else. Or not something else, but, you know, bend into the shape of something that's…easier." He let go of her hands. He was fucking this up. "Shit. That was a terrible speech."

"That was the best speech I ever heard."

He looked up. "Really?"

Could he have succeeded? He held his breath, afraid of getting his hopes up.

She looked around the room. "I don't think all this stuff will fit in a carry-on. I'm pretty militant about packing light, you know."

"Really?" he said again, but this time his voice cracked.

"Really."

"I love you." It got easier each time he said it. "I've never said that to anyone but Jane and my mom."

She stumbled a bit, and he had to steady her. "I love you, too." Her eyebrows rose like she had surprised herself. "And I'm not that far behind you. I've got an aunt in there, and of course there were my parents but that's about it."

"Is this the part where we kiss?"

She laughed. "This is the part where we kiss."

And they did.

They kissed until they heard a symphony of throat clearing and overly loud door opening.

When they parted, Jane launched herself at them. "Eeee! You guys! This is the best wedding present ever!"

Elise and Gia had come in with Jane, and after hugs were exchanged and tears brushed away, Jane put her hands on her hips, looked at him for a long moment, then shifted her attention to Wendy and said, "You need to get dressed. I'm getting married in fifteen minutes."

Right. Wendy looked around and spotted her bag. "I'll go change in the bathroom."

"I'll help you." Noah wagged his eyebrows at Wendy. Because all this emoting was fine. It had been necessary. But he was, ultimately, a man of action.

"Oh no, you won't," Jane said. "I'd like to get married sometime this century if you don't mind."

They all laughed, and as Wendy left, she said over her shoulder to Jane, "You want us to take these backdrops down? Noah can do it while I change."

"Nah," Jane said. "It's okay. This is a low-key wedding."

—◌◞

"Why are there so many goddamned children here?" Noah asked, leading Wendy through a line-up of families waiting to get on a ride.

"Because this is an amusement park?" Wendy laughed, relishing the feeling of his hand grasping hers. Relishing even more the idea that the feeling wasn't fleeting—it was going to be like this now. She was now a person who held hands.

She didn't hate it.

"You and your goddamned logic," he huffed.

"I try."

The wedding had just ended. It had been perfect. Low-key even. At least in the sense that when the officiant asked if anyone present objected to the union, nothing happened except she and Noah looked at each other and tried not to laugh.

"Keep up, old lady," he said as he picked up the pace.

"Hey! That's my line!"

In truth, she was so glad that their newfound...status, their emotional breakthroughs, or whatever you wanted to call it, weren't going to change the essential rhythm of their relationship. She was handing Noah her heart, and to do that, she'd had to give up the fears she'd been using as emotional crutches for years. She'd had to remake herself once again. Become yet another new person.

But there was one thing she was glad wasn't changing: the mock-fighting that she and Noah did. The competing and bantering. There was nothing she loved more. And the idea that she would get to do that forever? It made her shiver with happiness. She was pretty sure she'd never shivered with happiness before.

"Are you cold?" He shrugged out of the suit top he'd worn with the kilt for the ceremony and slung it over her shoulders.

"Yes." She snuggled into the overly large garment. "I'm very, very cold. I'm so terribly in need of warming." She didn't make it through the whole sentence without laughing, but it didn't matter, because he growled and pulled her behind a concession stand.

"I love this dress." He lowered his mouth to her neck and let his hands slide down her body, over the slick taffeta.

"Yes," she said. "I'm just a bonny Scottish lass. A bonny Asian Scottish lass."

"What you are," he said, just before he lowered his mouth to hers, "is mine."

They kissed for a long time. It had never been this way for her, her body jumping to attention like this, going from zero to sixty so incredibly quickly. It was like she *was* his. And he was hers.

"Get a room!"

The voice was loud enough to intrude. And the fact that it was a repeat of what someone had said to them that night in New York cracked her up. She pushed him away as she laughed. He grunted his displeasure. But it was just as well. She'd basically been about to stick her hands up his kilt.

"We can't just do it right here," she said.

"We can't?"

"No." She smoothed her dress. "Besides the fact that they'd probably arrest us—"

"Hey, I know the best defense lawyer in Toronto."

"I have my period, remember?" she said. "Things are..." She gestured at her nether regions. "*Happening* down there."

"Hey, I'm a modern man. A little blood doesn't scare me." He grabbed her hand again, and they started walking. They walked in silence for a few moments before he said, "It would have been okay, you know."

"What?" She wasn't sure why she was asking that. She had heard him fine.

He shrugged. "We're doing everything out of order; that's all I'm saying." Something sparked in his eyes. "So a baby would have been okay. We would have made it work."

She squeezed his hand, unable to speak.

He wasn't kidding about the out of order stuff. She'd

gone from being jilted by Noah to having sex with him to being...his girlfriend? And now, instead of dating, they were going to travel the world together. It boggled the mind.

"Let's go on that." He pointed to a carousel, an antique one featuring beautifully painted horses bobbing up and down.

Glad for the change of subject—she'd had enough life upheaval today without needing to add in conversations about procreation—she agreed, and soon they were seated side by side on a pair of fine mounts.

It was impossible not to grin while riding a merry-go-round. They were both doing it, just looking at each other with stupid smiles on their faces until—

"Wendy! Noah!"

That was Jane's voice. Wendy looked around, trying to locate her friend.

Noah pointed. There she was, jogging along with the carousel in her wedding gown, the entire wedding party loping alongside her.

"You guys took off too fast after the wedding!" Jane yelled. "You missed the vote!"

"What vote?" Noah called, laughing as Jane panted to keep pace with them.

"Who gave the best party!" Cameron shouted, jogging alongside Jane.

Oh yeah. She'd totally forgotten about that, given all the drama that had come after Vegas.

"The winner is...." Gia trailed off as Elise made a drum roll noise. "Wendy!"

"Hey!" Noah protested.

"Don't even bother," Jane said. "Majority rules."

"Dude," the usually silent Jay said. "They had a stripper. They *totally* won."

Wendy pumped a fist in the air as her horse bobbed up and down. She turned to Noah. "Enjoy Josh Groban."

"Anyway!" Jane waved her bouquet over her head and shouted, "I'm really here because I forgot to give you this!"

"What?"

"I think she wants you to catch her bouquet," Noah said, and sure enough, Jane was lifting her bouquet over her head.

"She wasn't doing a bouquet toss!" Wendy said. It was part of the wedding's low-key-ness. What had happened to low-key?

"It certainly looks like she is," Noah said.

"I don't want that!" Wendy shouted. She turned to Noah. "No offense."

He grinned. "None taken."

Jane either hadn't heard her or was choosing to ignore her. She retracted her arm like a pitcher doing an elaborate wind-up.

"Don't throw it!" Wendy shouted.

Jane threw it.

And because Jane was a comic book nerd and not an athlete, it was aiming right for the little boy on the horse in front of her.

Dammit. Wendy had to lunge for the bouquet to protect the kid.

"Ha ha!" Jane called as Wendy's fingers closed around the damn thing. Then she spun on her heel and ran away.

Wendy thunked her head against the pole she was holding on to.

"Here." Noah reached for the flowers. "I'll get rid of those for you."

Ugh. She didn't want the damn bouquet. It was too much pressure. But she didn't want to offend Noah, so she said weakly, "It's okay."

"Give it here. We'll save it for later. Maybe until after we've had our first date. Oh, actually, hang on. I'll trade you."

"What?"

He dug in his pocket. "I forgot. I got you this. It was my backup plan."

"Backup plan?"

He used one hand to tug the bouquet out of her grasp and extended the other one to reveal...a Pez dispenser.

This one had the heart-eyes emoji face.

"In case the New York backdrops and a heartfelt speech didn't work. I thought, well, there's always Pez. I preloaded this one and everything."

"Yes," she said, because it was almost painfully right. A perfectly calibrated gesture. She plucked it off his hand, clicked the head back, and ejected a tart, sweet candy onto her tongue. "There's always Pez."

Don't miss the next book in the Bridesmaids Behaving Badly series!

Bridesmaid Gia Gallo is on a mission to get her friend Wendy's wedding dress to Florida in time for the ceremony. The only problem? Her flight is canceled when a massive snowstorm shuts down the eastern seaboard and strands her in New York.

Best man Bennett Buchanan can't miss his friend Noah's wedding. After all, Bennett has the rings. Determined to rent a car and drive to Florida, he's not ready for the prickly but oh-so-compelling bridesmaid who invites herself along.

When Gia and Bennett are forced to stop fighting and start driving, this unlikely pair might discover that their inconvenient road trip could just be the trip of a lifetime.

Please turn the page for a preview of
THREE LITTLE WORDS

Available in early 2019

Chapter One

$\mathcal{T}$he woman throwing a hissy fit at the gate had to be Gia Gallo. She looked the part: tall, thin, and in possession of one of those huge ugly handbags that cost more than most people's rent.

She was also stunning, but that wasn't relevant.

Helming a successful Manhattan restaurant in an increasingly hip neighborhood meant that Bennett Buchanan had encountered his share of models. The funny thing about models was they usually weren't that good-looking up close. They were all angles and bones and overly exaggerated features that probably photographed better than they came across in real life.

Gia, though, with her shoulder-length, wavy, honeybrown hair, her heart-shaped face, and her plump pink lips, was almost unnaturally beautiful.

Or she would have been, if she hadn't been using that gorgeous mouth to yell at the poor beleaguered gate agent who had just announced that their flight to Tampa had been canceled.

Bennett didn't go for entitled. He'd seen enough spoiled princesses in his old-money Southern youth to last a lifetime. New York might rub him the wrong way a lot of the time, but one thing it had going for it was that debutantes were few and far between. Or at least their New York equivalent, the society ladies, didn't make their way up to his little Cajun place in Hudson Heights.

"Listen to me," the bad-tempered beauty said to the gate agent as she held up a garment bag. "This is a wedding dress. It needs to get to Florida *now*."

Yep, that was definitely Gia, one of the bridesmaids in his best friend Noah's wedding.

Bennett got up from where he'd been sitting and headed over to the desk to try to run interference.

A second agent had joined the first. He looked like he had a lower bullshit threshold than his colleague and was rolling in to play the role of Bad Cop Gate Agent. "A bridezilla. My favorite kind of customer," he said under his breath, but not really, because Bennett, who was still a few feet away, could hear him.

"I am not a bridezilla," Gia said.

"Honey, that's what they all say."

"I am not a bridezilla, because I am not the bride. I *am* a bridesmaid, though, so if you want to call me a bridesmaid-zilla, go right ahead. I will totally own that." She leaned over—she was taller than both the agents—and got right in the face of the one who'd called her a bridezilla. "This is my friend Wendy's wedding dress. Actually, it's her *dead mother's* wedding dress. And Wendy? She hasn't had the easiest time of it. So I have made it my personal mission to make sure her wedding goes off without a hitch. This dress will make it to Florida if I have to walk it there myself." She sniffed and straightened to her full, imposing height. "And *don't* call me honey."

"Well, you'd better start walking, *honey*, because they're about to close the airport."

"What part of don't call me—"

"Gia?" Bennett interrupted, pasting on his "the customer is always right" smile. "Are you by chance Wendy's friend Gia?"

She whirled on him, and she was *pissed*. Her eyes, which were a gorgeous amber that reminded him of his nana's cinnamon pecan shortbread, narrowed. They were flanked by long lashes and heavy eyebrows. The powerful brows contrasted sharply with pale, flawless skin marked by two blotches of angry pink in the centers of her cheeks. Jesus Christ, that kind of beauty was a shock to the system, equal parts invigorating and painful, not unlike when you burned yourself in the kitchen in the middle of a manic dinner shift.

"And you are?"

The question dripped with disdain, which was good because it reminded him that the karmic scales tended to balance beauty with sourness. She was like the abominations northerners called peaches: vibrantly pinky-yellow and fragrant on the outside, hard and woody and unyielding on the inside.

Still, he would do what he could to rescue these poor gate agents from her clutches. The monster storm that was bearing down on the eastern seaboard was going to make their lives unpleasant enough without the addition of an indignant model who refused to believe that the laws of nature didn't apply to her.

He stuck his hand out. "Bennett Buchanan at your service, ma'am." He let his drawl come on strong. That always charmed people.

Gia was not charmed.

She rolled her eyes.

But she did step away from the counter, enough that the next customer in line took her place.

"You're Noah's friend."

"Yes, ma'am."

"Don't call me ma'am."

The thing was, he was pissed, too. She wasn't the only one whose flight had been canceled. She wasn't even the only one who had been charged with transporting an item essential to the wedding ceremony. He had the rings in his pocket. Noah and Wendy had tacked their wedding onto the end of a six-month trip around the world. They'd dropped into New York a few months ago for dress and ring fittings and had left their friends custody of the properly sized final products.

So, yeah, he was pissed.

And cold. So freaking cold.

Top of that list of things about New York that rubbed him the wrong way?

Winter.

You can take the boy out of the South and all that...

Damn, he hadn't realized how much the idea of getting on that plane and emerging in a few hours into warm, humid air of a *civilized* temperature had gotten its hooks into him.

But unlike Gia, he was capable of holding his temper when things didn't go his way. He was an adult. A fact he reminded himself as he checked the impulse to start calling her "honey-ma'am."

"The wedding isn't for another week," he said. "We'll be able to rebook. Let's head back to the city, and we can try again when this storm passes. We can share a cab."

Which was the last thing he wanted to do, but if they

were closing the airport, taxis would be in short supply, and Bennett was a nice guy.

Well, okay, he *wasn't* a nice guy, but he'd grown adept at faking it. And if he could behave, so could she.

Instead of answering him, Gia elbowed her way back to the counter and started demanding a hotel voucher.

"We don't give vouchers for weather delays," the first agent said.

"Good luck finding a hotel room anyway," said Bad Cop Gate Agent. "Storm of the century, they're saying."

Gia puffed up her chest and opened her mouth. Bennett cringed. What did she think? That they could magically wave a wand and, like Harry Potter, repel the foot of snow that was set to dump down on them?

He would just leave her to her little tantrum, then. He was only so good at faking this nice guy shit.

But before he turned away, something interesting happened. Something subtle that probably no one else noticed. Gia's body, which had clearly been ramping up to escalate her fight just sort of... deflated. Her chest sagged as her spine rounded, and her chin came to her chest. He didn't miss her eyes on the way down. They were filling with tears.

Shit.

When someone needs help, you help. That's what separates men from monsters.

Chef Lalande's refrain echoed through Bennett's head. His mentor's mantra was a giant pain in the ass most of the time, but it was the philosophy that had saved Bennett, and that Bennett had embraced. Pay it forward and all that.

It wasn't a philosophy that could be invoked selectively—that was the pain in the ass part. When you changed the kind of person you were, you had to be all in.

"Hey, hey, Gia. It's going to be okay. I promise." He moved toward her, compelled to touch her for some insane reason, but he checked the impulse.

"How can you promise that?" The belligerent tone from before was gone, replaced by resignation. "Can you make this plane go?"

"Look." He pulled a small velvet pouch from his pocket. "I have the rings." He wasn't sure what his point was other than to demonstrate that he was on the hook for getting there as much as she was.

"Can you divert this storm?" She started walking.

He followed. "It can't snow for a week. Worst thing that happens is we miss a few days of lying on the beach." Which was a goddamn tragedy—he shivered thinking about heading back out into the winter—but it was what it was.

She started walking faster. She was almost as tall as he was, and he had to hoof it to keep up with her.

"Can you make a hotel room magically appear in over-booked New York City?" she snapped as she pulled out her phone. The pissiness from before was creeping back into her voice.

"No," he said sharply, suddenly done with her—he tried, but even on his best days, he was half the man Chef Lalande was. He wasn't responsible for this woman. "I can do none of those things." He stopped walking.

It took a few seconds before she realized he wasn't with her anymore. She stopped and turned. Looked back at him.

Then she did that deflating thing again. She reminded him of a pizza oven. You opened it and a blast of heat escaped and the temperature inside dropped by several hundred degrees.

"I'm sorry," she said. "I don't even know why I'm being like this. I'm just so..."

Mean? his mind supplied. *Arrogant?*

"...hungry."

He barked a surprised laugh. "Well, ma'am, that I can fix."

About the Author

Jenny Holiday is a *USA Today* bestselling author who started writing at age nine when her awesome fourth-grade teacher gave her a notebook and told her to start writing some stories. That first batch featured mass murderers on the loose, alien invasions, and hauntings. (Looking back, she's amazed no one sent her to a shrink.) She's been writing ever since. After a detour to get a PhD in geography, she worked as a professional writer, producing everything from speeches to magazine articles. Later, her tastes having evolved from alien invasions to happily-ever-afters, she tried her hand at romance. She lives in London, Ontario, with her family.

Learn more at:

Jennyholiday.com
Twitter @jennyholi
Facebook.com/jennyholidaybooks
Newsletter: jennyholiday.com/newsletter/

Fall in Love with Forever Romance

USA TODAY BESTSELLING AUTHOR

DEBBIE MASON

Sandpiper Shore

"Heartfelt and delightful!"—RAEANNE THAYNE,
New York Times bestselling author, on *Mistletoe Cottage*

SANDPIPER SHORE
By Debbie Mason

USA Today bestselling author Debbie Mason's latest novel in the
feel-good and charming Harmony Harbor series. Jenna Bell loves
her job as a wedding planner...until she meets with her newest
clients and discovers that the groom is the man she's loved for
years. For Secret Service Agent Logan Gallagher, seeing Jenna
after all these years brings back feelings that he's fought hard to
forget...and makes him wonder if getting married to someone
else would be the biggest mistake of his life.

Fall in Love with Forever Romance

COWBOY ON MY MIND
By R. C. Ryan

Welcome to Haller Creek, Montana. Ben Monroe has always been the town bad boy, but when he becomes sheriff, he puts the law before anything else and stays away from trouble... Well, until Becca comes back into town. Don't miss this special 2-in-1 edition that includes a bonus Western romance novella by Sara Richardson!

Fall in Love with Forever Romance

IT TAKES TWO
By Jenny Holiday

In this hilarious romantic comedy, *USA Today* bestselling author Jenny Holiday proves that what happens in Vegas *doesn't* always stay in Vegas. Wendy Liu *should* be delighted to be her best friend's maid of honor. But it means spending time with the bride's brother, aka the boy who once broke her heart. Noah Denning is always up for a challenge. So when Wendy proposes that they compete to see who can throw the best bachelor or bachelorette party in Sin City, Noah takes the bait—and ups the stakes. Because this time around, he wants Wendy for keeps.

Fall in Love with Forever Romance

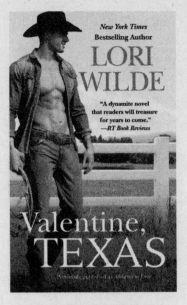

VALENTINE, TEXAS
By Lori Wilde

From *New York Times* bestselling author Lori Wilde comes a heart-warming story about love, second chances, and cowboys...Rachael Henderson has sworn off love, but when she finds herself hauled up against the taut, rippling body of her first cowboy crush, she wonders if taking a chance on love is worth the risk. Can a girl have her cake and her cowboy, too?

* Formerly published as *Addicted to Love*.